Joan Eadith lives in the [...] Manchester, where she [...] nurse. She also worked in the University Dental School and Royal Eye Hospital, and as a nursing visitor. She has served her time as a wife and mother, and now considers writing her career.

Dasia

Joan Eadith

WARNER BOOKS

A *Warner* Book
First published in Great Britain in 1992
by Warner Books

ISBN 0 7088 5424 9

Typeset by Leaper & Gard Ltd, Bristol
Printed in England by Clays Ltd, St Ives plc

Warner Books
A Division of
Little, Brown & Company
165 Great Dover Street
London SE1 4YA

Contents

CHAPTER ONE

Manchester, 1926

Dasia could hear her mother and father clearly through the large hole in the floor boards of her ornate bedroom. It was the same old gramophone record: 'Day-see-YA! Do you want dragging from that bloody bed? Do you *like* your poor father and me losing our voices screeching at you every morning?'

'Don't bother with 'er any more, Alice. She's a right little nowt. It'd do 'er good t'ave t'gwowt t'work, properly. There's lasses 'er age slogging away in factorries in their millions. A good dose of medisn for 'er ud be 'avin t'work as an apprentice like our young Tommy at Westin'Ouse.'

Dasia lay there defiantly, like some princess, in her own vast domain, with her red-gold hair strewn in natural waves of fine mesh across plump feather pillows. She wished she *was* their Tommy – four years older than herself and lodging in Stretford out of the family clutches. Men always got the best end of the stick. Tommy; only twenty – yet their three much older sisters still living at home ... and herself – the worst off of the lot.

Suddenly, with an impetuous gesture she leapt out of bed, as if it was a sunny spring day, and heaved at the large sash window, trying to free it from its damp, jammed permanency with all the strength of young muscles and grim determination. And at last, it happened. A great gust of sleety snow met her full in the face and drenched her new, bright blue pyjamas, as she gasped at the coldness of it, and gazed with growing hatred at the efficient red trams already on the move, far away behind gigantic oak trees whose branches, even in December, still clung to pale gold leaves.

She continued to stare out of the open window with icy drizzle spraying in. Here, in The Grove, Manchester had dissolved almost entirely into meadows and winding country lanes, with just the suggestion of a canal tow-path. And in this inner sanctum of The Grove's back gardens, with their half-acre orchards now full of black-branched, chubby, leafless apple trees, and their fine pony paddocks, the land was alive with six-bedroomed mansions similar or even larger in size than theirs, and well kept up; full of people with magnificent Ford cars and garages to match, and even servants.

Suddenly she shivered and began to pull the window down again. She turned away and stood there on the cold red lino, dreaming of some escape before she had to go and work at their hellish pawn shop! Then, sniffing and blowing her nose on a crumpled handkerchief from her pyjama jacket pocket, she hunted miserably for her ribbed cotton vest, as all the warmth evaporated. Then, peering round in a daze of distaste, she looked for her underskirt, and her pale green celanese knickers. Her clothes were in an untidy heap, half under the bed where she'd thrown them. And the elastic had gone in one of her knicker legs.

The sleet was getting worse and water was dripping through the leaking roof and streaming towards a bulging mildewed hole in the once magnificent, embossed ceiling paper. It was plopping on to a chair, just missing the strategically placed, chipped floral china po. A grey tubular oil heater lay spitting away next to the empty fireplace.

Mother and Father were mad to have moved from their respectable terraced house in Moss Side – to this. For although deep down she loved the lavishness of it all, her common sense told her it had been another foolhardy step her father had taken. Oh yes, they were now in what amounted to a palace compared to general everyday standards, for Father had bought it as a dropping-to-bits bargain which needed costly repairs. As usual, the family comfort had been sacrificed for yet another of his brainwaves for recouping his financial losses – brought about by his insatiable appetite for inventing things, while hopefully relying on the backbone of Mother's very small income from the pawn shop (which she'd inherited) to keep everyone afloat.

Sometimes Father actually made money on his inventions. His motor-bike/side-car patent had produced enough cash for a Vauxhall saloon car. But the car vanished for ever when he moved on to the expense of trying to produce an electric lawn-mower called The Greenbow, after their surname. This, he said, had been a bit of bad luck, because he was 'before his time' and there was no mass market for electric lawn-mowers when most working people in northern industrial towns lived in streets where backyards were more common than green lawns, and where many people had hardly heard of electricity and still used gas mantles in their lights, and the gasman went round lighting the gas lights in the streets. And so his glorious electric Greenbow resided in the graveyard of his other disbanded prototypes – in the large garage of their present dwelling – until he came up with a better, more profitable scheme.

As if to torture herself, Dasia stood in front of the mottled, pitted mirror of the huge mahogany wardrobe and looked at her own image in the sombre gloom: a small, pale-skinned, bare-breasted, innocent maiden – with one leg of her drawers hanging down loosely, and the other one all pouched up. Her hair suddenly glinted in a stronger ray of morning light, as she grabbed the rest of her clothes, put on a kimono, and hurried to the bathroom before anyone else got there.

The pawn shop looked quite cheerful when Dasia arrived on the early morning tram to open up.

Sleeting snow disguised the grime of the street. Horses and carts no longer rattled on the cobbled sets, for the sound from metal-bound wheels became soft and muffled in a world fast becoming a true Christmas fairytale.

Father and Mother had put up Christmas decorations before locking up last night. She knew their individual styles. His was HAPPY YULETIDE made into an ornate tableau with old piano wire and red-berried holly from the garden of their vast new home. He could make anything out of anything, yet always in the past when he aimed to make a million he fell flat on his face. And Dasia wondered whether it would soon happen again ...

Mother was different. She was hard, shrewd and ruthless. Dasia gazed at her mother's handiwork, and noted the tactless way she'd put a skimpy piece of last year's tarnished silver tinsel round Mr Cook's sacred lifeline – his expensive Kodak camera which popped in and out of the shop regularly, from his bare little home near Knott Mill railway arches.

She got on far better with her father than with her mother in spite of them both taking sides against her; for underneath her father's broad northern accent lay the heart of a sympathetic and literate man, hen-pecked into

4

convention yet never succeeding to conform properly when he was in the midst of it. Well aware of the plight of those around him, he was always two rungs short on the ladder when it came to trying to help.

Mother and Father, and Andrina, who was forty-one and their eldest daughter, all worked shifts in the pawn shop, along with Dasia. Yet Dasia's own working stints seemed to be getting longer and harder, while theirs were often broken up with the luxury of other 'pressing matters' so that she was constantly holding the fort, while being persistently criticised and nagged.

She even felt that her mother watched how much she ate, and resented her having a normal hungry appetite. Mother was always making rude remarks like: 'If you shovel down as many spuds as that in a meal, at *sixteen*, how can you ever hope to grow into a proper lady? You'll just be a sack of oats with a string round its middle!' or, 'At least the rest of us don't sup our tea like horses drinking from a trough. If I ever catch you cooling your tea in't saucer again, Dasia, I'll pour it down your bodice!'

But the one important thing in her life she could never really forgive her father and mother for was making her leave school at fourteen and work in Mother's pawn shop, instead of being sent to Miss Green's Junior Secretarial College, at a time when Father was having an affluent patch and could have afforded the expenses. She envied her sisters: at least – they weren't *completely* chained.

Apart from Andrina, there was thirty-five-year-old Louise who worked on the glove counter of Baulden's High Class Emporium at All Saints. She had a regular follower called Mr Arnold Kimberley from Crightons, the well-known drapers on the same side of All Saints Square. He was nine years younger than Louise. But in spite of Louise referring to him as her suitor and telling everyone they were courting, Mother still claimed she was 'on the shelf' along with poor Andrina – and that 'cradle snatching' would get her nowhere.

However, Mother always softened up a bit when it came to blond-haired Rosalie who was thirty-four and rather a flirt, with a big bust, and who dared to wear false eye-lashes. Rosalie worked in the Servant Registry at Sale, on the Cheshire side of Manchester. Many rich people went there to find suitable domestic help, so Mother always had hopes that at any minute Rosalie would meet a wealthy, gout-ridden doctor, or an earl wanting staff from the registry for his shooting parties – having, of course, called to see about it personally and been immediately swept away by voluptuous Rosalie's mellifluent charm. Whereupon she'd be married and installed in a large country house, with an estate like Dunham Park, and the whole of Dasia's clan as constant guests!

Dasia walked quickly through the shop and opened the door to the backyard. They always checked everything when they opened up in case of attempted break-ins. With a quickly beating heart she checked the old whitewashed lavatory, and the old washhouse, with its square brick 'copper' in the corner, which was now used as an extra junk store.

Twenty years ago the place had been an ordinary street house, until her mother's sister, Robina Floss, a widow with eight children, started it off as her own bit of flea market by buying up dirty sheets and bed linen, washing it all back to decency herself and then reselling it as second-hand goods. Although she clung to the income from it until middle age, her three surviving children all emigrated and tried to ignore the hardship of those days, and it was finally left to Dasia's mother – Alice Greenbow.

Thank goodness everything was in order. Dasia shook

her rain cape and put it in the scullery along with her wellingtons, which she left to drain in the old, shallow, brown slop-stone sink.

She always kept well covered up when working: thick lisle stockings, good stout lace-up shoes, and white replaceable elasticated sleevelets on her blouses – which could be washed and replaced fresh each day. The amount of unwanted life amongst much of the junk was terrific; she could recognise a flea or a bug almost before she saw it, and many a hurrying black beetle was crunched to death under her foot as she hastily emptied and reset mouse traps in strategic positions.

There wasn't much sign of the up-market Three Brass Balls here, with their neat metal grilles over glittering plate glass windows full of heavily jewelled watches – and gold and silver necklaces, and beautiful enamelled brooches, and emerald rings, and wonderful tea services.

For, although the Greenbows had their occasional silver-knobbed walking canes, mucky-looking eternity rings were thicker over the counter than large, solitaire diamond tie pins.

The weather was now so atrocious that customers seemed most unlikely – even though she knew that some of their best trade had come on hopeless days of rain, hail, and gales. But in spite of the conditions, and her early gloom before she set out to work, she couldn't help hoping there would be a grand fall of real snow, and that it would become a traditional Christmas, especially as her own birthday was on Tuesday, the twenty-first, which was less than a week away.

'Sweet seventeen and never been kissed' people always said … but mainly it was mothers or optimistic older men who mouthed the words.

She began to open the letters, still thinking of snow: its soft, white purity. Most of the post consisted of letters

7

of complaint, thinly veiled demands, or sly coaxing for money. 1926 was an uncertain year, what with the ten-day General Strike earlier, and the coal dispute still dragging on. The world was full of hardship and horror, so it was best not to dwell on it.

She stopped brooding, and then looked down at the last letter. It was penned in a large flowing hand. Carelessly, she took the ivory-bladed paper knife and slit the top edge of the crisp, creamy envelope. It had a fine, pale green lining, and she realised too late that it was a very private letter to her father and addressed him as 'My Dear Brace' – Brace was a boyhood nickname from his early school days; his proper name was Horace Bernard Greenbow.

Dasia felt a sudden flood of fear. Nothing annoyed her father more than having his personal mail opened. She heard the bell suddenly jangle on the shop door and pushed the letter hurriedly into the drawer of the old wooden ledger desk behind the counter, just as her sister, Andrina, walked in: 'Andrina! You're so early . . .!'

'I know. Mr Tankerton wanted to be at his office extra early about some legal work. And also to bring his mother in to meet her friends for elevenses at the Cafe Royal, and last minute Christmas shopping, followed by lunch . . . So I arrived in style in their car. I feel really sorry for Mr Tankerton still being unmarried and living alone in that huge house with his widowed mother. He must be at least fifty, and men rarely take the first plunge at that age . . . He was telling me on the way here, in their beautiful buff-coloured Ford, that he was bald at twenty-two. But his mother hastened to add that being bald had made him a *very* successful solicitor, because older clients had far more faith in him.'

Dasia smothered a smile: Andrina never gave up hope . . .

8

Andrina took off her sealskin coat and her crimson felt hat, and placed them both on a coathanger hooked behind the door. Then she patted her chestnut-coloured ear-phone coils with a towel, and turned up the oil stove: 'Can't see us getting many in today. Anything interesting in the post?'

Dasia showed her what had come, but was careful not to mention the personal letter for their father, which was hidden in the ledger drawer. Andrina was far too good at chewing over Dasia's mistakes and enlarging them.

Andrina looked hard at Dasia's hair: 'You can't go on having it half-way down your back once you're seventeen,' she said. 'You'll need to get it neatened up and put into proper coils like mine when you're working, instead of always tying a silly turban round it for protection. It looks far too outlandish!'

Dasia smiled: 'Don't worry. I aim to have it all neatly cut off into an Eton Crop at the beginning of next week, in the interests of shop hygiene, and fashion.'

Andrina stared at her disbelievingly: 'You wouldn't dare! Whatever will Mother and Father say? They'll think you're a flapper! At your age! It's not really quite decent ...' Andrina began to hunt round, vaguely, for the book of coarsely printed, numbered receipt tickets; the ones they always fastened to the goods. She was often absent-minded, but invariably blamed it, these days, on The Change. 'I don't know which is worse,' she'd groan, 'The Curse, or The Change.'

Andrina suddenly stiffened. She was holding something from the ledger drawer: 'Dasia ... This letter ... Did it come this morning?'

It was Father's letter ... Dasia looked away uneasily: 'Yes – I put it there by accident when you arrived at the shop. I thought you were a customer.'

'It's been *opened*.' Andrina looked at her accusingly: 'You know he'll go mad. Surely, you could *see* it was

9

his?' Then she hesitated, as curiosity killed the cat: 'Have you read it?'

'No, I didn't really get time. What I mean is . . .' her voice faltered as Andrina swiftly drew the letter from the envelope and began to read it aloud in a rather triumphant voice:

'Dear Brace. Please forgive this intrusion . . .' Then, a look of bewilderment spread over Andrina's face and she began to mutter the words so quickly that Dasia could hardly hear them: '. . . must be well nigh sixteen years since we met . . . and I myself am now reduced to an invalid chair due to an accident . . . I had trouble tracing you so thought it best to send this to your business quarters. I've sad news to impart. My son Blennim . . . BLENNIM?' Andrina's voice rose in horror as she went deathly pale: 'Passed away . . . *Dead?* . . . Oh no!'

She leaned back against the wall with a groan: 'Last week in Canada. He was forty-one – the same age as . . .' Her voice faded and she crumpled up the letter.

'What are you *doing*? It's *Father's* letter!' Dasia lunged towards her and tried to grab it, but Andrina was too quick and pushed it into the side pocket of her skirt.

'I just don't understand you,' said Dasia tearfully. 'Only a few seconds ago you were blaming me for opening it – and now . . .' She was completely lost for words.

All that morning there was an uneasy silence between them, as Dasia brooded on the letter. Why had her sister suddenly crumpled it up? What was there in a letter to their father to cause such a terrible reaction? Some old friend of father's – from times long before she was ever thought of . . . Someone with a son as old as Andrina, but now dead . . .?

While they were having a cup of tea and a ginger biscuit later in the morning, she said: 'Andrina . . .?'

'Yes?' Andrina tried not to look at her and sipped her

tea in a very concentrated fashion.

'About that letter addressed to Father – we can't just destroy it! It could be something of extreme importance. And I was responsible for the post, remember? I was the one who gathered it up and it was sheer fate that it happened to be in the ledger drawer when you came in.'

'It was not "sheer fate",' said Andrina with a cold, simmering calmness. 'It was a piece of deceitfulness on your part: you'd already opened that letter!'

'I know, but it was pure accident. I just did it automatically, then left it there, because the shop door bell went ...'

The silence between the sisters was heavy, and beyond the window of the shop the snow was thickening to large, clinging flakes.

'I shall *have* to tell Father a letter came for him, Andrina. I could never live with the idea that it had been deliberately lost.'

'Do what the Devil you like, you stupid little fool!' Andrina stood up quickly and fixed her gaze towards a framed trading certificate in the wall: 'Anyway, I've got other things to think about. I've got some extra shopping to do at Baulden's before this weather gets too impossible. And while I'm there I'll be having something with Louise in the restaurant at midday. So you won't need to get me a pie from Mrs Mattison's. I'll be back about two – and I'll make it up to you by letting you go home a bit earlier.'

Dasia stared silently as Andrina got ready to go. What on earth had got into her?

Never before had Andrina called her a stupid little fool. Insults like that usually came from Mother under a heap of other labels, such as: most troublesome, most emotional, most disobedient, and – according to Mother in her very worst moods – a blight on their old age.

So now, as usual, she was going to be on her own

again in her role of Chief Can-Carrier. She began to busy herself – polishing some of the brass and silver items which were for sale.

At least Andrina still appeared to have left the crumpled letter in her skirt pocket, because its stiff corners poked up slightly through the grey striped material. Maybe she'd show it to Louise while they had their dinner in Baulden's. The two of them were always very close.

When Andrina was finally wrapped up against the elements, Dasia went with her to the door of the shop, hoping in a ridiculous way that the letter would be mentioned again, and that Andrina would relent and tell her more – perhaps even turn back and take the letter from her pocket, and smooth it out and save it for Father.

But it was not to be. As she opened up her black umbrella and stepped out into the sleet and snow, she was met quite suddenly by a wave of slush, stirred up by a car pulling up outside the shop. In seconds she had collapsed to the pavement, her umbrella swept into the road, and she lay lifeless on the slippery, uneven pavement.

In a panic, Dasia stepped towards her, moaning her name, and her own heart all a-flutter. But before she had even bent down to give aid, the man from the car was already by Andrina's side.

'She's my sister!' sobbed Dasia in mounting fear. 'She'd just left our shop.'

'And it looks as if she'd better go straight back,' said the man with a huge grunt as he bent down and carried her back to the shop door like a rather heavy sack of grain – hitching her almost over one of his shoulders.

'Put her on that sofa.' Dasia's eyes were full of tears. She could see that Andrina had either fainted or knocked herself out.

'Flat on the ground's best,' said the man. He was tall and hefty, like a rugby player, and she suddenly realised he was quite young. He looked even younger than her own brother, Tommy, who was twenty. But he was a different type entirely: a bit like a gentleman farmer with an Oxford accent, although he wore a thick, blanket-check overcoat, and a blue striped bow tie. His dark black curly hair was uncovered, and his hands were well manicured.

'Do you think I should fetch a doctor?' Dasia stared at the man. He had greyish blue eyes and no smile.

'It's entirely up to you. Actually I was just calling in to redeem a pledge from a few weeks back. A medic pal of mine popped his binoculars. But I'll come back some other time.'

In seconds he was out of the shop, and his car had vanished.

'Don't you dare to fetch a doctor!' said Andrina suddenly recovering. 'I'll feel fine once I've got all these sopping clothes off. I'll put on that summer dress in the cupboard and the old jersey of Father's, and one of Mother's aprons. And you'd better go and get me a pie from Mattison's after all. But first, help me off with all this lot. My leg's killing me. We'll shut the place early and both go home by taxi. Call at Renshaw's and order one.'

Dasia did as she was bid with trembling hands, and soon Andrina seemed to be her usual self again as she sat sipping tea.

There was an old laundry bag in the back kitchen, and Dasia bundled the clothes into it ready to take them back home. Then she stopped. The letter – was it still there? She grabbed at the striped skirt and felt in the pocket. Then, with a huge inward sigh of triumph and relief she drew out the crumpled letter in its envelope and put it safely in her own leatherette handbag. Then

13

off she went for the two pies, and to order the taxi.

The savoury pies from Ma Mattison's were always piping hot and running with succulent gravy, and when Tilly Mattison heard about the fall, she added two extra pieces of bread and margarine, free.

Andrina was quiet as they ate their meal, then after a while she said, 'I wonder who that boy was, who carried me in. It was very kind of him to help us. Quite a young gentleman, he was. One of your real Upper Crust, I shouldn't wonder ...'

'He wasn't kind at all!' said Dasia irritated by her sister's grovelling attitude to a young man of substance who wore a bow tie. 'It was his car that caused all that extra slush you slipped on. It was his responsibility to help us, and any decent human being would have done the same!'

'Except that some human beings aren't "decent", Dasia.' Andrina gave her a cryptic, almost woebegone, smile as she finished her meal, got up, and began to hobble round the shop before the taxi arrived to take them home.

As soon as they were home, Dasia hurried up to her bedroom, took out the letter and smoothed it out carefully. Then she sat on the rickety, faded velvet boudoir chair and read the whole of it.

The address was the South of France, yet the envelope had an ordinary George V three-halfpenny stamp with a London postmark:

Dear Brace,
Please forgive this intrusion into your life as it must be well nigh sixteen years since ... I have sad news to impart ... Blennim passed away last week, just before his return to Canada. He was 41, and the same age as Andrina. He had been ill for some time.

14

His last wish was for his only child to receive various items, of sentimental value, with the stipulation that she collects them personally. He has left money to cover her travelling expenses for this purpose, and there is no particular date for this to take place.

When I receive your reply to this letter all will, hopefully, be legally signed and sealed.

How is the child? A bonny young woman by now, one assumes?

Yours in all sincerity,

Adrien Shewfield.

Dasia stared at the letter, then slowly, with complete puzzlement, she read it again ... Obviously there was some young person her father was aware of, who was unfamiliar to the rest of their family.

Her father was a strange man. You never did quite know how many deep secrets he kept. Never in a month of Sundays would she have guessed that her father had such an old friend with a son the same age as Andrina, yet Andrina must have known this son when they were small children, before Dasia's time. Why else would she have been so upset by the news of his death?

'Day-see-YA! ... How much longer are you stopping up there? The meal's ON'T TABLE!' Her mother's piercing yell filled the room through the hole in the floor. The water had stopped dripping from the ceiling. She looked at the wonderful flock wallpaper from its days of plenty – still covered in glowing creamy pink camellias, but now damp and peeling with an unpleasant smell. And the great double bed – all her own, to stretch in, and roll about in. A bed with its headboard of warped, walnut veneer all covered in a white bloom of seeping damp.

She put the letter under the pillow, and went downstairs.

They always had what was really a 'High Tea' with something savoury – a cross between a dinner, a tea, and a supper. Dasia breathed with nervous relief. Everyone was in a good mood. And Andrina was making the very best of the story of the stranger who carried her into the shop after she'd slipped on the slushy pavement.

'He was so *kind* – such a perfect gentleman, yet so *young* . . .'

'An' what sort of shoes were you wearing, Drina?' said Mother suspiciously. 'Not those rubber overshoes, surely, from Alf Simpson on't market? Why you keep being swindled by him I shall never know. I'll bet the soles were as smooth as a baby's bottom.'

Mother began dishing out some Lancashire hot-pot from a brown earthenware oven dish, while Louise carried in the vegetable tureens, and Rosalie put a mountain of white, delicately buttered bread next to the sugar bowl on the mahogany dining table – a piece of furniture left behind in the house when Father bought it.

''Ow did the shop go?' said Father digging into his meal with appreciative gusto. 'Not much doin' in weather like this, I'll be bound. Now that's one of the good things – 'avin that shop. Your poor Robby Floss came up trumps for you, Alice. What we'd have done without that shop, I just do not know.'

'*You* might not know, but I bloody well know,' said Mother acidly. 'If I hadn't been left that bloody shop, you wouldn't have been able to play about like some overgrown lad with all your silly inventions – bringing us all to ruin. You'd 'ave had to try and get a proper job.

'And another thing, whilst I think of it, Horace Greenbow – never let me hear of you sloping into that White City to the greyhounds any more. We don't all work to support *that*. You were seen by Mrs Fearnley when she passed by in their Lagonda. I could hardly believe my own ears. "Oh yes", she says, "ay knew it was eeem. I'd recognise those green cordyew roy troisers any w'hair."'

Everyone started to laugh, and Father began to choke slightly on a piece of carrot from the hot-pot and buried his head deep in a damask dinner-napkin, from a very nice set once brought into the pawn shop to sell.

'I hope you've cooked the rice pudding long enough tonight, Mother,' said Rosalie, clearing the first course plates away. 'I'm going to Redman's tonight with Arthur Bowlingshaw, the one who used to be on the Servants Registry books as butler, and now works as a railway porter after that terrible row ...'

Mother ignored her, and Dasia could see that Rosalie enjoyed seeing Mother annoyed. Rosalie often went to Redman's, in Stretford, dancing with Arthur Bowlingshaw. But unfortunately he was far away from Mother's dream of Belted Earls – even though he could turn on an impeccable accent and perfect manners when the occasion called for it.

Suddenly Dasia remembered the letter resting under the bedroom pillow, as she edged her spoon round the blue and gold border of a bowl of hot, creamy rice pudding. She glanced swiftly towards Andrina who was now leading an open discussion on whether she should stay in and rest her leg, or go to carol practice at church.

What would happen if the letter was mentioned? Now was as good a time as any, while everyone was in a good mood ...

She put the spoon down and, trying to be as unconcerned as anything, said, 'Oh, by the way, Father, a letter came for you today from one of your friends. I accidentally opened it. It was a pure accident. It's upstairs in the bedroom. Shall I go and fetch it?'

'What friend was that then?' said Father smiling

slightly. 'Some'd say as I 'aven't many friends left.' His teeth suddenly sparkled in the light. He had good teeth for his age and took pride in the fact that he'd never smoked. 'Go and get that letter then, lass. 'Ow do I know 'oo it is till I see?'

Dasia glanced quickly to where Andrina was finishing her pudding, and saw her push her bowl aside and stand up hurriedly: 'I think I *will* go to the carol practice ...' She moved from the table swiftly, avoiding Dasia's gaze.

'Are you sure, Drina?' said Rosalie, who was already covering her blonde hair with a fur-trimmed hat and rouging her cheeks in the sideboard mirror. 'You look perfectly ghastly – you're as white as a sheet.'

Dasia left the room with deep down relief and hurried upstairs. She stood in the bedroom waiting a while to allow Andrina time to get her coat and hat on, and go out with Rosalie. Then, as if luck was on her side, she heard Louise saying she was off to meet Arnold Kimberley, to go to the pictures. When she arrived downstairs again, there was only Mother left in the scullery, washing the dishes, and her father drying them and putting them on the shelves of the huge kitchen dresser.

Father smiled at her: 'Your mother's a right lucky woman. There's not many men as acts as kitchen skivvies for their lady loves.'

'And don't you be leading him astray with that damned letter,' warned Mother. 'He can't look at that piffle until he's dried and put away all this lot.'

Then, as if sensing Dasia's unusual interest in the letter, she said, 'Just leave it on the bloody table, child. No need to hang around forever. Your dad's correspondence is nowt to do with you, and it was very careless of you to have opened it. Why don't you go and get a few of those stockings darned, and repair some pillow slips?'

18

With sudden rising anger, Dasia scowled at her mother and stamped out of the kitchen to the small parlour – meant for non-existent servants, but used by the family as a sewing room. She pulled a woollen sock from the mending basket and found the wooden mushroom to push down to the toe where the hole was, but all the time she was listening to judge when the washing up was finished. Mother and Father never expected help with it in the evenings unless they specifically asked, or unless they themselves had been out.

Hastily, she cobbled together a bit of a darn, and put the sock to one side. When she walked back into the kitchen, Mother and Father were sitting at the large, scrubbed deal table with the letter lying there between them, next to its green-lined envelope.

She smiled, but they both looked at her solemnly: 'Did you happen to read all the letter, then, lass?'

'Yes Father ... I'm truly sorry. I didn't realise it might be private. Andrina was very upset when she saw it.'

'Our Andrina?' Mother and Father looked at each other with almost fear in their eyes.

'How come Andrina never mentioned it?' said Mother.

'I think she must have forgotten, because of the fall she had at dinnertime. She must have been very upset, with it being about someone she knew when she was little. I know *I* would have been ...' said Dasia sympathetically.

'YOU!' said Mother. 'What experience of life have *you* got? You're hardly out of nappies!'

'Well I must say it's all a great shock,' muttered Father, pulling at his collar and tie as if they were starting to choke him. 'A very great shock. Never in my worst moments did I suspect I'd hear from Adsy Shawfield again. And as for his son dying ... Well now.

That's a real blow. No wonder our Andrina felt bad.'

He and Mother looked at each other silently, as if they were struck dumb and didn't know what to say next. Then Father sighed and said to Dasia, 'Well, love, we'll just have to answer the letter won't we? But when you'll be able to get over to a place like Canada to collect these so-called items of sentimental value, the Lord alone knows.' He stood up and patted her affectionately on the shoulder.

Dasia froze: 'Me, Father ...?' Had he gone completely mad? There was another silence ... 'Aren't you getting muddled up?'

No one said anything. Whatever was wrong with them both? How could Father be mistaking her for some person who was clearly the child of this friend's son from years ago?

'The fact is, Dasia dear –' Her mother, calling her *dear* ... She never did that unless something exceedingly unpalatable had to be swallowed. 'Well – the fact is that Andrina ... is not *quite* the unmarried sister you thought she was.'

'Do you mean to say that she's been married?' Dasia's face brightened with sudden curiosity. She'd never imagined straightlaced Andrina as anything but an ever-hopeful, ageing spinster.

'Oh, no. She never *married*, dear. She never did that ...'

At this point Father slipped out of the kitchen almost unnoticed; one of his well-practised movements when Mother was taking control of a family situation.

Mother's colour suddenly rose and her normally pale face, haloed in greying hair piled high and full of hair pins began to show signs of perspiration on her forehead – almost like a hot flush – and she began to speak very quickly: 'You've got to know it sooner or later, and this letter's brought the whole sordid business to a head. My

God, and about time too! The years I've suffered from all this damned deceit. But now the truth's out. Our Andrina's baby was born on the 21st December 1909.'

'But that's *exactly* like me! Don't say I've got a twin hidden away somewhere!'

'You're very like your father,' said Mother, still gabbling. 'He had the same gingery gold hair as you, and the same unpredictable temper. Blennim Shawfield was an awkward, unfeeling young man and Andrina was well rid of him. But there you are. We mustn't speak badly of the dead.'

At first her words just didn't register at all – Dasia stared at Mother as if she'd seen a ghost. Stared at this plumpish woman in her sixties with the sharp, shrewd grey eyes set in the squarish, heavy-chinned face. Stared at the mouth which was never at a loss for the timely and caustic comment, with the lines at each side of it denoting a dry sense of humour. Stared at the soft wrinkles round her eyes which could, on occasion, melt to a motherly compassion. Stared now at a mask; a stone statue of the face of someone bereft of further words or emotion.

Dasia turned, and with a long gulping sob of anguish, rushed upstairs to her bedroom, taking with her the terrible letter from where it rested on the kitchen table.

CHAPTER TWO

Aunty Dolly's

All that night, Dasia never slept a wink. It was the first time in her life she had even known the meaning of insomnia, for usually she was so active and full of youthful energy that she was asleep in a flash. But now that time of comfortable security had vanished for ever as she went over and over the events of the past evening. Was she imagining it? Was she just dreaming? Was it all some terrible nightmare?

Or was it truly and inevitably correct that she was Andrina's one and only illegitimate child, and that Mother and Father were really her maternal grandmother and grandfather – which meant that Louise and Rosalie were her aunts, and even twenty-year-old Tommy was no longer her brother – but her uncle! She was now changed to an 'only child', in a few hours of a family secret – finally revealed.

She lay there worrying, and turning from one side to the other in the huge bed, clenching and unclenching her fists and even getting up and walking round the cold, damp room, and peering down at the dark gardens in the light of a half-moon.

How could she ever face any of the family again? How could she face Andrina? How could she possibly go to the pawn shop in the morning as if nothing had occurred? How could she ever face Father again, knowing what she now knew?

She switched on the light and looked at the small bedroom clock set in greenish onyx marble. It had stopped at 11.10 p.m. She'd forgotten to wind it up, yet she knew that it was well past four in the morning by the chimes from the local church tower.

She picked up the letter again from next to the clock and began to read it once more: her own father dead at forty-one, after living in Canada. Andrina's unmarried husband ... And this letter written by Adrien Shawfield, her true paternal grandfather; a letter with a London postmark, but an address in the South of France.

She flopped back into bed and lay there helplessly as if all energy had left her. What on earth could she do? She had hardly the money for a stamp to get in touch herself with Adrien Shawfield. And yet, in the scene last night, Mother and Father had left the letter lying there as if they wished to have nothing to do with it, and rather to pretend it had all never happened.

She got out of bed, for the fourth time, and began to look in her handbag to see how much money she really had. It amounted to one pound note, two sixpenny pieces, a half crown, a threepenny bit, ten pennies, three halfpennies and six farthings. She looked in her savings book from the Penny Bank and saw that there was four pounds and ninepence in it.

Then with a deep, sad, half-sobbing moan she found her cardboard suitcase and began to pack it with belongings: her kimono, one pair of best silk stockings, knickers and vests, two wool jumpers, two skirts and a silk crepe-de-chine party dress. By the time she'd finished, she had to sit on it to close it and she fastened it

23

with a stout leather strap and buckle.

Then, getting fully dressed, she made her bed, even though she knew it was bad to make it without an airing. Finally, she took her best pale green Harris tweed coat from the damp, mothballed wardrobe, and put it on with her favourite silk-velvet beret.

She took hold of the heavy suitcase and, after one quick, sad goodbye glance round the room, made her way silently downstairs, hardly knowing what she was going to do once she had left the house.

She halted briefly in the kitchen to rest the heavy case. Tears came to her eyes as Periwinkle, their black and white mongrel terrier, stirred from his dog basket near the warmth of the Esse anthracite cooking stove and wagged his tail sleepily, and Daisy the cat blinked through her striped tabby fur from her wicker basket on top of the corner cabinet.

The place smelled of home baking and the slight scent of cinnamon. The old grandfather clock ticked deeply in the corner with a steady sonorous beat, next to the old wooden rocking chair with its red cushion. There was a pencil lying on the mantel-shelf, next to the shopping list and Order Book.

She hesitated. Perhaps she hadn't better just vanish in the night – in case they sent the police to find her in the morning. Maybe she should leave some sort of note.

Nervously she took the Order Book and pencil to the kitchen table and sat down. Then carefully she tore a page from the small notebook, with its long grocery lists on the other pages, and began to write her farewell:

Dear Family,
By the time you read this I shall have gone for ever. I could not face seeing you all again and pretending that nothing has happened, so I'm going to Aunt

24

Dolly's in Stretford. Please don't try to get in touch as I've no intention of coming back and it would only cause a terrible scene if you tried to force me. Aunty Dolly will no doubt be telephoning to Mother (I mean Grandmother) and Tommy will still be coming back home so he can keep you in touch with everything.

Your ever loving, grateful grandchild,

Dasia

Love to my aunties and my new mother: Andrina.
I forgive everyone and wish you all a Merry Christmas.

Dasia propped the letter up against a tea-pot, then she went to the back door, unlocked it and made her lonely way down The Grove in the cold winter dawn with, far away, the sound of a rumbling milk cart.

The snow had melted and now she was glad.

She knew there would be no transport at this time in the morning to Stretford, but she was a good walker and the morning was looking dry and crisp. She felt slightly exhilarated, and after three miles of fresh, quiet, early morning winter air, she felt happier, but very hungry. She prayed fervently for a dairy or a corner shop to lift up its blinds, although she knew she'd have to be careful about parting with the small amount of money in her handbag. She stopped for a few minutes and sat on a low, red-brick wall to rest. It was amazing how quickly she'd managed this distance, especially for a person with – with a s...! Her stomach contracted and she felt faint; her SUITCASE! Still at home in the kitchen! No wonder she'd managed so well ... Oh, my God! What now? Not even any night attire or a change of clothes. Yet it was

25

impossible to go back, for she had virtually burned her boats.

Never would her pride allow her to go slinking back to collect her suitcase, even if she had to sleep in the nude and wear her clothes till they became rags. Her only slight consolation was that her handbag was here and it held her Penny Bank-book and all her most personal belongings, such as the small silver-framed photograph of the whole family, taken in Whitworth Park on May Day two years ago. She suddenly thought about her birth certificate. Funny how things like that had always been thought of as special legal matters linked only with Mother and Father and still hidden in a locked family deed-box.

Dasia realised now how well Mother had checked her natural curiosity in all matters of the world with phrases like: 'That's *enough*!', and 'Don't be cheeky!', or 'Little girls should be seen, but not heard.' And how often, on her more exuberant days, Father had said, 'A whistling woman and a crowing hen'll drive the Devil from 'is den ...' Well, there would be no need for *that* any more.

By the time she reached Aunt Dolly's in Derbyshire Lane, Stretford, she was dropping from hunger and exhaustion. It was now well past breakfast time and most people were already at work, including, she knew, her brother-cum-uncle Tommy, who lodged with Aunty Dolly during the week.

It was nearly a year since she'd visited Dolly's, and then it was just for afternoon tea, with Mother – and Aunt Dolly had spent half the time fussing round in the kitchen getting the meal prepared for her three lodgers.

'I should never have become a landlady when poor Oswald died,' she'd moaned. 'I should have taught music instead. But now I'm trapped with them, and even when I put the charges up they still want to stay.'

Dasia walked timorously towards the three stone

steps leading to the front porch with its decorated fretwork, and its panels of stained glass purple irises. She moved her hand towards the shiny circle of brass which held the door bell, and pressed.

Her Aunt opened the door. She was wearing a forget-me-not flowered overall, and a kitchen mob-cap. 'Dasia love! What on earth are you doing here at this time in the morning? Come in ...'

Dasia followed her through the hall into the dining-room, where a man in a brown suit wiped his moustache on a napkin before leaving the room.

'Mr Corcoran. Last one out. Commercial traveller,' said Dolly. 'Have a cup of tea? Did you take the tram?'

'No, I walked.'

'Have some of that nice toast he's left – while it's still hot, love ... You *walked*? Whatever for?'

'I've left home. But I left my suitcase behind by accident.' Dasia felt her eyes prickling with misery as she nibbled a piece of toast.

'Have a bit of that nice home-made marmalade on it, dear ...'

Dolly sat down: 'Left home? Did I hear right? Whatever's gone wrong? Don't say your Dad's turned into a tipster and 'ad to make a run for it, and it's broken up the family 'ome, because Alice 'as throttled 'im. Your dad's brother, Charlie, did just that! He became a bookie, and changed 'is mind again within twenty-four hours. He and 'is pal, Ronny, 'ad to quit, pronto – because Black Diamunda won at hundred t'one, and the crowd chased 'im and Ronny right down Stretford Road because they couldn't pay up.'

Her round, smiling face and joking patter belied the serious look in her dark brown eyes. 'So how will you do without your things if you've left 'ome? You can't sleep in the buff, lovey, not at your age ... not with lodgers about. Even though my particular gents are thoroughly well mannered and young Tommy is pure as driven snow. But always remember, Dasia dear, every man has his darker moments and it's often in a broom cupboard with a bit of fluff.'

Dasia stared at her pleadingly: 'I just *can't* go back. Somehow I've just *got* to manage ...'

'But why, child?'

'Because since yesterday I've changed to an entirely different person. I've found that our Andrina is ...' she began to weep ... 'm-my ... m-mother!'

Aunty Dolly pulled her chair close and put two firm arms round Dasia: 'You poor, poor bairn. I've often brooded on whether you'd ever get to know. It's shameful the way Alice and Horace kept it all a secret. And your father, Blennim, was such a nice young lad. His misfortune was he had a spitfire of a mother who sent him away to Canada as soon as she heard whisper of it. He was twenty-four, and was supposed to be a bit delicate, with hints of TB, and she insisted that his death was imminent and that he'd only survive with the pure fresh air of Saskatchewan. You know what it's like, love – the old story of the creaking gate that outlives everyone ...'

'But he hasn't outlived everyone, Aunty! Father received a letter from Blennim's father to say he's just died. He lived in Canada, and he left some things for me to go and collect.' Dasia opened her purse and showed Dolly the letter.

'Glory-be! I can hardly believe it. What a very strange set-up! And all expenses paid ... I'd jump at that if it was me.'

'But how can I? I can't go this very *second*.'

Dasia went silent. She didn't tell Dolly she had virtually stolen the letter from the kitchen table. In reality it belonged to her father, but she knew full well that in his state of mind the letter could be swept away

28

and lost forever and he wouldn't care.

'I expect what you need is a bit of a job,' said Dolly, thoughtfully. 'Trouble is, I can't ask you to stay and help me here, because I've got it all worked out with Mrs Wainscott, oo does me charring.' Her chubby face suddenly brightened: 'There is a faint chance that Marcia Mullander, next door but two, might need a maid. She has a new one about once a week. Anyway, get yourself up to the attic to the Put-U-Up and get a bit of shuteye. You look washed out, love. I'll wake you up at midday for a proper meal. You'll find one of my nighties in the top drawer of the tallboy on the landing. Marcia's a bit on the fast side, mind,' said Dolly as they both plodded up two flights of stairs, 'but I'll go and see her right now, an' I'll ring Alice about your clothes. There's plenty of hot water, now the men's out. And nowt's on t'slot meter here.'

The settee bed was paradise, and Dasia was asleep in a few minutes. What a blessing to have a relation like Aunt Dolly . . .

Dolly was true to her word, for when Dasia woke up it was gone midday, and Dolly had rung Alice Greenbow and after a great argy-bargy had arranged for her to come round in the afternoon with Dasia's suitcase. She'd also been round to Marcia's and fixed up for Dasia to start there, helping out, the following morning.

'You must have read it in the tea cups,' said Marcia to Dolly, drifting her long fingers about as she waited for the silver nail varnish to dry. 'I was nearly having kittens when Lizzy walked out at six this morning with my best fur coat on her back.'

Dasia was all on edge during the afternoon. She was dreading seeing her grandmother. She peered through the front window, endlessly wondering how Alice Greenbow would arrive with having the case to carry.

Would she come by train to Edge Lane and then get a bus? or – surely not a taxi all that way? They could never afford that! P'raps she would just trundle here on the tram.

Then – just as she'd turned away from watching – she heard the sound of a car pulling up and Dolly's voice bellowing cheerfully, 'Don't for God's sake leave him there in his own car like a common chauffeur – bring 'im in.' And into the room trouped Alice, in her best fox fur drape, following by Andrina with Mr Tankerton behind them, carrying the suitcase. And never a sign or whisper of Mr Tankerton's usual ever-present Mother.

'We aren't stopping, Dolly.' Alice's voice was shrill and tense: 'It's tragic the way you've been disrupted by this little minx. But we've brought the little baggage her baggage – and that's an end to it.'

'It is *not* an end of it,' said Andrina bristling up, and clutching her artificial pearls, as they all stood about in Dolly's front room. 'I know you're overwrought – and no wonder. It was a big shock for everyone to find that note left against the tea-pot, in our kitchen this morning ...'

They all, except Samuel Tankerton, glared at Dasia.

She was standing like a statue, her red-gold hair cascading to her shoulders and her face pale from inner fright.

Then Samuel passed his hand slowly and calmly across his faintly freckled dome, gave a polite placatory cough, and sat down in a metal-studded leather armchair – tapping slightly with his index finger on the brass ash-tray, with its ribbon of fringed, weighted suede draped across the arm of his chair.

Dolly relaxed and smiled reassuringly at Dasia: 'Sit down on the tapestry stool, lovey.' Then she turned to the others: 'She's just as upset as you are. Worse in fact. *We* all knew about it all along. It's been a terrible shock for her. Anyway, I've got her a job – starting tomorrow, helping out next door but two, with Marcia Mullander, and she'll always have Tommy here as a bit of company.'

'Never mind Tommy for company,' said Alice sharply, 'what about *us* and *work*? What about the pawn shop? We can't afford to get some girl from outside. When she's twenty-one she can do as she damn well pleases, but until that day she'll do as *I* say!'

Dasia saw Andrina suddenly go scarlet: 'She will not do what *you* say any more, Mother. She's *my* daughter, and if she wants to stay here, she can.'

'If I agree ...' said Dolly swiftly, with warning glinting in her eyes. 'I'm not going to be a soft touch, even for your Dasia. No one's going to make a mug of me. I've got enough to do looking after my gentlemen – and it's only out of the goodness of my heart I took your Tommy in. I'm certainly not here as a common lodging house for a tribe of Greenbows!' She suddenly noticed Samuel Tankerton gazing up at the white embossed circle of plaster laurel leaves round the electric light.

Andrina said, 'It was very good of Sammy to bring us. He's a lawyer with a very busy practice near Albert Square ...'

'I'll make us all a cup of tea,' said Dolly, rushing from the room. 'Come and help me, Dasia.'

After a cup of tea, when everyone had calmed down, Andrina said, 'We may as well get it all settled, Dasia. You're welcome either to come straight back home with us now, or come back later. Either way, you can always visit us any time you want. We all know it was an awful shock, and Dad'll miss you terribly. But it's up to you. P'raps the break here, with Aunt Dolly'll help to smooth things out. Especially if you're already set up with a nice little job helping Mrs Mullander. What a stroke of good luck ... Anyway, don't forget, dear, that I am your

31

mother and will always try to help you. In a way, it's much better to have it all out in the open.'

Alice Greenbow seemed lost for words, except to say, 'Give Tommy our love ...' Then Samuel Tankerton stood up, complete in his grey spats, and holding his bowler hat and brown pig-skin gloves, and they all stepped out to the Ford and drove away with lots of polite waving.

'Your Tommy usually gets in about five thirty for his evening meal,' said Dolly a bit later. 'You'll just have to explain the whole situation to him yourself, because I'll be very busy looking after my gentlemen.'

While Dasia thankfully unpacked a few things from her case in the attic, she wondered what she would say to Tommy. He was four when she'd been born – so could he remember that far back, and did he know already that Andrina was her mother?

'What are *you* doing here?' he said when he saw her. 'What's up?' He was a tall, thin boy, with neatly cut brown hair, and his face had fallen a mile.

'Nothing's up, Tommy. But there's been a sort of change in the family and I'm not living at home any more. It's quite a long story.'

Tommy tried to hide his displeasure, as they both tucked in to tripe and onions with great lumps of buttery potatoes in the thick white sauce.

'I'm only staying here till tomorrow, anyway,' said Dasia with her mouth bulging. 'I know you don't want me here, cramping your style. Anyway, Aunt Dolly's got me fixed up to help out with her neighbour, Mrs Mullander.'

Tommy almost choked, then bending towards her he gulped in a low voice, 'You can't go *there* ... She's a loose woman. But why did you leave home in the first place? A girl's place is at home.'

Dasia felt her temper rising. 'Look, Mr Clever Boots

– if a girl's place is at home, how is it that she can be conveniently transported to that bloody pawn-shop every day? At least you're training for a proper job with good pay – but girls "at home" get nothing but slavery!' Dasia swung her arm out so vehemently that the vinegar from the cruet went flying through the air and narrowly missed Mr Corcoran who was just about to sit down.

'For God's sake, calm down, Dasia,' hissed Tommy after he'd picked up the bottle and apologised. 'Keep your hair on! Look, how about coming with me to Redman's tonight and you can tell me the whole story?'

Dasia's heart lifted and she nodded, and smiled. She'd never been to Redman's Dancing Academy before. It was in King's Street, not far from the white marble-fronted Picturedrome. It was a very respectable place where people learned to dance, as well as enjoying general dancing and refreshments. Even Andrina had been there on occasions. She took a deep breath of delight. Thank goodness she'd packed her party frock.

They arrived about eight-thirty, which was quite late because Aunty Dolly had made her help with all the washing up. 'At least Grandfather and Grandmother at home sometimes wash up between them,' she grumbled to Tommy as they finally got out.

He was staring at her with a very puzzled look on his face: ' ... *Grand*father and *Grand*mother? What on earth are you wittering on about? They all died – years ago!'

So he *didn't* know ...!

Dasia said no more until they were inside Redman's. They had been given tickets to claim their refreshments, and she sat down at one of the small tables round the hall which were covered with red and white check tablecloths – while Tommy went for the tea and cakes, and potted-meat sandwiches.

She felt quite special in her pale blue, crepe-de-chine

33

party dress with its bunch of silky fabric violets pinned on the shoulder. Her eyes shone with sudden happiness.

'Excuse me, but, even in this light, I think we've met before. Only yesterday in fact – at the shop – in all that awful slush and snow.'

She knew the voice immediately and she gazed up at the strong-featured face beneath the thick mop of dark curls.

'How did your sister go on then? I called back today to find out, but the place was closed.'

'She's very well, thank you.' Dasia stared at him, dumbfounded. He was carrying a tray with refreshments on it. Was he *working* here?

He seemed to read her thoughts: 'I'm just over there on the far side with –' he hesitated imperceptibly, 'my pal from the hospital and his girl friend, and another girl who's her friend. I'm really acting as gooseberry.' He laughed and showed a perfect set of teeth.

Dasia stared at him silently. Then quickly she glanced across to where he'd pointed. The two girls both had their hair in short shingles, and she suddenly wished hers was modern and more grown-up, instead of just hanging down in loose waves. 'I'm here with my brother. He's meeting two friends. I've just left home to work in Derbyshire Lane – helping a friend of my Aunt's. They probably closed the shop because they were short of staff.'

He nodded and then strode off to the other tables, just as Tommy came back.

'Who the Dickens was that?' said Tommy. 'I thought you said you didn't know anyone round here.'

'I don't. He came into the shop yesterday. His car caused Andrina to slip in all the slush and churned-up snow. It was at dinner-time when she was setting off to see Louise in Baulden's, and he carried her back into the shop. It sounds as if he works at a hospital somewhere.

34

He didn't seem to be very hospitably when he carried Andrina in ... He never even bothered about whether we needed a doctor or anything.'

'He looks as if he's part of a Fast Set,' said Tommy primly. Then he said, 'And there's just no sign of Eustace and Joey. They swore they'd be here. It's just as well I've got you to hang around with.'

'Thank you *very* much ...' Dasia was just going to add, mockingly, 'dear brother' when she remembered it had all changed, so she said, 'Well, it's good they've never turned up because it'll give me time to tell you what's happened.'

By the time she'd finished telling him, Tommy looked like a wet week, and the evening was nearly at an end. 'I can hardly believe it,' he groaned. 'Fancy me having a *niece* as old as you!' Then he brightened up. It was a lady's choice waltz and a girl he knew, called Monica Tremelow, was advancing towards him with her dance card to sign. With a huge sigh of relief at escaping from Dasia he hurried towards the dance floor to the strains of 'Two Little Girls in Blue ...' while Dasia sat there on a plain bentwood chair feeling rather self-conscious. Everyone seemed to be dancing except herself, and it was really up to her – with it being a lady's choice. She looked at her card. It was completely empty. There was hardly anyone else sitting there, and the hospital man with the dark curly hair was going at it hammer and tongs with one of the girls from his table, who was nearly chewing his ear off, and was pressed close enough for suffocation. Dasia sniffed jealously. She wouldn't like to be squashed as near to a man as *that* in a public place.

Hastily she got up and went to the only male left sitting there. He was almost as old as Grandfather, and had what was called 'a huge corporation'. His large red face beamed with happy surprise and she was soon hooked against his stomach, as if she was clinging to some gigantic round boulder, and almost whisked completely off her feet in a sea of perspiration and wobbling fat, as he quickly took to the floor. He obviously prided himself at steering, and Dasia had the awful feeling that it wasn't the dancing, or even the music, he enjoyed but the ability to weave in and out of the crowd missing them all by a fraction of an inch, while using his feet on delicate satin slippers as if he was trampling grapes.

Until, all of a sudden he ran full-tilt into a pair of dancers, with poor Dasia attached to his midriff like the buffers on a train.

'Look out, you old fool!' The girl's voice was muffled in the mad collision as all four of them toppled on to the floor, and Dasia to her total astonishment found herself lying in the arms of the hospital man, who was now laughing his head off – but not for long.

No one else was laughing and, to her horror, Dasia felt her hair being grabbed and almost torn from her head by the girl who had been the hospital man's partner.

'She contrived that, Henry! She deliberately planned for old fatty Spenkinsop to steer himself over here and smash into us!'

'Rubbish, Hetty. Absolute bilge!'

By now others had charged into the fray, including Tommy, who was trying to get to the aid of Dasia. Hetty now turned on fat, elderly Mr Spenkinsop and began to bat him about the head with a gold-sequinned handbag. By the time Tommy got through the mêlée, Dasia had been whisked right out of the dancing academy, through a back window, by the hospital man, Henry.

They rested outside in the darkness, breathing in the cool, quiet air, and listening to all the noise still going on inside. Then Henry said, 'I'd better see you home right now. The quicker we're away the better. I don't suppose I'll ever be going there again. It's the first, and last time. I might have known Hetty Edwyns would cause a scene. It's one of her favourite pastimes. So, where was it you said you were living? Derbyshire Lane? I don't even know your name.'

'Dasia, she muttered it shyly, 'and yours is Henry . . .'

'Only when I'm out with Hetty. My name's Henry Wrioth, but all my real friends and relations call me Hal.'

'And my name's Dasia Greenbow.'

'Pleased to meet you, Miss Greenbow.' They stopped near Queen Victoria Park, under the bare branches of a sycamore, and shook hands.

'Pleased to meet you, Mr Wrioth.'

'Do you think we can ever meet again in better circumstances?' said Hal. 'I'd better say first – I'm a medical student, and we work very funny hours. On call, and all that sort of thing; lots of lectures to attend. Do you happen to be on the phone by any chance . . .?

'My Aunty Dolly is. She'd always pass on a message if I wasn't there.' Dasia's heart began to beat excitedly.

'Would you allow me to kiss you? You're so . . . beautiful.'

She hung her head as if she was ashamed. She somehow felt that people shouldn't be kissed just because they were supposed to be beautiful. She would have liked it better if he'd not said anything. Then she said, 'I'd rather not – if you don't mind. I've got to be up in the morning early, to start my new job. But I'll look out for the phone call.'

He saw her to the front door of Aunty Dolly's, but when he'd gone she went upstairs feeling her heart would break. What on earth had she done – telling him not to kiss her – when it might mean she would never see him again in her whole life?

There was a tap on the attic door. It was Aunty. 'Are you all right, Dasia?'

'Yes, quite all right, Aunty. Come in, if you want.'

Dolly came in and looked at her, curled up under the eiderdown. 'I was just wondering what happened to Tommy. He doesn't usually stay out this late because of getting up early in the morning for work. Did he meet someone?'

Dasia tried to wriggle away from Dolly's gaze. Whatever could she say?

'Did you come home with someone else, Dasia? I thought I saw a tall young man with you. A very athletic-looking one. I know it sounds old fashioned, but don't ever let them go too far, love. And *never* let them kiss you on the first time out or they may take advantage. Men aren't quite the same as us; they have what are known as "urges" all the time.'

Dasia closed her eyes tight, and said in a muffled sleepy voice, 'He was quite all right, Aunty. He was the man who looked after Andrina yesterday, when she slipped on the pavement outside the pawn shop. He's a medical student at the Manchester Prince Infirmary, and he lives in special student lodgings. There was a bit of a fuss at the dance because my partner crashed into someone by accident and Hal rescued me and brought me back here. I expect our Tommy stayed on with a girl he knows called Monica Tremelow ...'

Luck was with her, for at that very moment, at eleven-fifteen, there was the sound of a key in the front door, and it was Tommy. Then a bit later as he came to bed he nipped up and whispered her name. She went to the door and opened it gently: 'What on *earth* happened to you, Tommy? Aunty was going mad, wondering why you weren't back.'

'Because of *you*, that's what!' said Tommy, breathing angrily. 'The local copper arrived just after you vanished, and we were all nearly going to have our names and addresses taken, until poor old Spenkinsop said it was all his fault, and a storm in a tea-cup. Anyway, I walked Monica home after that – and I'm taking her to the Picturedrome next Wednesday. And she let me kiss her – even though it was the first time I'd ever walked her home.'

'Tommy! You shouldn't.'

'Why ever not?'

Dasia bit her lip, she was just going to tell him what Aunty had said – then thought better of it, and said, 'Sleep tight, and mind the bugs don't bite' instead. And soon she was sound asleep herself.

The following morning she was up bright and early, all washed and spruced up in her jumper and skirt ready to go and work at Marcia Mullander's.

'She won't be expecting you as early as this on the very first day,' said Dolly, looking at the clock, which said eight o'clock. 'She knows I'll be going round with you to get you started, and we both have our own gentlemen to attend to first, so calm down and have another cup of tea. Then get your apron on and help me a bit with all the pots.'

Not all that washing up, yet *again* … Then, in a sudden flash of insight, Dasia realised that this would be the pattern of her life, for all the time she stayed with Dolly or Dolly's friend, Marcia. And she began to wonder whether it was going to be any better than working in the family pawn shop? At least in there she'd been her own boss for quite a lot of the time when the shop was quiet. But here, it was plain to see, she would have hardly a single moment of privacy; never a second to herself as she ran round in circles looking after a lot of lazy lodgers.

'Always remember, love,' said Dolly as they washed

and wiped the dishes together, 'men need a lot of looking after, and boy babies are always harder to rear than us girls. They even take longer to get out of the womb, and they're always trying to get back in it ... You *might* think my gentlemen appear rather idle, and that I wait on them hand and foot. But don't forget they're on the road morning till night, in their little Tin Lizzies, trying to sell goods to people who don't want to buy 'em.'

By quarter-past-nine they were ready to go, and Dasia breathed with relief as they walked along to Marcia's.

The house was detached and bigger than Dolly's. It had lined, deep blue velvet curtains at the front windows and heavily draped lace curtains, with an Edwardian look about them.

'Her name's *Mrs* Mullander, but don't *ever* enquire about her hubby,' warned Dolly. Then she said, 'And get your hair cut as soon as you can. It's safer.'

Dasia gave a rueful smile. It was certainly safer if it was going to be grabbed and tugged out like it was last night at the dancing academy.

They didn't go to the front door. Dolly took her along the gravel path to the back, and waved to Marcia who was in the kitchen as she knocked at the door.

'What a blessing! Come in,' said Marcia in a deep gushing voice, her eyes as heavy as full green pea-pods. 'It was just like a bolt from heaven when you said your niece was here and could come and work.' She gave Dasia a long, searching all-over look: 'What beautiful hair you've got, dear.'

'I've been telling her to get it cut, Marcia. She doesn't want to be having to tooth-comb it every night. There won't be time ...'

'Oh! ... I don't know. Some people love hair like that.'

Dasia gave a slight shudder. There was something

about the way she said it. She looked quickly towards Dolly, but Dolly seemed cheerfully oblivious, as she remarked on the terrific size of the aspidistra in a big green bowl like a chamber-pot, on a bamboo what-not in the corner.

'Will she be able to live in, Dolly? It'll be so much handier, especially with it being so near Christmas, and party-time.'

'She'll be delighted, won't you, Dasia dear?' said Aunty swiftly, as she beamed at her. 'It'll help her in her first steps to independence; she's always lived at home until now.'

'The wages are ten shillings a week, and all found,' said Marcia. 'And what anyone gives you in tips is your own affair.'

'That seems very fair to me,' said Dolly, smiling at Marcia as one landlady to another. 'She's a lucky girl to be in such nice surroundings.'

Dasia's heart sank. It seemed a hundred years since she'd been lying in her own vast bed in their wonderful wreck of a house, and working in the family pawn shop. Yet it was only two short days ago. She had been well educated. She was used to better than this, but what else could she do? She'd come to Aunt Dolly in an hour of need and this was what she had been given to keep her going. Well, at least it was better than some people ... Better than people with large families, living round Ancoats and actually starving. Some folk would no doubt regard her as a spoilt brat from a wealthy background, having a home address like The Grove, but that was now gone for ever.

Marcia had brightly hennaed orange hair, cut in a bob – and she contantly wore three lots of powerful looking beads which drooped towards her thin bosom. Her lipstick was very dark red and her eyelashes were black as coal, about the pale white-pouched eyes and green eye

41

shadow. Dasia had to admit she was fascinated by this older woman who was like a viper compared to her sister, Rosalie, and *her* rumbustious make-up.

'From half past five in the morning until three in the afternoon you must always wear green needle-stripe dresses, white starched aprons, and a dust cap,' purred Marcia. 'I've got quite a large stock to fit your size, chick, because for some reason I've recently had a batch of really naughty girls who've hardly stayed here a second. So I hope we won't have any more problems in *that* quarter ...'

'I'm sure you won't, Marcia,' beamed Aunty Dolly. 'What could be nicer than a guest house to start off in life? None of your working men's hostels round here, or those really common lodging houses, or nasty commercial travellers' places full of ill repute ... No, just good fun and a homely, friendly, refined atmosphere. A lovely start for any young miss in this modern age.'

'And from three in the afternoon till eleven at night you'll wear black sateen dresses with a broderie Anglaise bib and white frilly afternoon apron, with black stockings and shoes, of course ... plus a white frilled head bandeau slotted with black velvet ribbon. I don't mind about the length of your skirts, it's up to you.'

'I advise you to keep them *very* long, dear ...' said Dolly hastily.

'That all depends on what lengths have been left behind by other wearers,' said Marcia coldly. 'Most of the girls have been even shorter than Dasia, and the only tall girl was like a rhubarb stick and her dress would reach to Dasia's ankles!'

There was a heavy silence, then Dolly said to Dasia, 'And, of course, you won't be working *all* those hours at once, Dasia, love ...' she looked at Marcia: 'It'll be split shifts ... Surely?'

Marcia scowled slightly then nodded hypocritically.

'Oh! yes ... but of course. Except in a desperate emergency. And it always *is* much, much busier at Christmas – with all the parties and things. And, of course ... if there was a flu epidemic or something. But as you know, there is other help; there's Mrs Wainscott who chars for me and you, Dolly. And I have a daily cook called Mrs Parsons.'

'That's all right then,' said Aunty with a happy sigh. 'You've really saved my bacon, Marcia.'

'And you've saved mine, Dolly,' murmured Marcia.

'I'll love you and leave you then, Dasia,' said Dolly. 'But always remember, I'm only a few doors away. I must get back; Mr Corcoran might be in at midday.'

'And we all know what that means,' murmured Marcia, as she showed Dolly out through the front door.

It took Dasia only a couple of days to get into the pattern of Tweeny Jill of All Trades, at Marcia's. She had hardly time to breathe or gollup down half a mince pie. And never even a *second* to think about her own Greenbow family in The Grove, or whether Hal Wrioth might have rung Aunty Dolly's to get in touch like he'd promised.

Life was turning out to be hectic, working from five-thirty each morning, until well past eleven o'clock at night with never a proper rest during the day.

'You're the best and most refined help I've ever had, dear,' Marcia cooed, 'and all my Sugar Daddies agree with me ...' Her guests, all men, numbered more than Dolly's three, for she had eight of them of varying ages, but none of them less than forty, who all seemed to be heavy spenders – judging by the tips Dasia kept finding, with innocent delight, underneath saucers and tucked about on breakfast and drinks trays.

Because she was kept so busy, and she was so young and energetic, and because the air was so full of the festive season with the traditional Christmas excitements and yet more flurries of snow, Dasia was swept along in a flurry of sheer delight. So much so that when her own seventeenth birthday arrived on the twenty-first, she'd forgotten about it and was only reminded by birthday cards and presents being brought round by Dolly.

She noticed with a sort of shrewd sadness that they were only 'token' presents, and not half as lavish as last year's. It was a sure sign that she was now in another, adult world. Silk stockings from Rosalie, Yardley's lavender soap from Grandmother and Grandfather. Gloves from Louise, a machine-knitted scarf – with a flaw in its pattern – from Andrina. A bottle of Barker and Dobson's barley sugar from Tommy, and a box of handkerchiefs from Aunt Dolly.

'I never *realised* it was your birthday, dear,' said Marcia in honeyed tones. 'People aren't seventeen *every* day. We must have a little celebration. It's only right to do *something*, seeing there's no way you can have any time off at present ...' For a brief moment Dasia felt a surge of anger. It might be all right just now, but she wasn't going to accept such long working hours for such terrible wages for ever. Surely Marcia would let her have the New Year off in lieu of all the extra work she was doing at Christmas?

A picture of her worst tasks rose before her mind's eye: emptying Mr Tonker's old-fashioned shaving mug with the beautiful roses on it, which he used as a spittoon and was always full of green phlegm; brushing up all the moustache clippings and toe-nail snippets from Mr Batril's bedroom rug; and cleaning out the lavatory when posh Mr Rainsly had covered the floor like a heavy April shower. She even had to sew up large rips in Mr Tomlington's flannel pyjamas, which one would imagine might have withstood even an Indian sabre, and put all Mr Dornay's five-pound notes away in

the wardrobe from where they often lay, on the floor –
in case he should accuse her of theft.

'Many Happy Returns of the Day, Dasia!' said
Marcia. 'We'll have a nice piece of cake and a small glass
of sherry each after supper tonight, to drink your health.
Before my guests go off to their other varied pursuits.'

It was fortunate that Dasia wasn't there when Marcia
announced it at the start of the evening meal. There was
a mixed reaction and a lot of grumbling, as they all
started their soup. 'What the hell's got into her –
wanting us to drink a toast to a little skivvy?' said fifty-
year-old Freddy Frandle. 'She's never been as fussy as
this before with the others. She's got a damned cheek
expecting us to conform to all her little whims like a load
of bloody school kids!'

'Be charitable,' said Marcia sweetly. 'We've all got
this dear little girl helping us, and it's her birthday this
very day ...'

'What's special about that then? We all have to suffer
those,' said seventy-year-old Berty Rainsly – slurping
away at his Cock-a-Leekie.

'Nothing's special, Mr Rainsly. It's just to show a
seasonal mark of our affection. She's seventeen and just
starting off on life's road.'

'As long as she doesn't hang around at the jolly old
street corners on the way, ay – what?' snorted ex-army
officer Tomlington. 'Keep 'em on the move – that's
what I say.'

'Be fair, you chaps,' said Mr Batril, who was a debonair
forty-five. 'We must always be polite to lady folk, whatever
their status, and I'm always ready for a free drink.'

At the end of the meal, with grim determination,
Marcia showed her guests who was boss by giving them
all a small piece of fruit cake and a small glass of sherry,
while she stood in front of the door, with an embarrassed
Dasia by her side.

That night Dasia felt a bit sad. Her thoughts went back to the night at Redman's when Hal had wanted to kiss her and she had refused. How different to all this ... She went into the kitchen and began to refill Freddy Frandle's stone hot water bottles. She screwed them tight, in the hope that they wouldn't be leaking in the morning, then put them in their red flannel covers and took them, one at a time, upstairs. She usually put one in the middle of his bed and one at the bottom. She was glad to get it over and done with ... and had just finished when, to her complete amazement, the door opened and Mr Frandle came in, in his dressing gown and nothing else.

She pretended not to see, and stood there, politely, ready to get out of the room as quickly as she could.

'Seventeen today then?' said Frandle, with such heavy, stertorous breathing that Dasia thought he must have been running up the stairs.

He was staring at her with a very strange look on his face. Then he went to the bed and ripped back the covers, and removed both the hot water bottles, putting them on the floor.

Like an innocent fool Dasia went towards the bottles to ask what was the matter, and maybe to put them back again. But as she bent down, he was on her and had thrown her back hard on to the bed.

For a second Dasia lay inert – then, with super-human strength and fury, she jabbed him straight in the face with a small, snaking fist, brought up her knee to thump him in his tenderest parts, bit his arm – and jumped off the bed. Then, like a frenzied maniac, she got one of the stone hot water bottles and hurled it at the dressing-table mirror. 'How DARE you,' she screamed. 'How *dare* you treat people like that, you disgraceful old donkey!' She was amazed at her own language for, unlike Grandma, she was rarely rude to people.

Then she stamped downstairs and, trembling all over, walked into the now empty dining-room and, finding the key to the drinks cabinet, took out some orange juice and added a very small teaspoonful of whisky to it – just like Rosalie did when she was under pressure. It tasted horrible! and she swore from that moment on to be teetotal.

'Whatever was that awful crash from upstairs?' gasped Marcia, rushing into the room. 'It sounded like breaking glass!'

'It was coming from Mr Frandle's bedroom,' said Dasia with deathly calm. 'It was the stone hot water bottle hitting the mirror. Seven years bad luck ... He tried to rape me.' Then she collapsed in a heap and began to sob.

'Tried to *rape* you, girl?' Marcia's voice was like ice, and so were her eyes. 'You're letting your imagination stray too far. Your birthday has gone to your head! My guests aren't like that!'

'Freddy Frandle is, and that's a fact,' said Dasia, reviving as the teaspoonful of whisky coursed through her veins.

'Freddy Frandle is the kindest, most likeable man in the whole place,' lied Marcia, wondering if she would be able to outwit this sharp little red-haired child, and cursing the moment she ever decided to employ her. 'How dare you say things like that! How disloyal can you get – after all your Aunty and I have done for you?'

Marcia's brain raced ... she was trapped in an awkward situation. If she turfed Dasia out right now, she knew the awkward little tyke would go round hollering Rape! to everyone who'd listen – though she doubted if Dolly would believe her story because she, too, only took in 'Respectable Gentlemen'. And, also, it was going to be impossible to get someone decent to work over Christmas for such long and unsociable hours.

'I don't want to hear another word about it, Dasia,' she said through tight lips. 'You'll just get up those stairs and get all the damage cleared up. Tell Mr Frandle I'll come up and see him when it's been done, and he can sleep in the spare bedroom. And if any real damage has been caused it'll just have to come out of your wages.'

Dasia listened in stony silence. She was in as much of a dilemma as Marcia. Where on earth would she go if Marcia kicked her out? She knew that Dolly wouldn't want any trouble, and Dolly herself could be extremely awkward and hasty when she chose to be. No, she certainly didn't want to get in Dolly's bad books, or have their Tommy carrying tales back home suggesting she had turned into some sort of loose woman. For, after all, Tommy had tried to warn her, right at the beginning.

When she got upstairs there was no sign of Freddy Frandle, and although the stone hot water bottle was in perfect condition, apart from a few glass splinters in its red flannel cover, the mirror was shattered to bits. Yet it was too awkward for her to move, and she could hardly call on the chivalry of Mr F. Frandle to help her move it. How could she ever face that awful man again?

Next morning, after it was all sorted out and cleared up and Freddy was in the spare room, and she'd got to bed at two a.m. – to be up again by five – the men were as quiet as little lambs as they all sauntered down for their breakfast and wished her a respectful 'good morning'.

The following evening Freddie Frandle looked her in the eyes and said calmly, 'By the way, Miss Greenbow, I wonder if you'd get me two *rubber* ones tonight, and don't screw 'em quite so hard. We don't want any more of 'em accidentally flying out of your tender little hands ...' And from that moment, until she finally left, they never spoke to each other again.

CHAPTER THREE

Hyndemere

Hal was coming home for Christmas after all ...

Cynthia, Lady Wrioth, was full of hope, as she stood in the library at Hyndemere Hall gazing out at the landscape. The light of her life, her one and only child, Hal, had just phoned to say he'd fractured two fingers when dealing with a sixteen-stone man who was coming round from an anaesthetic.

'So I'll be back pretty soon, Mother. No hospital out-patients, after all. Bit of a bind about the hand, but it shouldn't take too long to get back to normal.'

Thinny Wrioth (for that was her pet name) looked at the snow. It glowed smooth as icing sugar in the wintery gloom. Herds of deer dotted thousands of white-clad acres, amongst ivied oaks, and ancient ash trees. The slim, iron-railed boundaries of Hyndemere Park were etched to needlelike fineness. It was indeed a perfect Christmas card.

'Our poor lamb,' she murmured to her husband Bazz. 'Why ever he chose to defy perfectly sound family convention and involve himself with all that sordid nonsense at Manchester Prince Infirmary, we shall

49

never know.' Thinny tugged irritably at her three rows of perfect, salt water oyster pearls, then she marched off to look for Travers the head gardener in the vinery to give him her orders about orchids. She was a thin, frail little thing – determined on orchids for Christmas, as she was about every other detail in her well-tailored life.

Her dark eyebrows were beautifully curved, like her thin curved legs with their bony ankles in the pale grey kid shoes. Authority ran in her veins like Stephenson's blue-black ink, but whenever she and Travers met it was a Greek meets Greek confrontation.

'Orchids are impossible, M'Lady.' He gave her a malevolent glare from beneath his silver thatch of hair.

There was always a deep wound in his heart at the way she called the gardens hers, when all she did was walk round and admire them with her friends, as if she did all the donkey work herself. And now, her favourite phrase was ringing like Christmas bells in his ears: *Nothing is impossible* . . .

'Nothing is impossible, Travers. How many times a week do I have to tell you that nothing is impossible?'

She tried to freeze him out with a cold look, but his blue eyes met hers like hard blue cannon balls 'All't pipes in't' greenouses – OFF! An' don't blame me. All tampered with and buggered about by unknown 'ands. Stone cold for more'n six perishing hours – so there'll be no orchids for Christmas.'

He strode away heavily, stamping his toe-capped leather working boots noisily. But he didn't drown out her ladyship. His ears were always sharp enough to hear the song of the nightingale – as well as her 'Stubborn old sod' floating after him in hallowed female accents from the hot-house air.

Yes, Cynthia Eleanor Joanne Christiana Maria Wrioth, and her husband Lord Henry Basil Lancelot Eugene Wrioth were extremely confident people. Their bible was Debrett's Peerage. They were part of a steely mesh guarding their island jewel set in a silver sea as decreed by divine right.

Thinny and Bazz were a handsome couple. He was a long-legged, well-preserved man of fifty-six, with a hawkish nose and deep-set grey eyes. Wiry grey hair curled round his vivid, fresh-air ears which were as pink as boiled ham.

Hal was very like his father. They were both intelligent, awkward, tough and jealous-minded – with the Spartan spirit lying like a playful, dormant flame in their souls.

Lord Henry (Bazz) Wrioth had been married before, but tragedy struck early in his life, with the loss of a young wife and two small daughters in an earthquake abroad. Nineteen-year-old Hal Wrioth was his only son and heir, from his second marriage. Because of the profound local sympathy this had evoked, the village people, who made up the bulk of Bazz's servants, had over-cosseted him throughout the years – and he had become spoilt and over-demanding. As a consequence there was a steady turnover of new servants who were all personally vetted by Thinny – though it made not a jot of difference to the merry-go-round.

Thinny's favourite uniform as chief of the domestic household ranged from Macclesfield silk to angora wool jumper suits, plus personal jewellery consisting of small flowery brooches of diamonds, sapphires, emeralds and rubies – set in solid gold and silver.

Bazz's wardrobe was carefully nurtured by his personal man, Archie Smith, who tried to guide him away from the combination of fox-brown silk corduroy trousers and a black barathea morning coat worn while practising his golf.

Bazz Wrioth was unusual in that he had relinquished Huntin', Shootin' and Fishin', soon after his first wife

51

died, and now spent happier, more solitary hours in the old stables designing and making – with the help of fourteen-year-old Boots Boy, Dicky Brent – wrought iron trysting gates for his rose gardens. 'Though who you'd expect to see trysting in 'em is a bit of a mystery,' said Thinny with dry affection, for secretly she considered herself quite lucky to have a well-occupied, if slightly peevish Lord who was happy at home.

And what better too, to have one perfect son and heir, instead of the complicated ramifications of a large family tribe, full of petty jealousies about property? Yes, she had made a good catch when she finally hooked old Bazz.

Hal Wrioth packed his heavy pig-skin bag ready for Christmas at Hyndemere. He was extremely annoyed about fracturing his fingers. How could such a thing have happened so quickly and easily? He felt a complete idiot, and chided himself for not being swift and competent enough to deal with Mr Popinjay – the sixteen-stone man being given ether.

To be perfectly candid, he would secretly have preferred being on duty over Christmas with the other medical students, instead of submitting to the formality of festivities at Hyndemere and its matriarchal smothering. But he put a cheerful face on it, smiling broadly at the quips of his friends as, with his two splinted fingers and his arm in a sling, he accepted a lift through the freezing rain in his friend Kenny Saville's two-seater Sunbeam on his way to catch the train to Chester.

Chester, the nearest railway station to his home, was an ancient county town he knew and loved, with its reassuring aura of ages-old history and security, and the vast stone walls of the city resting so peacefully on the northern bank of the beautiful river Dee.

'Wish I was going with you, old boy,' said Kenny,

peering at him affectionately through pebble-like lenses as he blew his nose on a huge paisley-designed, fine lawn handkerchief. 'Wish I'd never taken up this doctor lark. Not cut out for all the gore and guts and bloody starched-up old Matrons – and those dragons of Ward sisters. Must have been tanked up – K-lied – when I signed the pledge. Don't be surprised, old sprout, if I blow mi top when old Perky Johnson shows us the finer points of a smallpox pustule, and walk out for ever! Drop me a few coppers in the cap, old chum, when I'm pleading on the stones in Mosely Street. Give me a kindly smile – and don't, for God's sake, smudge mi chalked-out pavement painting of the left-handed Aortic System.'

Hal nodded wryly. He knew the feeeling . . .

They were passing through Stretford, along Chester Road, near the Naked Child Inn at the river Mersey. They'd passed the Derbyshire Lane, King Street, Victoria Park area where Redman's dancing academy lay. It was miserable weather and nothing but grey smoky slush and sleet drifted through the sky to join blobs of swiftly melting snow as they ploughed noisily along.

Suddenly, Hal thought of Dasia. The phone call . . . No, he'd never got round to ringing her. But he'd make up for it as soon as he got to Hyndemere, he really would. She was a sweet innocent virgin. She deserved more respect than he'd bothered to give her by not keeping his promise. Her delicate features and bright perceptive eyes beneath the curling red gold hair welled up in his mind's eye – and stayed there so hauntingly that in no time at all they were in Altrincham, where he was to take the train to Chester.

'The *cars* they have these days,' cooed Aunt Dolly wondrously to Dasia amidst the coloured balloons strung across the ceiling. 'When I was out just now, I saw this little two-seater sporty one, with two real young blades in it, tearing along Chester Road as fast as any train. I'll swear it was going at thirty miles an hour!' Her beady eyes were round with excitement: 'That's the young monied classes for you!'

Dasia was preparing some boiled, potted shrimps. She was sealing them on top with melted butter which was planned to set solid like sun-yellowed ice. The shrimps were from Southport – brought by Aunt Dolly's favourite lodger, Mr Corcoran, who'd had a night of sin away from his loving, iron-gripped landlady.

Dasia took a deep breath. She felt suddenly defeated. Here she was on December 23rd amongst holly and mistletoe, having an hour's rest from Marcia's – which meant helping Dolly instead. For there was now a new format in her lifestyle. After the recent rape attack by Freddy Frandle, Aunt Dolly and Marcia had hastily agreed that Dasia should stay back with Dolly again, but fulfil her obligations on the servanting side at Marcia's until the fourth of January, which covered for Christmas and New Year, including cleaning up afterwards.

'I must say she's been a *great* disappointment,' sighed Marcia as she and Dolly chewed over the episode for the umpteenth time with renewed relish, disguised with suitable expressions of mock misery, while they parked themselves comfortably in the front room next to the Christmas tree. 'My old boys'll take a long time to get over it all. Freddy has refused his porridge two mornings on the run; Mr Tanker's broken his shaving mug, and Mr Batril's accidentally cut his stupid toe. Mr Rainsly complains all the time about the lavatory chain not pulling properly. No ... there's no sign of true Christmas spirit *anywhere*!'

'I just can't think what came over her,' commiserated Dolly as they both sipped port and lemons, and guarded their teeth slightly from the effects of rock hard mince pies. 'She was just asking for trouble to bend over in *any* gentleman's bedroom – never mind poor Freddy's. But there again, Marcia, if I remember right, you did once call him a sex-starved nincompoop deserted by three wives and forever observing women's combinations on washing lines.'

Marcia's slinky green eyes quivered slightly at the rebuff, and she changed the subject a bit: 'What'll she do when she finishes?'

'She'll just have to go elsewhere,' said Dolly. 'I was prepared to be kind. I did my best for kith and kin. And you helped, Marcia, love. We couldn't have done a stroke more ... Their Tommy can stay with me. He's *no* trouble – But *she'll* have to go! Quite honestly, I see a path of trouble for her wherever she goes in life. She's quietly stubborn. She hasn't even got all that hair cut yet. Oh yes – she was all for being Miss Modern when she was sixteen. And now, only a few days later when she's seventeen she's turned quite different. It was that late night out that did it – at Redman's. That's what's at the bottom of it ...'

'Y-you d-don't think she ...?' Marcia's teeth grated against the pastry in a shock bite, and she winced slightly.

'Oh no. Glory me! Nothing like *that*. Both she and Tommy are unblemished. NO ... It's hard to say ... but she has a very hard little core.'

Then the two of them stroked their faces, smoothed out their skirts, checked their stockings, and departed to their own domains, being careful to remove all traces of cigarette ends, and taking the ash-trays with them for Dasia to clean.

Danny Elvers the chauffeur had just collected Hal from Chester. He was a tall, quite handsome man in a peaked

cap. He wore a grey livery, tailored almost in the style of
an army officer with knee breeches, leather knee boots,
and brown leather gloves.

The snowy lanes knew nothing of Manchester's
murkiness, as the large dark blue Bentley approached
Hyndemere.

The house was set like a Yuletide cake, with whorls of
sparkling, frosted sweetness twisting casually along the
tops of its Tudor chimneys and rows of mullioned
windows that overlooked all its grand territory.

'First class, isn't it sir?' said Elvers cheerfully. 'Quite
brings a lump to the throat. Where else could you find
such an avenue of copper beeches as this, stretching for
a quarter of a mile?'

Hal nodded: 'Two worlds,' he said ruefully.

There was a sudden quietness between them. Then
Elvers said, 'But nice to belong to them both, eh – sir?'

Hal nodded again. Elvers, who was thirty-one and
seemed quite old to him, had fought in France in the
trenches of the Great War – when those around him
were all dying from cholera and dysentery in the mud-
filled dykes of a bloody and terrible battlefield.

'Nice to have a bit of peace, with views like this, sir –
don't cha' know? Good to be alive in the twenties, in
spite of strikes and strife. Nothing comes easy, Hal ...'
The more they talked the more Danny lapsed into an
equal footing.

Nineteen-year-old Hal nodded respectfully. In some
ways he felt relieved that he, too, now knew another
world based on his small amount of hospital experience
– even if it was a place of constant tuberculosis, infant
mortality, and family funerals. It was a gloomy saga, but
at least it was worth knowing about.

Even so, there were times when Hal wanted to forget
the white faces and red snivelling noses, the barefoot
urchins, and the chronic sick who queued so patiently on

the dark wooden benches, with the heady odours of pine disinfectant and creosote and ether and carbolic filling their city lungs, and the echoing sounds of footsteps in the long hard, cold corridors.

The car began to slow down, and as it drew up to the house, he acknowledged his own comfortable station in life and gave silent thanks as he planned always to try to help those worse off than himself – in spite of having a pater and mater who believed in the god given right to certain chosen people to be in charge of all the nation's land and property, for ever and ever, Amen.

'I always like the season of Goodwill to All,' smiled Danny as they pulled up at the intricately carved main entrance. 'Yes ... what I say is – it brings out the best in all of us and shows that, for a few seconds in our lives, we all mean well.'

Then the two men smiled at each other in a cool and knowing way, and Danny Elvers helped Hal with his luggage and relapsed back to 'Sir'. And Hal asked Elvers how his wife Enid was.

'How's her heart?' Enid had suffered from heart trouble after getting rheumatic fever as a child and regarded herself as lucky to be alive and to have borne five children – with all of them still alive and healthy.

'Fine,' said Elvers. They both knew that survival here in a spacious family house on the estate, with Enid helping out occasionally, was a far better bet than living in Ancoats like Enid's sister, or being a starving hill-side farmer near Macclesfield like Danny's brother.

After his arrival, when all the family greetings and general fuss had died down, Hal went up to his room. He was on the first floor which was just as well, as the flights of stairs in the house including the winding back stairs leading to the servants' quarters totalled over two hundred steps.

He looked round, and felt a sense of relief. It was all exactly the same. Although there was a private dressing room and bathroom with gleaming brass taps and delicately designed Minton tiles on the wall, in pale blue and greens with a border of dolphins, his bedroom itself was a museum to the past. An eighteenth-century silver-handled shaving brush stood on an old marble-topped wash stand with a Wedgwood water jug and washing bowl; toys from bygone nursery days still lay undisturbed on white-painted wooden cupboards by the side of a small, ages-old scratched and strangely gouged bookcase full of children's books – from as early as the seventeen hundreds.

He unpacked his belongings alone. These days the fuss of servants made him impatient, and all he longed for was complete privacy. But it was in short supply now, as guests and relations began to arrive for Christmas. There were his maternal grandmother and grandfather Petheridge, both aged eighty-seven, his father's aunt Felicity from Iffley, Oxford, his girl cousins Alicia and Madelaine, and his cousin Cedric. Cedric and Amanda's two noisy little brats called Belinda and Arthur ran up and down the picture gallery sliding about on the polished light oak floors, and screeching like a couple of screech owls.

And lastly, the most annoying and uncalled for guest of all: simpering Cordelia Cadwallader-Fenchurch-Brighton, who was as little like King Lear's youngest daughter as a sponge is to a pearl-handled toothbrush. There she sat in her pointed, pink satin shoes, spreading herself out like a huge, fluffy, angora cushion as she spoke in animated tones to Thinny: 'Oh yes, I had the most marvellous journey and they both send you all oodles and oodles of love and kisses and think Hal's absolutely spiffing to be braving medical school in a place like Manchester, ... and so do I ... ectually ...'

'And how's your dear Ma, Cordy, dear?' smiled Thinny with toothy radiance as she proffered both her elegantly bony hands in genuine affection. 'What ages since Taddle and I last met and talked about our own youthful Coming Out days. It's sweet of you to be here; Hal so desperately needs gals of his own set, and age group. He's a bit lost in the awful hub-bub of the medical world. You'll put things in perspective more ...'

'You Mas are all the same, Thinny,' said Cordelia with the bouncing confidence and sage worldliness of the totally ignorant. 'You want the best for Hal, and Mummy wants the best for *me*. That's why they went off to Monte with a clear conscience – knowing I was to be at beautiful Hyndemere ...'

Her pudding face beamed complacently. She could afford to be slightly smug, because she'd already discovered the true secret of the mature male's desire: a gal with a bit of good flesh on her. Unknown to Thinny or Hal she had just such a desiring male prominently placed in her engagements diary. It was Sir Crombie Delter's fourth son Leonard – a large cumbersome cricket player, who was spending Christmas drying out in a private nursing home – on a special healthy-life menu involving nothing stronger than exorbitantly priced fruit cordials at one and threepence a glass – after a costly binge with some of his more wayward friends.

In his former inebriated state, Leonard had – in a fleeting moment of sheer madness – given Cordelia a ruby ring he found somewhere, as a token of his eternal love, after covering her in soppy wet kisses and calling her a Bouncing Spiffer and a Good Old Prune. Cordy, herself, blessed her lucky stars at hooking one of the richest bachelors in Britain – even though it was a deadly secret, and even though he was now anxiously claiming that the secret betrothal should last at least ten years, if not for life, in case he had made a terrible mistake.

'Ah,' said Thinny, 'here comes Hal ...' she waited serenely, 'I knew you'd soon get together ...'

Hal stared towards the pink pointed satin slippers dolefully. Why on earth couldn't his mother see her matchmaking was a complete failure?

Cordelia advanced towards him like a fluffy embryo mother cushion: 'Hal – how wonderful. Doesn't the house look a dream?'

Lady Wrioth left them and walked away smiling. One had only to mention the beauty of the house and the password to her heart was found.

Hal tried to be sociable. He forced a slight smile: 'I should really be at the hospital, working.' He turned away slightly and looked down at his calico arm sling then towards the growing throng of guests.

There were loud discussions floating through the air about the village carol singing. It was to be held in the hall round the huge open fireplace with flames from the logs roaring and crackling up the massive chimney and finally settling to a late night glowing richness, bathed in the scents of larch and pine. He knew it would be wonderful, and he realised that the giving of presents and cuts of venison to the ordinary villagers was a praiseworthy Yuletide gesture. But a huge restlessness was already welling up inside him, after only a couple of hours. It was always the same – he was captivated by the sight of home, and the thought that it was still all there, and all going well, including his mother and father. But that one glance was all he needed before he got back to the swiftly moving real world that he bore in a strong love-hate relationship ... Dasia's world ...

Why was she haunting him all the time with her natural innocence – in this of all places?

Cordelia's voice stabbed the air: 'I'll look after you,

Hal. I'll be your hand maiden. I'm here all the time Mummy's in Monte Carlo, and I won't leave your side for a second.'

'Good for you,' murmured Hal through gritted teeth. Then he smiled cheerfully and said, 'Incidentally, Cordy, what's this rumour about your being secretly engaged for life to poor old Lenny Delter? Bit of a *faux pas* – wouldn't you say – or are congrats the order of the day?'

'What absolute balderdash!' She went as pink as her satin shoes.

'Sorry, Old Pickle – just some mad tale from Hetty Edwyns who said Lenny pinched her ruby ring when they were at a dance, and gave it to you by mistake.'

'Complete and utter tripe, Hal! I wouldn't be seen *dead* in anything she'd worn – even if it was the Koh-i-Noor. She's a cheap little trollop, and her father's a scrap iron merchant.' Cordelia's blue eyes flashed like steel above large flushed cheeks, as Hal moved away swiftly and disappeared to his own bedroom again.

He'd brought with him a new recording of Franz Lehar's Gold and Silver Waltz for his mother's gramophone collection, which she kept in the lacquered, mother-of-pearl inlaid cabinet in her dressing room. It was her hoarding place for secret delights, behind the black and gold papier-mâché screen which had been designed a century ago by Bazz's grandfather. The screen incorporated the family crest of the sharp-eyed serval with its tufted ears. And round it was spread, in a flat meandering ribbon of Latin: LIVE ONCE BUT PLAN THREE TIMES FOR FAMILY, HOUSE, AND GOD.

Hastily gathering all his Christmas presents together, Hal decided to put them behind the screen in his mother's room and flee the place, for a sudden primitive desire was entering his soul: the desire to be unhampered, and free to make his own choices without being bound to the age-old customs of Wrioth autocracy.

Once he'd made his first secret resolution he decided to re-pack all his belongings and slip, unseen, to the telephone downstairs and order a private hire Sunbeam all the way back to Chester, at a price that would have kept some poorer families near the Manchester Prince Infirmary in food for a whole month. Then – if needs be – he'd spend the night alone in Chester and travel back early in the morning to his student quarters.

By now there were three other creatures who sensed excitement in the air, the Wrioth family spaniels Punch, Judy, and Toby, who were following him everywhere with delighted and faithful interest, as he struggled to pack his suitcase again with one arm: *hors de combat.* Hal groaned quietly. The least attention at this moment, even from family pets, the better. So he decided to phone from his mother's own telephone in her room. After that, the escape would have to be a swift *fait accompli.* He could see it all in his mind: the announcement of the hire car by Belvers the butler – with Hal himself hovering unobtrusively near the front entrance, his luggage hidden behind the shooting sticks, umbrellas, walking sticks, and folding painting easels in their four foot six Chinese porcelain umbrella vase. Then, goodbye to the whole bally lot before they'd even realised it: 'Sorry and all that, Father, but just remembered about some vital medical treatment, due for an elderly patient in Denmark Road. Must dash back. I'll give you both a buzz when I get there, and try and return again tomorrow eve – if humanly poss ...'

The plans of mice and men ...

No sooner thought out, with the Sunbeam nicely ordered and due to arrive in half an hour, than the spaniels were on happy alert for their beloved mistress. Hal's mother appeared: 'Where on earth –? Cordelia said you'd completely vanished, and the children are

62

playing hide and seek trying to find you!'

'Bit of a problem, Mater. Things to attend to back in the big city. I'll try my best to be back from the hospital again tomorrow evening. I swear it.'

'A *problem*? How can you possibly have a problem when your arm's in a sling? Surely the whole of the medical staff isn't waiting for one mere student with two fractured fingers to go back and set all the cogs moving again.' She glanced at him shrewdly.

He glared at her with growing anger: 'It's a question of one's own conscience and integrity, Mother ...' he felt guilty at the way he was trying to make such an artificial case for escaping, all based on poor Mrs Taylor in Denmark Road who'd be sure to be dealt with by others in his absence.

Lady Wrioth gave a melancholy sigh: 'What a blunder it was to have gone to That Place when your life is already mapped out. Your place is here, Hal – as sole son and heir. Here, with us, being fully trained by Bazz to take over this whole estate, and producing a worthy family to carry on the family traditions. *That* is your true duty, and never forget it.

'Thousands of people are worthy of becoming doctors, but only one person in the world is the heir to all this, and it's you, our son.' Her face melted to a gentle smile, and he felt totally wretched.

Part of what she said was quite right. This was his heritage, and many large country estates since Edwardian times had faced a new era of survival and change. The Great War had caused costly losses within the great landowning houses of Great Britain. Many estates had been sold and divided, with portions sold to tenant farmers. Yet here at Hyndemere they had escaped.

'I honestly am sorry, Mother. But the car's about due – so I'll have to get moving. Anyway, no real harm done.

Only a few brief hours away.' He slipped a light kiss across the top of her head: 'Maybe I'll bring a friend back with me tomorrow to share it.' He didn't know what on earth had induced him to say it. It was as if the plan had been there all along and he was sealing his own fate.

At first a smile of relief lit his mother's face, then her look changed to consternation: 'A friend? What sort of friend? Is it one of the other students? Is it your friend Kenny Saville?'

He gave a faint smile and shook his head.

'Christmas is a family time for *close* friends ...' She stared at him: 'You seem to be behaving very strangely. I just don't understand you.' Then she looked at him coldly, and said, 'I'll tell them to prepare the emerald bedroom for him.'

Hal managed to get away without even seeing his father. It was a happy release, and already his mind was admitting its true intention, which was to ring Dasia and ask her to spend Christmas at Hyndemere as his guest.

He stayed at the Grosvenor in Chester and rang her. At no time did he even contemplate anything but an acceptance to his invitation, for there was – quite unwittingly – a streak of male aristocratic command, coupled with the natural assumption that Dasia would be conscious of the honour he was bestowing on her.

CHAPTER FOUR

The Fancy Dress

Dasia could hardly believe her ears when Dolly told her there'd been a phone call that evening from Chester, while she'd been toiling away at Marcia's.

'Someone with a very funny second name,' said Dolly. 'They said they'd ring again about nine this morning, but of course – seeing as it's now going on quarter past six, and you're due at Marcia's by half past, and aren't even out of bed yet – you'll be missing him again, because I've no intention of giving him poor Marcia's number, knowing what she's had to put up with, all through this busy and terrible time – and you, due to leave her in the lurch at the end of it all ... in the New Year ...'

Dolly was standing there with pouched eyes, in an old green mob-cap holding a chipped cup and saucer and a plate with half a slice of toast on it. She'd finally come upstairs to try and urge Dasia out of her Put-U-Up bed to start another grim day with merciless Marcia.

Later that morning, when Dasia was reluctantly stationed back at Marcia's donkey-stoning the front steps (which consisted of rubbing a block of honey-coloured sandstone across them, after they'd been washed so that they were immaculate until the next dark footprint appeared), she began to think miserably of her fate. She was reduced to donkey-stoning steps for next to no money, and was even regarded as some sort of criminal, because she'd fought for her maidenly honour against a hard-baked old imbecile; one of Mrs Mullander's 'gentlemen'. And no way, now, could she wait around for Hal's second communication, if he ever did try again ...

Suddenly, she stopped scrubbing, stood up and shook her mane of red hair, for she'd already dispensed with the tightly banded servant's cap she was supposed to be wearing. She stood there for a moment, watching people bustling along the winding lane, in a fever of haste to get set for Christmas Day.

It would soon be time for the distant clock to strike nine. Dasia lifted up the bucket of water by her side, and with one big swoosh, she flung the warm sodaic contents into the laurel bushes in Marcia's small acid-looking front garden and followed it with the bucket itself. Then she marched right through the wrought-iron gateway, and back to Aunty Dolly's.

'In heaven's name whatever's happened now?' groaned Dolly as her face went the colour of putty. 'Don't say you've upset the gentlemen again!'

Dasia stood facing her, next to all the chromium-plated toast racks in the kitchen. Then she took off her Hessian apron and said, 'Cheer up Aunty. They'll never annoy me any more because I've left – from this second onwards.' And the moment she uttered the words it was as if her fate was sealed because the phone in the hall began to ring, rather weakly in stops and starts.

With a huge surge of optimistic relief, Dasia rushed to answer it, followed half a pace behind by Aunty.

'You leave it alone, Dasia Greenbow! It's MY phone.'

66

There was a slight tussle as Dolly grabbed its long black Bakelite handle and heard the crackly voice of Mr Konrad the coalman promising some coke as soon as was humanly possible.

Dasia was in a fever of disappointment. Suppose the coalman had already blotted out Hal's call to her and she was doomed never to hear from him again! But her fears were allayed as it suddenly rang out again – just as Dolly had trundled back to the kitchen to watch some toast.

'Hello?' She put her hand firmly over the mouthpiece as she heard Hal's voice and called to Dolly, 'It's all right, Aunt. It's my message from the young man.' Then she took her hand away from the mouthpiece and gasped, 'I thought you'd never ring . . .'

There was a shy silence.

'I didn't forget.' His voice came and went in waves just like stormy weather. 'I've been thinking about it a lot . . . In fact I want to ask you a special favour.' His voice almost vanished. 'I know it sounds most frightful cheek at such short notice, but would you like to come home with me for Christmas? I expect it seems a bit mad, really, a bit of a shock.'

Dasia was stunned.

'. . . Are you still there?'

'Yes . . .'

'Well – would you?'

She felt herself going hot and cold in turns: 'Yes . . . Well . . . Yes, I'd love to. Oh yes . . . I mean . . . I'm not doing anything else.' She was nearly going to say, 'I've just walked out of Marcia's and chucked her bucket in the laurels,' but she thought better of it.

And she'd no idea where he lived, though when they were at Redman's he'd muttered something about it being near Chester.

She smiled with joyous excitement; what a wonderful and sudden adventure. The fact that she had only met him once in what was generally thought of as a respectable but fairly common provincial dancing academy gave her not a moment's anxiety, for it was apparent now that she'd burned her boats for good as far as Derbyshire Lane was concerned. Even her own family was fading a bit. They seemed to be under the impression that she'd left them for good and was totally in the clutches of Aunty Dolly's friend. Not one single soul had been in touch, although her brother Tommy did mention in a half-hearted way that Andrina was looking forward to seeing her, and that there were some presents waiting.

Presents ... Would she need to give Hal a present? Would she need to take a gift for his parents? And however could she afford it?

Would her one and only party frock be suitable? For it seemed that there wasn't even going to be time to get any more clothes from home – even if she wanted to.

'I'll call round at eleven then.' His sudden authoritative voice took her by surprise. It was a complete change from his first tremulous request.

'I'll be hiring a car from a lucky blighter of a friend, who happens to have two,' said Hal.

Two cars ... Dasia felt quite weak, even though she was used to cars because of her own father's lifelong interest, but only a few days at Marcia's had somehow taken the stuffing out of her. She was in a new world now that she was on her own, with hardly a penny in the whole world.

She replaced the receiver like someone in a dream; barely two hours, and she'd need to be packed up and away from here for ever ... Though it wasn't the moment to think further than that.

'Whatever does she think she's playing at?' said Marcia to Dolly in a tight, high-pitched voice full of tension.

'She actually threw my best white-enamelled, blue-rimmed bucket into those awful laurels, in full view of Mr Batril, Mr Rainsley, and Mr Frandle – who were standing by the front window waiting for their kippers.'

'Hadn't their breakfasts arrived on time, then?' said Dolly making a jab at Marcia's overall efficiency.

'SHE was supposed to be doing those kippers, Dolly! But I sent her to do the steps because that ghastly little skivvy, Milly Hopkins, suddenly left last night. Apparently she was very, very rude to poor Mr Rainsley, and told him to stop his fountain displays on the wall of the second WC, and he said either she went or he did.

'She was an absolute little horror and I was glad to get rid of her – and it works both ways as there's no Christmas Box to pay out, thank goodness. There's plenty more waiting for good-class jobs like we offer, Dolly.' She pulled out her glass-jewelled, gold-plated cigarette case and took a Craven-A, from the two narrow rows of fawn elastic inside. 'I will say one thing; at least your Dasia ...'

'She is not MY Dasia, Marcia. God help us all. I started off feeling sorry for her in her awful predicament about her not knowing who her true parents were, but now I can see that my sympathy is wasted ...'

'No. What I meant was, dear, that at least your Dasia and that brother of hers do have a spark of *culture*, even if she is a bit heavy handed with her fists.'

'Thank you Marcia. And I don't want to seem ungrateful, but I do acknowledge that there is far more than one spark of it in my relations. Her grandfather is a brilliantly inventive man. Brilliant. And if I'm not mistaken you once described your own uncle Frederick, who discovered gold by sheer accident in South Africa, as a moron of the First Order.'

They both tried to stare each other out through rings of smoke. Then Marcia made a conciliatory move and said, 'If it wasn't for her short fuse, she'd be the best maid-of-all-work I've ever come across. But that temper is very disturbing, Dolly. It makes her act just like a man, sometimes, and that's a very bad sign. Because when all's said and done – we are The Gentle Sex.

'Mr Tomlington says she has very sharp, jabby elbows when she feels like it. And he should know, with being in the army as an officer. In some ways I'll be sorry to see her go in the New Year, because most of the gentlemen are more respectful, now.'

Dolly tried to interrupt her: 'She won't be –'

'Yesterday, Mr Batril actually started to use his *Manchester Guardian* for catching his moustache and toe nail clippings. It shows they care at heart . . .'

'She won't be here in . . .' Dolly's face was anxious. She didn't want to break the bad news, for a good relationship with Marcia was worth more than pearls. But she was saved in the nick of time, as Dasia herself appeared, complete with suitcase.

'I'll be off shortly, Aunty. I've left a note for our Tommy and he can deposit anything I've left back at home, and tell them I'll call some time. My young man has asked me to spend Christmas at his home.'

They both gazed at her through their blue, tobacco haze. They were completely flabbergasted.

Then Marcia said, 'She's off her rocker, Dolly! Tell her to get back to my place. Today's one of the busiest times in the year, and there's all the vegetables to prepare, and the chestnut stuffing, and the puddings to check – and the turkeys still need plucking. There's the pork pie pastry to be finished too, and the ham and tongue to be done. And what about all my extra polishing of the brasses and the cutlery. And carting wine up from the cellar?

'Nobody but you and I know, Dolly,' said Marcia with dramatic pleadings, 'nobody will ever guess what we do

70

for the more respectable and homeless men of this world. Not a single one of mine has been invited out to have his Christmas dinner elsewhere. Not for them the sudden tinkle of an invitation from some young lady or refined dowager. There is no other place for them – no refuge in this universe except with me . . .' She wiped the corner of her eye with a slight dab of her lace-edged hanky, and blew her nose like a trumpet.

Dasia tried to be calm. She felt a bit braver wearing her own clothes, instead of those of a servant, as she hovered there in her pale Harris tweed coat and her emerald green, silk velvet beret next to her battered cardboard suitcase which held her best crepe-de-chine party frock.

'My young man is coming for me any minute, Marcia – so you'd better give me my money now, before you forget.' Dasia held her breath slightly, and her heart began to thud with inward terror – mainly because it was so important to have at least a few shillings in her purse in case of emergency.

'WHAT?' exploded Marcia. '*You*, ask *me* for money – after the way you've behaved in *my* house? I can hardly believe my ears!' And with no more ado she stamped out of the house.

When she'd gone, Dolly actually smiled and said, 'She'll come round, but you'll never get your pay – *never*. Not after all the trouble you've caused.'

'But it wasn't my fault, Aunty. Would you really have liked me to have lost my honour to one of her nasty old lodgers?'

'Of course not, lovey. But you must try to be more tactful.' Dolly was feeling more relaxed now than she'd been since Dasia first arrived. Her natural loving instincts began to swell once more – now that a young thorn in her flesh (even if it was a budding rose) was clearing out for ever and leaving the original status quo

71

intact. Brother Tommy was still king, and her star gentleman guest, Mr Corcoran, was still completely oblivious to callow young girls, as he stuffed down her savoury dumplings, toad in the hole, spotted dick, and bread and butter puddings.

'Now mind how you go, Dasia dear,' said Dolly getting fussier and fussier as the moment arrived for their final parting. 'I'll let them know at home for you. But *do be careful*; medical students can be very funny people – especially the ones who aren't really students at all ... So don't let this one examine you, or try to fumble with your private parts. And whenever you visit a strange household for any length of time, wear your thickest navy blue serge bloomers and never have fancy garters on as they can be very enticing. Just wear plain black elastic.'

'Auntee ...'

Dolly gulped to take breath: 'Yes dear?'

'There was just one *little* thing ... Hadn't I better take some small Christmas gifts, if I'm staying there over Christmas? Do you happen to have anything your lodgers have given you that you want to get rid of? He'll be here in a minute and it's too late to go to the shops.' She knew it was a half-lie – for the truth was she couldn't even afford to buy anyone anything.

'What are his parents like, pet? What about one of your pots of shrimps with a ribbon tied round. I could manage that for his Ma. And a packet of strong mints for his Pa? And there's a brand new wool vest one of my lodgers left behind three years ago when he eloped with one of Marcia's maids. It might be just right for your young man if he's nice and narrow built. And anyway it's the thought that counts, chick. I'll put them all in a nice big brown paper bag for you.'

Then she said, 'Is it Chester you're going? Well, jot down their name and address as soon as you arrive, and write I WAS HERE on it – then put your own name and address on and stick it under the insole of your shoe ... just in case they're part of any white slave trafficking. And see that they give you a decent single bedroom; don't let them fob you off with sleeping with his sister or someone. And watch out for bugs under loose wallpaper. Also, love, don't let the family cats or dogs anywhere near you with their mange and tape worms. I'll pack you a nice big tin of Keatings flea powder in the paper bag. Sprinkle it on your bottom sheet and if they say the sheets look a bit yellow from the powder, dab some Eau de Cologne on top and tell them you upset your new face powder. Now, is there anything I've forgotten to tell you?'

'No, Aunty.' Dasia's eyes were wide and solemn, for she knew from her own experience of working in the family pawn shop that much of what Dolly said must be treated with respect, even if it was a bit old fashioned.

Then, to her delight, Dolly went to the sideboard drawer, unlocked it, and carefully drew out a pound note: 'There you are, chicken, that should keep you going a bit.'

'B-but Aunty, I can't!'

''Course you can, lass. An' don't say I never give you owt.' Then Dolly muttered humorously to herself, 'It's worth a good bit more'n that to get shut of you before I gets a heart attack.'

When Hal and Dasia had finally gone, she rang Marcia and said, 'Gone at last, Marcia. And you'd never believe it – he's only got his arm in a sling and fractured his fingers. They're trying to get there in some battered old jalopy hardly fit for a trip to Urmston and back; one of those light little open roof two-seater things a bit like your Mr Batril's Singer with a Dickey Seat. Thank God her family didn't see her!'

★

73

Lord Wrioth had cut himself shaving, and little bits of cotton wool fluff still clung to his huge chin. He cursed silently. He should have let his man do it for him. Perhaps he should try one of those new safety razors with a fresh slither of fine steel blade sandwiched like a small vice in a T tool?

He nodded and smiled slightly, but never in his innermost heart would he admit that his own ham-handedness was caused by the thought of Hal bringing this unknown young female home; some young sprat hardly out of nursery, to be foisted on them all at Hyndemere. A girl who appeared to have no antecedents of any consequence whatsoever, but who, nevertheless, would have to be treated as one of the family guests. Thinny had drummed it all into him, until he was quite worried and irritated. It wasn't like Hal to do a trick like this. But his father tempered his own criticism with caution; many a man had gone overboard for sparkling eyes with limpid depths, and a good pair of curvaceous legs – and even Thinny's hadn't been too bad in the old days.

Dasia was as quiet as a mouse on the long tedious journey to Hyndemere with Hal. She was overcome with shyness and the feeling that everything that happened in her life henceforth was in the lap of the gods and guardian angels – specially with this partially disabled driver of unknown skills.

The little green car he'd borrowed was completely unsuitable for wet, muddy winter weather. It was also in a poor state of repair, and twice Hal had to get out and lie underneath it in all the slush and rain, with car tools spread on a piece of ragged towelling by his side, and just his oil-skin trousered legs poking out. And twice, because of his arm which he'd now removed from its sling, Dasia had to get out and help him as he worked – which meant her best Harris tweed coat was ruined with grease

74

and grime. No wonder his friend had two cars if this was a sample.

Six times poor Hal and herself had to get it to restart by fixing the starting handle to the centre bottom point of the bonnet, then jerking the wretched thing with all their power, almost wrenching their guts out to get the engine spluttering into life again.

The whole journey became so excruciatingly boring that some four and a half hours later Dasia neither knew nor cared where they were, and never even realised they were now in the long beech avenue leading to the house. For Hal had been very vague about describing where he actually lived – except to say that there would be a warm, friendly greeting, and they would soon be able to get changed and dry.

'Another few seconds,' smiled Hal, his face glowing with pride, 'and we'll just be in time for the ceremony of the pikelets. Then, after dinner tonight, there will be a Christmas Eve fancy dress party – interrupted by the villagers being invited to sing Christmas carols and being given a glass of punch at the end of it all.'

The small, mud-spattered, snow-covered car pulled up noisily. Its wheels churned the gravel and there was a belch of fumes and a grinding of gears.

'The final Frontier ...' said Hal. 'And all done with an arm that had to disband its sling pretty early on, in some very tricky bits of repair work, managed only with your help ...' They smiled at each other with a bond of true affection.

'What a perfectly ghastly journey you must have had, my dear,' said Lady Wrioth to Dasia. 'Your poor coat was in a dreadful state, but – not to worry – Mrs Pierpoint the housekeeper will make sure that it's returned to all its former glory in next to no time. And Melanie here will show you to your room and see that your luggage is brought up.

'You've both arrived in nice time for our Hyndemere speciality: hot toasted pikelets and gorgeous strawberry jam.' Then, with a slight but polite and kindly smile that covered a multitude of secret observations, she drifted casually away to speak to her son, Hal.

'You're in the Emerald Bedroom, Miss Greenbow,' said Melanie respectfully, as she showed her the way.

Dasia stared at the crossed and interlaced creamy ceiling. It was a far cry from the one at home in The Grove – with water dripping into a po.

There was a small four poster bed here with bright velvet curtains fringed in gold silk, and the room looked out to the rose gardens, which were entered by wrought-iron trysting gates.

Dasia gave a silent trembling sigh of pleasure as she walked cautiously into her own private bathroom for the first time in her life. Then, undressing completely, she turned the big brass taps on, and watched the piping hot water gushing out into the huge, man-sized bath with its great claw feet. What a luxury it was after her un-forgettable mud-spattered journey. No need here to heat your own water first, or even use the same bath water as the person before you, or get out an old zinc bath in front of a kitchen range, on the peg rug with a soot-covered kettle by your side to heat the water up.

As she dried herself on the white Turkish bath-towel she wondered what was best to wear. Hyndemere Hall was bubbling with a Christmas house-party: friends, relations, and guests; a private, new world of warmth, comfort and cheer quite different from her own at home. Not better ... But different ...

She looked at her meagre clothes: her lovely crepe-de-chine dress had suffered a huge muddy water mark from their terrible journey, getting here. So what should she wear? Should she be in her plum-coloured crocheted jumper with its tie-string neck and bobble-ended ties,

76

coupled with her oatmeal tweed skirt? Or should it be her dark blue V-necked cashmere jumper suit that Andrina had once passed on to her? It had a flaw in one line of the knitted welt, which Andrina had assured her was completely unnoticeable and looked almost like a special sign-mark of quality in such a beautifully made garment.

At first she was swayed by quality and the accordion pleated skirt. Then she looked again at the crocheted jumper – worked in a fit of begrudging kindness by her grandmother, Alice Greenbow. It fitted her beautifully and moulded itself to her figure like magic, and the bobbles were gorgeously carefree. It went well with the light oatmeal skirt. She felt happy and confident as she put them on and then, as she glanced at herself in the mirror for a second, she tossed her head in triumph. Her glinting auburn hair was damp and curling as she hurriedly combed it and pressed it into flattened waves with her fingers. Then, slipping on her best grey kid shoes with four leather bars buttoning across her insteps, which she fastened with her new button hook, she took her small network reticule, once rescued from the pawn shop and of unknown ownership, and she was ready to meet the other guests.

She walked back down the broad, richly carpeted, stairs, feeling shy and awkward, and suddenly extremely lonely. Never before had she been away from home in such an independent manner with no one else in the family close at hand, and not one of her close relatives even aware of exactly where she was. Usually it was the exact opposite and she'd always felt hemmed in and over-sheltered. It was a complete contrast and even quite frightening.

She felt a flutter, of complete panic, but already Hal was beside her – almost like a knight protecting a maiden in distress from her story days when Horace

Greenbow the man she had always known as her father had read her tales of Una and The Red Cross Knight.

Hal smiled and she realised, here in the warmth and grandeur of his family surroundings, what a handsome, dark, curly-haired portrait of sheer male elegance and beauty he made; for his eyes sparkled and shone with delight, and his whole frame emanated the vigour and enthusiasm of health, wealth, and security. She gave an involuntary shiver of strange fear. It was as if someone had suddenly walked over her grave. Was it really true that she, seventeen-year-old Dasia Greenbow, was here with him as his specially chosen guest? And then the fleeting shadow was gone, as he murmured in a slightly comic *sotto voce*, 'Watch out, here comes The Ceremony of The Pikelets . . .'

They both sat down on a sofa and waited, while two small serving maids clad in afternoon waitress regalia (similar to Dasia's own – only yesterday at Marcia's) stood by this baronial fireplace in the great Tudor hall, with large plates of pikelets – those small round, thick muffins punctured with holes the size of fine knitting needles through which melted butter could ooze, once they were toasted.

The girls stood at either side of the gigantic chimney piece, facing a very complicated, revolving iron spit. This spit, which had been designed and made by none other than Lord Wrioth, was poised close to the hottest glowing embers.

Jenny, the plain, dark fourteen-year-old, fixed twelve pikelets to a row of spikes, and in some complicated mathematical way Dasia saw that Lord Wrioth had worked out blank alternating rows to enable pikelets to be toasted and replaced for as long as was needed. Meanwhile, Phyllis, the other fourteen-year-old at the other end, took off six toasted pikelets at a time and buttered them like a young demon as if all hell was let loose, and she herself was being prodded with the devil's own toasting forks. Then the pikelets were placed in a heated, insulated cabinet on wheels which looked like an ancient converted barrel organ. While Lord Wrioth, the aristocratic inventor, beamed in complete and sweating happiness from the intense heat of the fire at his own wonderful toasting machine.

Following this, two more maids appeared, to shepherd everyone into the converted Anne of Cleves orangery, where tables were set out for afternoon tea with pikelets and strawberry jam. Some tables were round and seated six, and others were for four.

Hal lead Dasia to a table for four, close to the tall windows – and immediately to his chagrin he saw Madelaine, one of his cousins, and Cordelia Cadwallader-Fenchurch-Brighton walking over quickly to join them, with huge fixed smiles on their faces.

Dasia noticed rather gloomily that they were wearing the most wonderful short, heavy silk afternoon dresses of beguiling simplicity. Each dress had a square neck, and on hers the chubbier girl named Cordy wore a lilies of the valley corsage which Dasia knew was a token of beauty. The other one, Maddy, wore violets for modesty at her waist – even though she looked like the flappiest of flappers in her flesh-coloured silk stockings, dangling earrings, and beads as long as a skipping rope, and a cigarette holder like Marcia's – except it looked like solid gold. Oh yes, they were just like the most expensively dressed female dummies in Baulden's Dress Department – a level often aspired to by Dasia, but never actually attained in real life.

They both waved their hands in vague directions and sat down as Hal introduced them. Then Hal excused himself for a moment because his father had beckoned to him, and within seconds Madelaine and Cordelia were so busy trying to weigh up Dasia and prise information out of her that she felt like a poor little shell fish being forcibly removed from some small sea-washed rock which was its life-support.

'So where did you meet dear old Hal, then?' winkled Madelaine, narrowing her eyes slightly and smiling as she blew a smoke ring from her holder.

'At Redman's,' said Dasia.

'Redman's?' drawled Madeleine, 'What in heaven's name is Redman's? Is it an oyster bar?'

Dasia flushed slightly. The only oyster bar she'd ever seen was the one in Oxford Road in Manchester, and it was only used by men – or so people said. Was this Madelaine person hinting that she worked in one as some sort of servant ... or even worse? 'Redman's is a local dancing academy where they hold tea and supper dances. It's in Stretford.'

'Stretford?' Madelaine looked puzzled. 'Do you mean Stretford-on-Avon, or Stretford in London?'

'Stretford near the river Mersey – near Manchester,' said Dasia.

'The canal and the railway run through it,' said Cordelia, swiftly. 'It used to have wonderful Trafford Park there, owned by The Traffords in the Middle Ages, but now it's all been sold out to heavy industry: Westing House and all that jazz ...' They both turned their noses slightly upwards and looked away from Dasia.

Then Cordelia said cheekily, 'And what do you do, when you're not at Redman's?'

Dasia hesitated then said, 'I've been helping my aunty for a while. She runs a guest house.'

'Really?' Cordy's plucked eyebrows arched even higher. She was stuck. Obviously she couldn't enquire as to the exact grade of guest house, which might have been a respectable haven for retired gentlefolk such as parsons' widows, but there again might, God forbid, be a bordello, frequented by wayward medical students.

80

Cordelia's glance suddenly met Madelaine's; then her face lit up slightly and she said to Dasia, 'Do you ride to hounds?'

Dasia shook her head, then added, 'A lot of people where I live ride ponies, and one of my sisters, Rosalie, can ride a few yards as long as it's not up hill as some horses can be very stubborn.'

A repressed glimmer of a smile forced its way to the corner of Dasia's lips as she remembered the handful of lessons Rosalie had kicked up such a fuss for, when Rosalie was twenty-eight and Dasia herself was only eight. It was at a time when Horace Greenbow was quite opulent after a bonus from inventing and patenting a new kind of tin-opener. Rosalie had gone on and on about her lean childhood years and how it was soon her birthday and there was a chance she might soon be riding to hounds with a belted earl if only father would present her with the wherewithal to get a few lessons on a cuddie. But her bottom was so sore after bouncing up and down a few times, even though Mr Jorrocks at the stables congratulated her repeatedly on her firm and wondrous seat, that Rosalie forswore the quadruped for ever and said she preferred horsepower in a car driven by a handsome man – with a fur rug over her dimpled knees.

While Dasia was remembering all this, the other two were ignoring her completely as they talked about Paris, and walking in the Bois de Bologne, and going to the Comédie Française. Followed by an intense discussion about Michael Arlen's novel *The Green Hat.*

Dasia breathed a sigh of relief as she saw Hal coming back, just as Cordy was asking her if she knew anything about badgers.

'Sorry to be so long,' Hal smiled at them all, and at their plates with only pikelet crumbs and smears of jam left. 'Father wanted me to say hello to Nanny

Binnington.' He turned to Dasia: 'She looked after Father when he was small. And me! She's nearly ninety-five.'

Later that afternoon, in the blackness of the coming night, it started to snow again thick and fast. Dasia gazed at it all through the window in her bedroom – alone. She'd excused herself on the pretext of resting before dinner, but it was really because Hal kept getting button-holed by so many people.

Later tonight there would be the fancy dress party, and the carol singing. Already 'In The Bleak Midwinter' threaded its words and tune into her mind while she looked at the white frozen world beyond the window. '... Earth stood hard as iron, water like a stone. Snow had fallen snow on snow, sno-o-ow on snow. In the bleak mid winter, lo-o-o-ng ago ...'

Here inside it was warm and mellow with tradition. Hal said that later tonight there would be bowls of punch mulled with a hot poker, and games of bob-apple. Tomorrow would be a day of church blessings and thanksgiving, coupled with Hyndemere feasting and joyous relaxation.

She felt a sudden wave of home-sickness, longing now to be sitting safely with Andrina and Louise, Rosalie and Tommy and her grandparents in their own comfortable family kitchen, with Daisy the tabby cat and dear old Periwinkle the black and white mongrel terrier. She remembered the simple excitements of their own true life, as they all delighted in Christmassy things, like home-made bread sauce, flavoured with cloves – and fussing about whether the baked potatoes were golded and gluey and roasted properly in the baking tin. She saw in her mind's eye the cheerful red and gold crackers on the lovely heavy lace table-cloth in the dining-room, as they finally sat down in all their best clothes while

Horace Greenbow did the carving. Then, later in the afternoon when they'd all opened their presents, should they really have finished off two round boxes of crystalised slices of oranges and lemons with those small wire forks, and gobbled down so many chunks of soft melting turkish delight, and cracked such scores of walnuts and brazils and almonds? She remembered the dates straight from the sticky stalks and thought how white and furry they were inside.

Dasia slipped off her shoes and lay down on the bed. Supposing she was trapped here for ever, with only the pound note Aunt Dolly had given her? Even the prospect of being here with Hal didn't soften the idea, for it was, she admitted sadly, an alien land and she didn't really know any of them. It was probably all right if you had lots of money, even though Andrina once told her that the very rich never mentioned anything to do with filthy lucre as it was *de rigueur* . . .

Somehow Dasia couldn't imagine a place where you weren't allowed to mention money – especially if you were a penniless female. It was a bit like Oliver Twist not being allowed to ask for more gruel. And even if she wanted to escape, she wouldn't even have enough money to leave – unless someone was kind enough to provide free transport into Chester where she might find really cheap lodgings and then make a phone call to her own home.

Suddenly there was a gentle tap at her bedroom door. She sprang from the bed.

'Dasia . . .?' A male voice, a whisper . . . 'It's me – Hal. Can I come in?'

'Of course!' Her heart leapt with joy as she opened the door wide. 'It's a lovely bedroom. I've never slept in a four poster bed before, especially one with a gold fringe –'

They both burst out laughing then Hal looked serious

and they both sat down on the bed together. 'I'm sorry I've been neglecting you a bit. It's always like that in this place, but it'll be better tomorrow, I promise.'

'Tomorrow? But what about tonight for dinner, and the fancy dress, and –'

He put his undamaged hand across her shoulders gently. 'The fact is that Father wants me to do him a bit of a favour and take Nanny Binnington back to her residential home for retired nurses at Saltreach village about seven miles from here. It may take a while, and it would be churlish just to deposit her like a parcel.' Then he smiled and said, 'But don't worry, I'm leaving you in good hands with my cousin Cedric, and his wife Amanda.'

Dasia felt anxious, but she smiled and tried not to show it. The weather was still terrible. Suppose he was snowed up at the other end?

'Are you coming downstairs, then?' Hal smiled and gently stroked her hair for a fleeting second like a child touching forbidden property. 'All the time I was down there I kept wondering where on earth you'd vanished to.'

'I just felt lonely. I felt I didn't belong, and you were always surrounded by other people . . .'

His eyes smiled at her: 'Believe me, Dasia, even I feel lonely in this place when it's full of specimens like Cordelia C.F.B. and stuffy relatives and dreadful friends of Pater and Mater who do nothing except discuss people they know who cheat at cards, or live in India.'

Then he said, 'I'll get back as soon as is humanly possible from taking Nanny to Saltreach, and from then on we'll stay together like milk and honey.'

They went downstairs together and he held her hand, and as he did so he suddenly caught sight of his mother fixing them with a penetrating, cold gaze. Then she turned away and began a laughing conversation with her

84

cousin Lady Fernfeather who was trying to make the best of her only daughter wanting to become a nun, just at a time when a very rich Scottish laird had asked for her hand in marriage.

There was a tall, slim, older man in livery waiting inside the main entrance, holding a peaked cap and wearing light-coloured gloves. He was smiling, and to Dasia at that moment he looked the most human person in the whole world – apart from Hal. But of course he was much, much older; he was surely into his thirties . . .? He seemed to Dasia as sturdy and firm as a lighthouse, beset by scores of small ships all buffeted about in a Hyndemere sea.

'Danny's already waiting for me,' said Hal as he and Dasia walked to the front door. 'The quicker Danny and I get away, the sooner we'll be back.'

He introduced Dasia to Danny, who took off his glove, and bowed almost imperceptibly. As their hands met in a handshake, she looked up at his face and was held for a long second by his frank, grey eyes – as an arrow of love shot through her. She knew instantly he was the sort of person she could trust with her innermost soul.

It was rubbish of course, and she knew that Aunty Dolly would have had a fit to think she was willing to trust a stranger with her whole life, after one handshake. ('And never be swayed by any sort of uniform, either, even if it's the king himself,' Aunty Dolly had once said. 'Men are men the whole world over . . .' Then she'd dabbed herself with Ashes of Roses, and gone back to sousing some herrings for Mr Corcoran.) Yes, this man could be the most evil villain in all the world for all she really knew.

Little did she know, either, that the touching of hands had had almost the same effect on Danny as he greeted her with impassive cordiality – appearing completely

85

unmoved by this first meeting yet, secretly, flooded with a sudden protective awareness which took hold of him entirely as he perceived in seconds her youthful, lonely vulnerability.

'I'll just take Dasia across to cousin Cedric and Amanda,' said Hal, guiding her towards them. Then, explaining everything, he left her to their tender loving care and made his way towards Danny Elvers the chauffeur and the family automobile.

The Christmas Eve fancy dress party was in full swing and Hal still hadn't returned from Saltreach village. Dasia sat there during the evening, mostly with Amanda by her side while Hal's cousin Cedric cavorted about in a Harlequin costume, surrounded by Bo-Peeps, elderly gauze and muslin, tinsel-ribboned fairies, and people dressed as jesters and comic opera characters from Gilbert and Sullivan.

She herself was now attired as Cinderella – a role so unpopular that she was the only one. She hadn't wanted to be Cinderella, but the moment Hal had moved away in the limousine, Cynthia, Lady Wrioth, was immediately by her side and taking her over.

'You'll make a simply spiffing Cinders, dear. Hal brought a young girl like you home once before ... It was just at the time of one of our other parties. She had lovely long curling hair, just like yours, and I rigged her up in an old brown georgette thing of mine cut to shreds round the hem with a few patches tacked on it. It was absolutely perfect. Young people of your age can wear anything – and still look stunning.'

Dasia smiled politely. She was completely at Thinny's mercy. She hadn't known anything about Christmas in a place like Hyndemere, and no way could she have dreamt up a suitable garb out of her own personal belongings. She stared at the richness of it all: people in huge, tall pompadour wigs, and a woman in a pale blue satin crinoline, and a diamond tiara ... Rosalie had once told her that they hired them all from theatrical costumiers and that they often cost as much as someone's wages for a whole year, working as a machinist in a Manchester sweat shop ...

At first she politely stalled the whole idea of asking if it would be possible just to wear her ordinary clothes, but Thinny was adamant. Her thin, oval face registered total shock: 'We can't have that, dear. Supposing everyone decided to opt out! We really and truly would be up a gum tree then, wouldn't we?'

Dasia nodded with a smile on her face, but inside she felt glum and suspicious: Hal – bringing back a girl like her once before? And this female having to be arrayed in this same dreadful costume? There was something slightly unsavoury about it. Surely his mother wasn't putting her into the poor, ragged, servant role deliberately?

Was there anything significant about Lady Wrioth herself being dressed up as The Queen of Hearts? Dasia suddenly realised that she had no idea what Hal planned to dress as; then her optimism got the better of her and she began to hope that Lady Wrioth wanted her as Cinderella so that Hal could come along as Prince Charming and make her his own true love ...

But there wasn't much sign of that happening at this particular moment, for now she was on her own again – a real Cinderella – while Amanda, dressed as Columbine, was asked to trip the light fantastic with a huge man dressed as one of the three bears.

Dasia tried to look really happy as if she was enjoying every moment of it, yet all the time feeling like Piffey on a rock-bun, and wishing and wishing for Hal to come back. Then to her relief she saw Cedric making his way towards her, walking as if he was on the deck of a listing ship, but on watch for a safe harbour. Even in that state it was nice to have him sitting next to her as moral support.

'How you enjoy-yinit – Dace – ya?' he mumbled. Then he hiccuped and said, 'Ay think ay'm a trifle squiffy, old bean. Too much champers puts on the dampers ...' Then he sat down very carefully with all his weight leaning against her young, but thankfully resilient, slimly curved shoulders. Wiping a salivary drip from his moustache, he asked her to accompany him outside for some 'Fraysh Are' ...

She hesitated: 'Do you think it's wise to go out? It's terribly cold, and there's heavy snow. Why don't you sit here for a while and wait for Amanda to come back?'

Suddenly, his mood changed. He stood up and snorted and lowered his head, and glared at her balefully from beneath his brows. 'Are y'tellin mi warradooo?' He grabbed her by the wrist and pulled her towards him. She was powerless to resist because she knew that even the slightest scuffle of resistance might cause some terrible scene, as people with too much drink inside them were completely unpredictable. So she let him lead her from the room, pretending, on the way, that they were the best of friends, but praying all the time that Amanda his wife would arrive and rescue her.

He dragged her with determined, drunken effort down a labyrinth of passages to a small green baize, metal-studded door which led to a private glass conservatory full of dried up palms and rickety old cane tables and chairs. 'Howzatt ay?' he babbled. 'Fraysh are, but not out in all the bloody old snow, ay what?' Then before she could say another word he grabbed her in a hair-tearing clutch and, mumbling, 'Darlin', little Cinders,' he tried to kiss her.

Dasia was in a panic. She had no idea what part of the house she was in and he was almost squashing her to death as she struggled to escape. She was pressed so

88

hard against his chest that shouting for help was a wasted effort and her ears were completely blocked from hearing whether any other human beings were at hand to be of help. Then fate suddenly came to her aid because, in his sozzled enthusiam, Cedric fell backwards over a decaying wickerwork chair, dragging Dasia after him, which cushioned her fall and allowed her to escape. She rushed to the door and was just in time to see a tall, gaunt figure disappearing along the passageway, clad in a Robin Hood costume.

It was Lord Wrioth . . .

Robin Hood and the Queen of Hearts were deep in conversation in the corner of their magnificent library, which had a secret passage door disguised as leather book spines with gold leaf titles – like so many of the other books. And this disguised opening was where Lord Wrioth had emerged from the scruffy old semiderelict conservatory, for it was a direct but obvious route to and from the servants' quarters.

'They were embracing,' sighed Bazz.

'Embracing? Who was embracing? Was it wretched Cedric or amorous Amanda? They spread their favours about like the flu . . .' Thinny's heavily rouged cheeks registered deep and utter scorn as she tapped the big red heart on the front of her white satin bodice, irritably.

'No, Cynthia . . . It was Cedric and that girl Hal's brought back. They appeared to be at it hammer and tongs in the glass house. I just came upon them by accident on my way to seeing your Melanie about a bent toasting fork. I must say I was jolly surprised. Somehow I didn't think she was the type – more like a virgin in disguise and all that . . . '

'There's many a young strumpet hidden behind a dairymaid's complexion, Bazz,' said Thinny knowingly. 'You'll have to speak to Hal about it the moment he arrives back. We can't have the poor darling living in a fool's paradise. My God, Henry – our own parents, God bless their noble souls, would have sent her off with a flea in her ear in two secs, as nothing but a common little go-getter. We're all so much more liberal minded these days. It was the last war that did it. Having to have all those women in the munition factories and actually driving vehicles. I know they're my sex, but you really do have to watch 'em. It's always the worst ones that get above themselves.'

'There's always the possibility she was led astray by Cedric,' said Lord Wrioth without much conviction, but anxious to hang on to his image of liberality. 'He's a bit of a Jekyll and Hyde once he's had a skinful.'

'No female is ever led astray completely against her will, Bazz. Any intelligent woman would use her savvy not to get into a dangerous situation in the first place.'

'But to be fair, old bean, she is only a young slip of a gal – and she was left in the old wolves den by Hal.'

A trace of a smile lit Cynthia's thin mouth: 'Stop making excuses, Henry – or I'll begin to think she's got *you* in the palm of her hand, as well as our beloved son.'

Then they both trundled from the library shaking their heads with ages-old wisdom.

CHAPTER FIVE

Christmas Dinner

Dasia took ages finding her way along the tortuous winding corridors again, towards the Christmas activity in the main part of the house. It was fast getting to eleven o'clock now, and she was tired, disillusioned and fit only for a long night's sleep. She dreaded what Christmas Day would be like tomorrow. And just supposing, the worst nightmare of all, that she had to face it with Hal never turning up because he'd stayed overnight at Saltreach.

She was just traipsing up to bed, when suddenly she heard his voice, and soft steps behind her.

She turned to see him, and her whole being flooded with joyful relief. He was standing there in his heavy dark Abercrombie overcoat with traces of snow on it, with a mixture of smiles and concern sweeping over his face: 'It's been a fiasco of a night, Dasia. It was awful having to leave you for so long, but they insisted on making us so welcome. They had all the photograph albums out, and it was so hard to escape ... You know how it is.'

A simmering flame of temper rose within Dasia; what

a pathetically lame explanation. Was she just a write-off? Didn't he even give her a second thought, once he was away from her side? Ever since she'd arrived here she'd been treated like something the dog brought in. It looked as if he was regretting ever having asked her to come back with him to Hyndemere.

come down again with me and see Christmas Eve out,' he pleaded.

She looked at him coldly 'I'd rather not. I'm very tired, and your cousin Cedric wasn't in the least gentlemanly. He seems to me to be just a boozer, and as bad as any of the gentlemen my Aunty Dolly's friend knows ...' Then her heart suddenly melted a bit, and she walked down with him.

He smiled quizzically as they sat in a dimly lit corner underneath the stuffed, holly-covered head of a huge elk gazing mournfully from the wall. 'Boozing is a universal pastime, Dasia: the infirmary out-patients is full of the final results. I'm lucky to be missing all the drunken brawling – and the blood and vomit. But we're all guilty of it at times.'

'Well I'm not – and that's for sure,' said Dasia with firm conviction. 'Only one small birthday drink has crossed my lips since I met you at Redman's. And that's how it's going to stay.'

'Good for you,' said Hal with a certain brusque steeliness. Then, softening a little, he gave her hand a brotherly squeeze and said, 'But don't sign the pledge just yet ...'

She stared at him. Where was all the romance going? There was a shallow smooth surface now, in everything he said to her, and a sort of awkwardness. Or was she just over-sensitive and tired? Tired of this whole terrible place.

He looked at her face: 'Cheer up, Dasia. The world's not as bad as that. We'll join in "Auld Lang Syne" then we'll go and look at the stars from the glass observatory. It's turning into a good clear night for shepherds. And then – yes, then you can go to bed.'

'Thank you very much.' She meant it sarcastically but her heart suddenly melted and she smiled up at him. In a fraction of a second she knew by his glance that true love was back again – only to be caught and destroyed like some ethereal will-o'-the-wisp as they both heard Lord Wrioth's voice.

'Hal. Can I have a word with you in the library, please? At once!'

Her happiness vanished, as he left her yet again and followed his father. She continued to her bedroom and got undressed with gloom once more descending, but the bed was so wonderfully warm and ready prepared for a good night's rest by the servants – with a blue, rubber hot water bottle with the name Boots written on it and a special velvety cover – that her natural optimism returned, and she began to look forward to tomorrow.

Both his mother and father confronted him when Hal reached the library.

By now, the scandalous story of Dasia and Cedric had been wonderfully garnished with damning details by Lady Wrioth so that Dasia sounded a real little tart – a fitting term to be used by a woman still wearing her Queen of Hearts fancy dress.

'I just do not believe it!' Hal protested. 'She's not a girl like that. She's completely young and innocent.'

'It's you who's the innocent one,' said his mother bitterly. 'You're just completely besotted, just like you were with that other one who called me a cow and broke a Ming vase. Believe me, Hal, when that bovine word fell from Enid Shufflewick-Milton's lips I knew I'd been right all along about her coarse background. She was a black-haired vixen!'

'She was only a schoolgirl, Mother. It was years ago. We were both only fourteen ... And she wasn't from a coarse background. Her aunt's cousin was third Lady in Waiting to Queen Mary.'

Lord Wrioth himself remained silent most of the time, but now he sprang to Thinny's defence: 'We've both lived on this earth much longer than you, old chap. Young female adventurers are out there in abundance – just waiting to waylay rich, naïve young men. For make no mistake, Hal, you are very rich by today's standards, and you have a responsibility to this estate as my sole son and heir. And don't forget your actual age of nineteen boy. Twenty-one is the official age of independence ...'

Hal felt his hackles rising. His parents were so stupidly rigid and hide-bound. His face paled with rage. Was he to be blackmailed all his life just because he'd been born heir to Hyndemere? Was he, too, destined to be locked in this prison of family dynasties?

His father's voice softened: 'I understand a bit how you feel, my son. The world's a hard place – and you've been graced, by unknown forces, into a dominant and responsible position.

'Surely you can see all this when you work amongst all the poor and starving Manchester wretches, who visit your hospital?'

'They aren't all starving wretches, Father. And even the worst cases have their human pride, just as we have. You're bringing red herrings into our conversation. The main point is that Dasia is not an adventuress. She is my guest here, and she's had her character blemished because of the drunken antics of Cedric.

'I can see that the only thing to be done is for me to remove Dasia immediately from all this dishonour. We shall both get away from here as soon as possible. Within the next hour, to be precise.'

94

'WITHIN THE NEXT HOUR?' They both stared at him in horror: 'You must be mad!'

He didn't reply, but in a way he *had* gone mad as he strode up to Dasia's bedroom and thumped on the door.

She sat up in bed with a look of terror. What on earth was going on now? She could hardly believe it. What time was it? She'd just fallen sound asleep and wasn't even sure for a few moments where she was. She looked at the small clock. It was nearly midnight ...

'Open the door, Dasia. It's urgent.'

She did not reply but sat there rubbing her eyes sleepily trying to work out what all the fuss was for.

Hal tried the door knob. The room was unlocked, for she hadn't seen any reason for locking it. She was wide awake now, poised and tense – like some forest creature ready for flight.

Hal was struck with wonder at her sensitive natural beauty. Her burnished auburn hair tumbled to slim shoulders against her pale blue flannelette nightie.

'Whatever's happening? Is it a fire?'

'Get up and pack your case. We're leaving!'

'Leaving?' She gaped at him, dumbfounded. Was it, after all, a dream ... Or a sudden awful nightmare? 'But it's midnight. I was sleeping.'

He lowered his voice and spoke quickly: 'Trust me. You'll come to no harm, but we've got to go – this instant. We just aren't welcome any more; and when a place doesn't welcome you, you have to quit. Something's happened to make it hopeless for us to stay for Christmas Day; "Goodwill to All" would be just hollow mockery.'

Dasia got out of bed timidly and stood there so helplessly that Hal felt like lifting her up in his arms and reassuring her – or even taking her, and himself, back to the big goose-feather mattress beyond the fringe of gold. But instead he said, 'I'll be back in ten minutes when you're ready. Don't be long.'

When he'd gone and she was fully dressed, deep misery took hold of her as she realised she was of no account to anyone at Hyndemere. God forbid that she should be the cause of Hal having to leave his own home, for she now felt like some helpless slave. She could see no other option than to obey him in this unplanned midnight future. Was her life always going to be ruled by others?

She took one last look into her purse to make sure her pound note was still there, and in doing so she saw the letter she'd taken from home. The one to Horace Greenbow about the strange inheritance overseas. And immediately she felt a wave of intense comfort and hope. There was a whole world waiting out there. One day, surely, she would reach it.

Within twenty minutes they were out of the huge house and back into the terrible two-seater, open-topped car. Her teeth were chattering and she was numb with cold, as growing fright of the unknown took over. But she comforted herself by trying to think of all those who were far worse off than herself. The picture came to her mind of some tinkers they'd seen on the road as they'd come here. They had been on a open cart which jolted along in bare, snow-streaked poverty. A young man in his twenties with a black moustache drove the small scraggy chestnut nag, while next to him was a ragged boy of about twelve with lank fair hair. Behind them on the cart, huddled on some sacks with two brownish grey whippets, was a young woman with shiny black hair, an infant grasped against her bosom, a skimpy shawl sheltering her head and shoulders and a small bundle of a baby fastened against her back like a flat, grubby parcel.

She was like a parcel herself at the moment – not knowing what was going to happen from one moment to the next, driving along on a strange Christmas jaunt with a young man she hardly knew. Cut off from her own family in more ways than one, fearful to go back to The Grove to face the new family circumstances, fearful even of meeting darling Horace again because he was no longer her father but her grandfather, she pulled a hanky from her pocket and dabbed, silently at the corners of her eyes.

'What's the matter?' said Hal above the roar of the engine. 'Are you feeling the cold? Should we stop somewhere and shelter for a bit?'

She tried to smile cheerfully but shook her head half heartedly. For goodness sake let him get the journey over and done with – for at least they were away from Hyndemere, and maybe in the morning she'd pluck up courage and ask to go home for Christmas Day – even with Hal if needs be.

But where was he taking her *now*?

They were back in Chester again, with the gas light glowing in a greenly lit network of winding lanes and narrow gunnels; sometimes brightened by street flares from ragged ever-hopeful Christmas Eve traders. And still Dasia did not know what Hal's plans were for the night. She began to wonder if they would end up sleeping under the tarpaulin in the car, for not once had he suggested going to a reasonable hotel to book rooms until the morning. All they were doing now, after leaving their car parked in a narrow street at the back of the grandest hotel in Chester, was to drift about, seeing the lights and shadows behind the curtains of scores of small street houses, almost as if Hal himself didn't quite know what to do.

She plucked up her courage: 'What exactly are we going to do, Hal? Are we driving back to Manchester through the night? Will we have enough petrol?'

He shook his head. 'We can't drive back again now! We'd be out for the count! And I don't want to check in

97

anywhere where they know me. It would be a slur on your reputation ... Gossip travels round Chester faster than a comet.'

'But we've got to arrange something ...' Dasia was at a loss for words. Here she was with the son of a lord who within his own domain was decisive and knowledgeable, and where she was hardly more than a piece of dandelion fluff. Yet here, in the ordinary streets of Chester, in the now early hours of Christmas Day, for it was now long gone midnight, he was as lost as she was.

Secretly she would like to have suggested that they should ignore the gossips and both have a good night's sleep in salubrious surroundings before setting off again tomorrow, but how could she with only a single pound note between her and the workhouse?

For a few moments they stood together, hesitating outside a row of small, terraced houses, with the sounds of merrymaking in their tired ears, as a door right next to them suddenly swung open.

They were taken completely by surprise as a middle-aged, bald-headed man in a striped collarless shirt still sporting brass studs waved a large glass tankard of ale at them with intoxicated fervour.

'Come inside,' he cajoled. 'Come into the warmth and comfort of a good fireside, with a lonely old man. Come and drink to the blessings of the season. For it's bloody perishing for you two, standing there like a couple of skinned rabbits, to be sure ...'

Dasia flinched and drew back, closer to Hal. But Hal revived, as if the sound of another male voice, even at its high level of inebriation, was a sound as good as a heavenly choir.

'Thanks a lot, old chap,' he said, grasping Dasia firmly by her hand. 'We're in need of a bit of warmth. We're trying to get to Manchester, but the old tin lizzy's let us down. Confounded and bloody nuisance –

especially with having my young cousin in tow ...' He gave Dasia a silencing look, as cautiously they followed him into the tiny living room.

It was all decorated with paper streamers in pink, blue, yellow and green, with paper lanterns dotted about, and Christmas cards in a higgledy-piggledy mess on the sideboard. On the wooden kitchen table was a piece of newspaper, three empty beer bottles, and two half-eaten mince pies on a plate; with further bottles of refreshment in an old shopping bag in a corner of the room.

'Make yourselves at home,' the older man said. 'What's mine's yours. Have as much to drink as you like. Stay the night if you want. In fact you'd be doing me a real Christian favour if you stayed with me tonight ...'

Dasia heard his invitation thankfully. Her impressions of him had changed. He was a harmless, lonely old soul, and the only sounds of true yule-tide festivity came through the thin walls from his neighbours on each side. At least she knew that the offer of a night's rest was based purely on hospitality.

'We'd be quite ready to go to bed right now if it's all right with you?' she said.

Hal glanced at her sharply. Plainly he was taken aback by her sudden forwardness. Yet under the circumstances there was nothing he could do, except to stress that, as cousins, they would certainly need separate sleeping arrangements.

The man, whose name was Mr O'Driver, looked gloomy when Hal said this. Then he took another drink and said, 'Sure an' it's Christmas an' it's what Mary herself would have wished, before she left me. I was a rotten husband to be sure, but none of us is perfect in the sight of God. Sir, I'll sleep down here on the floor and the darlin' girl can have my very own little room; and you, son, can have the big room with me own true wife, for sure she doesn't want a drunken lout like me breathing fumes on her – on the day of Our Baby Lord ... And not a word about money. Like I says; sure the young lady can sleep in the little room, and you young sir can sleep with the wife while I kip down here.' He smiled at them toothlessly through a beery haze.

Hal recoiled slightly, but tried not to show it: 'We'll take up your kind offer for the rest of this night, then, and set off again for Manchester at crack of dawn tomorrow. Do you have an alarm clock?'

'Indeed I do, sir,' said Mr O'Driver quaffing the last dregs from his tankard. 'Little do you know what a blessing this visit has brought me, for now my wife will have a partner all the night and I'll get some true rest. But it's a nice scenty room, sir. Her favourite flowers are there. Carnations from the best florists ...'

'I think I'll go up to your little room now then – if you don't mind,' said Dasia. Surely the man's wife wasn't still in the same house ... though there were cases of married people who weren't even on speaking terms but still lived under the same roof. Then a flood of sudden horrified shock coursed through her body as she remembered an overheard conversation between Marcia and Aunty Dolly about nymphomaniacs, when Marcia was discussing one of her fleeting maids of all work. 'She didn't just *make* the beds Dolly – she used to *lie* in them and wait for my gentlemen. She was a complete nymphomaniac and I caught her at it when she was waiting for poor Floddle to return with a new duster for his black boots – though she swore me black and blue she'd gone all faint from her monthly visitor.'

The more Dasia thought about it the more upset she got. Surely with Hal being a medical student, he would know the danger of casual liaisons and the risk of disease? For even in the ladies' lavatories there were white enamel notices warning you of the terrible hazards.

'I'll bring your case for you,' said Hal to Dasia, hastily.

Dasia nodded, then burst out passionately: 'My cousin can sleep in *my* room, Mr O'Driver. I'm quite willing for him to sleep on the floor – for neither of us will be actually undressing properly or wearing night attire. Then you can be back in your rightful place by your wife's side, Mr O'Driver.'

Mr O'Driver looked slightly ashamed. 'You're quite right, Missy. But with her having gone – the strain of me being in her room on my own is getting too much.

'So – if you don't mind – I'll show youse both up the stairs.' Then, just as they were reaching the small landing, he suddenly beamed with happiness and said, 'Sure, 'tis the best stroke of luck since she died, for me not to be on mi own wid 'er ... over Christmas night. For who wants to be at a wake at this time of the year? No one round here and that's for certain.

'All you needs to do, son, is to be in the room with the coffin, an' you can snore to the blessed heavens, for I've already had a bucket full.' He turned pleadingly to Hal, and repeated, 'Who in hell's name wants to be at a wake on Christmas Eve? An' if you knew my wife when she was alive, sir – God rest her soul a hundred times – sure she drove me mad for forty years with never a kind word passing her lips. And me getting her a good wood coffin.

'Take my place, son – you can snore your own self to heaven or Hell, for there's a good camp bed there ...'

'You don't mean to say you've both driven all the way here, *this very morning*?' gasped Andrina staring askance at Dasia and this young, rather hollow-eyed young man beside her. (Surely she knew his face from somewhere? ... was it the pawn shop?)

Dasia nodded ... What paradise it was to be back home seeing them all. Her heart flooded with love, and she said, 'We set off very early indeed. I was home-sick. I wanted to be back here for Christmas Day, and Hal agreed.' Little did the Greenbows know the real ramifications of leaving Hyndemere, and the journey back here ...

The car was resting, at last, at the back of the Greenbows' rambling and decrepit home, and Dasia and Hal stood thankfully in the warmth of the family kitchen, which was full of female fuss and pandemonium in the annual panic of cooking the Christmas dinner.

By now it was half past twelve, the goose was being carefully basted, and the head of the household, Horace Greenbow, was well away out of the house, having a glass of claret and a game of chess in old Esau Bartholomew's front parlour with old Esau – who collected foreign stamps, didn't celebrate Christmas, and lived on his own in a small agricultural labourer's hovel alongside a rather dried-up brook half a mile away.

Esau's parlour was packed with at least six escapees, including Horace; some sitting on the floor in their best clothes, some smoking pipes full of thick twist or puffing at Christmas cigars and all arguing about the state of the country, the League of Nations Union, the Great War, and the awful state of a local billiards saloon.

So it was with some surprise that, when Horace arrived back at the carefully timed hour of two o'clock which, from years of experience he knew to be the exact second for everyone being ready to eat, and with Alice having had to carve up the bird instead of himself, he saw Dasia sitting there with a strange young gad-about ...

'What's all this, then, Lass, an' where uv y' been? We thought as 'ow you'd flitted for good.' He gave Hal a shrewd glare over the top of his glasses: ''Ave we bin introduced then? Or is it a charity dinner for the poor and needy?' His eyes perused Hal's well-cut tweeds.

'Where do you work, then, lad? The Fifty Shillin' Tailors?'

'He's my friend . . .' Dasia hesitated uncertainly.

There was a second's suspended tension in the air as she spoke the words and all the family, including Tommy and Dasia herself, knew why – it was a case she called Horace Greenbow 'Father' by mistake. And for a moment Horace himself felt a sad stab of emotion.

'He's a medical student . . .'

– All the Greenbows held their breath –

. . . 'Grandad . . .'

He relaxed and his face creased into a smile, as he went to take his coat off and wash his hands while they put his dinner out.

Joviality reigned as they all sat round the table with its heavy lace cloth, and golden crackers – with their paper hats on, reading out Jolly Gems from the mounds of paper now littering the cloth: 'If you've got a good wife, keep perfectly still, and thank God every twenty minutes for it . . .'

Alice brought in the Christmas pudding and Tommy – in a new Fair Isle pullover and white shirt-sleeves rolled up – poured brandy on it and set it into blue flames, before they all started to eat it and find the silver threepenny bits hidden in it.

In the afternoon it was warm and sunny, and the snow patches were melting away. It was almost as if they hadn't had any bad weather at all. But, then, in England it was always incredibly changeable.

'Why don't you stay the night with us all?' said Dasia, as she and Hal took a breath of fresh air along The Grove. 'You're not on duty or anything, and at least you'd get a proper night's sleep – instead of like last night, with that coffin in your bedroom, and us getting up at an unearthly hour.

'It wouldn't take you long to get back to the infirmary

103

in the morning ... It's been so nice. I'm really happy again, now.'

Hal smiled, then agreed to stay. He was glad she was happy. It salved his conscience after the indignities she'd suffered at Hyndemere, through no mistake of her own.

'When my fingers are out of their splints,' he said, 'I'll return the compliment, and we'll have a really good night out on the town. A visit to the Opera House, then maybe a dinner dance at the Midland ... Would you like that?'

Her eyes shone and she nodded. Yet, deep down, there was a feeling of uncertainty as she wondered what would happen next now that she'd walked out of Dolly's, and deserted Horace, Alice and Andrina in the pawn shop.

CHAPTER SIX

Shop Girl

On Boxing Day, after the Greenbows had paid their
final friendly Christmas dues to the postman, the
dustman, a local lamplighter, the milkman, the butcher's
boy and the paper lad, Alice Greenbow said quizzically
to her granddaughter, 'So what was it like at Hal's
house, then? He seemed very quiet about his background. Our Rosalie even wondered if he was an orphan
. . . If we didn't but know better. Does he live somewhere
grand or summat?'

Dasia was helping her to sieve and strain the remains
of the Christmas goose carcass for making a wholesome
broth. At first she didn't reply, but knowing what a
needler for information Alice was, and how she was
always hoping for the miracle of Royal and Noble
marriages for all her daughters, Dasia couldn't resist
telling her.

'He's the son of a lord.'

Alice Greenbow looked as if she'd been pole-axed.
She dropped the wooden, hair-mesh sieve she was using
and sat down on a kitchen chair in stupefied silence for a

few seconds. Then she said, 'The son of a lord? Don't you *dare* do any silly romancing with me, madam!'

'He is! It's true. He's the only son of Lord and Lady Wrioth of Hyndemere Hall near Chester.'

For the first time in her life, her grandmother was bereft of speech.

Then Dasia said perkily, 'There's no need to look so stunned. They're no better than we are. In fact some of them's worse. His cousin was nothing but a lecherous drunkard, and his mother is as tough as old boots and could sell an igloo to an Eskimo. She even tried to change me into a real Cinderella so as I'd know my proper station in life. But then – we can't choose our backgrounds, or our parents – can we?'

There was a moment's quietness and they both looked secretly sad. Sometimes, Alice's heart bled for young Dasia – but she never showed it. Her finding out about the true family set-up by accident had been a terrible shock all round — masked by all the Christmas festivities. But now all that was over, and here the child was, back home again. But as for all this sudden story about the lordship ... well! Alice didn't quite know whether to take it with a pinch of salt. Maybe Dasia was saying it because she wanted to try and be the centre of attention again, as she had been before with being the youngest one in the family.

Alice Greenbow belonged to an older generation where class was class, and never the twain must meet – unless her lot were expendable servants of the other lot. And the only way of becoming part of that other lot in past Victorian days was to be seduced by the Lord of the Manor – and so to increase his family by an extra birth or two.

Alice's mind was working overtime. Maybe Dasia was right? So it might be that this Hal person could be appearing on the scene again, especially as Dasia had said something about going to the opera house with him in the New Year.

A purr suddenly appeared in Alice's voice ... 'Well, all I can say, love, is that it's quite amazing and dumbfounding, and I would never have imagined it in a month of Sundays. But always remember, Dasia, he's always welcome here. And if he'd like to spend any time staying here instead of his quarters at the infirmary he'll be nobbut welcome.'

Dasia was really touched. She went to Alice and flung her arms round her: 'Oh Mother, it's been such a terrible Christmas, until I got back here.' She started to cry and the crying flooded into huge sobs that shook her whole body. 'Oh Grandma – if you only knew! It was all such a terrible shock and I didn't know what to do. I thought I would go mad. Then when Hal came and took me with him to Hyndemere I thought it would all work out happily, and it didn't ...'

Then she cried and cried, until the whole of her dress bodice was damp, and said, 'Why didn't Andrina ever say she was my mother and I had another father? How can I stop thinking of you as my real mother still? And Andrina as my sister like it all was before? All the time I have to try and remember. And yesterday at dinner I was terrified I would still call granddad Father ...'

'There, there now, child. Have a good cry and get it out of your system. You've got me at it too.' Alice took out a big hanky and wiped her eyes as they both held together in a firm, fondling embrace. 'You will always be our youngest child, and it doesn't really matter about whose child you really are.'

'But it matters to me, Grandmother.'

'Yes. I know it matters to you, love. And in one sense I expect it matters to us all – but what I meant was that our love all remains the same underneath. Names is just names, love. It's the people behind them. Nothing's changed in one way. But in another way, everything's changing all the time because of our ages and what we do. Like you bringing this young man home. So cheer up, chucky. I know I go on at you at times, but it's all been for your own good.' Alice gave her cheek a gentle kiss. 'Go and wash that face. Get it all blooming again – for the New Year.'

When Dasia came back from washing her face and combing her hair, she felt much better. They both went on with preparing the broth as if nothing had happened when Alice said again, 'And remember to tell your young man he's always welcome.'

Dasia smiled and nodded. Secretly she knew that Hal would never want to come here. He was as awkward here as she'd been at Hyndemere, and she knew he hadn't been his natural self when he'd stayed the night. She'd tried to unite him and Grandfather by explaining that Hal's father was just like Horace Greenbow because they both invented things, and she had described Lord Wrioth's pikelet toaster; but Horace listened with polite but guarded scepticism, while Hal retained an embarrassed silence.

Then, just as Dasia and Alice had finished the broth preparations, Alice said in her usual rather aggressive way, reminiscent of her sister Dolly, 'And if he ever takes you out to any posh eating places, never eat truffles. An' I'm not talking about those chocolate-box ones from that Belgian hand-made chocolate shop in Oxford Road ... I mean those so called delicacies they dig up from under oak trees where pigs roam about – that do no good for man nor beast, and heat up all the sex glands.'

Dasia nodded solemnly. She'd never been warned about truffles before.

Then Alice added hastily, 'Of course, if you were actually married to a lord it would be quite different,

108

because it might help you to get a good family. But most of these things are strictly for married women only ...'

Dasia was back in her own bedroom good and proper now. And nothing had changed one iota. It was as if she'd never run away at all, except that the room looked shabbier and slightly smaller after her cursory, toe-dipping excursion to Hyndemere. Even the po was still there to catch the drips from the ceiling although the ceiling was dry now – watermarked by a strange billowing cloud effect in pale brown sepia, its voluptuous curves and circles from past floods almost resembling the start of some historic ceiling sketch before the actual picture was painted.

A New Year due ... never in her life before had she given it much thought except for the old traditions of being rid of the old, and welcoming the new – with church bells, ships' sirens, and train whistles. And there were their own family customs; like Horace Greenbow (who was nothing like the required 'tall, dark, stranger') being pushed out of the house before twelve o'clock, with a piece of coal in his pocket ready to bring it back as a token of warmth and good luck, a piece of bread and dripping with salt sprinkled on it for plentiful food, a bottle of home-made ginger beer for all-round friend-ship and hospitality, and a farthing to keep debt from the door – which was usually impossible.

But this year, on Saturday the 1st January 1927, as Dasia sat filling in a new diary which Andrina had got her at a reduced price (because the whole of February was missing) she began to give earnest consideration to her New Year Resolutions.

Usually, it was the familiar ones: 'Must flatten my bust more ... Must not show my temper ... Must use more polite and ladylike words ... Must try to play the ukulele ...'

But this time, 'Must think about getting a job' (or as most young ladies in The Grove put it, 'Going Out to Business') headed her New Year list.

She noticed that no one in their house had ever mentioned her going back in the pawn shop again, and Andrina said they were to employ a fourteen-year-old boy called Arthur Stubbs to take her place – who had his leg in an iron caliper, and was willing to work for practically nothing just to have something to do, instead of being at home with his widowed mother the whole time.

Then, to her delight, on Monday the 3rd of January, thirty-five-year-old Louise arrived back from working at Baulden's to say she'd been promoted to the job of assistant buyer in the gowns department and that there was a vacancy on 'Gloves'.

'If you're really interested, and swear not to disgrace the family name,' said Louise with some asperity in her tone, 'I'll fix you up with an interview to see Mr Mildew.'

A job at Baulden's – it was all Dasia could have ever dreamed of.

'And there's no need to look so joy-struck. You haven't got it yet. Mr Mildew is *extremely* particular about his staff. He usually prefers more mature people – especially for the gloves.

'Miss Davina on the gloves is very fussy too. The female glove counter caters for very cultured customers.'

Then Louise went bright pink, pressed her dainty, well-manicured fingers nervously against her chestnut-coloured fringe, and said quickly in a low voice, 'Tell him you're twenty-one. He always forgets to ask for people's birth certificates, but it will add to your chances of employment, even though they'll have to pay you about a farthing extra, based on age.'

Dasia was quite shocked. She hadn't realised that

tender, honest, conscientious Louise would ever actually stoop to suggesting deceit. She didn't answer – but nodded gratefully. She would decide for herself when the time came.

The following day, Louise came back from work with the news that Mr Mildew was willing to interview Miss Dasia Greenbow at ten o'clock, prompt, on Wednesday morning.

The whole family was delighted.

'Try and look as if you mean it, our Dasia,' said Alice Greenbow drily. 'From what our Tommy said went on – over at Dolly's at Christmas – employing you is worse than a fire hazard.' Then she relented a bit and told her to plait her hair so she didn't look like The Wild Woman From Borneo.

'Never speak unless you're spoken too, either, and always let the man make the first move.

'And never walk through a door first unless it's obvious that he wants to show you how polite he is, and bows slightly – with his face looking pleasantly in your direction, love; with one arm stretched out like a sign-post.

'And if he actually shows his teeth in a smile, always note whether it's a fatherly sort of smile and not a come-hither leer. And even that is difficult with these new big dentures like tomb stones. You can't always tell – especially if they has bushy eyebrows and wears glasses.

'And *never* smile back at him!' said Alice – now in full, excited flow. 'Give 'em an inch and they'll take a yard in places like Baulden's where they're all supposed to be so select and prissy. Just lower your eyelids slightly, and keep your lips firmly together. It's not the same manners there as working in our pawn shop where we're all normal.'

Dasia set off for the interview with mixed feelings. She was fast becoming taken over by Alice and the rest of them again. They'd even decided what she should wear.

Not for her the chance to borrow Rosalie's new mustard velour ragamuffin hat with a huge pheasant feather sticking up from the petersham ribbon round its crown, or borrow silk stockings from Louise. Instead, she was attired like some ancient dame, in an awful navy blue serge suit, hastily borrowed from a very thin cousin, along with a cotton pin-tuck blouse which was heavily starched, a deep, navy hat which almost buried her eyes, thick grey lisle stockings, a black handbag – and black lace-up shoes.

'You look lovely, love,' said her grandmother as she hurried off to catch the train. 'You look really respectable. There's nothing better than a young woman in a proper hat.'

Dasia sat like a statue on the brown bentwood chair in Mr Mildew's poky little office – with its picture of men in walrus moustaches and beaver beards on the wall.

'I think that's all I require, Miss Greenbow. Twenty-one years old, eh? The age of consent ...'

Dasia nodded politely.

'I'll take you to The Gloves and introduce you to Miss Davina. She's been with us over thirty years – and she'll soon put you on the ropes ...'

They shook hands solemnly. Surely she should have only been shown the ropes ... not put on them? She hardly dared to look too closely at Mr Mildew because of Alice Greenbow's instructions – but he was a slim-built man of about forty with very bright eyes, a moist mouth and large, yellow, hungry-looking teeth.

He walked to the office door just like her grandmother had described, and stood there smiling at Dasia with his arm pointing out of the office like a signpost.

She walked through the open door and lowered her

112

eyelids slightly, and as she did so she felt a huge nip, as if the back of her skirt had got caught up on a hook, and she turned quickly. 'Whatever was *that*?' she said in a loud voice. 'I mustn't get this skirt caught on anything. It belongs to my cousin.'

'Does it indeed?' said Mr Mildew – completely taken off his guard as he put both his hands hastily behind his back.

January sped along now she was in a real job, and she felt proud and independent for the first time in her life. It was much more tiring work than being in the family pawn shop because she was on her feet for hours on end, and most older people in Baulden's haberdashery complained of varicose veins like bunches of purple grapes and even piles from sitting on frozen chairs – though it must be admitted that this last claim was from a lady who often claimed her bottom was numb from just sitting down typing for Mr Mildew.

Dasia looked on the Glove department as refined and civilised, and some of the gloves were wonderful. There were display cases with continental gloves in them embroidered in the finest bead work. And even some with gold thread and tiny jewels.

Miss Davina was extremely kind; she was crippled with arthritis and often sat on a polished beechwood stool with a cushion on it, soothing the pain with swigs from a small, leather-covered flask which she kept in her voluminous, tapestry cloth handbag with its big amber-coloured bone clasp. She would take out the bottle when all was quiet and say, 'Of course, it's only cold tea, dear, but it helps.'

Miss Davina knew many of her customers extremely well, and had their hand and finger measurements written down in a large ledger – including the hand sizes of their children, which were crossed off and altered as the children grew bigger.

'Thank God, lass,' she said, 'that people from birth to the grave keep losing their blessed gloves, and coming back to Baulden's for more ...' Then she gave Dasia a lesson on how to use the glove stretcher, warning her to be careful not to harm the actual fabric and seams of gloves by over-stretching them, as the staff were liable to pay for any damage themselves.

One day when Dasia was looking in one of Miss Davina's notebooks, with its list of customers' orders in it, she noticed some very small initials in pencil by the sides of some of them.

'What does MP mean, Miss Davina?' Dasia had even imagined it might mean the woman's husband was a member of parliament, knowing how high-flown Miss Davina's clientele was.

'It means, Mucky Palms, dear. You'd be surprised how some of them never wash their hands properly after eating bread and butter or an orange. And any small LFs stand for long fingernails that can rip delicate gloves to bits.'

She also warned Dasia to watch like a hawk for people like rich Mrs Mottershead who was forever forcing her podgy fists into the tightest tissue-like openings of kid gloves when she thought she was unobserved.

'– But we can see them through the mirrors, dear, and they never realise it. So if any of them look as if their hands aren't properly washed, love, or their nails are all black or bitten, or chewed – or as long as a Chinaman's – don't on any account let them try the expensive ones. Persuade them either to consider the leatherettes or to get some cheap wool and shoddy from the Penny Bazaar.

'Most of their sort never intend to buy in the first place. The nearest they ever get to proper gloves is a pair of cheap cotton mittens.'

Then, at the end of all this she said, 'But always remember, Miss Greenbow: The Customer Is Always Right ...'

'That rich son of a lord doesn't seem to be courting you very much since you went to work at Baulden's,' remarked Alice, one Sunday morning when Dasia was helping her to get roast beef and Yorkshire pudding ready for dinner – while Andrina was off to church with Samuel Tankerton, the solicitor, and his limpet mother, in the Tankertons' Ford.

'You never seem to have mentioned that wonderful night out at the Opera House again. A youthful young man of noble intentions, no doubt – until they turn to addled eggs.'

Dasia's colour rose. Her grandmother's sarcasm was often very hard to bear – especially as it was still only January and Dasia's resolution not to show her temper hadn't been operating very long.

'There's no need to *worry* about it, Gran. It's not all that easy for him; he works very long hours, and I work long hours too, only different ones. So there isn't much time for gadding about.'

'Then how did he manage to be gadding about when you met him at Redman's before Christmas?' asked Alice shrewdly.

Dasia flared up and glared at her: 'Don't ask *me*! I'm not his blinking keeper. And I am only seventeen ... You tell me *that* often enough. So, for your information, I don't want to "grab" anyone yet – even if they are a lord. I don't want to marry till I'm at least thirty; until I've collected that inheritance from my true father.'

She stopped dead. Alice was staring at her with a frozen look on her elderly face, and pain in her grey eyes.

'Life's not as simple as that, love,' said Alice quietly.

'It all depends on which side of the blanket –' Her voice became more steely: 'For your information you slept in a wooden drawer when you were born, because our Andrina never admitted you were even there, and just said it was either extra weight from a passion for jam doughnuts – or, if it didn't improve, it might be a cyst and she'd have to go to the doctor's.

'Then, one night, the lump *did* disappear. Every bit of it of its own accord and with a lot of roarings and heavings, and not even goodbye. And there you was … howling away like a little purple giant with rope hanging from its belly button.

'And we put you in the big mahogany drawer out of that sideboard in your bedroom, wrapped in Andrina's best pure wool combinations, until we'd all sorted ourselves out …'

Dasia felt herself trembling as if someone had suddenly hurled a rock at her. Was Alice deliberately trying to destroy what little self-confidence she still had and which had slowly been improving since she got her job?

She gave a huge, shuddering sigh as she felt tears coming to her eyes. No wonder it seemed to be every girl's aim to marry a rich man, for how could any of them manage on their own slender means? She thought of her ageing aunt, and her mother Andrina: how ever could they rely on Horace Greenbow to give them a good send-off? What it would amount to with him, kind as he was at heart, would be a cheery glass of sarsaparilla, a jam butty, and shanks's pony to the nearest registry office. And as for dowries – and all that 'something borrowed, something blue' stuff – it would just be a case of sorting out a few bits of junk from the family pawn shop.

With leaden heart Dasia began to face up to the awful truth – she was never going to fit in properly at home

116

again. Not with both her dominant grandmother, and her quietly stubborn, strait-laced mother whose only real passion was wasted, now, on Sammy Tankerton.

'Stop looking so miserable, child,' said Alice briskly. 'Dinner's what we've got to think about. We don't want that Yorkshire pudding ruined. They'll all be back soon.' Then it was, 'Oh my God. Drat that telephone! It always rings at the wrong time. Get away and answer it – and if it's Mrs Trencher, say I'm not interested in the Darning Day at the Mission Hall or the Ironing Day the following week, even if it is for helping others. Especially not since that Pastor Peach tried to cash all those false cheques then did a flee from his creditors, taking blind Mr Dibworth's sixteen-year-old daughter with him to play the piano accordion.'

That afternoon, when most people in The Grove were lying in over-heated, snoozing torpor and were heavy with home-made rice pudding, or boiled marmalade suet roll, Andrina noticed how sad and depressed Dasia seemed as they sat alone together in the big family kitchen.

'What on earth's wrong, Dasia? You look perfectly dreadful. You've even got some spots coming up on your chin.' Andrina went to the kitchen cupboard and began to hunt for the brimstone and treacle – a thick, sticky, dark brown concoction often used as a spring cleaner for the system.

Andrina turned and gazed at her daughter. The brimstone and treacle was in a large round carton and Andrina had the spoon ready. 'You don't look as if you've had a decent night's sleep either. There are dark rings around your eyes and your hair is as lank as wet hay. Maybe even a dose of castor oil would help.'

Dasia was suddenly filled with fury: 'Save it for polishing the piano, Andrina,' she said scornfully, 'I'm not your little baby now, lying in the drawer wrapped in

117

your best combinations. In fact at the moment I just don't know who I am, or where I'm going and I don't care!'

Andrina went as white as a ghost: 'You've been overworking at that terrible Baulden's and you've only been there two minutes. But I knew all along it would be worse than working in the pawn shop.'

'All the same – you never even asked me to go back to work at our own shop, did you?'

'Of course we didn't. None of us thought you'd ever want to again, after the way you suddenly left home. And anyway, little Arthur Stubbs has taken to it like a duck to water. He'll probably land up as top class valuer.

'All the same, I only wish you looked happier after your short stint in that wretched glove department.'

'I'm perfectly *happy* in the glove department, thank you –'

'Then what's all the fuss about? And why were you trying to get at me with all that talk about being in a drawer when you were a baby? Some people have suffered far worse fates than that – including my poor dead Blennim – *your* father ...

'How do you think *I* felt when I saw the news in that awful letter addressed to Horace? How do you think *I've* felt as your secret mother, during all these terrible years when I would for all the world have liked to claim you as my own little girl, and talked about you to other people and been proud – when all along it had to be hidden. And for the sake of stupid respectability Alice had to take over, while my rightful motherhood was hidden in shame and disgrace.' Andrina began to cry and go quite hysterical as years of simmering agony and anger were released at last. 'And for why? I'll tell you for why, young lady, it was because Blennim's mother was a bitch. That's for why.' Tears streamed down Andrina's thin nervous face.

118

'She shoved him off to Canada on health grounds before we could get properly betrothed. And it was impossible for me to go after him, because I had no money – and that's the truth of it.' She bent her head and arm on to the hard wooden table as she sat there, and groaned softly.

Dasia was shocked and contrite. It had been like having a huge bucket of cold water suddenly tipped over her own emotions, as a great wave of guilt flooded over her. For now she saw that Andrina had lost more chances of leading her own life than she herself was likely to do – including that of bearing another child, even if she'd wanted one, because she was too old, so that her joy of motherhood had been killed before it even began.

'I think I know a bit – how you feel, Andrina ...'

'*You* know?' her mother turned on her like a ferocious tiger with eyes of fire. '*You* know nothing, my girl!' And she got up and left the kitchen without another word.

At first, when she'd gone, Dasia herself felt like collapsing into tears, but she knew deep down that they would be tears of self-pity about the whole sorry state, and with a deep sigh she stood up and decided to go for a walk. At least the whole thing had now been aired properly and was now in the open.

She realised that these innermost feelings that had welled to the surface had cleared the air for the future – for the whole family. Then she became sad again, for she felt so lonely. She was the one, virtually the only one, who had suffered the greatest change of all and the greatest shock, because the rest of them had been aware of the whole situation for the past seventeen years.

She put on her thick coat and scarf and new knitted hat and set off – glad to be away from the house for a brief half hour as she walked along The Grove and past The Cedars where Sammy Tankerton and his mother lived. Further on, branching off to the right was a small field path and a wooden stile leading towards the brook. It was a pleasant and popular walk, used by all and sundry for afternoon strolls and short cuts towards busier suburban roads. It finished along an unpaved tree-lined avenue that led to a busy, curving lane with small cottages at the other end.

Dasia had just passed the cottages when who should she see – all dressed in her Sunday best with a small puppy on a lead – but Aunty Dolly.

'Aunty Dolly! Happy New Year. Better late than never ... Fancy seeing you here ...' Dasia stared at the small, white, smooth haired terrier with a black spot on its back.

'It's called Spot,' said Aunty Dolly a trifle mournfully. 'I just don't know what Mr Corcoran was thinking of to have given it me as a Christmas present. It's a complete menace. Just look at it this minute, getting all tangled up in its lead and trying to chew it all. No, dogs don't suit me, Dasia, but it was my own stupid fault. Just after you'd gone off with your young man, I was talking to Mr Corcoran about the dangers of the single woman left to cope with life on her own, without a good husband – and this was the result.

'But what can one do? I know he meant well.' She looked at Dasia with a long morose look, then smiled down at Spot and gave his lead an almighty jerk and tightened it enough to make him yelp. 'You have to be very firm with them, Dasia. So what are you doing now, love? I'm just here taking Spot to cock his leg up.

'Mr Corcoran and I are on a short run in the car to see Mr Corcoran's friend who's just bought a chip shop, but doesn't live on the premises. Which way are you going, dear? I'll walk a little of the way with you. How did you go on with your young man after you set off in all that dreadful weather? Always remember, Dasia, you're welcome any time as a guest, but come in the afternoons when they're all out. It's best to ring first really, in case Marcia's about, as I don't think she'll ever quite forgive you for leaving her in the lurch. She's had a *dreadful* Christmas ... And the New Year hasn't been much better.

'When Mr Corcoran and I came out this afternoon, Mr Batril had broken six of her best dinner plates – helping her to wash up. And her new maid was accused by Mr Dornay of stuffing one of his five pound notes into the top of her black silk stocking and showing her garters.'

Dasia glossed over her time at Hyndemere, and concentrated on the fact that she was now working at Baulden's.

'I'm so glad for you, dear. And I hope you have a really good fresh start this year, after all you've gone through.' Then they went their separate ways and Dolly hurried off into the distance with her troublesome charge on his lead.

As Dasia turned to go back home she felt completely normal again. Her cheerfulness had revived like a ray of sunshine because of meeting dear Aunt Dolly.

'You'll never guess who rang up when you were out,' said Alice, with quite a kind look on her face.

Dasia's heart thudded with heartfelt relief. The world was right at last.

CHAPTER SEVEN

The Day Out

It was nearly the end of January and the weather was
frosty and bright with heavy morning mists.

Much to Alice's amazement, Hal had become Dasia's
young man. It was an unspoken, unofficial acceptance
by the Greenbow family. He came to the house as often
as he could in his time off from the hospital.

He had more than fulfilled his promise of taking
Dasia to the Opera House, and to a dinner dance at the
Midland Hotel in Manchester, for they had also been to
the talkies, and even to see Charlie Chaplin in his latest
silent film *The Gold Rush* (for Charlie had not ventured
into talkies as his comic style told it all without words).

They'd also been back to Redman's, dancing, and
they'd seen Miss Horniman's Gaiety Theatre Company
in some plays at The Green Room.

Dasia's life was thoroughly transformed.

And on this last Sunday in January Hal had invited
her to go for a run in a proper car with a waterproof roof
to Alderley Edge, beyond Wilmslow; a beauty spot with
a high, red, sandstone ridge which gave wonderful views
of all the countryside for miles around.

Alice pressed her lips together with relief. At least he wasn't vanishing into thin air.

The change in Dasia had been quite astounding; her eyes shone with joy, like some small child being given a wonderful pot doll with jointed legs from Wile's toyshop.

'We're going to the spot where the Wizard sleeps with his enchanted warriors,' Dasia said.

Alice smiled. It was a good place to go for a nice winter's day out if the weather was fine, because the vistas of the Cheshire plain could be seen as a vast panorama unimpeded by leafy trees. And on a really clear day you could see the line of hills in Yorkshire, rising above other high ground, called Blackstone Edge.

'I expect he'll take you to the Wizard,' said Alice, 'but don't drink anything stronger than ginger beer.'

The Wizard was an ale house. It stood beneath fir trees facing towards the Cheshire plain and was a popular countryside rendezvous. It had a distinctive inn sign with a painting of the Wizard on his white horse.

Legend had it that a local farmer on his white horse was crossing the heath along the top of Alderley Edge when he came to a spot now known as Thieves' Hole. Here, he was stopped by an old man in flowing robes who was a wizard. The wizard said he would buy the farmer's white horse, and led him to a place where they seemed to hear the sound of horses neighing underground.

The wizard touched a rock with his wand – and immediately, before the farmer's eyes, rose a pair of iron gates.

The gates opened and they led to a cave where the farmer saw many men – all with white horses, and fast asleep.

In an innermost cavern, there was a mass of treasure, and the wizard told the farmer to take from it the price for his own white horse, for without the farmer's own

123

white horse the magic would not be strong enough to wake the slumbering horsemen and their steeds to fight a great battle for their country.

So the farmer left his horse, and the iron gates closed with fearful sounds. From that day onwards, no one has found the iron gates again.

Hal knew this story, which he told to Dasia on their way to Alderley Edge.

'There are lots of different versions,' he said. 'P'raps it arose from people working in the copper mines, and mining cobalt and lead there. Perhaps there *were* iron gates, but so long ago that they've now rusted away. The legend still lives on with a forecast that a battle will be fought when George the son of George the Fifth is on the throne.'

They both laughed with youthful delight, glad to know that the 'war to end all wars' was well and truly over, and that they were part of a newer, better world.

They parked their car in Alderley village and made their way towards the Edge itself – with its sandstone outcrops and pebbly footpaths. There was a beacon at the top, near castle rock, and about sixty yards below the beacon was the Holy Well of Alderley Edge.

Dasia and Hal gazed up at the huge clefted rock where water emerged – gleaming like streaks of silver in the deep mossy greenness – and they stood and kissed each other in the cold bright winter's air. They nuzzled each other with their noses and gave butterfly kisses with their eyelashes. Then holding hands like Babes in the Wood, they helped each other downhill along the narrow uneven track to the point called Stormy point and viewed the smoke of distant Manchester.

On the way back to the car, Hal said, 'Come back to my place, before I take you home. We never seem to be alone together for very long. Surely we've known each other long enough by now ...?

Dasia smiled at him, and looked searchingly into his smooth handsome face.

'But I thought you once said you weren't supposed to entertain young ladies in your quarters? I thought it was supposed to be the worst sin you could possibly commit?'

In her brain, his last sentence rang in her ears ... 'Surely we've known each other long enough by now ...' What exactly did he mean? After all, they'd only really known each other for a month even though it seemed like forever, and many people courted for years and years – like Rosalie and Louise, and even Andrina.

Apparently, after the first year some men began to get quite nasty; even though they weren't willing to get married, they tried to convince the girls that 'A bit of what you fancy does you good ...'

But a bit of what *they* fancied was often a far cry from the engagement ring that the girls had in mind.

She suddenly relaxed, and chided herself. Perhaps Hal wanted to take her back with him to propose?

Maybe he had a ring tucked away somewhere. But if he had, it would certainly need some thinking about, because she hadn't actually planned to marry anyone for a few years; and after only one short visit to Hyndemere she suspected that being married even to a lord was no better than being married to anyone else.

And besides, she was saving up now she had her job at Baulden's so that one day she might have enough money to go and claim the inheritance which her other grandfather, Adrien Shawfield, had mentioned in the letter to Horace Greenbow.

Hal was looking at her pleadingly: 'There's no one about on Sundays and it's not as if you're coming to visit me late at night. It's all perfectly respectable. Surely you weren't thinking I might –?' There was amused devilry in his eyes.

'Certainly *not*!' Dasia was truly shocked. She had no

illusions about deflowering ceremonies, and first nights of the honeymoon. Many of the tales were like horror stories as far as the female victims were concerned, and jokes about men leaping from the tops of wardrobes were manifold.

Hal's room in the student quarters was quite civilised. It had a small desk and book shelves, and a firegrate with his own kettle on a hob in the fireplace.

There was a good big cupboard with kitchenware in it, and a small gate-legged folding table. On the comfortable-looking, three-quarter-sized bed was a large thick fringed woollen travelling rug – which acted as a counterpane over the top of his eiderdown. And in the corner was a floor-to-ceiling built-in cupboard, which acted as a wardrobe.

The sash windows were covered in net curtaining and looked out on to similar rows of net-curtained windows on first and second floors.

'Shall we have a drink? Cherry Brandy . . .?' Hal took a half bottle from the kitchen cupboard along with two small glasses, and put them on the table.

Dasia felt tired now, after the day out in the cold fresh air of Alderley Edge, and she began to wish she hadn't come. Her eyes felt like lead in the sudden warmth. As she looked towards his bed she wished she could lie down like a complete log, and relax – like she could at home in her own bedroom.

But she knew it was impossible. How could any girl in a man's rooms suddenly flop on his bed and lie there all relaxed – with a man anxious to ply her with cherry brandy?

'No thanks, Hal. A drink like that'd make me feel too drowsy after all the fresh air. And besides, I'm supposed to be keeping away from drinking. It doesn't do people any good.'

'Good Lord, Dasia! It's only one minute cherry brandy. I'm not out to make you legless. We can have fruit juice if you prefer it. Or even a cup of tea.'

'I'll just have a drink of water, please, Hal. I like water.'

'Water? What's come over you? Do you feel all right?'

They both smiled at each other, then Dasia gave in, 'Go on then; but only *one* very small one ...'

Carefully, Hal poured her out about a teaspoonful, and himself something four times bigger. Then he said, 'Come and lie on the bed. Come on ... Never stand when you can sit, never sit when you can lie down!'

He pulled her gently towards the bed. She was completely in his power. She'd never find her way out of the building without his help, and Sunday night wasn't the best time for transport, or for being alone on Oxford Road. Yet to refuse would be tantamount to saying she didn't trust him. And if he really was her young man, there had to be trust – else what was the point of going out with him?

They lay peacefully on top of the tartan travel rug; Hal with his hands folded behind the base of his neck as he stared up at the ceiling, and Dasia lying quietly by his side.

Suddenly Dasia felt truly relaxed and happy. She closed her eyes drowsily. Then she opened them and looked at Hal. His eyes were closed too, and his black curling eyelashes looked, to Dasia, like an angel's.

But just at that very moment of truly innocent paradise, there was a sudden violent rattle of the door knob and a strident female voice rasped, 'I know you're in there, Mr Wrioth. Can I come in please? I don't want to have to use my own keys!'

He sprang up like a Jack-in-the-box, and in seconds he'd pushed Dasia into the clothes cupboard behind coats and trousers: 'Coming, Mrs Butters ...'

He strode to the door and swung it open calmly, with a deliberately surprised expression on his face.

'I'll come in if you don't mind, Mr Wrioth.'

'With pleasure. Do. Take a seat . . .'

'I'll stand if you don't mind. The fact is – you've been reported as bringing a young woman to your room, and you know very well it's against the rules.'

'I can't see anyone,' said Hal. 'And even if there were, it's an extremely stupid and uncivilised rule.'

'But it is a *rule*, Mr Wrioth. Ours is not to reason why . . . If I find you are entertaining females in your room, I shall be obliged to report you.'

Hal's temper started to rise: 'All right. Get on with it, then . . . I am entertaining one!'

The look of triumph passing across Mrs Butters' gaunt face was almost unbelievable as she snooped swiftly about, peering here and there for damning evidence: 'Where is she then? Tell me *immediately*!'

'Right here. In front of me, Mrs Butters. A female . . . *you*, Mrs Butters.' Then, before she could gather her wits together, he ushered her outside and closed the door firmly, making sure it was locked. Then he went to the clothes cupboard to release Dasia.

She was nervous, trembling and angry as she fell into his arms. She felt completely diminished. Fancy having to be hidden in a cupboard as if she was secret contraband – like a refugee slave.

'I want to go home,' she sobbed. 'I'm never, *never* coming here again.'

'There, there . . .' he cradled her in his arms with her red, glowing hair tangled against his chest, and put the blanket over both of them as they lay on the bed again while he murmured soothing words of abject apology. 'Just relax for a few minutes my sweetheart, and then we'll go,' he said. 'And I promise you we'll never be together in this room again.'

He stroked her hair lovingly and smoothed it away from her forehead, smiling into her eyes, and in return she smiled back and stroked his dark curls, running her fingers delicately round his ears, little realising she had lit the tinderbox. For in next to no time she knew the moment had come for the final act and she accepted it, not in any passionate love at this instant, but as part of her own education. The yearning somehow to get it over with and find out what it was really like.

Looking back at that first time, years later, Dasia marvelled at her own naivety, and Hal's – even though he was a medical student. For this first act, immediate and unplanned, without any thought of contraception, was in its forthrightness nothing to do with the true world of consequences. Hal was her lover – yet not loved by her in this mutual sex act, as she felt him on top of her, groaning with male joy and excitement then rolling away from her in happy relief – leaving nothing to show, except seminal fluid and a show of her own slight trace of blood beneath her.

Was this all it was ever going to be? This kind of giving …

Rosalie had once told her that when the time came she would realise the joy of it. But at the time, all she wondered was how on earth a single woman like Rosalie could be so certain?

The only thing *she* was certain of now was that she had lost her true innocence, and would never be a real child again. And all done in seconds; for when she went back with Hal that night to The Grove, she would be different.

She felt a shiver of fear in case any of them would somehow notice it with the deep intuitive knowledge of adults.

When she and Hal stirred themselves from each other's arms, and were ready, finally to leave his room, it was nearly nine o'clock. And as they walked hastily along silent stone corridors – both hoping not be seen by anyone in authority – they suddenly came face to face with the housekeeper: Mrs Butters!

Dasia noticed she wore grey, with black stockings, and a large white starched bonnet on her head with a bow under her chin – like someone from a hundred years ago. She was standing talking to a heavily built man in a black morning jacket and grey striped trousers. Her face said it all, as she saw Hal with Dasia.

'Professor Ruxtable ...' murmured Hal with a hollow groan as they both hurried past – praying they wouldn't instantly be recalled.

Hal didn't stay long, as he deposited Dasia at home. Both of them felt guilty, and Dasia was wondering desperately whether her grandmother would try to wheedle a whole detailed report of her outing with Hal – including why they were back so late. But her fears were groundless because Alice was busy elsewhere – and the house bustled with the noise and activity of the rest of the family.

Quickly – with a glass of hot milk and two ovaltine biscuits – Dasia went upstairs to bed, and lay there shivering slightly between the icy sheets, for there was no hot water bottle. Then, thinking of her love making, she fell asleep.

Little did she know how Hal was faring as she kissed him goodnight, in a sleepy attempt at mental telepathy.

And it was just as well ...

CHAPTER EIGHT

The Proposal

Hal was very thoughtful on his way from taking Dasia home. And as he neared his own quarters he thought of their time in his room, and its implications.

It was absolutely clear that she'd been a virgin, and although there'd never been any doubt of it right from the beginning of their friendship, he knew that no man who called himself a true gentleman ever divested a girl of her maidenhead without a formal promise of engagement and prospective marriage, especially if she was under twenty-one. And even though he was only nineteen himself, he knew it was an act regarded as an inhuman and unscrupulous ravishing of unsoiled and unsold goods – even though, in their case, it had been an inevitable coming together of youthful passion, curiosity and romance.

He hurried to his door, glad to be back, and was astounded as he put his key in the lock to find Mrs Butters standing behind him, literally breathing down his neck.

'I've been waiting for you,' she said. She pushed her way into his room after him, and stood there accusingly. 'You deliberately flouted the rules, Mr Wrioth!

'Professor Ruxtable is adamant that none of his students should entertain any woman whatsoever in their rooms without first asking permision of me, Mrs Wilhelmina Butters the housekeeper, in a prior arrangement – and then only between certain civilised hours of any day except the Sabbath, ending before seven in the evenings.'

Hal stood there dumbly. He knew she was perfectly correct, but he was uneasy about the hate in her eyes. He felt a stab of fear as he remembered a fellow student Perry Saltburn being sent down for disobeying this very rule; although the *official* reason was Professor Ruxtable's perpetual claim that Perry had no idea how to sew up human flesh satisfactorily.

'So what have you to say for yourself?' sneered Mrs Butters with a malevolent glare. 'Both the professor and myself saw you with her in the corridor, earlier on.

'Come on, Mr Wrioth – where's your honour? Admit it. We weren't all born yesterday, sir.'

Hal's temper rose, and he said coldly, 'You saw no one in this room when you came to look, before, Mrs Butters. And well you know it.'

'Unless she was *hidden* somewhere,' said Mrs Butters with a triumphant gleam, as she marched across to the wardrobe cupboard. 'Unless she was in there …' She pointed her long decisive finger: 'It isn't unusual, Mr Wrioth …'

Hal stood and watched her. He was nonplussed. The less said the better … Just let her natter on and hope she'd go. Then, to his horror, she spotted something on the floor beneath the gate-legged table. It was a small mother-of-pearl button, quite often found on ladies' underwear – and Mrs Butters was in such joyous haste to grab it that she bent down too quickly and gave her face a mighty crack on the oak table right across her cheeks and the bridge of her nose.

She staggered back with shock, and her nose began to bleed. She began to groan loudly, as Hal helped her across to his bed, and administered first aid with genuine concern.

But that only seemed to make matters worse: 'Take your hands off me,' she shrieked. 'You've done enough damage for one night. Professor Ruxtable will hear about this!'

The following morning it was obvious that Mrs Butters had wasted no time in striking while the iron was hot, for instead of Professor Ruxtable ambling in for an eleven o'clock lecture, he was striding round with righteous indignation at half-past eight with Mrs Butters, and her two awful black eyes. Messages were delivered to Hal to report at two o'clock that afternoon to the boardroom – to go before an extraordinary meeting of some of the senior medical school staff, headed by Professor Ruxtable.

'Do not attempt to leave your own room, or converse with anyone before that time,' said the officially typed message on a piece of flimsy Memo paper which was obviously a copy of some more permanent document which they would no doubt file, as a life-long historical fact against him. 'Midday food will be sent to your room by a porter.'

Hal felt like a condemned man as he brooded in silence, unable to concentrate on anything but the wretched and, to him, trivial episode.

But deep down he knew his fate was sealed. He'd never got on very well with Ruxtable. Hal was incapable of showering flattery and adulation on his elders and so-called betters. And although the professor could never fault Hal on his standards of work as a medical student, there was a barrier of mutual dislike, and even envy between them.

★

Precisely at twelve o'clock midday, there was a tap at Hal's door, and a porter was standing there with a billy-can containing mutton and vegetable soup, and a large white bread balm-cake in a paper bag.

And at two o'clock precisely, Hal – clad in a charcoal grey, fine flannel suit with matching waistcoat, and a bow tie of blue, silver, grey and green stripes on navy blue round the neck of his snow white, starched shirt – walked meekly into the boardroom prepared to meet his doom.

There were five of them there, along with Professor Ruxtable's secretary, Miss Penn, who had a hearing trumpet, and her shorthand pad out.

There was Professor Ruxtable in a stiff white, winged collar and maroon cravat with a diamond tie-pin. Doctor Longbottom with his monocle and his Royal Engineers' tie from the war. Professor MacVarty who was nearly ninety and wore plus fours and a green velvet smoking jacket. Doctor Slicer with his bright ginger walrus moustache, and Mr Carradyce – a young consultant surgeon of thirty-six, a bald-headed man with gold-rimmed glasses, and a short, black, clipped tuft of hair on his top lip which resembled an enlarged Victorian postage stamp.

'Step forward, Wrioth,' said Ruxtable in genial triumph. 'Don't hover near the door. This isn't The Star Chamber, so sit down in that empty seat where we can all get a good look at you.

'Every word spoken in this room from now on is in complete confidence, and any decision which is reached between us all will go no further. Is that understood?'

Hal gazed at them all. He sat like a statue, but his mind was racing. Surely he was entitled to legal representation in a case like this? For he could see now it was a Kangaroo Court; an unofficial meting out of 'justice'.

134

'We are here to investigate a complaint about your appalling behaviour yesterday evening, regarding – number one: the harbouring of a common prostitute in your room, and number two: a brutal assault on Mrs Butters herself in the course of her carrying out her rightful duties.'

Hal was speechless with amazement and disbelief.

'What have you to say to these two accusations?' said Ruxtable in oily tones.

'They're both completely false, sir. First, I have never in my life harboured and consorted with a common prostitute. Secondly, Mrs Butters found no other person in my room except myself. And, thirdly, I never laid a finger at any time on Mrs Butters except to render first aid when she accidently tripped and hit her nose on the table in my room.'

There was a heavy silence, then a blowing of noses and coughing and rustling of paper, and the heavy, warm smell of cigar smoke.

Then Mrs Butters herself was ushered into the room and a place was made for her right next to Professor Ruxtable, where she sat and stared at everyone like a sad, newspaper cartoon of Horlicks Night Starvation, except that the black circles round her eyes were twenty times worse.

'Oh yes, sir, there's no doubt about it. As soon as I said he'd had her hidden in his wardrobe cupboard, and I'd found the evidence of a button from her most intimate underwear on the floor near his bed, he attacked me good and proper – as you can all see.

'Then – as if that wasn't enough – he tried to smother me with one of those terrible sponges that some times smell of chloroform.'

This final accusation caused much puzzlement and academic discussion about a chloroform sponge – which, much to the annoyance of Mrs Butters, veered away from her own dramatised predicament and became a general one on the quality of natural sponges, with Boots, and even Marshall and Snelgrove mentioned. Then Hal was asked to leave them all and retire to the ante room again. To him, it seemed like waiting for hours ... Surely they were reasonable men underneath ... Surely they would see that it had all been a ghastly mistake. Surely they wouldn't take every single word uttered by Mrs Butters as gospel truth.

He was waiting there exactly five minutes before he was called back.

'We've come to our decision, Wrioth,' said Ruxtable briskly, 'you are henceforth dismissed as a medical student due to conduct unbecoming to this establishment. The vote was unanimous, and you can leave as soon as you like.

'An official letter will be sent to your home address. That is all.'

Hal was as white as death when he left the room. His brain was in a whirl. It was unbelievable!

How could this group of senior men snuff out his whole career so easily on such a trumped-up charge? This time yesterday, he'd been with Dasia at Alderley Edge on one of the happiest days of his life – and now it had all turned to hell.

What on earth would his parents say when they saw the letter? They'd be sure to want a full explanation, and if they thought he was truly innocent they'd be prepared to make a court case of it.

He began to tremble slightly from the shock of it all. Just imagine it in the papers ... his family and Dasia's; The Wrioths and the Greenbows all mixed up in a scandal with inferences of prostitution, and the assault of an innocent and conscientious housekeeper trying to curb the mayhem in the Rabelaisian students' quarters ...

No. Surely not all that! A thousand times no. Neither he nor Dasia would be able to stomach it. Better to accept the verdict and disappear as quickly as possible. Settle down with Dasia somewhere – for at least she knew the whole truth of it, and surely, together, they could cope?

He realised now she was the only proper support he was going to have in this terrible time of crisis, as his mind went round and round with the idea of actually marrying her, and so at least legitimising their new relationship; for no one dared to show disrespect to an honourably married woman, as long as the husband was close by.

'Do you mean to tell me, old sprout,' said his loyal friend Kenny Saville the next day, 'that you didn't even know that old Willi Butters is one of Ruxby's paramours?

'I'm absolutely staggered, old son! She always was a lying bitch, and there's no two ways about it.'

He was watching in horrified fascination as Hal packed his bags. He was a peaceful person, an easily depressed soul who suffered the tortures of being a medical student in a plethora of agony. 'Fancy you having to scamper away – when it's always me forever expecting to meet my Waterloo.

'Trouble is, Hal old fruit, I'm so bloody frightened of the gentle sex that I miss out on all the complications, or should one say combinations? And as for buttons, old chap, it takes me all my time to unravel a simple calico bandage. Although when those darling girls get to over sixty, they all seem to adore me! They like the perfume from my heady Parma Violets brilliantine.'

Hal began to lose interest. Life was too serious for all this prattle – until he suddenly heard Kenny say: '... they're all maiden aunts, you see? And they own rows and rows of property round these streets – just like toothpaste coming out of tubes. So I'll soon find you another kip, for next to nothing.

'In fact, I guarantee you'll have a place by tonight, scrubbed out and clean – with all the windows in, and all the slates on the roof – somewhere round Denmark Road.

'My Great Aunt Celia in particular – always keeps some respectable emergency dossing at hand for deserving cases of all classes. She's very religious and rents a pew in Didsbury Church.'

That evening when Hal was finally in partly furnished accommodation in Denmark Road, and had met Kenny's Aunt Celia, and been given his own key and a religious tract, with only a peppercorn rent to pay, he rang Dasia. He didn't tell her the full story, but said he'd left the officially approved student digs and was now at this new address.

'So shall we meet again tonight, so you can see for yourself? This time, we really will be free of inter-ference.'

'But won't you be working? I thought you said you were extra busy studying anaesthetics?'

His voice changed abruptly: 'There's been a sudden altering of plans ... I *must* see you, Dasia. It's urgent. Thank God I've still got the old tin Lizzie, and a place to park it nearby in this new place.

'I'll call round for you tonight. Tell them we're going to the cinema.' He rang off, and as he replaced the receiver his hand trembled and he was sweating.

Dasia was very disturbed by the call. Something terrible must have happened since they parted. She could tell by His voice changed abruptly: 'There's been a sudden got his little car – just as if everything else had been taken away from him. It wasn't like him at all. He was usually so humorous, and passionate, and confident.

'Who was that on the phone then?' said Alice.

'Hal. He wants me to go out with him tonight, probably to the cinema.'

'But I thought you said he was busy working at present?'

'He is, but maybe it's a case of all work and no play making Jack a dull boy,' said Dasia quickly.

'There's not much chance of that where he's concerned,' said Alice drily. 'I hope he doesn't expect you to dash off without proper food inside you. He may be the son of a lord, but you weren't put on this earth just to run round at his every beck and call.'

Hal drew up outside Dasia's. He was very calm, and as pale as alabaster as he walked up the drive to the front door and rang the bell.

Alice greeted him: 'You look as if you need a bit of time off from all that study ... So where's it to be?'

He tried to look cheerful: 'Probably Buster Keaton at the Picturedrome. Something frivolous.'

He faltered ... What did he care about what it was; all he wanted was to take Dasia back with him to Denmark Road.

Alice frowned slightly. There was something terribly wrong somewhere. He'd never before looked as white as that. But all she could do was be on her guard and hope for the best.

Then Dasia came into the room wearing her new brown knitted skirt and jacket, and her long scarf with turquoise stripes in it, and her matching woolly hat with two woolly bobbles over her left ear. Alice looked at her with appreciation. It was fitting that Andrina had knitted it all, and it looked perfect on Dasia.

Alice Greenbow watched Hal and Dasia get into the small two-seater car, and waved to them with heavy foreboding in her heart. There was something up for sure – and as soon as her granddaughter got back she meant to wring the whole story out of her: 'Don't be late, you have to be up early for work. *Both* of you . . .'

Her voice was drowned in the noise from the engine as she watched them vanish down The Grove.

About half a mile further on, Hal stopped the car near some allotments which were now lying dormant in the frosty winter air, with dark silhouettes of thick stalked Brussels sprouts and hardy cabbages.

He parked the car next to a wooden hut near the water tap, with only the light from nearby houses: 'I've got something terrible to tell you, Dasia.'

He related what had happened, and she listened in shocked silence, shivering slightly and holding his hand.

'. . . so it's up to you to decide what you want to do. We can either part, right now, and I'll take you home – and we'll each make fresh starts. Or we can just stay good friends, and make this night a visit to the flicks – to a talkie, and let things cool off . . . or . . .' there was an agony of hesitant silence – then he said in a sad, flat voice: 'or – we could marry.'

'Marry?' Dasia was completely taken aback.

'Though you won't be marrying the son of a lord. You'll just be marrying me, ordinary Hal Wrioth, with no money, no prospects, cut off from my family and in total disgrace.' He gave a slight sob, and cursed himself for being so soft in her presence.

'But it was a travesty of justice, Hal! You're completely innocent of all the awful things they said!'

'Try and prove it,' he said bitterly. 'The medical profession is a closed shop, and although they apply the highest ethics, and are governed by the Hippocratic Oath, they are a law unto themselves.' Then, in a sad disillusioned voice he began to recite parts of the oath:

'I will give no deadly drug to any, though it be asked

140

of me, nor will I counsel such, and especially I will not aid a woman to procure abortion ... Whatsoever house I enter, there will I go for the benefit of the sick, refraining from all wrongdoing or corruption, and especially from any act of seduction, of male or female, of bond or free.'

Without another thought, and completely carried away by his awful predicament and the desire to show her love and loyalty, Dasia flung her arms around him and said, 'I *will* marry you. Of course I will! Even if we haven't got a penny. Even if we might starve. Though I don't think it'll come to that because my family would always help us out. I'm sure it'll all work out in the end; I'm certain of it.'

Denmark Road was a very long street in Moss Side, full of well-built family houses with attics and cellars. It started off quite small at Bradshaw Street, then widened out a bit, running between Greenhayes and Whitworth Park, and finishing at Oxford Road directly opposite the infirmary.

But the house which Kenny's great Aunt Celia had given Hal the key to was a much smaller, older one, yet quite sufficient for a first home. In fact it was complete luxury when one considered people with lots of young children living in a single rented room, or in basements or family attics.

Some of the small houses in Manchester had no inside lavatories or indoor water systems, and families had to share an outside water tap. While many of the bigger houses with indoor plumbing were split up into flats and bedsitters, with everyone paying rents to the landlord, and often sharing a single, filthy scullery, with one sooty black kettle and a blackened iron frying pan for communal use – and with one horrible stained and broken down WC.

141

But this wasn't true for Dasia and Hal. Hal showed her round the house and its backyard, and stressed that they would be allowed to live there for next to nothing until his fortunes changed for the better, thanks to the good works of Kenny's Aunt Celia.

Dasia's spirits rose. It had a glass fanlight at the top of the faded green-painted door, with coloured transparent paper stuck on it to make it look like stained glass. And on the door, below the white enamel number plate and brass door knocker, was a wooden name plate with the name TIPPERARY in painted black letters.

As they drove home again to The Grove that evening, after drinking to a better future with a bottle of Dandelion and Burdock from Tittlepenny's ever-open corner shop, Dasia said she'd visit Hal the next day during her dinner break.

But later on, when Hal parked the car back at her home, Dasia began to wonder what on earth she'd done to have promised to become his wife, and what on earth she would say to them at home this time . . .

Her heart flooded with unease, and fear.

CHAPTER NINE

Tipperary

The following morning, after Dasia had visited TIPPERARY in her break from Baulden's glove department, with two large newspaper bundles containing savoury ducks, chips and mushy peas, Hal outlined plans for them to go up to Gretna Green to get married.

'It's just over the English border in Scotland to the west – not far from the border city of Carlisle. It's the only place we can go easily, without needing parental consent. All we have to do is to declare in front of witnesses that we wish to be man and wife, and we can be married by Mr Richard Rennison over the anvil in the Old Blacksmith's Smithy. What do you say to that?'

She didn't know what to say. Gretna Green was to her like some strange fairy tale.

All she knew was, she couldn't stay at home much longer with secrets in her heart, like this awful one of Hal being kicked out of medical school, breaking away from his rich family background, and then suddenly suggesting they should both marry in haste in a blacksmith's shop in Scotland.

'... Marry in haste, repent at leisure' – she could just hear Alice Greenbow spitting out the words with triumph, for although her grandmother welcomed the idea of society weddings in her family, they had to have all the right trimmings.

'You look quite scared, Dasia.' He gathered her up in his arms and kissed her. 'It's perfectly legal ...' then he added, 'and although I know we'll both be very poor until I find myself a job, at least we've got a few pounds from what's left of my quarterly private allowance – even though it'll be the final end of it all.'

His voice suddenly became very strict – like a headmaster talking to a child. 'What you must do now is to get ready for us to go to Gretna next Monday to get married ... and tell them at Baulden's you're not very well, but hope to be in the following week.

'Get your Louise to do it for you ...'

Dasia stared in disbelieving horror: 'But it'll mean all the family will know! I just couldn't bear that! It'll be enough disgrace as it is.' As soon as she'd spoken she could have bitten her tongue out as she saw Hal's colour rise and his eyes flash with anger.

'Please yourself,' he said with cold malevolence, 'but I didn't somehow imagine your family would like the idea of you here, in this little tin-pot dwelling, with a disgraced ex medic.' Then he thrust his final dagger: 'And you didn't exactly try to stop me – when the moment came ... in that room ... did you?'

She could hardly believe her ears. Was this her lover, her sweetheart, her true gentle gentleman? Was this the person she was willing to forsake everything for – the man who had offered his life to her with straightforward humbleness?

Her own temper began to bubble. Who did he think he was – treating her like some little child, issuing instructions about what she should tell them at Baulden's and how to arrange it at home, when he'd hardly even set foot in the shop in all his life except to

144

buy a pair of cut-price cuff-links, nor even seen where she worked in it or how it was run.

'I'm very sorry about what happened ...' Her voice broke in a flood of tears, and she found herself screeching at him in sheer uninhibited anger: 'but you'll have to understand here and now that you aren't my keeper.

'I've got a brain the same as anyone else – and don't you forget it. And if I want my family dragged into it all, I'll decide for myself. What *they* think, and what *they* do has nothing to do with what we're going to do.'

His face lit up and his brow wrinkled in smiles: 'So you are still coming to Gretna then, boss?'

'You'd look a bit of a fool, alone. But – I will *not* be *bullied.*'

'The same applies to me,' he warned. Then he shoved a hanky at her to dry her eyes and they both laughed with relief.

When Bazz and Thinny received the brief typewritten communication about their son being kicked out of medical school, they were absolutely stunned.

'What the hell's going on?' exploded Lord Wrioth as he tried to telephone Hal, for an explanation.

'I'm terribly sorry, sir,' said a smooth male voice, 'Henry Wrioth is no longer here.'

'No longer there? What the devil are you talking about?'

'He's no longer a student, sir. He moved out yesterday.'

'Can you repeat that, my man?'

'He moved out yesterday, sir. That's all I know.'

'Surely you can't make a fellow just pack his bags and go? I've never heard such damned nonsense! It's a bloody disgrace! Put me through to Bingley-Stringfield, the Dean, immediately.'

145

'I'm terribly sorry, sir, he's up in Edinburgh but I can pass a message to his secretary, Miss Noble, when she gets back from the lecture theatre with Dr Walford.'

'Forget it!' Henry Wrioth slammed down the phone while Cynthia stood there clasping and unclasping her hands in anguish.

'There's been a terrible miscarriage of justice, Bazz. A terrible, terrible miscarriage of . . .'

'Yes, yes, yes. We know that. But *how*, and *why*? And where *is* the young fool?'

'It looks as if Elvers'll have to run me up there to find out.'

Dasia was sitting in Andrina's bedroom at home, while her mother showed her the small gold brooch Sammy Tankerton had bought her. 'He's ever so kind and thoughtful. That's his trouble really. That's why his mother's always managed to have such a grip over him,' said Andrina.

Dasia was plucking up her courage to tell Andrina her plans. 'Andrina . . .'

'Yes?' Andrina looked up from the brooch – slightly worried by the sound of urgency in Dasia's voice.

'You remember saying that because you were my mother you'd always try to help me?'

'Did I? Oh well, I expect I must have done if you say so . . . As long as it isn't anything too awful.'

'I'm leaving home again. I'm going to Scotland with Hal on Monday. We're getting married at Gretna Green. There! It's out!'

'Gretna Green . . .' Andrina looked askance: 'you can't be serious, Dasia. All that Gretna stuff's a complete load of nonsense. It's just not done – to pretend to be properly married in a smithy, over an anvil! It's the sort of tale they turn out for rubbishy news stories.'

146

'It *isn't*. It's *true* ... Hal said. And he'd never lie to me ...' a look of misery spread over her round, young face as she pushed back some tendrils of coppery gold hair. 'The truth is, Drina – he's not a student any more.'

The story began to flood out: 'He was dismissed instantly, the other day ... He was got rid of by this terrible dishonest dragon of a woman who's the friend of a really dreadful professor with lots of power – and they accused Hal of things he's never done.

'He was completely innocent. I swear it!

'Anyway, his friend Kenny's Great Aunt Celia's found him this little house called Tipperary, and Hal's asked me to marry him straight away by going up to Gretna Green ...'

Andrina hesitated. Her face was getting calmer as she got older. She enjoyed her affair with Sammy Tankerton. In some ways, his being tied to his mother had its advantages; it kept them both independent – no mad flings for them!

She began to dwell on her own fate all those years ago when she and ginger-haired Blennim Shawfield had been young, passionate lovers, and it had all been nipped in the bud by his jealous, interfering mother who'd never lived to see her illegitimate granddaughter born.

And now the wheel had turned full circle – and here she was, herself, turning into another interfering mother ... for Dasia.

Suddenly she made up her mind: 'Do what you really think is best for *you*, dear. How can any of us ever know what fate has in store? All I can do is wish you good luck, and love – and tell you I'll always be here to be of support.' Then she said, 'What will you say to the others?'

'I can't bear to say anything. I'll leave you to tell them all I've gone into rented accommodation nearer to Baulden's. And tell our Louise that I might not be in to

147

work for about a week. She's good at pouring oil on troubled waters – and after all, it was she who smoothed the way when I told Mr Bottom-Pincher Mildew I was twenty-one, instead of seventeen.'

Andrina nodded. Louise was secretly far more expedient than any of them.

And so, very early on Monday morning, Dasia packed her bags and left home for the last time – knowing that this was her journey to adulthood – as Hal waited for her at the end of The Grove in his car.

And it was on that self same day that Lord Wrioth ordered Danny Elvers to pull up outside the small street house called Tipperary – only to find there was nobody there ...

February around Manchester and Salford was generally a depressing month of darkness and gloom as people clad in mufflers crowded into doctors' waiting-rooms – people, patient as owls, perched on hard bentwood chairs and gazing down at brown lino as they waited for the sound of the buzzer and their turn to see the doctor.

But away from the smoky, fog-blighted parts of north-west England, with its gales and heavy rain, there were snowdrops pushing through rich brown blankets of last year's fallen leaves – with here and there a slight hint of something better as hawthorn hedges showed slight pearls of green on their knobbly twigs – and green-budded daffodils speared their way to the sky.

Although Dasia was now married to Hal, they never let it be known to any outsiders, but kept to their single names – except on St Valentine's day when Hal brought her some anemones home, and a card with real lace and ribbons on it with two red hearts entwined, addressed to 'Dasia, my darling wife'.

Alice and Horace didn't take too kindly to her second

dash away from them, for neither Louise nor Andrina revealed anything other than she was going into rented rooms nearer work.

'It's becoming quite an 'abit with 'er,' said Horace as he tinkered about with a bit of copper wire for some sort of new electricity circuit he was re-inventing.

'She's a rum lass. But at least she seems 'appy enough with all them gloves in Baulden's. An' I 'spect she'll soon come running back 'ere again if she finds life in them back streets is getting 'er down.'

'She'll do no such bloody thing, Horace Greenbow! She's not using this house like a perishing railway station. She's made her bed for the last time, and now she's got to lie in it. That girl hasn't even had the decency to leave us her address. And no way am I going to try finding it out. Talk about the gratefulness of the younger generation ...'

Horace looked across at Andrina who was making out a list of items to give up for Lent, like chocolate marzipans, and face powder. 'Where's she at, then? Andrina ...'

'A little house, somewhere off Bradshaw Street,' replied Andrina vaguely (though she knew the real address off by heart and had already called to see them both).

She also knew that Hal hadn't yet found a job, and had refused to see his parents – and had sent them a short letter stating again his entire innocence in the student episode, and that he wanted to forget the whole thing and had no intention of having it dragged through courts.

'It all seems *very* peculiar to me,' sighed Alice Greenbow. 'Very bloody peculiar ...

'I know she can be a little bat out of hell when she wants, and is well capable of fending for herself – according to our Dolly. But there's few respectable girls

149

of her tender years as can even afford to live alone in rooms, of whatever kind even if they were in some small house.

'I hope she isn't disgracing us all by starting off life as a kept woman – just to let that son of a lord take advantage of her. I'd never lift up my head again if that were true.'

'Well, it isn't true, Mother,' snapped Andrina. 'The rooms she lives in are in a small house owned by a god-fearing woman who rents places out to those in need – including young women, single or otherwise.'

Alice's face fell: 'But surely not to *single* people of opposite sexes?'

'That's exactly what she does do, Mother. She believes we are all equal in God's sight.' Then Andrina added cattily, 'Dasia could even be sharing with a Chinaman and an Abyssinian, just like anyone else in a house cut up into private rooms and let out to rent.'

Alice opened her mouth to protest, then thought better of it. All she could do was pray that Dasia had been brought up with sufficiently high standards to encounter even a male Eskimo lodging in the next room without flinching.

On Shrove Tuesday, pancake day, it was a joyous time in Manchester, for it was students' Rag Day – a few brief hours of the year when the general public was beset by well-meaning horseplay and clowning. It was a day of riotous festivities – usually at the expense of stern authority – in order to raise gargantuan amounts of money for medical charities.

Thousands of families came to watch this disrespectful pageantry, with its humour akin to bawdy sea-side postcards, as red nosed 'doctors' with over-large stethoscopes tried to tackle struggling hospital 'matrons' attired in stout pink laced-up corsets, their huge, bony, male knees carefully covered in matronly navy blue bloomers.

Other tableaux specialised in doctors and nurses carrying out operations with tree saws on false legs dripping with bright red liquid as students mingled in the crowd collecting money in bottles and bedpans.

But for Hal the day was salt in the wound – for he was no longer part of it all. He hurried through Deansgate, well away from all the jollification taking place round Piccadilly Gardens.

He was on his way to an interview for a job. But in his heart was deep foreboding. In desperation he'd answered an advertisement in the somewhat seedy columns of a medical journal with a rather small circulation.

The few weeks of isolated unemployment had come as rather a shock – as had having to accept Dasia's meagre wage as part of their subsistence. After exploring every avenue – including that of a night watchman, for which there were three hundred applicants, and a job as a gardener in a posh house in Northenden, where they were immediately suspicious of both his accent and his Tin Lizzie, he was at his wits' end grasping at straws – like this one advertised as Box 509 of the journal of The Enlightened Benefits Association for Female Difficulties.

It appeared that people with slight medical experience were required for confidential work, salary to be mutually agreed.

He hadn't said anything about himself or his background, but received an immediate response – asking him to meet a person called Mrs Torsque in number six of a small, elite apartment block with its own uniformed door man. It was in the area between Deansgate and Albert Square behind some attractive trees of a small green which had survived from Georgian days.

Hal ran lightly up the plush-carpeted stairs to the

second floor where glass chandeliers hung from the high ceiling in the corridor. The extremes of wealth and the poverty in the surrounding city streets were amazing.

A maid opened the door, and he was shown into a small, dark, oak-panelled study with an Adam fireplace. The ceiling here was decorated in a Wedgwood style and a naval chest with brass fittings, and a large mahogany kneehole desk dominated the room. Upon the walls were engravings by Hogarth which hung from oak picture rails.

He somehow expected a large motherly woman with a rosy complexion to greet him, but the person who came forward was like the Madonna herself with smooth, silky black hair parted into a glossy, narrow halo round her ivory forehead.

She was about twenty-five, small and neatly built, and was wearing a navy-blue tailored dress and dark shoes and stockings.

A great wave of innocent relief welled up inside him.

'Do sit down, Mr Wrioth,' she said in carefully modulated tones.

He smiled and sat down. His spirits rose even higher. The whole ambience of the room was in keeping with his early childhood. He noticed she had his letter, written on blue notepaper, on the desk in front of her.

Then she smiled and said, 'I expect you're wondering why you received such a prompt invitation to visit us.'

'Well, no ... As a matter of fact, I –'

'It was your name, Mr Wrioth. My employer seemed to know your name quite well.'

He stiffened. Her employer? What a strange way to put it. It took away the cosiness immediately – especially as she never mentioned her employer's name.

'Are you by any chance a medical student?'

He hesitated and became extremely uneasy. 'That's right. I *was* ... but due to circumstances beyond my

152

control I've recently changed horses mid-stream, so to speak.' He smiled wanly, only wishing now to escape.

Mrs Torsque smiled reassuringly: 'What we're looking for is a really reliable person to help us with anaesthetics, Mr Wrioth.

'Obviously, you would have a qualified doctor with you at all times, but the work is extremely confidential. It is concerned purely with women's complaints.

'We need someone we can rely on utterly, and the salary for your services will be extremely good. We deal with a very rich clientele.'

Hal glanced round. The place was completely quiet, peaceful, and private.

'This part is, of course, a personal apartment; the whole of the next floor is my employer's private clinic.'

'What's his name then – your employer?'

'Mr Smith.'

Smith ... He gave an inward sigh. There were numberless consultants and physicians called Smith. It was one of the commonest names there were.

'So do you think you might be interested, Mr Wrioth?'

'I might be, but not knowing what the complete set-up is makes it hard to judge.'

'Mr Smith is away at present, but I could show you round the clinic if you wish and let you read a couple of sample case-papers.'

Reluctantly he nodded, and was soon led to the third floor where an ante-room was unlocked, leading to the whole unit.

'As you will see, it comprises of a small operating theatre, a recovery room, three curtained cubicles, bathroom, lavatories and sluice room – plus our main consultation office and three private bedrooms for our patients, not to mention this beautiful kitchen.'

He surveyed it all with swift concentration. It was

absolutely immaculate. The floors shone like the mouse drawing advertisements for Mansion Polish. The private bedrooms all had bell systems connected to the office, and were also attached – Mrs Torsque assured him – to her own private flat which was part of the premises.

She took him into the consulting office which contained imposing bookcases full of leather-bound volumes. One of them was by the ever popular Nicholas Culpeper: a copy of his directory for midwives 1651, and nearby was a book by John Snow who had the honour of administering chloroform to Queen Victoria in 1853 at the birth of Prince Leopold.

Then she showed him the two sample case-papers stamped CONFIDENTIAL in red ink, and 'For Teaching Purposes, only'.

In the names and addresses section, both were marked M.T.B. Nonesuch, Blank Street, Blankshire. One set of notes was for a Miss Nonesuch, while the other one was for a Mrs Nonesuch.

Miss Nonesuch was diagnosed as suffering from a (query) small cyst which would need examination under general anaesthetic and removal. And Mrs Nonesuch was suffering from (query) fibroids, which would need an examination and perhaps some treatment under general anaesthetic.

The treatment included such items as enemas, douches, ergometrine, and dilation and curettage (not necessarily in that order or indeed all of them) and it finished up with a cheerfully reassuring report that no cysts or fibroids were found in either case while the patient was being examined under anaesthetic.

The case notes of Miss Nonesuch's medical history said she was due to go up to London for her Coming Out Ball this year and wanted to be perfectly healthy and fit. And the notes on Mrs Nonesuch's said: 'She needs to be able to take up riding again as soon as possible.'

Both females had to have a signed consent form for the administering of the anaesthetic, and if they were under twenty-one, it was usually the male guardian, or head of the family, or their husband who signed it.

The consent form said: I hereby give consent for M.T.B. Nonesuch to be given an operation under anaesthetic, and for Dr. . . . to do whatever he considers to be necessary.'

Hal was just turning away, in depressed despair, when Mrs Torsque smiled brightly and said, 'We aren't monsters you know. Please don't be too hasty, Mr Wrioth. The pay's remarkably good considering you're unqualified and are only a general assistant. Believe me, our books are full all the year round and, if you fit in well with the organisation, you could be earning as much as a qualified doctor – starting almost immediately.

'Our cases aren't messy ones. They are quick and straightforward, and performed within the highest standards of medical care. Our patients return to their own homes and receive private nursing care for ten days afterwards.

'We have had some ladies back two or three times for effective treatment, and never once have we received a complaint.'

Then she murmured casually, 'Surely better than what the general public have to suffer, Mr Wrioth – with all their shady back street abortionists?

'Think it over, anyway, and drop Doctor a line. There's definitely a place waiting for you if you're interested.'

On the way back to his new home, Hal was pale and drawn. Surely shortage of money wouldn't drive him to accept this? Helping the rich out of their sexual slip-ups?

He began to brood on all the cases of real hardship in women's wards of general hospitals: those genuine, haunting miscarriages which sapped their health and energy and whole nervous systems. And of women who'd spent their married lives praying that they might at last conceive – only to have yet another 16 weeks' miscarriage, with all its anguish.

Then he thought of all the cleaning up jobs the medical staff had to do for desperate women worn out by large families with not enough money to feed themselves properly, and at their wits' end to know how to cope. Women driven, by the crudest methods of knitting needles, Penny Royal, and constant trips on the Blackpool Big Dipper to try and shift the small, ever-growing, arrival inside them – until eventually they lay in a collapsed state in some gynaecological ward suffering from septic abortion.

Hal suddenly felt as old and grey as the hills. All he wanted now was to escape to the quietness and privacy of the humble threadbare little home he now shared with Dasia – away from the world of decisions, and back to the scent of blue hyacinths in a simple bowl, brimming with innocent beauty on the window ledge.

CHAPTER TEN

Looking for Work

Baulden's always did good trade on pancake day, and Dasia was kept going all morning on the glove counter – brisk business combining with comic intermissions when students managed to waylay some of the customers, even to the point of threatening to kidnap Dasia herself and put her in the furniture department with a view to a ransom. But fortunately this ominous idea was nipped in the bud by Miss Davina, who put two shillings out of the petty cash float into the charity box and sent Dasia off to early dinner.

What a blessing to work for Miss Davina, thought Dasia, as she hurried to the corner bakery for hot meat and potato pies on her way home at midday. 'How would Hal have got on at the interview,' she wondered.

'Well,' she smiled and looked at him questioningly as she answered the door, 'any luck?'

'It depends what you call luck,' he said cautiously, as he kissed her.

She looked so innocent and enthusiastic, standing there all flushed and beaming. He hadn't the heart to say what was really on his mind – about the job being at a clinic for wealthy private patients who wanted un-official and unlawful abortions.

He knew full well what happened if you were found guilty at that game – you were sent to prison, and your life was ruined.

'Come on then – tell me all about it ... Was there a chance of steady work at something you'd be good at?'

'It was a private clinic for women needing small amounts of surgery. They needed an assistant to help with anaesthetics, and the pay was said to be excellent ...' he hesitated, with the horror of it and its ramifications still lurking in his mind.

'And?' Her eyes sparkled; 'Tell me quickly. It sounds ideal! Just what you wanted. A chance to use your medical experience.'

'Except ... well – except I felt there was something crooked about it ... Nothing that could be proved, obviously, but it seemed to me to be very much like an under-cover abortion clinic.'

Dasia looked horrified. It was completely outside her life's experience. She hadn't had the misfortune even to visit a hospital during her seventeen years, and as for abortion clinics, they were some vague shady place which cropped up sometimes over the years in some terrible newspaper scandal. In fact there wasn't a personal friend or relative she knew who even uttered the word abortion. It was always 'miscarriage' whatever the circumstances.

She suddenly recalled a time when she was about thirteen and Aunty Dolly was talking to Alice: 'Oh yes, Alice, she had a terrible do ... It was prunes and figs and Scottish country dancing all the way, and in the end she had this miscarriage, God help her.'

All these years hence, and only now did Dasia see the significance of Dolly's cheerful approach as if the 'miscarriage' had been a happy release – when all the time Dasia had thought the woman must have been suffering from dire constipation.

Hal was staring ahead with a white-faced impartial look, trying his utmost to be calm and reasonable. 'Of course, I may have got the wrong end of the stick – but . . .

'And some people in medical quarters do say in private that it might be more civilised to let all women have the right of –' He stopped suddenly: 'Dasia? Are you all right?'

Dasia was as pale as he was, as she sat there on an old wooden kitchen chair: 'Hal – how *terrible*! How can anyone want to get rid of their baby?'

He sighed wearily. 'Lots of very good reasons. It's never as simple as it sounds. And sometimes it's actually done for genuine medical reasons such as saving the life of the mother.'

'I would never want it to happen to me,' said Dasia vehemently. 'I would cling to my pregnancy through thick and thin.' Her eyes flashed with pride.

'Sometimes it doesn't work out like that. Sometimes all the love and wanting in the world isn't enough to stop a miscarriage.'

They both became silent as Dasia put their meat and potato pies on warm plates and Hal made a pot of tea.

'You can't possibly take that job then – can you?' said Dasia as they finished their meal: 'How can you risk being branded a criminal – for that's what it would amount to if you helped.'

He nodded, then sighed with open relief. 'That's what it looks like. Put at its most venal, we need the money, but I'm a coward and not willing to take the risk, because it's illegal. But as far as the actual rights and wrongs of it go – I have an open mind.'

Dasia was secretly shocked to hear him admit he was a coward. She didn't think he looked a bit like one. And then she suddenly realised she didn't know what a coward was although she was apt to think that men who pounced on women or pinched their bottoms on the sly were leaning in that direction. But she was a coward too – she was always living in fear of something.

Her latest fear, which had suddenly occurred to her this very moment, was what would she do if she found she was expecting, and had to leave Baulden's and Hal *still* hadn't got a job?

It was Easter, and all the churches were decorated with spring flowers. Families, spurred on by the children, painted and decorated eggs usually by boiling them in onion water which turned the eggshells a beautiful, bold yellow. And then they went out on Easter Bank Holiday Monday and found hills and slopes to roll their eggs, in egg races.

But Dasia and Hal were feeling lonely, and even a bit depressed – though neither of them admitted it.

Neither of them had dared to visit their respective homes, and they didn't know anyone who was part of the ritual of chocolate Easter eggs and excited children clutching small, fluffy, yellow cotton-wool chickens with thin wire legs and bright orange beaks. Then, just as they were strolling out for a walk around Platt Fields, who should they meet but Perry Saltburn along with his wife Clarinda and three young children.

Perry was an ex-medical student like himself who'd suffered the same sort of fate, meted out by Professor Ruxtable almost a year ago.

'Hal Wrioth, or I'm a Dutchman! Fancy meeting you after all this jolly old time,' roared Perry jovially from behind a massive curling beard.

He pointed to the dark-eyed infant in the pram: 'This one in the bassinet's Benjamin. And that one in blue reins with bells on is Karlotta, And this little titch,

160

holding my weary old finger, is Ruby.

'But take heart, old boy; only the one in the pram is ours.' He turned to his thin, fair haired wife: 'Isn't that true Clarry?'

She smiled and nodded as Hal introduced Dasia. 'These other two are my sister's children.'

Dasia smiled back, but with a sinking heart noticed that Hal introduced herself as merely his friend. Yet, even though she wore no rings, she was his true wife and wished he'd introduced her as that – even though she never wore her wedding ring, because of wanting to remain single at work. Louise had impressed on her that singleness was a better proposition and that some employers even refused to consider married women for employment.

'Why don't you come back with us for a meal?' said Perry cheerfully. 'We usually have tinned salmon when we have to fend for ourselves at tea-time: tinned salmon, tinned pears, tinned Ideal Milk, and loads and loads of bread butter and jam ... How does that suit?

'We have been known to be more exotic, but when you have to do all the bloody stuff yourself and the baby's yelling its little noddle off it gets a bit fraught.'

The two males strode happily ahead as Perry quickly abandoned Ruby to the women and gassed forty to the dozen to Hal, while Dasia was left with Clarinda.

Dasia soaked in Clarinda's appearance. She was deceptively young-looking because of her bean-pole figure but Dasia judged her to be at least twenty-five.

She was quiet and unassuming as she strolled along with the three children: 'Yes, poor old Perry got the push from medical school too. I was known to have been in his room twice, and it was made out to be a harem by the time they'd all finished. And also Professor Ruxtable disliked him. I was quite pleased in a way that Perry escaped it all.

161

'As you can see, he's a large, outgoing, good-natured type, and the job he's got now, as a local traveller in medical supplies, seems to suit him.

'We also live in quite a big house as you'll see when we get there. It was left to Perry when his Aunty died, and we let out the top floor to a doctor friend of his. We use the ground floor and basement.

'In the basement he's got a small laboratory where he turns out his own brand of ointment for healing and soothing the skin. It's called Perry's Perfect Unguent, and he's just started to take samples round with him when he's calling at chemists' shops with his other supplies.' She smiled gently at Dasia: 'Mind you, it is a shock when you suffer the mortification of being driven out of such a hallowed group as the medical profession. And it's hard if you're actually married – because if you survive in the profession it goes without saying that you're secure for life. But if you get turfed out, you're grovelling away, most probably in poorly paid employment like most of the rest of humanity with your capabilities completely stunted.'

Then she added, 'I advise you to stay single as long as you can, my dear. Being a wife isn't all it's cracked up to be if you're stumped for cash.' She laughed, and began to play a peek-a-boo game with her son as he sat in the pram chuckling his head off.

Dasia sensed it was just to show that all she'd said was half in jest – and to forget it. But Dasia was anxious to correct the other woman about her own marital status.

'I'm a wife too!' she said triumphantly, 'and most of the time I love it. Hal and I were secretly married at Gretna Green, this year.' Then she related all that had happened since she had first met Hal. And by the time they reached the large soot-blackened residence of the Saltburns, the two women had become friends for life.

★

In April Dasia realised with deep certainty that she was pregnant. No monthly period had arrived in March and, apart from always seeming to want to wee more than usual, there was one day at Baulden's when she went very faint and had to go and lie down.

'It's either pernicious anaemia, dear,' said Miss Davina bluntly, 'or else you're expecting a little stranger. I've had so many girls working for me in this department over the years that I know the symptoms inside out. And I always feel extra sorry for the unmarried ones like you.'

Dasia blinked her eyes as she rose from her swoon – how on earth could Miss Davina be sure, when *she* didn't even know herself?

Yet, now, as she gazed out of the window at home and watched a rag-and-bone-man cloppeting by, with bowls of live goldfish, and saw the sun coming out after a sudden rain shower, and a flower-seller wheeling her old barrow full of daffodils and tulips, she knew for certain, and felt calm and happy.

Life was getting more sorted out at last, and Perry Saltburn had managed to find Hal a job as a travelling salesman in rather lurid Home Medical Books, for the general public to expand their knowledge of ailments, even though the human anatomy portrayed in them had all sex and reproductive details carefully missed out. Most of the other contents concentrated on steam tents, blanket baths, and instructions on whooping cough and croup; plus pages of advertisements for Friars Balsam inhalers, Carters Little Liver Pills, Parishes Food, best quality castor-oil, bottles of syrup of figs, and large leather trusses – and one very small advertisement which said: '*Perry's Perfect Unguent* will soothe away every spot of bother'.

Eagerly, Dasia waited for Hal to get back from his travelling. He always managed to call back home, very

163

briefly, at midday, but today there was no sign of him and she had to take her lunch completely alone, then hurry back to the gloves.

Whatever had gone wrong? It was the first time it had ever happened.

Then, just as she was back at work putting some kid gloves between fine layers of tissue paper, it suddenly struck her that for the past two or three days he had seemed a bit absent-minded. One day he wouldn't put any sugar in his tea, and the next minute he was putting in three full teaspoons. And even their sex life was a bit erratic – though she hadn't bothered much about that, as it always seemed to be a bit over-much, especially when she was so busy working.

Even in the short time she'd been married it came home to her pretty smartly that the joys of so-called 'creative love' were weighted towards the whims of the husband. No more those single-girl days of romantic celebration where one could decide that canoodling would be allowed on a certain evening – all prepared and relaxed and hopefully dressed up to one's own film star standards. Instead, it was a case of being there, on tap at all times. And as Josey, one of the girls at Baulden's said, 'Thank your lucky stars he doesn't want *you* every dinner-time – along with his meat and potato pies.'

The hours at Baulden's that afternoon dragged on, as Dasia worried about getting back home. And when she eventually put the key in the door of Tipperary there was still no sign of Hal.

By now she was getting really alarmed. Supposing he'd been killed in an accident? Or supposing he'd had some sort of brain storm and wandered off – never to be seen again? A cold shiver of fear ran down her spine as she began to prepare an evening meal to put in the oven – just in case he did, hopefully, turn up.

By ten-thirty that night there was still no sign of him

as, tearfully, she made her way to bed.

Then, just as the local church clock struck the half hour past midnight, she heard his step at the front door, and the sound of his key.

Immediately she got up and put on her dressing-gown and slippers to go and greet him. But as she went down the steep wooden stairs she smelt the heavy fumes of ale and cigarette smoke all round him, and when he spoke to her his speech was slurred.

She froze in terror. He was a changed personality.

'Wherever have you been, Hal? I've been out of my mind with worry. Whatever happened?'

He tried to smile at her, then flopped on the couch helplessly. 'I've done it,' he muttered.

'Done what? What have you done?'

'New job, mi darlin'. New – better paid job. Starting tomorrow ...' He suddenly sobered up a bit: 'Fact is, Dace ... the chravelling librey job folded at the begeening of the week. It washant paying its way.' He gave a huge belch, then hiccuped. 'Shree of us – meaning the whole bloody shute – were shacked. So this week I've jush bin trailing round trying to find somshing else, each day, but it's absholutely hopeless ...'

He gave a final groan of desperation: 'Sho in the end I got in touch with that private abortion playsh again, and I shart tomorrow ...

'Quite frankly, after being there earlier in the day to shign up and get a proper briefing, I was show depreshed that I downed enough ale to shink a ship – then staggered round trying to walk it off, along with a few more drunkards.' He grinned ruefully.

Tears came to Dasia's eyes as she brought him some Andrew's Liver Salts in a cup of water, and tried to console him.

'You can't go there Hal! Not after what you told me. You mustn't. There must be some other way ...'

165

'There is no other way. I *must* have a job – a job with decent money.' His voice began to return to normal and he sat up properly and stared round the room then stood up and walked carefully to the whitewashed lavatory in the yard outside to have a wee, and a bout of vomiting that seemed to go on for ever, with Dasia hovering anxiously by the lavatory door ready to help him back inside where he began to get back to normal.

About two hours later, and both of them completely tired out, he said, 'We'd better get all this sorted out now, Dasia, because in a few hours we'll both be on the job circuit again.

'The only thing I've got any real knowledge of at present is anaesthetics. And there's the question of references too, from all those well-known people who are pillars of respectable society. No chance for me there ...

'Oh – I daresay if I got in touch with them again at home my father, after a grim lecture, would do me proud and welcome me back to the fold to work on the family estate. But I can't trade on that.

'We all have our individual dignity, and if my personal liberty rests on carrying out work related to abortions, then that's how it stands.' Then he said despairing, 'Come on, Dasia, for God's sake let's get to bed.'

'Until you land up in prison – and your unborn child has a jail-bird father!' yelled Dasia hysterically as they started to go upstairs. 'And what about *me*? We're supposed to be bound together as man and wife – yet you never consider that. What about *my* individual dignity?'

Hal sat on the edge of the bed and gaped at her. 'Your what ...?'

'*My* individual dignity ...'

'No – before that. About a child ...'

She said nothing.

'Your unborn child ... *our* unborn child! You don't mean ...?'

'I certainly *do* mean ... and while you're at that terrible place tomorrow ruining all our lives – *I* shall be sitting in Dr Fotheringill's waiting-room for confirmation of the pregnancy. And let's hope *that* doesn't meet its Waterloo!'

Then she went all the way downstairs again and made them both a small drink of cocoa, and brought him up a tiny bit of stew, and warned him not to dare to be sick in the night.

'If you're ever sick in the same bedroom as me – from drinking,' she said, 'I shall sleep in another room for the rest of our married life.'

The following morning, Dasia saw Hal start off very early for his new job and, although her heart was gloomy, she had within herself a new streak of excitement and adventure as she made her way to see Dr Fothergill.

CHAPTER ELEVEN

Expecting

The private clinic was a very strange place, for although Hal was introduced to Dr Smith who ran it, Dr Smith always happened to have a white, well-tailored fine cotton mask over the bottom of his face, and be wearing a theatre cap which stretched almost to his greying eyebrows – impeded only by a pair of horn-rimmed glasses. This garb also applied to the anaesthetist, except his outfit was green instead of white, and he was addressed as either G.A. or Pongo.

'Pongo sometimes needs to go away,' explained Dr Smith. 'That's why we need a reliable assistant to be here at all times to take over, and be with our two nursing assistants, Miss Mina, and Miss Dolores.'

Hal noticed that even Mina and Dolores wore white masks which never left their faces, and that the only exposed physog in the place was the madonna-like apparition of dark-haired Mrs Torsque, which made him swiftly blot out his own features with a mask, and make sure it stayed there ...

There were four cases listed for that day, and the first two were wheeled in and out of the small theatre in the equivalent time of having a few teeth out, as blood and tissue scrapings fell into white enamel kidney-shaped dishes.

But the third case was different ...

The woman was larger, heavier and more pregnant. And she needed a longer anaesthetic.

Skilfully, Pongo got her to sleep with a few whiffs of chloroform breathed in from the powerful concoction, sending its choking fumes from a small metal half-hoop of a mask, covered in double gauze where he had sprayed it. And then – quite out of the blue – he suddenly asked Hal to take over: 'The calls of elderly nature, old chap ... Got to dash – Smithy'll keep you right.'

Hal took over Pongo's seat, and with long, trembling fingers held the sides of the woman's jaw in firm position to keep her air flow unrestricted.

But all of a sudden, she stopped breathing.

'Oxygen! Give her oxygen,' muttered Smith, as like two demented demons the young nursing assistants removed her spread-eagled legs from the metal stirrups.

'External massage to the heart. Get the Coramine. Tilt the table!'

It all took place in seconds as the woman lay white and lifeless – just as Pongo came ambling back and took over.

'She almost looks a gonner,' he observed calmly as he put his ear to her chest, then held a couple of fluffy feathers near her mouth and nostrils to see if any breath emerged – finally ending with the stethoscope from round his neck as the ultimate verdict.

'You do sometimes get sudden collapses with chloroform,' he said, as the woman gave a wild snorting gasp and began to recover as she went purple in the face, 'and of course, if the brain is starved of oxygen she'll be damaged for life ...' Then he dabbed his sweating temples with a bit of gauze and added: 'Not to worry, old bean – she didn't die, but it was a near thing.'

Afterwards, when the woman was lying in the recovery room, and they'd broken the news to her that she hadn't even had the operation – and that it wasn't worth risking her life to try again – Hal suddenly thought of Dasia sitting there patiently and full of hope for them both, in Dr Fothergill's shabby old waiting-room. And that afternoon, after only one small session in the private clinic – and without payment – he left it for ever.

He was just walking along King Street that self same afternoon when who should he bump into but the person he knew best in all the world – his father.

'Hal ...' His father's heavy face beamed with joy and relief.

'Father! Where are you off to?'

'Just off to meet your Ma in St Ann's Square then tea and chocolate eclairs at Meng and Eckers. She tootled round to visit cousin Mimi while I went to be measured for a suit and have a browse round.

'How's life then?' He looked at Hal shrewdly.

'Oh ... All right. Fine really. A relief to be alive.'

'And what means that, my boy? Not managing at all, no doubt.'

'Just between work at present ... was working for a sort of travelling medical library scheme, but it folded up last week and we were all sacked.'

'Still living in Denmark Road?'

Hal nodded.

'Still living with the girl?'

He nodded again with a certain proudness: 'She thinks she's expecting.'

'Whose is it?' said his father bitingly.

Hal was silent, but his temper shot up. How could he

have expected anything else but such a calculated jab at this one and only son who'd so seriously disgraced them?

'Goodbye, Father,' he said coldly. Then he turned and walked quickly away.

As Lord Wrioth marched along to the tea-room in St Ann's select and secluded tree-decked square to meet Thinny his wife, he grew scarlet with anger.

That little chit of a girl from nowhere was ruining his son's life – and this last bit of news was the final insult. His only son and heir was now placed in the dilemma of acting like a gentleman to a shallow little hussy who was hanging on to him like a leech, and draining away all his youthful potential.

Oh, admittedly she was an attractive and lively specimen, but there were plenty of those about, and most of them too cheeky for their own good and with grand designs well above their proper station. Thinny would vouch for that, she spent her life interviewing them for domestic work.

The danger point came when girls like this one who'd just trapped Hal began to crowd out better people of good breeding, who had more secure family back-grounds and property. And in this way the whole fabric of one's life was weakened.

She'd ruthlessly wormed her way into their Christmas gathering and completely ruined it. She'd made Hal run away with her and forsake his parents. She'd somehow been at the root of getting him kicked out of medical school – and now, after living in sin in a little slum house for a couple of months, she was actually crowing about being pregnant!

Lord Wrioth gave such a yelp of exasperated rage that two passers-by turned and stared at him with open mouths.

Bazz trudged towards the tea-rooms, the word

'pregnant' taking over his whole mind. Then he cooled down a bit. After all, many a slip twixt cup and lip – and there were quite often miscarriages with the first effort. And if that happened, Hal would be well rid of her and could settle down to a proper family affair, based on a bit of proper background and some decent breeding.

'You look a bit peculiar,' said Thinny when she saw him. 'Did you nearly get run down by horses?'

'Nothing quite as pleasant as that, Cynthia.'

Then, without another word he settled down to his afternoon tea and chocolate eclairs.

Dr Fothergill smiled reassuringly at Dasia: 'Oh yes, there's no doubt about it, but it will be better to verify in a further four weeks' time – judging from all the signs and symptoms, I'd say you'll be expecting your baby by late next December. The precise duration of human pregnancy is not known, but we always judge it to be approximately nine calendar months and seven days.

'And always remember, my dear, that pregnancy and childbirth are normal physiological functions in women, and should not be looked on as some sort of illness.'

Then he gave her a quick fatherly pat on the shoulder and showed her out of his room.

Dasia was over the moon with joy. Dr Fothergill was a middle-aged pillar of strength to all young, worried mothers-to-be. Anyone who went into his surgery came out ready to face the world with fresh optimism, and filled with sensible and kindly advice.

On the way home she went over his words about it all being a natural function. Clearly she would need to keep on working for as long as possible, and would have to keep it a complete secret from everyone except Hal and a few close friends – for neither his family nor hers (except Drina, Louise and Rosalie) even knew she was married.

But as she drew nearer the small green door of Tipperary her spirits flagged a little, as she remembered where Hal had gone to work.

What an irony that he was helping to destroy the very thing she desired most in all the world. But what was the alternative, if there was no money to live on?

She went in and stoked up the fire – as it was always built up in the morning with what was known as 'Nutty Slack' which kept it burning at a very slow rate behind the fire guard.

Then she made herself a cup of tea and put her feet up – resting her legs across a small stool with a cushion on top of it – and planned to get back to work this afternoon. She thought dreamily of prams and baby baths, and whether they could really afford a baby at all as things stood at present. Unless of course Hal was really well paid at the awful clinic.

When she returned home from work that afternoon, she was amazed to find him already waiting for her. And standing in a bucket near the slopstone was a huge bunch of daffodils and tulips. How on earth could he possibly have afforded it?

'How did you get on at old Fothergill's then?' He kissed her rapturously, as if paradise has arrived.

'How did *you* go on, first?'

'I chucked it ...' His face clouded over, and the moment of exuberance vanished as quickly as it had come.

'How do you mean?'

'I just couldn't stand it. It was awful; a woman nearly died. And I thought of you sitting there at Fothergill's with the seed of our child in your womb.' He sat down and covered his face with his hands. 'But the crunch is – how to manage?'

Dasia looked across at the flowers in the bucket. How indeed ... Then she put her arms around him in relief.

At least he was no longer party to all those terrible goings-on. 'We'll pull through somehow. There are millions of people far, far worse off. And at least I've got this Baulden's job.

'Dr Fothergill thinks the baby'll be due in late December. Surely by then the tide will have turned?

'Of course, I'll have to keep it all secret at work for the time being and put it all down to gaining extra weight ... And you'll have to be a bit like a housewife and do some cleaning and cooking, until you get some sort of job, yourself.' Her eyes shone with natural delight for she regarded herself as entirely equal – now that she was the sole independent wage earner, and pregnant into the bargain.

And so it was a shock to see the wave of consternation that swept across Hal's handsome face.

'Cooking and cleaning? And *washing*? Come off it Dasia. The world isn't as topsy-turvy as all that ...

'Oh yes, the odd meal, maybe. And a cup of tea in the morning or at night – that's understandable when you've been working all day. But not household drudgery. Certainly not that. It's completely demoralising for any man!' He began to smile at her as if it was a great joke.

'I'm serious, Hal; someone will need to do it – and with the hours I work at Baulden's, on my feet the whole time, I'll be completely exhausted if I have to do *everything*. I don't want to risk a miscarriage.'

'We'll just have to try and get extra help for you then – won't we?' he said with cold steeliness.

'But how can you afford that without a job – or money?'

She was amazed at his utter ignorance of the domestic structure of life. And yet he was so clever and knowledgeable about other things.

He stood up, shrugged his shoulders and went

174

towards the bucket where the flowers were: 'I brought you them from that old barrow woman. Stop talking a load of rot, and find a vase to put them in from the kitchen cupboard.'

She hesitated for a second – then, making the best of it, she did what she was told and smiled at him, consoling herself with the idea that he had more to learn from life than she had ... and that he didn't realise the half of it and probably never would.

And that night in bed she forgave him as he made love to her; and she to him. And he forgave her for still being an utter child, where true knowledge of men was concerned, as they sank back in relaxed contentment.

CHAPTER TWELVE

The Befriender

On the first day of May all the big working cart-horses in
Manchester were a truly glorious sight as, freed from
their hard daily work carrying all the heavy loads of
industry from bales of paper and cloth to beer barrels
and coal, they were bedecked in all their time-
consuming, skilfully planned, traditional finery with
plaited and beribboned manes and tails.

The heralding of May was indeed a happy time in
Manchester, for it was the gate to summer. Villages like
Knutsford were the place to go for family outings to see
the May Day celebrations, with their large maypoles on
the green, as people danced round them weaving
patterns with the beautiful coloured ribbons.

In Manchester itself the emphasis was more political
with equally beautiful and colourful displays as Trade
Union banners were carried aloft to join mass gatherings
in places like Platt Fields.

Even though the weather was often very cold and
windy at the beginning of the month, the sudden change
to long light evenings and periods of hot sunshine that

encouraged the delicately flowered almond blossom in town gardens made Dasia glow with love and delight.

It was also Hal's birthday; he was twenty. It had been a quiet, loving day, and she'd bought him a birthday card with gold lettering and sailing ship on it, and a cotton shirt from Baulden's.

Sometimes she even forgot she was pregnant at all, except for feeling sick in the mornings, which Hal assured her would pass – and the feeling that her breasts were expanding a bit beneath the rather tight dresses she wore for working at Baulden's.

'You're looking really bonny these days, Dasia,' whispered Mr Fanshaw admiringly. He was one of the maintenance staff and was called on whenever the lights went wrong, the heating went off, or the window blinds needed fixing. He was thirty-seven and said to have twelve children including two sets of twins. He made no bones about liking Miss Dasia Greenbow, but it was always in the best of taste, and with a fatherly concern for her general well being.

She was apt to be a bit over-talkative at times, and one day confided in him how worried she was that Hal hadn't got a job.

'So who's Hal then?' said Bert Fanshaw, with a sly sauciness. 'Is he your brother, or your young man?'

Dasia stopped in a nick of time before saying 'my husband', and said hastily, 'He's my friend. We spend a lot of time together.'

Then Mr Fanshaw said, 'So where does this young man of yours live, then?'

'Oh, he lives with me, naturally.' The moment she'd spoken, Dasia realised too late what a bloomer she'd made.

Mr Fanshaw's eyes bulged and widened in their sockets and his face went quite red: 'Oh aye . . .?'

'Well no. What I mean is – I don't think you quite . . .'

177

'Don't alarm yourself Miss Greenbow. I know exactly what you mean. Say no more ... Just our little secret eh?'

'I don't think you do, Mr Fanshaw, because it isn't a little secret, it's –' She closed her mouth suddenly. No way could she tell him, a complete stranger, that she was a respectably married young woman of seventeen, and hardly older than his own daughter who was now a children's nanny-cum-maid-of-all-work.

On the way home from Baulden's, Dasia thought affectionately about her husband, and thanked heavens for having met someone so kind and caring and understanding as Hal; for she was always aware of the old saying that the course of true love ne'er ran smooth. Even though Hal was suffering terribly at the moment from a feeling of hopelessness about the job situation, at least he kept the house tidy and clean and made their bed and washed the pots – which was quite unheard of in the case of most men, who even thought it was an insult to be seen wheeling a pram. In a way it was a pity there were these two extremes emerging in their lives, for Dasia was now full of hope and love and excitement for the future because of her pregnancy, and Hal – when she looked at him sometimes in his unguarded moments – looked sad and depressed.

She knocked at the front door of Tipperary, almost expecting him to have opened it even before she raised the brass door knocker, but today there was no welcome smile and cheerful kiss. The faded old door remained closed. With typical optimism, Dasia hopefully surmised it would be because he'd at last found a suitable job that very day and was away working.

She took out her key and went in, and as soon as she did she smelt the familiar sweet-sour tang of wines and spirits and saw her beloved lying on the horsehair sofa in a stupefied state, with a high pink flush on his face. He was snoring his head off, with sunshine streaming in through the window panes and the small fire grate still full of cold dead ashes.

Dasia felt an awful sense of foreboding and a faint sickness; surely this wasn't going to be a regular occurrence? In her own home there had never been any drink problems except for a bit of fairly harmless boozing in the local pub by Horace Greenbow, or her aunties getting a bit squiffy on occasions such as weddings and parties; and even then it was only to say things like, 'Aren't the lights bright?' and 'I think I'd better sit down ...'

She stood beside him, then bent down and kissed him on the forehead. His eyelids opened slightly and he groaned, then fell into a deep sleep again. As Dasia sadly straightened up she saw that the table was loaded with buff-coloured envelopes. There were hundreds of them in packets, and boxes of them under the table, and in one small pile next to a fountain pen on the sideboard were about a hundred already addressed, in Hal's own hand, to the little streets in West Gorton, next to Gorton Park. She saw now that other blank envelopes were in bundles waiting to be addressed; with a long list of names and addresses beside them – to streets such as Hinde Street, Hewitt, Mary, Joseph, Stanley, Egerton, Derby and Leach Streets. On and on, and on, went the lists. Then in the corner she spotted a huge cardboard box with its lid torn open, and in it were cheap, coarsely printed flimsy advertising leaflets for Agglethorpe's perfect answer to the common aspirin: *IS LIFE GETTING YOU DOWN? IS YOUR HEAD SPLITTING FROM HOW TO COPE IN THESE HARD DAYS? Forget all the taxes on tea, cocoa and tobacco. Don't worry about dog licences and the cost of ale. Just take one Agglethorpe's Pink pill daily with a*

179

dessertspoonful of water and within a week you'll see improvements.'

Dasia flopped down on a chair; what on earth was happening? Don't say Hal had got himself one of these notorious home jobs? It was hardly credible that someone of his education and standing should have been driven to this. It was usually the sort of work that women did and was a last resort when they were literally starving; for the pay hardly helped even to curb the starvation. Often the whole family including very young children had to be roped in to help in occupations such as assembling cheap and nasty toys, hand sewing garments or packing cheap bottles of highly noxious scent.

Dasia stared at all the envelopes again. Surely ... surely he wouldn't be expecting her to help him. Terrible thoughts came to her mind. Marry in haste repent at leisure – had she looked at him through rose-coloured spectacles the whole time? Was he the sort of man who would expect her to do this work in the evenings after she'd already worked at Baulden's, with the idea that now she was pregnant she could stay pinned to the house 'resting' whilst she, through wifely obligation, took on yet another boring and wearisome task. For the point about this sort of work was that it needed literate people who could read and write correctly, without a single blemishing mistake, and this took time and care and could never really pay its way.

Suddenly Hall gave a snort, a gasp, and struggled to sit up. He gaped at Dasia in disbelief: 'Good God ... What time is it?'

'Never mind that, Hal. What in heaven's name is all this? There isn't even enough room to set the table properly for a meal!'

He groaned and sat on the edge of the sofa with his head drooping, and his hands covering his face. 'I was a

180

bloody fool' he said, 'I followed up a tip, from Joe the barman in the local pub, about so called "medical" work as a house-to-house traveller. He introduced me to this bloke called Ackers from a small chemical set-up in Hulme, and Ackers drove me home with all this lot. Not only am I supposed to address all these envelopes, and stick leaflets in – I've also to trail round shoving them through all the letter-boxes within the next week ...' He looked at her sheepishly.

Dasia stared aghast: 'But it's impossible! How much is he going to pay you?'

'Two pounds, ten shillings. He said his competitors get it done for one pound, nineteen shillings and nine-pence.'

At last the sun broke through, and Hal actually smiled: 'I must have been completely off my rocker. But I had to do something, Dasia. I can't just sit here chewing my nails.

'This week I've tried for twelve jobs: warehouseman, kitchen porter, railway clerk, railway porter, road sweeper, hospital cleaner, boiler-man, caretaker, office clerk, rat catcher, grave-digger, and machinist. And – not a sausage ...

They both stared at the table. Then Hal staggered to his feet and began slowly to pile all the envelopes into one large heap in a corner of the room – as Dasia, with deep foreboding, waited to hear the dread words asking her to help him.

She heard him gulp.

Then he looked at her quizzically and said, 'I shall need your help, Dasia.'

She felt herself going slightly faint and light-headed from the strain of it all.

'You can stand by with a bucket of water in the back yard, just as a precaution, whilst I set fire to the whole bloody lot!'

'But you can't do that! If they found you'd done that the man who gave you the job would beat you up – or they might even bring in the police and accuse you of being an arsonist, or accuse you of stealing and damaging their goods. I mean – all these envelopes and leaflets will have cost them quite a lot in the first place.

'All you need to do is take them back.' She gazed at him with innocent honesty.

'TAKE THEM BACK?' He was horrified. 'I can't do that! I'd never get back alive!'

Dasia suddenly relaxed: 'I've just thought of something; there's this very kind man, Mr Fanshaw at work who has twelve children, and they're always looking for things to do ...' her voice faded as she saw his expression.

'But how old are they, Dasia? And can they read and write properly? It's not as simple as you think.' There was a miserable silence cheered only for Dasia by the thought that Hal was quickly emerging from his drunken state into harsh reality.

Then Hal said, 'It's no good. I've got to face the music. I'll do the bloody thing even if I drop dead in the attempt. But it's taught me a lesson.'

'Should I help you?' she said with an inward fatalistic groan. 'We could get quite a few done tonight?' She just couldn't bear to see him in such a jam.

He shook his head and said flatly, 'Worse trouble at sea, Dasia. I'll just have to grit my teeth and get up at five tomorrow morning, and keep on and on for the whole of this week. Then I'll take what I've managed to do of them round to the old sod who palmed it all off on me. Then at least I'll have a clear conscious. I'll have done as much as one normal human being can do – working all out for a week for a measly couple of quid. And if that doesn't suit ... well – hard cheese.'

Hal was true to his word, as all that week he toiled

182

away at the envelopes until his fingers were swollen from clutching the pen and his hand ached. Yet so determined was he, that he never took a single drink to cheer him on his way, except for mugs of strong, sweet tea. By the end of the week he managed, by working full out from five in the morning till eight and nine o'clock at night, to do half of the load ... never mind the final labour of trailing round shoving them through letter-boxes.

On the next Saturday morning, he packed the rest into the back of his car, ready to be deposited with Ackers at the factory, realising as he drove along how fortunate he was to have his own four wheels and what a difference it made in the day-to-day struggle for independence. For without any means of transport there was no way you could return the results of your sweated labour – particularly if you happened to be a penniless woman.

'Good lad,' beamed fifty-year-old Ackers with condescending sleaziness when he saw Hal arrive. 'There's nothing I likes better'n seeing young'uns oos not afraid of a bit of work, whatever their station in life. Did you manage with the bloody letter-boxes what some of 'em 'aven't got? Shove 'em under't doors – that's what I says. There's always a yard of draught under 'em to 'elp yer. 'Ope you didn't get minced up by any of them wolf dogs with no collars or licences. 'Ow people can claim to be starving and keep them around beats me. But they do say some of 'em's trained to pinch things from shops.

'Now 'ow much is it we owe yer? One pound, nineteen shillings and sixpence, if I'm correct ... and there's more work where this came from, for the likes of you.'

Hal nodded with satirical humour, then he said: 'I'll just bring in all the ones I didn't manage to get done in time. P'raps you'd like to help?'

Ackers was so puzzled that he followed Hal to the car and allowed his arms to be filled with a big, unopened box of envelopes. Then, as soon as he'd twigged the situation, he howled like a dervish for others to come and carry the rest of the boxes, muttering to himself: 'Am a dreamin'? What's 'appenin'?'

'Sorry I didn't get to shoving them under the doors ... you'd need someone good at crawling for that. But it's taken me sixteen hours a day to get this lot done legibly and correctly. So if you'll just give me my pay I'll get going. I shan't be doing any more, by the way; I believe in letting others share the good fortune.'

'Bugger off!' roared Ackers. 'You've got a bloody cheek if you expect paying for that stinking little lot. Gerrout afore you get kicked off the premises! I always was too bloody kind 'earted. I should a knowed better with the likes of your sort. It's always the same with you posh sods. Spineless. That's what you are. Give us a good woman any day if you wants a job done proper, an' no complaints.'

Hal strode to his car as a stone narrowly missed his ear, and as he drove home he philosophically regarded the whole episode as one of life's little lessons on how the poor live, and at the same time assuming himself that he at least had no intention of joining the happy band if he could possibly avoid it.

Lady Wrioth's cousin Mimi was a small slim maiden lady who weighed about eight stone, had pure white hair, rosy cheeks and a back as straight as a ramrod. She lived in a rambling old Victorian villa in Didsbury village, along with her resident companion, Miss Frinton, and a live-in tweeny maid. They also had a daily housekeeper, a charlady, a daily cook, and a visiting gardener.

Mimi was a staunch supporter of Didsbury church, which in her time had been dominated by strong men and true, with long sermons, restless choir boys and important people stamping down the aisles to their pews after the first hymn had started, which caused great rustlings of hymn books, and glaring. One of Mimi's friends was Celia Saville who was Kenny Saville's great aunt, and rented a pew close to hers. So when they met in the vestry to discuss the sale of the Sunday School building to Manchester Corporation in connection with some road widening operations their conversation veered to the more homely matters of Good Works. For both women had more money than they knew what to do with as, year by year, it gained more and more interest. So the present discussion about selling the Sunday School building for £250, which clearly broke their hearts, was superseded by more down-to-earth matters like helping the 'Here and Now'.

'Good repair and upkeep of what we already have, is the answer,' stressed Mimi to Celia in gentle and civilised tones. 'I can hardly foresee a time when there will be so much traffic on the roads that they'll all need widening, especially when we have such good tram and train services.'

Celia Saville nodded. Holding on to and acquiring extra property was a far better and safer proposition. 'They should be doing even more to help the homeless,' she said, 'in spite of the new Wythenshawe scheme for better housing away from the city centre.

'I could fill my own little rented-out terraces in Manchester a hundred times over with deserving cases. Only recently, my great nephew enabled me to help a young friend of his who'd been wrongfully dismissed as a medical student and had nowhere to go. His name is Wrioth. Even people in the upper environs often need help. We are all equal in the sight of God.'

'Wrioth?' said Mimi sharply. 'Where does he live? It sounds distinctly like someone from our family branch. My cousin was mentioning something of the sort only the other day when she called to see me. Something to do with her own son. But there was no address.'

Celia opened her capacious carpet-bag which always appeared to hold all her worldly goods including the bible, took out a small note pad, wrote Hal's address on it and silently handed it to Mimi who put it in her small reticule. Then they got back to the road-widening scheme.

The following Sunday morning, while Hal was out visiting his friend Perry Saltburn to see if Perry had any more ideas for furthering their own mutual financial predicaments, a large, dark blue, chauffeur-driven car drew up outside Tipperary, and Lady Wrioth with a neat silver mink collar on her pale tweed costume stepped out of it.

Dasia stood in the dim background of her small living-room behind the heavy lace curtains, her wrists still showing traces of flour from mixing Yorkshire pudding, and looked out with mounting alarm. What on earth did Lady Wrioth want, and how had she found out where they were living?'

Then, before she could think another thing, there was a sudden thud, and Cynthia Wrioth fell down on the paving stones. It was easily done; usually by the elderly for the pavements were notoriously uneven.

Lady Wrioth was a woman who prided herself on sure-footedness, and she felt an absolute fool. But here she was in alien territory and although she would never have admitted it she was a bit nervous. But in seconds Danny Elvers was by her side and – as if nothing had happened – they both walked towards the front door of Tipperary where Thinny gave a brisk, resplendent rat-a-tat-tat on the front door knocker.

Dasia opened the door. She hadn't expected to see Elvers there as well. She was in a fluster herself, as she'd rushed away at the very moment Cynthia Wrioth slipped over, to wash all the flour from her hands.

She gazed at them both from the doorway, in the bird-chirping, hazy sunshine, laced with the smell of dinners cooking – as neighbours gossiping at their own front doors or sharpening their carving knifes on steps ready for the Sunday roast, all looked on with cheerful curiosity.

'Ah ... Miss Greenbow? We meet again. How are you?' said Lady Wrioth.

Then Danny interrupted and said urgently, 'If Lady Wrioth could just sit down for a few moments. Her ladyship slipped ...'

'Don't *fuss* so, Elvers. I'm perfectly all right.' She glared at him warningly, as he and Dasia quickly got her seated.

She turned to Dasia: 'The last time we met, at Christmas, seems an age ago, doesn't it? And suddenly, on this wonderful morning, it's summer! I must say you do look very, very well.'

'I am very well ...'

Lady Wrioth gave a polite cough: 'Is Henry about? Could you tell him his mother's here, please. She'd like to have a few words with him.'

'I'm afraid he isn't ... I'm terribly sorry about the fall. The pavements round here are a disgrace.

'Would you like a drink of tea or anything? Hal's gone out to see his friends, but he should be back soon for his dinner. P'raps you like to stay and eat with us?'

'How very, very kind. But we must get back. Elvers has other work waiting, haven't you, Elvers? Perhaps some other time ...?'

'I'll have a cup of tea, if you don't mind, Miss Greenbow,' said Danny Elvers, 'and then if her Lady-ship decides to have one, it will be here.' He stared right at her, with a full, frank, gaze, and she felt the blood rushing to her face.

'Yes of course ...' she hurried into the small scullery ashamed that he should have had such an effect on her, and guilty that he'd called her Miss Greenbow – and that neither of them knew yet that she was Hal's proper wife.

Little did she know that the effect had been mutual. And that Danny Elvers was feeling slightly dizzy as he sat in the rather dark little room, gazing out at the brilliant sunshine and hearing the sounds of the street, while Dasia put two cups with matching saucers on a tin tray on top of a spread-out paper serviette, and found three lone ginger biscuits in the biscuit tin.

How had Hal been lucky enough to meet such a beautiful and accomplished young girl? Especially when the boy had been hounded all his life into the match-making circuit.

Miss Greenbow was just the sort of girl he himself would have fallen in love with, if he hadn't met his darling Enid. She brought back all the memories of his own innocent unspoilt youth, and when Dasia came in again, carefully carrying the tray, he had an insane desire to take her in his arms and kiss her.

'Anyway, please tell Henry I called,' said Lady Wrioth after she had sipped some tea, 'and ask him, if it isn't *too* much trouble, to get in touch with us at Hyndemere – today, if possible.' Then, smiling graciously, and shaking hands very limply with Dasia, she moved back to the car with a slight wave.

Dasia stood out on the pavement, watching as Elvers helped Lady Wrioth into her seat, and as he closed the door he turned. His eyes met Dasia's and they both knew they liked each other.

For two seconds she felt shy and embarrassed –.then it all vanished as swiftly as a summer breeze.

★

'Mother? Been here?' Hal was staggered.

'She said she'd like you to ring them at home as soon as possible.'

'Was she on her own?'

'She arrived with Mr Elvers, in a huge car.'

Hal tried to look as if he didn't care, but Dasia could see that somehow he was pleased.

After dinner, Hal walked to the nearest telephone call box, with his pocket full of coppers in the form of penny pieces, and asked the female operator to put him through to Hyndemere Hall. Then he put two pennies in the machine, and turned the handle. He breathed a sigh of relief – he was through with no trouble.

'Mother ... It's Hal. Dasia said you called this morning? What an amazing surprise. How did you find our address?' He heard her rattling on in her precise voice about Cousin Mimi ...

'But what I really wanted to get in touch with you for, Hal, was to say your father hasn't been too well. He's had what appears to be a slight heart attack.'

The phone had gone fainter and slightly crackly. Hal's own heart sank ... His father? Somehow he'd always regarded him an immune from mortal illness. He was a man who rarely even suffered a cold.

'How is he now, then?'

'Perfectly all right, but Doctor Morrison says he has to rest and try not to do too much.'

'But he never does do too much, Mother. He does just what he wants to do.'

There was a slight silence at the other end, then Cynthia Wrioth said, 'Quite frankly, Hal, I think it's all this trouble with you that's caused it.'

'With me?' A sudden anger rose within him. 'What have I done?'

'The way you've cut yourself off from us – living with that girl. Your father thinks your duties lie elsewhere,'

189

His heart began to thump with annoyance. This was sheer moral blackmail!

'I think you should at least come back and see him and sort something out. When all's said and done you are our only son. Anyway I don't want to go on too much on the phone. Visit us tomorrow. Goodbye.'

He heard the phone click at the other end. Visit them tomorrow. The royal command. No thought as to whether he had other plans. Just supposing he'd had a job to go to? Nothing of that sort ever entered their heads. No thought either of whether he'd even had the means to visit them in his impecunious state. Yet all the time, beneath his simmering hostility, he knew he would have to visit them tomorrow.

When he got back he told Dasia what had happened: '. . . A mild heart attack. So I'll have to go tomorrow and I'll be back – Wednesday.' He looked slightly embarrassed, then he said, 'It would be better if I went on my own.'

She nodded sympathetically, but deep down she was slightly hurt that he hadn't given her the option of going, now she was his wife. They would have to know the proper facts sooner or later, and in any case she didn't exactly relish being left on her own overnight and coming and going to and from work to a silent house. Although the neighbours were very friendly, she and Hal had kept a certain amount of distance, for Dasia knew only too well from her own family how little it took to have a constant invasion from others into your own little private domain – on the gossip-gathering routine of borrowing half a cup of sugar, allowing children to do errands, or putting the kettle on as soon as someone knocked at the door to ask if you'd seen the cat.

Hal put his arm round her tenderly: 'Do you think you'll be all right?'

'Of course! It'll be a sort of rest in a way. And even if

190

you'd asked me to go with you, I wouldn't have really been able to get time off work without pretending I was ill, and we're very busy at the moment with it coming up to Whit Week.'

His face suddenly brightened: 'How about me giving you a lift back to The Grove on the way, then collecting you again on my way back? We'd both be seeing our families, then? Perfect!'

'But I've broken off diplomatic relations with them – just the same as you did with yours.' Surely he realised that she couldn't expect them to welcome her with open arms? It wasn't as if any of her lot had suddenly suffered heart attacks or were pleading with her to visit them. It would be a case of, 'What's brought *you* here?' or, 'What do *you* want? Has he finished with you?'

'Stop looking so gloomy, Dasia. Going home to see them all might be a very good step, and it'll only be for a couple of days. It'll be good all round; I'll feel easier knowing I've not left you on your own – and you'll be fixed up for work because with Louise being at Baulden's, too, she can give you lifts there and back. And, best of all, we'll both be back on an even keel with our respective families.'

He gave a rueful sigh: 'So now, maybe, we can at least reveal to both lots, in a normal manner, that we're respectably married – and let them know how well the pregnancy is going. The only other thing we need is for me to have a decent job and be able to provide you with the style of life we both enjoy best.'

Reluctantly Dasia agreed. So that very evening she got on the phone to her own mother, Andrina, to tell her about Hal's father having a heart attack and suggesting that she, Dasia, and Hal would come round after tea that evening, so that Dasia could stay back at The Grove for a couple of nights while Hal was at Hyndemere.

'And I'll be able to come out in the open and tell Alice

and Horace that they'll soon be great-grandparents!' Dasia heard Andrina sniff warningly at the other end of the line ...

'Don't expect them to be *too* enthusiastic,' she said, 'you know what your grandmother is for looking on the dark side. But I think it's an excellent idea, and so will Louise. Needless to say we've never said a word about you being married – or expecting the baby. Anyway, I'll do a bit of spade work about you both coming round to-night. So get ready and be quick.'

Although Dasia had only been living completely away from her family in The Grove for a couple of months, she experienced a different perception when she saw it again. It was all so different from the bustle and noise and smells of the narrow city streets and the small darkened slate-roofed houses of the poor, as they breathed and gasped the smoke and fumes of coal fires and back-street businesses.

She realised how lucky she'd been to have once lived in The Grove in a place with orchards and huge gardens and ponies in paddocks, even if their own rambling house was dropping to bits, with water leaking through the roof.

People often said that when you went back to a place where you'd lived in childhood it looked smaller and tattier. But coming back here after only a few weeks it looked, and was, fresher and brighter and more uplifting, and she smiled with relief as Hal parked his car. They knocked at the back door – then opened it and walked in.

'We're here ...' She called out the words with forced cheerfulness as she waited to see what the reception would be.

'Oh you are – are you?' It was her grandfather, looking much the same as ever, and holding a block of wood with three holes in it which he was fixing to

192

something else, to bring forth yet another miracle of invention. He stared at them both over the top of his glasses, and Dasia moved forward and kissed him. Then she said in one quick breath, 'I'm a married woman now, you know, and we're expecting a baby. Did Andrina say?'

'She did an' all ...' said Horace Greenbow with a glimmer of a smile. 'Your grandmother's bin fussin' round cleanin' out your bedroom and movin' all my equipment out. Six 'eavy coils of wire and a lot of soldering equipment, plus a work bench with some crucial bits of stuff on it 'ave 'ad to go out.'

'She needn't have. I'm only here for a couple of days. I'm used to all your junk. I quite miss it at Tipperary.' She bit her lip; she didn't want to sound home-sick and disloyal to what was now her own beginning in Denmark Road.

That night, when Dasia was in bed in her old room, and Hal had continued his journey to Hyndemere, Alice said, 'I hope all this works out. Never in a month of Sundays will I regard going up to that Gretna Green place as a proper marriage. The Lord alone knows what we've suffered already in this house; what with Andrina being single when she had you. And I don't even know whether I really trust that Hal either, he's so young. And young men under twenty-seven – never mind nineteen – were never known to be ready to settle down for long at anything, never mind marriage.'

'For God's sake cut it out, woman,' growled Horace. 'I've never known such a one as you for always picking people to bits. The two of 'em's young, and in love. And Gretna Green, Alice, is a proper marriage whether you like it or not, at this present day. And not many others under the age of twenty-one 'as a nice little 'ouse just for two to live in. And 'e's supposed to be part of t'gentry. So what more does you want?'

'It's just that I didn't expect it all to happen to our Dasia. And so quick ... I always hoped that Rosalie –'

'We all know about Rosalie,' said Horace with a sigh. 'Your plans for Rosalie've 'aunted our lives. And she's not caught a Belted Earl yet, at that Servants Registry. An' I'm not surprised, Alice. Life catches you where you least expect it, and our children, an' gran'children, an' great-gran'children, for that account, has to work out their own ways. We can't expect to pry into their lives and rule their affairs for ever.'

It was a long speech for Horace Greenbow to make. And for once in her life, Alice was stuck for words.

It was very late when Hal arrived back at Hyndemere.

There was only Mr Marjoribanks from the house staff waiting up for him. Even next morning he breakfasted alone, with a maid placing great heavy silver-lidded dishes on the sideboard hot-plate so that he could help himself to kedgeree.

He'd just finished, and was gazing out through the leaded lights of the massive bay window towards the arboretum, when he heard his mother come into the room and felt a moment of sheer panic. He didn't turn round but instead tried to calm himself by absorbing the scene set before him outside: the wonderful collection of trees in the sunlit emerald glade of early summer, dappled with calm shading, as blackbirds and thrushes hopped placidly about the leaves and mosses.

His mother was immaculately dressed in her tweeds and pearls. She'd already breakfasted in her room.

She came towards the window and kissed him lightly on the cheek: 'I'm glad you've managed to come and see us at last. I was beginning to imagine we hadn't even got a son, never mind a son and heir.

'Your father'll be very pleased. All this trouble at the medical school has upset him dreadfully, and this extra

194

problem of the girl being pregnant has been a terrible shock.'

Hal suddenly looked his mother full in the eyes. His face was pale. 'If you ever chance to see Dasia again you will treat her as you would treat anyone else in our family. She is not "the girl", she is going to be the mother of my child. She is Miss Dasia Greenbow ...' He broke off abruptly knowing he had evaded the real truth. He was funking the real issue by not revealing that he and Dasia were married. But already he was comforting himself and justifying the deceit by the thought that if his father knew the whole truth in his present heart-attack state, it might well finish him off; and if that happened Hal would live with the guilt of it all his life.

His father looked better than he'd expected when at last he met him after breakfast, outside in the gardens.

'... So I just thought I'd come and see you both,' said Hal. 'I thought we'd better get things sorted out a bit, and I wanted to apologise about all the trouble I caused over the mess-up at the hospital, in which I was almost entirely blameless. But all the same, Father, I decided the fuss involved just wasn't worth kicking up about. It would have only dragged us all through the mud, and caused more family trauma than ever. And you've always said yourself that my true duty lies, eventually, here at Hyndemere.'

His father nodded and smiled: 'You are right. We must just forget the whole episode. What you must do now is to come back home as soon as possible, and look after the estate.' Then he said, 'And as to the young girl, we'll just have to arrange for her to have the baby, and make her a decent allowance.

'You haven't quite learnt as much about life as your mother and me, my son. A girl like her may appear to win your heart for ever by her youthful beauty, but really she is what they know in the States as a gold

195

digger. She's just out to grab personal riches, and who can blame them when they live in such a poverty-stricken world?'

Hal listened to him with horror and depression. It was as if his father was entirely divorced from reality. He seemed to acknowledge only two sorts of people: the very poor and the very rich. And the very poor were the ones who were employed by the very rich out of the goodness of their hearts, for the sake of king and country. Completely unknown to him were the millions of people in towns and cities like Manchester; people neither poor nor well off, who were happy and comfortable, who regarded themselves as independent individuals and had never had to suffer the fate of being servants for an upper, land-owning aristocracy.

That night in bed Hal hardly slept as he thought about the whole situation. Part of him longed to be back in his childhood home, here in beautiful Hyndemere – even though he realised it was all a sort of mirage from the past. If only it were easy just to obey his parents like some automaton, and forget Dasia for ever; even pretend that his disastrous sojourn in Manchester as a medical student had never happened. If only he could be the perfect answer for his mother and father as the proper inheritor of this house; a man set to rise from his roots like some great oak tree, to defend the political stage and contribute to public life – perhaps even ending up in some illustrious chair as chancellor or rector of a renowned university.

He turned and turned about, restlessly knowing that all he was thinking and dreaming was a load of fairy-tale nonsense that he wouldn't really want to happen at all – what was done in life was done; there was no going back.

Then, out of the blue and as if to chide him, a picture came to his mind of himself as a child of nine and his mother.

He was watching his mother open her jewel case. She was putting on a brooch, and as she did so she suddenly pressed a secret spot in the carved design of the box where there was a groove in a curving rose leaf. A panel moved and at once revealed a small disguised drawer in the jewel case; whereupon she took out a sparkling gold ring studded with huge diamonds, and a small slim necklace of smaller diamonds.

'These are yours, my son,' she had said, 'but not until the time comes. They've been handed down through the Wrioth family – always to the eldest sons when they marry. And the son gives it to his bride, but only for her lifetime, until the next male heir arrives to present it to his wife. It's a family heir-loom.' He saw his mother's beautiful oval face framed by the dark hair as he gazed at her in awe.

How strange to have thought of it now in the middle of the night, at this time of stress and indecision.

He sat up in bed, wide awake now. In the past three years his life had completely changed, and now he really was the eldest son and properly married, even with a child on the horizon. So this family ring and necklace really did belong to Dasia.

He got up and put on the light. Then, finding note-paper and envelopes from the small bedroom bureau, he wrote a note to his parents with the May 1927 date on it:

Dear Mother and Father,

    If this drawer is empty when you open it again, it's because I, Henry (Hal) Wrioth, your only son and heir, did take both the ring and necklace to give to my married, rightful, and officially registered wife, Dasia Greenbow, who is now expecting our child, and who is therefore the rightful receiver of these pieces of jewellery as laid down by Wrioth family tradition, and

197

which I am now taking with me to give to her for her life-time.

Signed: Henry Martinvale Eustace Wrioth.

Then he went back to bed and fell peacefully asleep.

The next day when everyone in the house was otherwise occupied, Hal folded the letter very small and slipped into his mother's dressing room. Then, opening the secret drawer where the jewels were, he lifted them carefully, complete in the drawstring kid bag, and replaced them with his letter. Then he went downstairs and ate a hearty breakfast.

He greeted his mother and father cheerfully. He suffered no qualms about his actions. He knew now that trying to explain or even argue with them was hopeless. They were frozen into a past and completely different era which had started to crumble, even in Edwardian times.

'I must get back now,' he said with, deep down, an impulsive and self-inflicted sadness, for his parents didn't seem to be a bit sad, and his father's heart condition was improving of its own volition.

'Think very carefully about what we've said to you, Hal,' said his mother warningly as she rearranged some delicate lemon mimosa in a blue and crimson Chinese Chun vase.

He nodded dutifully.

Then his father said brusquely, 'And unless you've finished with the girl the curtailing of financial allowances will continue, until such time as you might want some unofficial private assistance to be given towards the upkeep of the infant, if she has no other means ...'

Hal listened in silence. Shortly afterwards he left, swearing never again to set foot anywhere near his childhood home.

CHAPTER THIRTEEN

The Debt

The annual Manchester Whit Week was normally full of excitement, family pleasure, and religious processions. Flocks of shiny-faced children looking their most angelic, many of the little girls dressed in white, with white net veils and wreaths of small white flowers on their heads like small brides, trod the cobbled streets.

Boy scouts and girl guides, and numerous local bands, and youth brigades walked proudly by, along with church dignitaries in white surplices and rich cloaks, wearing vestments of scarlet. Thousands of ordinary adults for miles around wore their best and often brand-new Whit Week clothes, and small shabby streets became alive with visions of the Virgin Mary, on colourful silk banners, usually in bright blues, white, and gold.

But Whitsuntide and Whit Week in particular, apart from its religious significance, was also the true sign that summer was here at last. Those who could afford it often took their one and only week's holiday of the whole year, in special 'works weeks', and went off to Blackpool. Others took days out for a picnic in one of the many parks, or an outing to places like Boggart Hole Clough, or Bellevue Gardens or Wythenshawe Park.

Usually Dasia soaked it all up with carefree happiness, but this year there was uneasiness verging on misery, for Hal seemed incapable of keeping the same job for more than three consecutive days, always ending with the remark that he couldn't stand being a slave to some stupid drunken boss. And at one point, much to Dasia's horror, he'd taken on a job as a gigolo – a male dancing partner for older women at matinée dances at the large hotels in the centre of Manchester.

And it had all been because of Aunty Dolly ... and her friend Marcia.

'He's so young, and handsome, and clever, and athletic, I just don't understand why he can't hold down a decent job,' said Dolly to Marcia as they sat in Marcia's back kitchen in Derbyshire Lane one afternoon, repairing linen while their gentlemen were all out of the way. 'Why on earth doesn't he become a dancing partner at the tea dances in all the big hotels, or the dinner dances at the Midland? Especially with your brother Montague running that agency for them and knowing all the ropes.

'You told me yourself that some of them make a fortune, and to my mind he's even better looking than Rudolph Valentino. It's absolutely mind-boggling how Dasia managed to grab him.'

'Easy to grab but hard to get rid of, if you ask me,' purred Marcia glancing down at her purple nail polish. 'A man without a job is simply no use, Dolly, no matter how handsome he is.'

'Well then – what about what I just said?'

Marcia began to fuss about with her hair and poke about with her little finger at the edge of her false eye lashes: 'Montague can't possibly take on anyone else. There's a waiting list a mile long. Especially after that old trout Mrs Hollyboxer left two hundred pounds to that little sixteen-year-old lout who used to play wag everyday from school to go dancing with her. I wouldn't mind, but his poor parents thought he was studying the life cycle of the water beetle ...'

'Mmmmm ... I remember that, Marcia, and the little devil even had spots. What happened in the end?'

'He was sacked from school and within a year he was almost a millionaire from scrap iron. And now he lives out at Wilmslow and's married to one of the pork sausage people.' Then Marcia looked at Dolly's rather crestfallen face and said, 'Tell you what, though, why don't we invite your Dasia's Hal out with *us* one afternoon and sort of act as his dancing partners so that he edges his way in?'

Dolly began to look uneasy. It was all very well having a bit of harmless gossip and pretending to want to help, but she knew only too well that getting involved in family predicaments which had nothing to do with her was about the worst possible scenario. 'Er ... well I'm not quite sure, Marcia. After all, he is the son of a lord you know and if *they* can't even find themselves a decent job what hope is there for the rest of us? And supposing we did do it and he got involved with some loose woman or something? I would never forgive myself.'

The following Tuesday after this conversation, Hal was amazed to get a visit from Dolly while Dasia was at work.

'I've come for your own good, Hal. But mostly it's for dear little Dasia ... because I happened to hear how bad times are. I mean, are you keen to earn a few pounds to oil the wheels – or is it all too much below your standards?'

He looked at her drily: 'Depends what it is, Dolly. No one can say I haven't tried – but it all depends what it is. Every man has his pride.'

'And so does every woman, Hal. My goodness so does every woman – or else why do you think Marcia and me's so fussy about who we have as resident gentlemen?

'No – what I'm going to suggest, Hal, could turn out to be the best move in the whole of your life. People have got to Hollywood on less, and it isn't hard work. All you have to do is to be a dancing partner and be paid for it.'

'WHAT ...?' Hal couldn't believe it. 'You must be joking Dolly! I wouldn't even *think* of it!

'What you really mean is one of those confounded smooth-faced gigolos who con old biddies, and count the diamonds in every woman's necklace!'

Dolly gave a secret snort. You could tell he came from another world when he actually thought all elderly women had real diamond necklaces. The nearest she'd got to that with Mr Corcoran was what he called a very rare 'blue diamond' brooch which, when she took it to the corner jewellers to have it valued, had the setting removed to reveal a piece of blue sugar paper carefully glued behind a small lump of bottle glass. But she didn't tell him as it would have been such a terrible let down for him after spending (he'd assured her) forty-five pounds and threepence.

'It's not a bit like that; it's perfectly harmless! There's lots worse jobs. Surely you don't hate women so much not to ever dance with them? Surely you'd dance with your own dear mother if she asked you to?'

'Certainly not. It all sounds too unsavoury for words.'

'But you did meet Dasia at Redman's ...'

Hal groaned in desperation. 'Look, Dolly, do you think you could mind your own business for just two seconds?'

'If you were having to dance with *men*, Hal, I could understand it because it'd end in a shin-bashing contest. But just think of it, love ... sweet old ladies and the middle-aged, all in their best silks and satins, waving their fans and smiling – and pleasant music and the best hotels. And even *paid* for it, *that's* the main thing.

'Why don't you come with me and Marcia tomorrow afternoon,' she wheedled. 'Just think how nice it'd be to greet Dasia when she gets home all tired from work with a couple of brand-new white fivers in your pocket. I can even let you have a dress suit if you want, with black satin revers on it.'

In the end, worn down by the strain of trying to be polite to one of Dasia's relatives rather than attempting to strangle her, he allowed himself to be won over – to the extent of promising to turn up the next afternoon at the tea dance, at the Grand Savoy.

'But I'll choose my own type of dressing up,' he assured her.

Tea dances at the Grand Savoy were out of this world. Generally speaking, tea dances came in all shapes and sizes according to their vicinity. Some were family affairs with young children there, others sported nothing but flappers, and others were a general, homely cross section of the population. But the Grand Savoy was ten rungs above all that.

The place itself was ornately furnished with embossed ceilings and Egyptian columns, with plenty of gold leaf about. The private ballroom, where the tea dances were held, had a small balcony where orchestras and bands played, and the place was always in use for private functions. It could cater for hundreds of people at sit-down wedding feasts, and banquets, complete with flunkeys, and a master of ceremonies.

But on these afternoons it was a quieter scene as the more elderly age groups, all looking like dowager princesses and accompanied by elderly Lotharios, trod the light-fantastic, in feverish fandangos, with eyes flashing, and fans all aquiver with here and there the accidental glimpse of a garter, and ladies sitting on men's hands by mistake as the men claimed to be helping them to sit down.

Round the edges of the vast luxurious rooms, huge mahogany tables spread with snowy silk damask displayed hundreds of cups and saucers and huge urns – along with scores of silver-plated cake stands holding potted meat sandwiches, scones, and fancy cakes with hundreds and thousands on them.

'We'll sit just here, at this table for four, right on the edge of the dance floor where he can be properly seen,' whispered Dolly to Marcia. 'No good hiding his light under a bushel . . .'

They had both scampered round their housework at top speed that morning, in a real Cinderella act – from mob caps and overalls to fringed frocks and feathers in bandeaux, their legs covered in bright salmon-pink silk stockings, and rhinestone beads catching the light from the chandeliers.

Hal himself sat there calm and immaculate in the self-same grey suit he'd worn when he was up before the kangaroo court, but now he wore a dark blue silk tie with fine white spots on it.

He sat there with passive and humorous resignation – for quite honestly he couldn't really take it seriously.

'You take Marcia round for this waltz, then,' said Dolly excitedly. 'Get on the floor before anyone else and I'll guarantee that by the end of the dance I'll have you booked up for the whole afternoon.'

Hal chose not to hear her – as the strains of 'The Blue Danube' sounded in his ears and he waltzed off with Marcia in exaggerated rapture.

But Dolly was right, for within seconds a large lady in a glittering white sequin frock fit for a well-fed mermaid appeared at the table. Dolly quickly got out her notebook, took the lady's name, which was unbelievably

Gloria Swansdown, and wrote 2/6d by the side of it.

'It seems incredibly *expensive*,' grumbled Gloria in cut-glass tones. 'The usual one only charges one and sixpence ...'

'But he isn't "the Usual One" is he dear?' said Dolly coldly. 'He's the *Unusual one*, with his own teeth and hair, the strength of a panther – *and* he's the son of a Ruritanian Prince.'

By the time the afternoon had finished, Hal was sweating cobs and his curls hung damply across his forehead. His feet had been stabbed to death by scores of high heels; there was lipstick of various shades on his neck and ears, and face powder all over his lapels. While his one-time best silk tie hung like a bootlace under his collar.

'You've made four pounds, two and sixpence, take away our admittance fees, plus that marvellous IOU for ten pounds from that foreign lady who wants you to dance with her as her full-time partner tomorrow and wants to take you to Baden-Baden, later in the year.'

Hal groaned. He didn't say anything to Marcia and Dolly but he'd also seen two friends of his mother's there, and hoped to hell they hadn't recognised him. And to add insult to injury, some dago had sidled up to him and told him to beat it unless he wanted both his ears chopped off.

When he'd seen Dolly and Marcia on to a tram to Stretford he went straight into Tommy Ducks near Central Station and blew the takings on a few drinks, some flowers for Dasia on the way home, and a new, very expensive tie, in case he needed it for a proper job interview – plus some spot remover for his clothes. And yet another job idea bit the dust.

★

And still the general situation got worse and worse. Even though Hal kept hidden amongst his belongings the small leather drawstring bag containing Dasia's rightful ring and necklace, he still hadn't had the courage to mention them, for deep in his heart he knew the actual gift, which was worth enough to buy twenty small houses outright, meant virtually nothing to them in these hard times.

Then one showery summer's day towards the end of June, just as she was setting off to work at Baulden's, Dasia looked in her purse and found that her last farthing had gone.

Mournfully she set off earlier to work, knowing she would have to trudge all the way without a tram ride and aware that she had one single crust of bread and jam tucked away in her handbag for her midday meal.

As she walked towards the gloves department she felt quite weak with anxiety, for she hadn't even enough money to buy herself a midday snack, and it wasn't the first time either. Often these days she took sandwiches to work – so meagre that they'd hardly have kept a starving sparrow alive. Even though the motto for all pregnant women was 'eat for two', here she was without even the wherewithal, energy or enthusiasm to eat for one.

Her deep, expressive eyes welled with tears as she checked her stock, dusted all the glass display cases and made sure everything was in order for yet another busy day. It was a week during which there wasn't even the consolation of seeing Louise who always cheered her up with anecdotes about being an assistant buyer, because Louise was away on holiday to Hoylake with Arnold Kimberley.

So today Dasia followed her now all too familiar routine of telling Miss Davina and the rest of them that she liked to have more time to do bits of shopping during

206

her short dinner break, when really she would sooner have paid for a decent meal at staff rates like all the others did. Instead, with the weather being warm and fine she went and sat down outside in the square and had her snack, feeding a few crumbs of it to the starlings and pigeons.

'Mind if I join you, Dasia?'

It was Mr Fanshaw of the twelve children, and occasionally he came to join her on the seat and eat his own sandwiches. Today he opened up a huge pack, enough for a giant: 'Corned beef and piccalilli,' he grunted, as he opened his large cheery mouth. Then staring at Dasia's small crust he said, with his mouth full to choking, 'Want some?'

Before she was expecting she might easily have said yes, but these days at just over three months pregnant even the thought of corned beef and piccalilli made her feel quite queazy, along with such things as cheap sardines in oil. And the smell of fish being fried in lard made her feel positively bilious. 'No thank you, Mr Fanshaw, but it was a kind thought.'

He took a small bottle of lemonade and a white enamel mug from his khaki-coloured canvas bag, opened the wired stopper, and began to pour some of the fizzy, sparkling liquid from the thick, pale green, transparent neck. 'Want a drink? Surely you ain't doin' without even a sup of summat?'

She hesitated. She was quite thirsty. 'All right then,' she said.

He finished his own in one gulp and poured her a drop in the same mug – politely turning the mug to the other side for her to drink from.

'So 'ow's your young man goin' on then? I'll bet 'e's right proud to court a young lady like you.'

'He's not doing too well at present . . .' She was nearly going to tell him the whole sad tale but checked herself

207

just in time, and he noticed it instantly.

'It's just as well you aren't married yet, then – or you'd be the only bread winner ... and *then* you'd really have summat to worry about.' Then he said in fatherly and sympathetic tones, 'I know what it's like being young and in love and, even though I says it miself, never trust any man, for often they just can't 'elp their sels when't passion rises. So if you wants help or advice, always come to me.'

Dasia was overwhelmed by his kindness and concern, for until now she had always had a sneaking suspicion that he was not the paragon of virtue he claimed to be, and that his wife and twelve children might not be leading the idyllic and energetically fulfilled lives of hard work and prosperity that he painted for them all. For never once was there any mention of dissension in his household, and Miss Davina in the gloves department, who couldn't bear the sight of him and once muttered words which sounded like lecherous villain, often described his wife as a poor over-worked creature who was nothing but his under-blanket. But there again, as Miss Merrion from Straws which was part of the hats department said, You couldn't always take what Miss Davina said as perfect truth because she was an elderly spinster, and spinsters were always very jealous people – a theory which Dasia did not agree with, knowing that all her own aunties were still spinsters and seemed perfectly normal.

When Dasia got home again that day it was the same old sorry scene: no Hal, and not even enough spare coppers for coals in the grate. For although it was summery outside, a few small glowing cinders were a welcome in the rather small dark room which soon became chilled.

Bleakly she noted that everything was stone dead as usual, waiting for her to make it into a welcoming home;

a conventional wife's warm greeting for a man who, like millions of others in those hard times, had nought but tales of woe whenever he put foot across the threshold, and when he did arrive was laden with heavy beery smells from pubs as far afield as The Ivy Bower at Ardwick Green, the Gog and Magog, The Shambles near the cathedral and Yates Wine Lodge in Oldham Street.

Dasia laid her hands across her belly; there were hardly any outward signs yet of the swelling of her body, but when she had her clothes off the half below her belly button was tense and smooth, and curved outwards, defying her to keep her stomach in as she attempted to keep herself looking slim and wand-like, as the new life grew within her.

And that was what worried her, for she knew she must eat well and live properly for the sake of the unborn child. She shuddered to herself as she thought about all the cases of rickets, brought about by mal-nutrition and the new things called vitamins, which were, and always had been, in good fresh food and plenty of sunshine, but had been denied to so many in the past so that theirs was a heritage of stunted growth and weak, bowed legs.

The streets of Manchester lay witness to it ... God forbid that she and Hal would come to that. But it could well happen if she lost her job and they were both without means of support or employment, for even the house they now lived in was only a passing bit of luck from a charitable and rich woman.

And so the see-saw continued until Hal eventually found employment as a medical supplies traveller singing the praises of various orthopaedic tools used in bone oper-ations, many of which were as gruesome, large and heavy as anything to be found in a butcher's shop, and samples of which, plus heavy catalogues, he carried round in his small car.

But at the end of June the bottom dropped out of Dasia's world once more as he announced that his car had conked out. 'That's why I'm back so early. God knows what'll happen to the job. The only reason I managed to get it in the first place – out of fifty applicants – was because I had no transport difficulties. And believe me, Dasia, it's "Come a day – Go a day", with that little outfit. Goodbye, and bugger you, Mr Wrioth, and bring in the next victim with a car.' Then he groaned and said, 'Shanks's pony again ... Anyway thank God I've got Lizzie into Brindleworth's garage. It's going to need pretty extensive repairs.'

Dasia almost fainted: 'But how on earth can we afford it?'

'How on earth *can't* we afford it? It's absolutely essential for me when I go job hunting. It cuts down the odds against me by ninety per cent, even as a pathetic status symbol. All's fair game in job hunting, especially in the commercial travelling area. And if the worst comes to the worst we'll just have to pay the garage repair bill out of your wages. I expect if we were really starving, we'd have to go round for a meal to Perry Saltburn's, or even back to your lot in The Grove ... But let's hope it doesn't come to that.'

'But we already use all my money, Hal, on day-to-day survival. It's not just food and drink; there are scores of other expenses, like tram fares and shoe repairs, and laundry, and the new chairs we bought, and our pots and pans still to pay for on the never-never, and the decent blankets for our bed.' She looked at him in anguish. 'The accounts aren't working out ...'

He glared at her reprovingly: 'Well, we'll either just have to manage, or else Freddy Brindleworth'll just have to wait for payment. I'll give him a cheque; that should

210

shut him up. We've dealt with him for years ... Father often calls in to his place even now when he comes to town.'

'But how can you, now that your allowance has vanished?'

'He'll not know that! He sold me the damned crock in the first place. And by the time the cheque bounces we'll at least have had a few days' grace to get some financial settlement sorted out, and I'll also have our repaired car back to get work; that's the main thing.'

She felt sick with fear. She had suffered enough in the past, in her own home, with the precarious fortunes of her own grandfather, Horace Greenbow, so that all she longed for was the normal untrammelled, comfortable existence which hard work and honesty were supposed to bring about. But if a man started passing dud cheques, they were doomed.

'Don't do it, Hal. Please, please, don't do it. I couldn't bear you to get into real trouble, especially with our baby growing inside me. Surely something will happen that will save us.' It was hard to believe he had been a medical student, training to take on grave matters of life and death which entailed seeing the problems and weaknesses of everyone, for now he seemed a complete simpleton slipping back to schoolboyish truculent irresponsibility.

Then suddenly his mood changed and he looked at her gently, as he walked over to her and put his arm round her shoulders: 'I'm not quite the idiot you take me for, you know,' his eyes met hers knowingly, 'and we'll do as you say ... we'll bide our time. Meanwhile ...' he hesitated, then to her amazement hastened out of the room and came back very quickly, 'I've got a sort of present for you, here. For you and you alone.' With a mock gesture of allegiance he knelt before her and presented her with the small kid leather drawstring bag.

'Whatever is it?' she was completely startled as she stood there solemnly twisting some strands of curling red-gold hair straying across her smooth creamy forehead. She began to stare at him accusingly and the colour gathered stormily in her cheeks: 'Surely you haven't been buy –'

'No, of course not. Talk sense, Dasia. Open it. Whatever's inside belongs to you.'

Slowly and suspiciously she pulled at the strings holding the opening of the bag and felt inside. The tips of her fingers met the hard unyielding shapes of the jewellery. Surely, surely … it wasn't … it couldn't be stolen …? Inwardly she cursed herself for even thinking such an awful thing of her true love. But alas, the background experience of the family pawn shop, and the regular visits there from the police forced her to accept that no class on earth was immune from deviousness in times of crisis, and sometimes it even became a bad habit. Please God let this not be the case – and God forgive her for even thinking such a thing.

She took hold of the necklace with her finger and thumb and brought it out into the light, gasping at the sheer beauty of it as it lay there on the table, sparkling and glinting. Then she fished inside and took out the ring with its huge diamonds. She was absolutely staggered!

'Put them on. They'll cheer you up.' Hal was actually laughing at her.

'Where on earth did they come from?' She hesitated.

'Come from?' He bristled slightly and said defensively, 'Hyndemere of course. Where else? And they belong to you – to do what you want with in your own life time … to be passed on to the next Wrioth bride.'

'I just don't know what to say. It's an awful shock. Should I put them in the bank? But how could we afford to keep them there?'

'Do what the hell you like with them,' he said, now grown tired of the whole subject. 'Family heirlooms cause more damned trouble than they're worth. But you might as well have what you're entitled to.'

She nodded. She didn't kiss him or say thank you; it would have been demeaning. Instead she went away to think of where she could keep them safely in the house, so she just put them in her old cardboard suitcase, along with the letter about her inheritance, burying the small bag inside some rolled-up stockings, and willing herself never to lose the two pieces of precious jewellery.

That night in bed, after they had entwined their young and vulnerable naked bodies in loving pleasure and satiated their longings, she lay in the darkness thinking of the amazing jewellery, while Hal lay like a contented log beside her.

A small streak of shame rose within her, as the letter about her inheritance also came to mind. For she knew that even though the months were moving forward and she was now a married woman who should make all things known to her husband, just as he had made known to her the family jewels, she had never made mention of her trip to Canada in answer to the amazing letter which had already turned relationships upside down in the Greenbow family. When she first took the letter off the kitchen table when she left home, little did she realise how much life could change in only a few short months. For now, the vague dream of seeking out her inheritance was an adventure in her imagination, unrelated to true life. How could she take the journey now as a married person, with a baby to be born and a husband who was firmly rooted in England? How could she even mention the letter to him at present in these times of unemployment and turmoil?

Tonight in this humble little room they'd been true lovers, with the world their own, and the darkness enveloping them in comfort and happiness. But tomorrow the grimness of their true situation would be even worse for where would they get the money to pay for the car repairs?

Next morning, as usual, it was back to reality. But thankfully the summer warmth and lightness bred optimism. Not many people could be totally miserable in the long lazy days of these middle months, and even those inexorably trapped for long and tedious hours in factories, sweat shops and mines looked forward to a few hours of summer freedom. And in the closely knit communities of streets where Dasia and Hal were living, where the whole of family life from birth to death took place, the young and the old laughed and cried, joked, groused, and gossiped, quarrelled, and showed love and hate, fear and violence as they went about their regular pattern of living from day to day.

That morning at Baulden's Dasia thought briefly of Hal, as he had waved to her earlier and set off to Malton's Medical Equipment firm, to break the news to them that his car was now in dock for repairs. To Dasia it was scandalous the way he didn't even get an allowance for using his own vehicle or for car repairs.

She decided to go and sit in the square again at midday, and as she sat there leaning back with her eyes closed and her face towards the sunshine, she heard the familiar tones of Mr Fanshaw, and felt the wooden bench give slightly as he sat his huge bulky body next to her.

'Takin' full advantage of the nice weather then, Dasia? A swim-suit's what a pretty young thing like you should be wearin' with a nice little figure like yours.'

She opened her eyes and smiled politely. She knew he meant well ...

''Ow's your boy friend then? Still got 'is job as a traveller for Malton's medical stuff?'

214

Then, at about eleven o'clock at night, Hal came rolling home at last. He was staggering. His face was as white as chalk and there were traces of blood along the hair line of his head.

She rushed towards him as he came through the back door: 'What is it? What's happened?' Her heart thudded with anxiety and she felt a terrible weakness sweep over her as she steadied herself against the table. At first she'd been convinced that he must have been drinking, but now it was clear that he was completely free of the smell.

'You were right, Dasia,' he mumbled, as she got him to lie down on the small sofa, with his feet sticking over the end. 'That bunch of crooks sent me packing straight away the moment they found I'd no transport. We're back to square one again.'

'Shall I fetch a doctor?' She hurried away to boil a kettle of water to bathe his head. Surely he hadn't been in a fight? There were some parts of Manchester and Salford near the docks where even the most innocent passer-by could find himself short of an eye for life if they so much as glanced in the wrong direction.

She heard him groan: 'A bloody doctor? Don't for God's sake do that, Dasia. Only over my dead body ...' Then, as she returned with a bowl of warm water and some cottonwool and lint, he gave a faint, weary smile and said, 'I can't even claim it was a heroic injury. The fact is I fell just as I was trying to do a running jump on to a tram. But I missed and the damned thing kept moving along, with the conductor shouting "Serve you bloody well right" and threatening to report me for dangerous behaviour. Then I must have blacked out, because the next thing I knew some people in Jackson Street took me in and let me lie on a bed for hours to rest, and gave me sips of water and cups of tea, until I insisted I was fit enough to go. And the terrible thing is I don't even remember which house it was or even their names. I'll just have to put a letter in the evening paper tomorrow, addressed to Unknown Good Samaritans.'

But the next day, he was in no fit state to compose a letter to anyone. His head throbbed and his bones ached and ached, as signs of bruising began to appear all over him, and his face became a swollen, purple pudding.

Dasia was truly terrified. Was she doing right in obeying his plea not to fetch a doctor? Supposing he got worse or developed a temperature and suffered from concussion? Supposing he got worse and suddenly died and she was to blame?

'Never you mind, lovey,' said Mrs Binks next door who was well into her seventies and lived with her husband in the downstairs part of the house. 'I'll keep an eye on him while you're out. All men's stubborn, and if they wants to be idiots and not have specialist care it's not for us to worry. I'll come and stand for you, pet, if you're ever in't dock. They can't do you for being an obedient wife and carrying out your 'usband's wishes. After all, we are supposed to be their bloody goods and chattels aren't we?' She gave Dasia a huge, cheery wink.

It was now the beginning of July, and nature, along with summer sunshine and Dasia's nursing, combined with Hal's own inherent youthful fitness, had worked miracles on his recovery with never a doctor in sight, as he resumed his search for a job.

'There is one slight hope,' he said, 'and my car back from that garage would be an added bonus. I met Perry today and he knows someone at J & N Philips who could probably get me quite a decent little job there with real prospects – particularly with my own transport. He can get me an interview for next week. It'll be for relieving holiday absences at first, then could become more permanent.'

218

Dasia sighed with relief. Things were improving at last.

'What happened to that note they sent us from the garage about the car being ready?' said Hal cheerfully. 'I think I'll trot round and get it.'

Her spirits dwindled: 'It's over there on the mantel-piece just near the clock – but we can't afford to pay for it yet, not until you're actually back in work again. You admitted, yourself, the cost of repairing it might be almost as much as the price of the car itself.'

'Look, my little poppet, just you mind your own business for once eh? After all, it is my personal property, and my family and their retainers have been personal customers of old Freddy Brindleworth's since the firm built stage-coaches. I shall just ask them to send us the bill and we'll pay in due course . . . It's as easy as that.' He gave her a big cheerful kiss.

But was it as easy as that? Would it be as easy as that when Brindleworth's studied their customer's address more closely, or accidentally found out, through a highly coloured piece of gossip, that the owner of the small, washed-up two-seater was an out-of-work layabout without a penny in the world, and was in no way related to their most esteemed, ancient and now rare customer – Lord Wrioth of Hyndemere Hall.

Without more ado and riding on the crest of a new sparkling wave of confidence, Hal strode off to Brindleworth's and was back within an hour and a half with Lizzie – and the bill.

The bill was written on a big foolscap sheet of lined paper, and listed on it were all the numerous repairs in neat copperplate handwriting. At the right-hand bottom of the red-lined cash column was the total, which amounted to the frightening sum of twenty-three pounds, sixteen shillings and sevenpence three farthings. Immediately after Freddy Brindleworth's own wobbly

signature it said: PAYMENT REQUIRED IMMEDI-
ATELY OTHERWISE APPROPRIATE PROCEED-
INGS WILL BE TAKEN.

None of your 'Faithful and obedient servant', or 'I
am, yours respectfully', or 'At any time to suit Your
Lordship's convenience', on this one ...

Dasia set off to work at Baulden's the following day
with the car bill and its threat niggling away in the back
of her mind.

'What's the matter, then?' asked Mr Fanshaw as he
replaced some slightly rotted sun blinds at the department window. 'You're looking quite peaky, girl. Don't
say it's that young man of yours again.'

'Not quite, Mr Fanshaw,' said Dasia a bit off-
handedly, 'it's the bill we got from Brindleworth's for
those repairs. They're absolutely exorbitant. Some
people could almost buy a house for the price! And he
expects us to pay it all IMMEDIATELY.' The colour
rose to her cheeks and her eyes flashed.

'Told you so – didn't I?' crowed Fanshaw in excited
triumph.

'Well, yes ... I must admit you did. But it was too late
even then, because they already had the car in their
workshop. Anyway – we'll manage somehow, and Hal's
got an interview for a really good job this time at J&N
Philips.'

Mr Fanshaw got down from his ladder, looked about
dramatically to make sure there was no one about, then
slipped across to her and, whispering with trembling
passion-lipped vibrancy, said, 'Look here, Miss Dasia,
I've got a fair bit of money tucked away miself ...
money that's always available, see? Not money in't bank
or owt like that ... Proper money in one pound notes;
some of 'em big, white, five pound uns, and all – what
you 'as to sign when you pays 'em in at shops. I'm in
charge of all money matters in our 'ouse, see? So if you

220

wants that money this week to stop 'im sending the bailiffs in, just you think seriously about what I've just offered.'

The bailiffs ... Dasia shuddered. Surely not for a bill they were going to pay within the next two weeks? 'It's ever so kind of you, Mr Fanshaw –'

'Just call me Algie, Dasia.'

'I'm really touched – truly I am ... but hopefully it won't come to borrowing.'

'Never be too sure, my dear, never be too sure ...'

On Tuesday of the following week, when Hal had gone for his interview to J&N Philips, Dasia was startled to find a letter addressed to Hal tucked away behind the rest of the letters on the mantelpiece. It had been opened and had obviously arrived the day before without her knowing. A second letter from the garage ... She looked inside. It was a demand for the bill to be paid and was in bright red writing. It said that if the money wasn't forthcoming within five days, and paid in full, bailiffs would be sent to the house to make up the debt from goods collected from the house.

'But how can they do it, Hal?' she asked tearfully when he got home, 'and why didn't you tell me about the letter yesterday?'

He shook his head sadly: 'Isn't it clear to you why? Just look at you – all tears and fuss about a load of empty threats. You won't do the baby any good if you fuss so much about things of no consequence.'

'But it *is* of consequence, Hal. Mr Fanshaw at work warned me about Brindleworth's ...'

'And who's he when he's at home. I hope you haven't been spreading our private affairs all round that blasted shop!' His face was tense and angry. 'Don't say I've married some little gossiping trouble-maker. What does that idiot know about it? Does *he* deal with them?'

Her eyes filled with tears at his nastiness: 'No, but he

221

knows people who work there ... and he says they send the bailiffs in – in an instant. But the thing is, Hal, this isn't even our house. Just supposing they broke in, and damaged it?' She broke down into sobs and pressed her head against his chest. 'We might get chucked out, and have absolutely nowhere to go?'

He patted her hair impatiently: 'Dasia, for God's sake *shut up* ... You're just getting completely hysterical.'

'I'm not ... It's true ...' In vain, she pleaded and pleaded – but it only served to make him more stubborn and sure of himself.

Then he said with a big sigh, 'Look, Dasia, you've never even given me time to say that I've got that job at J & N Philips. I start a week on Monday, and I'll be paid weekly – with a week in hand. I'll be getting an official letter and a form to sign. So in another two weeks we'll be wondering why on earth we were doing all this worrying. And I'll be able to pay the garage bill in no time at all.'

She nodded miserably.

The next day at work, when she saw Algie Fanshaw again, she said, 'Mr Fanshaw, could I meet you in the square this dinner-time to ask you something ... something very important?'

'Course you can ...' Mr Fanshaw's face was plum-red with fiery enthusiasm. Then he whispered, 'Money – is it?'

She nodded self-consciously: 'Just a loan,' she whispered, 'for about two weeks. Hal will be settled in his proper job by then.'

'To pay the car repairs?'

She nodded again, then felt a slight shiver of unease ... as she felt his hand brush accidentally against her thigh.

At midday, when they were sitting on the bench in the square again, he said, 'How much was it exactly you were wanting?'

She took a deep, quivering breath, 'Twenty-three pounds, sixteen shillings and sevenpence three farthings. And I can pay you back the week after next.'

He took out a small note-book and wrote it down laboriously. 'I'll bring it for you tomorrow, then, Dasia ...'

She was so overcome by emotion and relief that she flung her arms round him and kissed him: 'Oh thank you. Thank you, Mr Fanshaw. You've saved our lives. You said all along what Brindleworth's were like, but somehow Hal just takes no notice. He doesn't seem to realise.'

'I expect once he's tucked up in bed with you at night it's all forgotten,' said Mr Fanshaw with sudden razor sharp swiftness disguised in joking slyness.

She was covered in confusion: 'Oh, no, it's not that. I mean – Well ... when we *are* in bed we –' she stopped dead, realising that she'd always evaded any crafty probings by Algie Fanshaw about her actual level of social intercourse with her 'young man', and had never breathed a word about being married or expecting a baby, for the sake of keeping her job.

'Yes?' Fanshaw was alert as a weasel. 'In bed? Then what?'

She lowered her eyes and refused to say. A terrible feeling had come over her. A feeling of disaster and the intimation that she had landed herself in the clutches not of her saviour after all but of a slowly uncoiling snake in the grass.

223

CHAPTER FOURTEEN

The Bailiffs

A few days later life was all sweetness and light, as Hal showed Dasia the letter he'd been waiting for from J & N Philips offering him employment.

'There you are ...! All our worries are over at last.'

He pressed her to him with joyous, playful kisses. But as she smiled and kissed him back her thoughts were turning to another envelope he hadn't mentioned.

'The other letter, Hal, what about that one?' She walked across to where it lay, half hidden by two small apples in a bowl; but he was there before her, and grabbed at it hastily. He knew full well who it was from and even that second was going to destroy it, only to find Dasia whipping it from his grasp as she vanished into the backyard to read it.

Her worst fears were realised ... The bailiffs would be arriving at half past ten tomorrow morning.

She went inside and flung the terrible threat towards Hal: 'Read it for God's sake!'

But he laughed and shook his head: 'It's just the

oldest con trick in the world, my angel. They wouldn't dare! And besides, our small bill is chicken feed to them. They don't employ bailiffs to collect paltry sums under fifty pounds. It wouldn't be worth it. Mark my words, we'll not hear another word. Apart from the fact, cherub, we haven't even had a police summons.'

He was so confident that her fears were allayed slightly by the time she set out for work. But as she walked along, threading her way through all the back streets in a short cut, she thought of all the people in these small houses like their own, where the strong arm of the law had caught up with them in the form of a six foot bobby in his tall black helmet, standing there with a wad of summonses on thick greyish blue paper ... 'On This Day of Our Lord ... and demanding the transgressors to appear in court for proceedings to be taken against them'.

Her spirits sank lower, for she knew that things weren't even done as formally as that ... There were always undercover thugs and hard men who managed the whole procedure quite successfully without all the official red tape.

Later that morning, with tear-rimmed eyes, she saw Algie Fanshaw and told him about the further threat; for although he'd promised to bring the money 'the next day' some days ago, it hadn't materialised and she'd tried to forget she'd ever mentioned it.

But now she knew she must take a chance. She must trust him. After all, he had always been extremely kind and cheerful to her. He'd worked at Baulden's for years, and was highly efficient and reliable, if accounts of his home life and twelve children were to be taken as gospel truth. (In spite of what Miss Davina had to say on the subject.)

'I never brought it when I said I would, Dasia,' said Mr Fanshaw, 'because I found that the wife, unknown to me, had landed us with a new mattress to be bought for our bed, and she needed the money for it immediately. But rest assured, I'll have your small loan ready for you almost this second. In fact I'll pop home at midday and bring it in. How will that suit?'

She was overcome with joy: 'What a friend in need you are, Mr Fanshaw; then I'll be able to take it round, myself, this very day to Brindleworth's garage. I'll ask Miss Davina if I can have a bit of time off this afternoon for domestic reasons, and then work extra hours later.'

And at midday, sure enough, Algie Fanshaw arrived as usual with his bait box in the canvas bag.

It was gloriously sunny but they both looked about carefully for the most secluded spot to sit and found an empty seat right in the corner under a huge sycamore tree which all the regulars had shunned – probably because of a filthy old tramp lying half buried in the grass nearby, in a grey ragged overcoat and who was either sleeping, drunk, or dead.

Mr Fanshaw opened his bag and carefully took out his brawn and pickle sandwiches, then he felt further down in the bag and produced a note book and copy ink pencil, which he slipped into his jacket pocket. Then taking a leather wallet out of his inner waistcoat he turned to Dasia and began to count out the twenty-three pounds in one-pound and five-pound notes, ending with a brown ten-shilling note, three florins, a sixpenny piece, a penny, a half-penny and one farthing from a small tobacco tin.

'There you are, Dasia, mi darlin', how does that suit?' His eyes were sparkling with happiness as he then opened his notebook, licked the tip of his copy ink pencil and wrote: 'Paid out to Miss Dasia Greenbow, as a loan', and the date. Then he asked her to sign it.

Silently and with trembling fingers she did as she was bid, as a strange and uneasy silence fell between them.

'That's it then,' he said, 'and don't worry your pretty little head too much about trying to pay it back too soon.'

'Oooh – yes, Mr Fanshaw. I promise you, it will be back in your own pocket again in less than ten days. I shall take it round to Brindleworth's right now. I've made that arrangement with Miss Davina to have some time off specially to pay the debt.'

'I 'ope you didn't tell 'er where you was getting the money from.'

'Good Gracious no! It's an entirely private matter.'

'And that's 'ow it needs to stay, mi dearie. No blabbin' of any kind. Just our own little secret, eh . . .?'

She nodded anxiously. All she needed to do now was to get away to the garage to pay the bill immediately, to forestall their threats. She began to stir, and tried to stand up, but his hand suddenly gripped her hand like a huge clamp: 'Aren't I even going to get one sign of proper lovin' thanks, Dasia? Like the time you once thanked me afore?'

She turned her face to him to try and speak, but the moment she opened her mouth she felt the full force of his heavy bristly chin grating against her skin. She shut her mouth quickly enough for him to be denied his bit of pleasure, and she felt herself going scarlet with horror and indignation. Was this how all women were treated when a man offered to help them out with a loan?

She struggled quickly to her feet: 'I shall be eternally grateful to you, Mr Fanshaw, but quite honestly I don't think it's quite right for us to be kissing in the park on this occasion. Just because I happened to kiss you once because you'd been very kind to me, doesn't mean that you can take advantage of me . . .'

Mr Fanshaw gave a huge melodramatic gasp: 'Take advantage of a chit of a young hussy like you? I never heard tell of such impudence! I just can't believe my own bloody ears that a little drubbins like you can make up such a tale about a respectable and God-fearing man like me with a wife and twelve children to care for who, out of a Christian act of mercy and compassion, took the fruits of 'is own 'ard-earned labour and bestowed on you the wherewithal to get yourself out of a very sticky situation. I just cannot believe it! Clear off – you bloody little varmint. The only time I ever want to speak to you again is when you pays me that money back as fast as you can next week.' And stuffing a huge lump of bread in his ever open gob he turned his back on her and stamped over to another seat where a rather elegant bit of fluff was sitting feeding the pigeons.

Dasia fled like wild fire from the square, covered in remorse and shame, for there was no getting away from the fact that he had come to her aid in her hour of need, and now she seemed to have wounded him deeply. Why was it she always seemed to spoil everything?

She arrived at Brindleworth's Garage in a flutter of fear and nervousness as she checked up the money, and the demand note and bill, which were all together in a fawn envelope.

Two young oil-covered mechanics in grimy blue boiler suits were playing football in the garage yard when Dasia arrived. They took not a scrap of notice. They were both imagining themselves to be young Albert Geldard, who last year made his second division debut for Bradford versus Millwall at the age of just under fifteen-and-a-half.

Dasia walked past them, dodging the hard, heavy, leather-laced ball and trying to avoid the dust and grit being swept into the dry air. She went towards a small wooden office which jutted out from the main garage, and peered through the mucky glass partition in the upper part of the rotting office door. She could hardly credit that this was a place where Lord Wrioth himself had often been a customer.

Inside, she could see a tall wooden desk with a small top and legs long enough for a person to wear stilts. It had a filthy old ink well on top and a groove along the back ledge full of pens and pencils. There was also a matching long-legged oak stool with a repaired bit of leatherette over the padded seat. And on the wall in front of it was a huge squared out calendar with a saying for each day like: 'A miser isn't much fun to live with, but he makes a wonderful ancestor', and each day was ticked off in blue pencil until the whole month was full. Hanging above it was a printed engraving of a Rolls Royce, the sort with glass partitions and speaking tubes.

Dasia stood there, still peering in. No one would think of it as the sort of place that sent the bailiffs in. It looked like it might be a casualty of the bailiffs itself ... She hovered outside the locked door uncertainly.

'Was you wantin' summat?' It was one of the boys from the football, pale and lanky with an angry red boil blooming on his forehead.

'I came to pay a bill ...'

'Mr Brindleworth's not 'ere.'

'When will he be back?'

The lad shrugged his shoulders, then the other one who was older came over: 'What's up?'

'It's a garage repair bill to pay. It's urgent.' Dasia stared at him beseechingly: 'Mr Brindleworth threatened us with the bailiffs in his letter. You can just tell your Mr Brindleworth that I think it's an absolute disgrace to threaten ordinary decent folk like that ...' Her look became challenging and the older boy gave a bored sigh, took a key from the top pocket of his boiler suit and opened the office door.

Dasia took out the fawn envelope with the money and the bill in it: 'And will you please make sure Mr Brindleworth receives it *immediately*, today, please?'

'Yes, Missus.' The boy in the office unlocked a black, metal cash box, took the money then put it in and receipted her bill: 'Thanks Missus, Tararr ...'

'You won't forget will you?' It was as if she was talking to thin air as the boy locked the door again, and within seconds was back playing football.

It had all taken about five minutes. Five minutes of complete uneventfulness. Yet when she thought of all the heartache and misery the whole event had caused right from the beginning it seemed quite mad.

She hurried back to Baulden's. Well, at least she hadn't taken too much time from her official meal break.

That night, as Dasia lay in bed, she felt a sense of relief flooding over her to know that she'd got the bill paid just in time. But it was coupled with almost agony at the way her simple friendship with Mr Fanshaw had turned out. He had saved them from a terrible fate with the bailiffs but now it appeared that he and Dasia were enemies. Perhaps she should have kissed him? Perhaps she had misunderstood his ways and all he desired was one small generous kiss of thanks for coming to her aid. Perhaps, with having so many children and such a lot to cope with, all he craved for was a small amount of affectionate acknowledgement for his goodness and understanding of the hardships of others. Then she thought of Miss Davina who called his wife his 'under-blanket', for no one could say he wasn't getting his oats ...

At breakfast the following morning Hal was cheerful and loving. The effect of him getting proper employment with a reputable firm had been wonderful, and Dasia felt that a huge black cloud had been lifted from their horizon as she set off for work. The only thing that marred her own life was having to see Mr Fanshaw when he was working in the department, knowing now

230

how much he hated her, and how she still owed him the money for another week, until they could finally afford to pay it back. There was also the fact that Hal himself hadn't even guessed that she had already paid the garage bill, for he seemed completely confident that the whole threatening exercise was a mere sham, and certainly wasted no sleepless nights over it himself. As he once said, 'Even if they did try it on, my beloved, how could they possibly rattle up even that much money from the belongings in this place, when hardly any of it is ours and belongs to Kenny Saville's Aunt Celia?'

Baulden's was pleasantly busy that morning, and everything went like clockwork. Added to which, Miss Davina was in her seventh heaven because three of her richest personal customer's (Mrs Palinthorpe's) daughters had all had offspring round about the same time, which Mrs Palinthorpe swore to Miss Davina was due to their husbands eating a lot of oysters last August. So Mrs Palinthorpe wanted all five of the infants (two sets of twins and one oversized girl called Clementina) put in Miss Davina's Glove Book.

Dasia was feeling that at last all was well with the world. Even so, she didn't chance going to sit in the square at midday, and decided to hurry home instead.

By the time she'd reached the end of the road she was quite breathless. Normally she realised she would never have been so. But at last the baby was beginning to make an extra weight in her body, even though it was not visible from the outside. She slowed down and began to walk at an ordinary pace and, as she did so she saw a group of women talking to each other, standing there in their overalls and aprons, some with head shawls on. Then to her alarm she saw as she drew nearer that they were standing right outside Tipperary.

Her whole body seemed to lurch from inside as she realised that her worst fears were about to come true.

For when she reached the women she saw that the front door of the house was wide open and almost off its hinges.

The women groaned at her as if to share her misfortune and made way for her as she walked into the house and viewed the chaos.

'Can any of us 'elp, love?'

She was lost for words. Then, swiftly, the whole picture darkened and faded away as she slumped down in the empty living room, with voices murmuring all round her and people trying to bring her round.

'You can't go back to Baulden's this afternoon – that's for certain,' said Myrtle Binks from next door as Dasia sat in the comfortable little kitchen, with its huge peg rug made out of all seventy-five-year-old Mr Binks's trousers and socks, and was mainly navy blue serge and black and grey with, here and there, a dot of red from one of Myrtle's own jumpers or a speck of bright blue from a scarf.

'Those bloody bailiffs want locking up – that's what! They're nowt but thugs and criminals! And the same goes for them as employs 'em.' She handed Dasia a mug of tea with a big spoonful of condensed milk in it: 'I expect young 'Al ud better come round 'ere when 'e gets in. 'Ow they could've done such a thing to a pair of young uns like you just beats me.'

Dasia told her about paying the bill yesterday: 'I impressed on the boys to let it be known immediately that the money was already paid ...' Then blowing caution to the winds she half sobbed, and said, 'I wouldn't mind, but I went to all the trouble of borrowing the money from a man at work to pay – just so that the bailiffs wouldn't have an excuse to do it at all. You see, Hal never even imagined they'd bother.'

'God knows where he's spent his life then,' said Mrs

Binks bitterly. Then she said with typical practicality, 'What does he like to eat? Will kippers and bread and butter do?'

Later that day, Mr and Mrs Binks and Hal and Dasia walked round the whole of Tipperary surveying the mayhem and pillage wrought by the bailiffs, for not even a bed had been left for them to sleep on; all the pots and cutlery had been taken, also a bookcase, carpet sweeper, all the chairs and every scrap of bedding. 'They've even taken my suitcase,' wept Dasia, 'a suitcase made of cardboard with only small items of personal value. What possible good could ...' She stopped suddenly and went the colour of death. She stared lifelessly at the ground not daring to look towards Hal. For she knew only too well what was hidden in the rolled-up stockings in the case; quite apart from her letter about going to seek her bequest in Canada, it was the Wrioth family heirloom – the diamond ring and the beautiful family necklace. Hal must never know, for it would surely break his heart, even though he professed not to care a fig for it except as Dasia's marital right.

'They can't get away with this!' muttered Hal in stunned disbelief, surveying the general scene. 'I'll be round to Brindleworth's right now, and if he's not there I'll go to his house and stay on his doorstep till he swears every single item will be brought back again.'

Myrtle and Lenny Binks gave each other a knowing look and shook their heads sagely. What a green young stripling he was ...

'Can Dasia stay with you, then, while I'm out?'

'Course she can, love. And so can you if it comes to you both having no bed for the night. Good Luck anyway, son. You'll certainly need it ...'

Hal drove round to Brindleworth's. What strange irony that the very item causing this furore, his own little Tin

Lizzie, was now happily chugging along there as large as life to help sort out all the trouble.

By some amazing stroke of good fortune, Brindleworth himself was still there. He was in fine fettle, sitting alone in his poky little office cabin with a bottle of Guinness and a cheese pastie – his walrus moustache covered in froth as he supped his drink.

He dragged the back of his hand hastily across his whiskers when he saw Hal: 'Hello young sir,' he joked, 'and what can we do you for? Nice weather, eh? Just had a couple of days in your neck of the woods; Chester.'

He glanced jovially towards the car. ''Ows it goin'? Good little runner, that. Should last you for years ... Thanks for settlin' up this mornin'. The lads let me know.'

Hal stared at him in a befuddled haze, and wondered if he'd gone crackers. How on earth could Brindleworth be looking so damned perky?

'I 'ear 'is Lordship's not been too well then? Sorry to 'ear about that. Mrs Brindleworth's sister Maureen's daughter who's in service in those parts, knows Elvers's wife Enid ... Would you like a sup of Guinness while you're here, sir?'

Hal nodded like a floundering flat fish. He needed something for the shock, as Brindleworth produced a glass and filled it with a rich dark liquid.

Hal finished it in two long gulps and said, 'Mr Brindleworth, I've called to see you on a very, very serious matter which I can only regard as an almost totally unbelievable and ghastly mistake.' He hesitated for a few seconds to let it all sink in: 'When I got home today I found that our house had been entered unlawfully. The door had been deliberately broken off its hinges to get in, and all our belongings had been removed ... In *your* name, Mr Brindleworth ...'

234

Mr Brindleworth looked totally stunned: 'I ... I – Well, bless me ... I just don't understand, sir – I ...' He wiped his brow with his hanky and was thoroughly flustered: 'Are you quite sure?'

'*Sure?* Of course I'm sure! And I'm so furious, Mr Brindleworth, that I shall be seeing my lawyer first thing tomorrow to bring charges against you for illegal entry, gross damage and robbery.'

''Old on there, son. There must be some bloody awful mistake! Never, sir, would I do such a thing to anyone coming from a family of your standin'. There's been some awful blunder. I was entirely unaware of any of it.'

With trembling hands he reached for a heavy dust-covered ledger from the small shelf and looked inside, muttering that his chief clerk Charlie Moffit now dealt with all this sort of stuff: 'It's mi eyesight, see, sir ... Cataracts. You see, Mr Wrioth, sir, I just can't cope with it all any more an' I 'as to trust others. I 'ad no idea it was goin' on ... And you'd even paid the bloody bill today, an' all. I'd a never sent bailiffs in for summat as paltry as that!'

'Exactly,' said Hal smoothly. 'So you'll need to get all the stuff back tonight, or my pregnant wife and I won't have a bed to sleep on. Where will it all be?'

'Stoway's Warehouse. I'll get in touch right this bloody second, sir. I'll even go round if needs be and get the damned key to the place from Cyril Stoway 'imself. An' I'll get the lads to 'elp us shift it all back. I can't apologise enough, sir.'

Later that night, Dasia and all the neighbours were amazed to see a huge brown pantechnicon drawn by two cart-horses slowly draw up outside Tipperary. Then Hal got out, followed by a stocky little man in glasses with a walrus moustache, another man like a prize wrestler with a face like a bulldog and bow legs, and two callow youths in boiler suits. Silently, with expressionless faces

235

similar to those of experienced poker players, they moved all the furniture back into the house again and muttered something about coming back next day to do repairs to the front door and any other accidental damage.

'Well I never!' gasped Mrs Binks to her husband: 'It's the first time since The Creation I've ever known this to happen after the bailiffs've been.' Then she turned to Dasia and said, 'Pr'aps your 'Al isn't as soft as we took 'im for.'

Dasia gave a deep sigh of heartfelt relief, it was all back to normal at last ... except for one small secret thing that no one on earth except herself must know about: her own little cardboard suitcase with the most important items of her life locked away inside it, in an old envelope and a rolled-up stocking. What was their fate?

By two in the morning she and Hal were safely installed in their own bed again, with great jubilation from the neighbours. But as they lay there, Hal said slowly, 'The only thing that puzzles me is how you managed to pay that bill?'

A nervous lump came to her throat: 'Don't get upset Hal, but I borrowed the money. I just had to, for my own peace of mind ... even though it didn't quite work out. A man at work lent it me.'

He sat up suddenly. 'You ... WHAT?' He tried to roar the words at her angrily, but the act was too tiring: 'You're a little fool, Dasia. I told you all along it would be all right. Why don't you ever trust me?' Then he turned away from her and left her to weep silently to herself in the night.

The next morning, Dasia asked Mrs Binks if she'd keep a look out for the men supposed to be coming to do the repairs: 'I hope they arrive on time, Myrtle; you know what they're like. They never seem to arrive when you're expecting them, and we need it all shipshape as soon as possible, before Miss Celia Saville gets wind of it. For sure as eggs are eggs the news'll travel . . .'

'Don't you worry, dearie, you've had enough to think about these past few weeks. Just you get to your proper work at Baulden's. It's as well you've got good employment these days, especially with you being such a young girl. I'm amazed they took someone so young to work in Gloves; it's usually slightly older people. Anyway, love, it'll feel like a complete rest – being there for a bit – after all this lot last night. I'll look after things, so don't worry.'

Just before midday at Baulden's, Dasia was surprised to get a message from Miss Davina that Mr Mildew wanted to see her in his office. Whatever could it be?

Even Miss Davina was puzzled: 'He rarely asks to see people again – once they've been interviewed and employed,' she said, 'unless it's to be dismissed, or promoted. And I don't think either of those options could possibly apply to you, Dasia.' Then fixing Dasia with her eagle eye she said bluntly, 'You wouldn't be pregnant, would you?'

Dasia felt her whole body going crimson, but before she could say anything Miss Davina said, 'Your secret is safe with me, dear. I've been in this department a very long time, you know. But I'll tell you this much, there'll be others only too glad to get someone else in your shoes and I should be very sad indeed if that happened, because you've been one of the best girls I've ever had working here. All my best customers speak very well of you.'

Then she said, 'I hope you won't think I'm being impertinent, but I noticed Mr Fanshaw making himself rather familiar with you, and although he appears very willing and friendly he once got a girl sacked from here after she'd borrowed some money from him that she couldn't pay back. Everybody blamed the girl, of course, and it was years ago but I've never trusted him from that day onwards. He and Mr Mildew are like blood brothers.'

Then Miss Davina walked stiffly away without another word.

'Come in ... Ah ... Miss Greenbow. You got my message?' Mr Mildew was smiling at her with his moist mouth full of hungry-looking fangs: 'No need to look so worried. Take a seat ...'

She perched herself on the edge of one of the familiar brown bentwood chairs.

'I was wondering if you could do me a favour this afternoon, Miss Greenbow. Miss Taylor in Travel Goods has to be away for a couple of hours, and I was wondering if you could help out ...? Only for a couple of hours mind you. You'll have Miss Lawson to help you if you need anything. That's all. You can go.'

She nodded, stood up – and went. But when she got back to Gloves and told Miss Davina, Miss Davina seemed to think it was all exceedingly strange.

'Never have I known that happen before, Dasia. And why haven't I, as head of the gloves department, been consulted about *my* staff requirements while you are away? I just don't like it. It seems very fishy to me. Anyway, all you can do is do as you're told in this case, and we'll just have to manage without you for a couple of hours ...'

For Dasia, two hours in Travel Goods was not a thing to look forward to after delicate Gloves. There were large displays of big cabin trunks and heavy leather suitcases and round patent leather and leatherette hat boxes, and special leather creams to polish your suit-cases. There were travelling irons you could put tablets in to heat them up, and great big wooden parasols, and mosquito nets and jars of cream for insect bites; all at prices that were beyond the pocket of any normal person.

And along the back of the department, close to where the long mahogany counter was, and the wires where the metal money cylinders trundled to and fro across the ceiling to the accounts kiosk, were about six screens all painted and designed with holiday scenes of sea and mountains and golf courses and tennis courts and boating, sailing and yachting.

And high up above all these colourful screens, was Algie Fanshaw, industriously cleaning the windows ...

Miss Lawson smiled at Dasia politely, then she whispered, 'I just can't think what's come over Mr Mildew – sending you to stand about here for a couple of hours when you need to be in your own department. We're quite slack this afternoon, and we've had much busier times when people in Travel Goods have been off, with no extra help whatsoever!'

Dasia smiled back, then just for something to say she remarked, 'I like all the screens with the holiday scenes on them.'

Letty Lawson nodded a bit mournfully, then she pointed to a small seaside bit on one of the screens with a rather highly painted and slightly wobbly yellow and purple beach ball glowing from it: 'That hideous thing,' she whispered, 'was painted on extra by Mr Fanshaw's eldest daughter Mildred who's sixteen and fancies herself as an artist. She was working as a nanny but it hardly lasted two minutes, because she was too clever for her job and refused to scrub floors. Anyway, with Algie working here so long ...' (She glanced up to Algie on his ladder and lowered her voice even further) 'he's asked Mr Mildew if she can start training here as soon as there's a vacancy. She painted that ball on the screen when all the rest of us had gone home, to show Mr Mildew just how artistic she is and how she'd make a good window dresser, and such ...'

Then Miss Lawson who was anything but artistic said, 'The reason I like the screens really, is that you can keep such a lot of junk behind them, and I can go there and hitch mi garters up or make mi corsets looser.'

Dasia stood there behind the counter wishing it would be a bit busier, and then because there wasn't a thing going on she walked over to the screen where the painted beach ball was, and stared at it idly. She was convinced that anyone even in the Greenbow family could have made a better job of something like that.

'Our Mildred did that,' said a voice right behind her shoulder. 'Did you get everything sorted out then, Dasia? Sorry if I was a bit off 'and with you when you last spoke to me but I 'ad a lot on mi mind. The wife 'asn't been too good recently. Did you get done what you wanted to then?'

'Yes thank you, Mr Fanshaw. It all went very well and I shall always be grateful to you. In fact I'll be able to pay you back straight away tomorrow as my husband is now settled into a proper job. He said I should never have borrowed it from you.'

Fanshaw's expression changed to a wary scowl: 'There was no need to 'ave told 'im ... People doin' good deeds feel fools if it's blarted out all over t' place, and anyways wasn't you off yesterday afternoon? Someone said as you fainted over and 'ad to be taken in by a neighbour.'

An expression of hypocritical innocence swept over his huge face, and it was now Dasia's turn to be wary as he said, 'I didn't know you was actually *married*, Dasia ... I allus thowt it was yer boy friend ye lived with. Ye must be quite a young pair I reckon.'

Dasia fell into his trap like the spider and the fly. She

turned to him and said, 'We aren't absolute children, you know, Mr Fanshaw. Hal's nineteen, and I'm seventeen. And there's many another young couple started a family at that age. Lots of people have slight fainting fits at the beginning, and by the time it arrives I'll probably be eighteen ...' As she finished speaking she knew by his face she had burned her boats, even more so as Mr Mildew himself suddenly appeared from behind one of the screens close to them.

'Everything all right, Miss Greenbow? Just thought I'd pop along to see how you were coping. Especially with you being off work yesterday. Mr Fanshaw here seemed to be a bit worried about you. Forgive me, but did I accidentally overhear you say something about the delights of expecting a little one later in the year?' Mr Mildew's dark eyes positively glittered. Then he murmured, 'I expect you do know the rules about that. Your sister will have told you ... No mothers-to-be are ever employed here and, of course, it goes without saying no one under the age of twenty-one is employed as an assistant, except for young trainee girls – such as Mr Fanshaw's sixteen-year-old daughter might be. Is that quite clear Miss Greenbow?'

'Quite clear thank you, Mr Mildew.' Dasia stared at the two older men. She was no match for them whatsover, especially as she knew all along that she'd claimed to be older than she was on Louise's instructions.

'Do you think I could go back to my own department now, please, Mr Mildew? It's very quiet here, and Miss Davina always needs help.'

'She certainly does, Miss Greenbow, and when you get back you'd better tell her that you'll be working a week's notice, and that your place will be taken by a trainee assistant called Miss Mildred Fanshaw – and that if she likes to come to my office immediately I'll explain it all.' Then both he and Algie disappeared behind the screens together and Dasia, with a pale, tear-stained face, went back to the Gloves department.

'Never mind dear,' said Miss Davina when she'd listened to the whole squalid story, and they'd both had a nip of Miss Davina's cold tea. 'You'll be much better off at home – especially now your husband's got a proper job at last. A home of her own is where every young mother should be – to prepare a really good nest for her little ones.'

But when Dasia got home to Tipperary again at the end of that memorable day she found that dreams of her nest had fast flown.

CHAPTER FIFTEEN

The Sack

A week's notice ...

All the way back to Tipperary it thudded in Dasia's head. The tables had turned. It was now her fate instead of Hal's.

Well, at least there was one good thing – she'd just got that money paid in time or it would have been even more of a catastrophe.

Mrs Binks was very tactful with her when she got back from work; she told Dasia the good news first ...

'They came as soon as you'd gone, dearie, and fixed up the door and all. And not a moment too soon either – because five minutes later along came Miss Saville. She's a sweet old thing, really, and she had a nice cup of tea with me and a chat. She asked how you were both going on, and said she was glad she'd been able to help at a time when you needed it most.'

With gloomy patience Dasia waited to hear the worst ...

'... Of course, love, we've known Celia Saville round 'ere for donkey's years. She owns streets of 'ouses and is a very good landlord, and very religious. She's always willing to 'elp those in a bit of distress.

'She wasn't 'alf mad when she heard about the bloody bailiffs ...' Myrtle hesitated. 'Someone must have given her the tip-off even before it took place, for her to be here so quick this morning, complete with 'er Bible.

'Anyways – I don't really know as I should be tellin' you all this, Dasia – but she seems to be of a mind that you and 'Al will 'ave to be lookin' round for summat else ...'

Dasia stared at her: 'Something else? How do you mean – something else? This is our home – and I'm expecting a baby. Surely she wouldn't turf us out *now*?'

Mrs Binks looked slightly rattled, for basically she saw the situation quite differently. She had brought up a big family herself and had lived in the same house for years right next door to this cheap haven that Celia Saville provided for those in need. She had seen tramps, alcoholics, starving abandoned mothers, badly done-to women of the street, demented and stranded old men and women and young people on the verge of nervous breakdowns – all being given a bit of a break under the roof next door. But that was all it was; a bit of support on life's ladder to heaven. And she'd also seen how often those who were the best off, and the fittest, always wanted to stay in the house as if it was now theirs for ever – even forgetting that they lived there for next to nothing.

'I don't suppose she'll turf you out without any warning at all, love, but I know she did say she was looking for somewhere to put a poor woman and her three little ones who'd been recently widowed and was absolutely penniless, and 'ad bin in 'ospital, for the removal of a growth.'

Mrs Binks saw consternation sweep across Dasia's pretty young face.

'How awful ... It's made me feel quite guilty. It's true

enough, Mrs Binks. Hal and I are going to be much better off, now he's getting the job at J & N Philips, and I know for certain that my own family would always take us in, at a pinch. But you must know yourself what it's like living with your relatives – all squashed up, Mrs Binks – when all you long for is a place to start off a family of your own.'

Myrtle nodded silently. She knew only too well as she gazed at the golden red curls and the honest young eyes. Ah, me ... It was hard to find how cruel life could be, and easy to forget that even here in the busy city streets they were mostly a lot better off than some poor devils.

'Anyway – don't bother yourself too much, Dasia, dear. It hasn't happened yet. And Lenny and me's enjoyed being of 'elp in the short time you've been 'ere. An' I 'ope we'll always remain good friends.' Then she put some more hot water in the tea-pot from the kettle on the kitchen hob and popped the woolly tea cosy back on it.

Celia Saville removed Dasia and Hal with the utmost politeness. She didn't come round to see them or even send them a letter, but it so happened that she invited her great nephew Kenny round for afternoon tea, and they had a delicious, oozing, jammy cream sponge cake together and a small glass of non-alcoholic fruit wine, while she explained about the woman with three children who'd just had the operation for a growth – and needed somewhere to live.

'Operation for a growth?' said Kenny suddenly alive with interest. 'What sort was it? Some of those fibroids can be big enough to cut a loaf of bread on. I sincerely hope she won't have had old Ruxtable's golden boy Doctor Slicer on the job.' His cheerful smile faded as he saw Celia hastily put some smelling salts to her nose.

A few days later, Hal happened to meet Kenny Saville

in town and Kenny told him about how his aunt had this very deserving case, but was too polite to mention it. 'I expect if you could both manage to clear out, old fruit, it would make matters a bit simpler all round. Would the end of the month do? Give you a bit of time and all that jazz ... And you'll be well ensconced by then if you've got this new job with some proper prospects.

'You don't know how much I envy you, old bean. Every night I have nightmares at that place about some old buffer chasing me round the ward with the wrong leg I cut off by mistake ...'

Working her week's notice was a nightmare for Dasia, and although Miss Davina and Dasia's friends among the other girls were loyal and sympathetic, she still felt a sense of deep shame at being sacked – especially when she fancied others had taken umbrage at the way she'd deceived them about her age and were walking past her and looking the other way.

As for Mr Mildew, he ignored her just as if she wasn't there, and seemed to spend a lot of time with Algie Fanshaw's daughter – showing her the ropes, before she started work in Dasia's place next Monday.

'Not long to go now, ay – Dasia?' said Fanshaw on the Thursday of Dasia's final week, while he was in Gloves checking a bit of fallen plaster from round a light fitting.

At first she didn't reply. She was so staggered that he was talking to her as if nothing bad had ever happened. And deep down she also felt perpetually guilty because she hadn't yet paid him back the money she owed him. It was proving harder to get it together than she'd imagined. For although Hal now had his new job he had to work a week in hand – and that meant living for a week still with no money.

Algie's powerful, confident voice boomed out: 'I was

just saying – you've not got long to go . . .'

'Er – no. Not long. It's the last day tomorrow. I shall be quite sorry.' Then, impulsively, she said, 'I'm sure your daughter'll like it in Gloves, Mr Fanshaw. Miss Davina is terribly kind and helpful. And what she doesn't know about gloves isn't worth knowing.'

He grunted, and lowered his voice: 'She's getting a bit too old for that job, Miss Dasia. She's part of a bygone age. Our young Mildred'll make two of her.' Then in the same breath he said, 'I'm right glad I managed to 'elp you in your hour of need, anyways. Will you be bringing it in tomorrer then? Mi wife'll be needing it for house budgeting. Oh she's a terrible one, the wife, Dasia. The 'ardest worker on earth but also the 'ardest woman on earth.

'I've seen times – all this is confidential, mind – when she's let fly with a solid iron pan at those that don't suit 'er. And there's nowt she dislikes more'n folks what don't pay up their debts – smartish. I'm just telling you now, Miss Greenbow, 'cos I don't want you to be shocked if she finds 'er way round to your place out of the blue . . . You understand?'

Dasia's heart began to quicken with a mixture of anger and fear: 'Yes, I quite understand, Mr Fanshaw, and I can't thank you enough for how you came to my aid. I truly, truly appreciate it and I can assure you – you'll be paid back in full.'

'Paid in full?' his voice became sneering and nasty. 'I should ruddy well thinks so, girl, or else there'll be a bit of interest to pay an' all!

'A working man like me isn't just a soft touch you know. There's not many men as ud come to the aid of a feather-headed female up to her eyes in debt. And there's certainly none as I knows of oo wouldn't expect to see some sort of return or thanks on the loan.

'Oh no, Miss Dasia, I'm not God an' I've never tried

to be. All I am is a yooman being, what likes to help others more 'elpless than 'is self, if and when required. So think on ...' And with these last warning words he picked up some ladders and left the department.

Dasia was now in a fever of terror. How on earth was she going to pay him by tomorrow, her last day at Baulden's?

That evening just as they'd finished their tea back at home she decided with heavy misgivings to mention it to Hal – who was now on the crest of a wave, with prosperity just round the corner.

'Hal ...'

The tone of her voice made him look up from the *Evening News*: 'What is it this time, Dasia? Surely not more trouble from That Place. I'll be glad when you're completely rid of it and can be a proper housewife.'

'I'll be rid of it the moment I've paid back all the car repairs money to Mr Fanshaw. He's expecting it tomorrow morning or his wife's coming round to beat us in with her iron cooking pan.'

'Like hell she is,' muttered Hal going back to the paper. 'The trouble with that type is that once they do you a bit of a favour they think they've bought you for life.'

'But he really was serious, Hal.'

'And I'm serious, too, Dasia. So he'll just have to wait for it, won't he? What's wrong with the man? Got ants in his pants?'

'He did help us, Hal ... I was desperate at the time.'

'Well you needn't have been. Your problem is, you take on matters which are well above your head that you know nothing about. Always refer all money problems to me. I'll soon sort them out. That Fanshaw bloke's got a bloody cheek getting at you all the time for a few paltry pounds.

'He should never have offered them in the first place.

Just ignore him. And we'll wait until he and his wife *do* arrive at the door with the old saucepan; preferably before we're out on the street again at the end of the month.' Hal smiled broadly, as his newly found confidence bubbled like a piping hot geyser.

But as Dasia cleared the table and began to wash the pots she knew she just had to try and find her own solution, just as she had with the car repairs; for her own peace of mind.

She swished her hands about in the soap suds. Maybe – after she'd dried the dishes – she should try catching a tram to The Grove and having a few words with Andrina about borrowing the money from her, for at least Andrina wouldn't be threatening her as soon as it was borrowed ...

But there again, would Andrina have such a large sum immediately available? She'd never known Andrina to carry such an amount unless it was to take it to the bank from the pawn shop.

And then if she got back there and they all started fussing and wanting to know what all the bother was about the fat really would be in the fire.

She sank back on a small hard kitchen chair, in a sudden wave of hopelessness. She was living in cloud cuckooland even to think of rushing round there this evening. It would take ages to get there for a start, and Hal would want to know what on earth she was up to.

Perhaps she should just try and relax and forget it all, and if she saw Mr Fanshaw tomorrow just tell him that she'd call in with the money as soon as possible. Above all she must have faith in Hal and do exactly what he said, which was to take no notice.

But all the time her conscience kept pricking her as she remembered how thankful she'd been for the loan and what anguish it had saved her, and how she'd so earnestly promised to pay him back within about ten days – if not before.

Then in the end she resigned herself to a compromise. She had at least to be practical, and she knew that what she needed above all else at the moment after working all day was a rest, and let tomorrow take care of itself. In the background another more reasonable idea presented itself – Maybe Aunt Dolly would help her ... she always seemed to have money concealed somewhere.

When she awoke next morning with the sun showing slightly and heralding good weather, it was as if all her worries of the night before had completely vanished – especially when Hal kissed her and said that today was celebration day, because she would be leaving Baulden's for ever ...

And that day at work, although she was on tenter-hooks with nervousness all morning, she saw never a sign of Algie Fanshaw or his ever present daughter. Neither did she see Mr Mildew and someone told her that Mildred was at home resting a sprained elbow and both the men had gone off to visit an industrial plumbing exhibition at the Free Trade Hall.

'Which means, dear,' said Miss Davina to Dasia, 'that when it's quiet we can have a nice little farewell party for you, without snoopers about.' And true to her word she produced a bottle of sparkling non-alcoholic grape wine and some petits fours for all of them, plus a present for Dasia – not to be opened till she was back home. At the end of the day Dasia departed with kisses all round and her eyes full of tears for all the kindness and happy memories, as she went home earlier than usual.

The moment she was back at Tipperary, she wrote a note to Hal saying she'd gone to Dolly's on an errand and not to worry as she'd be back soon, and it was cold salad for tea. Then, making herself a quick cup of tea and sitting down to rest her feet while it cooled down, she unwrapped her present from Miss Davina and the rest of them.

It was a beautiful pair of pale cream, kid gloves with 'good luck for the future' written on a small white card, and on the other side of the card was written: 'Your guardian angel from heaven above's/sure to like you in these gloves.'

She smiled, and dabbed the corner of her eyes to stop the tears. Then she got up and went to Dolly's.

'To be perfectly candid, you've come at a very bad time, dear,' said Dolly with a red sweating face as she hurried round in her pinny getting the evening meal prepared. 'I've had interruptions galore today. First the gas man about a suspected leaking pipe in the road who sat down and smoked all my cigarettes – and told me how dangerous it was to smoke cigarettes near leaking gas pipes. Then along came Mr Watts the window cleaner wanting boiling water for his billycan, so he could stir in his tea and condensed milk from his little paper packet. Then Marcia called round to say one of her maids had fallen down the attic stairs. And now *you've* arrived ... so here's a bowl of carrots to peel. Sit yourself down and make yourself useful.' Then she rushed away again, as the phone began to ring in fits and starts.

'That, believe it or not, was your Hal asking if you were here. He says he'll call and bring you home in about an hour. What a kind man. Be quick and tell me what you want, for nobody ever visits me without wanting summat – except Marcia for a gossip.'

Dasia felt as if she'd had the wind taken out of her sails. She viewed Hal's phone call and instructions with mixed feelings. It was a relief to know she wouldn't have to trail all the way back under her own steam but on the other hand she felt a bit like a naughty child who'd escaped; especially with Dolly being in such a rush. And no doubt the next demeaning thing to happen would be their Tommy suddenly arriving back from Westinghouse and asking her what the devil *she* was doing there. And if he found out he'd go and tell them all, back in The Grove.

Then, to her profound relief, Dolly said, 'Well at least there's one good thing, I've got two less for the evening meal; Mr Corcoran's gone to Stoke-on-Trent, on business, and your Tommy's found himself a girlfriend and gone round there for his tea. So what is it, Dasia love? You're peeling them carrots *very* slow ... What's wrong? – but be very quick.'

Then she hurried across to the kitchen dresser and, getting some plates, said, 'Is it to borrow something? I can always sense when people want to borrow.'

Dasia was just going to admit it, and stutter out her requirements when in rushed Marcia in a welter of rapturous excitement: 'You'll never believe it, Dolly, but Mr Frandle's won me five pounds on the greyhounds! There was one running called Merryfield Marcia and he put me a bob on it as a rank outsider. Wasn't it honest of him to give me the winnings? I think it's because I've put him in that large double bedroom, while I'm decorating – and he wants to stay there. Would you like him to put you any money on, the next time? He says there's one running next week called Dolly Daydream, but he needs the money first.'

'I'll let you know later, Marcia.' They gave each other a meaningful stare: 'I've got Dasia here at the moment ...' Then Dolly pushed her hurriedly out and there was a bit of whispering in the hall.

Dolly came back and, with a big sigh, sat down at last: 'Now what's it all about, love?'

In seconds the whole sorry tale came pouring out of Dasia like the Niagara Falls as she told Dolly all about the car repairs bill and about Mr Fanshaw and the loan, and how he was now about to turn nasty, and how Hal seemed impervious to people demanding money from them.

'And now I really need to try by some means to get almost twenty-five pounds together right away, aunty – before he comes round with his wife to harass us. And it's all very well for Hal to say not to worry, because *he'll* be at work when it happens and I'll be the one who'll have to suffer it all – even though I definitely know Mr Fanshaw'll get paid as soon as Hal's wages all get running smoothly. But with me having left Baulden's an' all, it probably looks to Mr Fanshaw like I've gone for good – complete with the money he lent me.'

Aunty Dolly looked Dasia over carefully, and frowned. Then without saying a word she disappeared and came back carrying a bundle of Bank of England Notes, a notebook and a copy ink pencil just like Algie Fanshaw's. 'Sit down and put your feet up, love, while we sort it out.

'Those ankles of yours are beginning to swell a bit ... Have you felt any movements yet? I'll bet you any money it's a boy. They're more tender to rear when they're born than girls. How much was it you wanted? I'll make it the straight twenty-five, but you'll have to start paying it back as soon as Hal gets settled down, at ten shillings a week. Just drill that into him will you, love? And tell him that Aunty Dolly can't stand them as don't pay their debts immediately. I feel quite sorry for that marvellous gentleman, Mr Fanshaw. Of *course* he wants it back quickly, Dasia, and so would anyone else in their right mind. And obviously you knew how to correct him when he started to get a bit heated down below – so there's no real harm done. Anyway, let's say no more about it – and it's our little secret as far as all the other Greenbows are concerned.'

253

The parting was hasty as Hal's small car drew up outside. Dolly excused herself from meeting him because she said she had to attend to her gentlemen – but also because she was furious underneath at the way he had treated Dasia by being so bone-headed.

'What the hell was that great dramatic dash to Dolly's in aid of?' said Hal on the way home.

Dasia pretended not to hear, and countered it with: 'Aunt Dolly says she thinks we'll have a little boy. They're supposed to be harder to rear than girls.'

'What absolute utter piffle!' said Hal in disgust as he proceeded to give her a lecture on obstetrics, as learnt as a student.

She sat there in quiet contentment as he rattled on with the whole nine months' gestation period of the human being ending by saying that it took elephants nearly two years to perform the same task. And by the time they got back he had entirely dismissed from his mind the reason for Dasia wanting to visit Dolly.

The very next morning, when Dasia was busy washing some clothes and trying not to worry too much about what was going to happen to Hal and herself at the end of the month when they had to find somewhere else to live, her worst fears were realised when she was confronted at the front door by Algie Fanshaw.

'Just got a Saturday morning hour off, Miss Dasia. One what was owing – same as you owe me that money, my dear.'

He was beaming all over his coy, bulging face as he enquired about her health and said how sorry he was she'd had to leave, and what a pity they'd missed each other yesterday, and what a lot of huge pipes there were at the plumbing exhibition.

'Baulden's won't be the same without you, Miss Greenbow. I shall really miss our friendship in the park ... and the way I was there to help you – just when you wanted it.'

His voice sounded so smooth and menacing that she went quite weak, even though she knew the money was there in the drawer waiting to be paid and that she'd planned to take it in to him on Monday.

Then, without warning, he pushed his great heavy boot through the front door and tried to step inside.

Her anger was so great that she instinctively barred his way with her own small foot and gave his boot a meaningful jab. 'Just put it back on the other side of that step, Mr Fanshaw, if you don't mind. My husband doesn't approve of people trying to force an entry. Wait there if you please while I go and sort out the money.'

He stood there grinning at her. The faint tap against his boot amused him and he was pretty sure she was up a gum tree at the moment with regard to his money ... But he could afford to give her another few weeks before he put on any real pressure. They were marvellous at that age when they were roused ...

Dasia rushed into the backyard and fortunately Mrs Binks was out in her own yard scrubbing a mat.

'Yes of course I'll come, this minute, love. He always was a cheeky devil. My brother Terry knows the whole family. Yes, of course I'll witness you paying him back the money. You just can't be too careful these days.'

They got back inside Dasia's not a moment too soon and found Algie already inside the living room, smiling smugly and sitting on the one and only best chair with a lascivious glint in his eye. His face fell a mile when he saw Myrtle Binks.

'Hello Algie, how's your wife? Still slaving away at all those marble floors and brass door knobs?'

He grunted gloomily as Dasia counted out the money on to the table and Myrtle watched it all. And this time it was Dasia who was first out with the copy ink pencil and notebook as she entered the date and fact that she'd just paid Algernon Fanshaw his money back in full – signed and witnessed by Dasia Greenbow and Myrtle Binks and not forgetting grateful thanks at the end. And Algie slid away looking thoroughly disgruntled.

Living with in-laws is not always the rosiest of situations, and Hal found this out to his cost as he and Dasia finally accepted a begrudging invitation from Horace and Alice Greenbow, to go and stay there for a bit till they were properly sorted out.

Everything was now in the open ... Alice accepted that her granddaughter was now a sort of married woman, even though Gretna Green was about the last sort of send-off she have wished on anyone. But it was better than nothing for a young girl with a babby inside of her.

But in the background, she privately simmered and nagged at poor old Horace so much that his latest design for a small electric washing machine was perpetually hampered; so much so that he could hardly invent anything practical at all except an imaginary device for shutting women up.

'I mean, Horace, I just can't bloody well credit it! It comes to summat when Andrina and me's still sweating away at the pawn shop and she's living here like Lady Muck with Hal. I wouldn't mind, but he's even worse than she is. He'd be quite 'appy to 'ave us all standin' on our 'eads for 'im – if we let 'im. And 'e's got an appetite like six damned horses. Yet never once has he offered to wash or dry a perishing plate in this establishment since the minute they landed themselves on our doorstep ...'

'Pr'aps they're just bein' tactful, love. You know you like to organise all that sort of thing yourself. Even I know that it's best to keep out of the way rather than try to be helpful when you're not wanted. 'Ow many times 'ave you told me to get out of t'road, or get from under your feet int' kitchen?'

'Yes, but you do help when it's required, Horace. And another thing – it's not good for our Dasia to be moping about round here all day long when everyone's out, now she's got the sack from Baulden's. I did hear tell from the midwife t'other day that scrubbing floors is good for pregnant women because all fours is the natural way to carry the baby. It takes the weight off the spine, and we yoomans wasn't ever supposed to have walked upright in the first place. She said it stretches the perineum and makes birth easier ...'

'What in heaven's name is the Perry-knee-um then, Alice? It's a new one on me, that is.'

'And me, love, but I think it's to do with our backsides, or in this case the second opening us women 'as where the baby comes out ...' And after this, thankfully, silence descended.

A couple of days later the gramophone in Horace's ear was getting even louder ... 'She just lolls about in the garden the whole day, Horace. Surely you can see 'er? That awful striped bathing costume Andrina gave her from the market and guzzling condensed milk and banana sandwiches as fast as she can get them, with never a bath robe to cover her state ... her belly's beginning to show for anyone looking out of a window.

'As soon as our Rosalie gets back from the Servants Registry tonight I'll ask if she can find her a nice little sitting down job out of harm's way 'elping out.'

And that night, in the old sewing room at The Grove, Alice Greenbow put her full weight on Rosalie in a threatening plea to take Dasia off her hands and carry her off each day to Sale, to work at the Servant Registry.

Rosalie was absolutely horrified: 'I can't possibly do it, Mother. It would ruin my whole, working schedule – especially when I'm just learning to use a typewriter, and we're very busy.'

'There you are then!' said Alice in triumph. 'This is

just the time you need her. She can do some filing, and answer the telephone, while you get on with learning your typewriting.'

It's not at simple as that, Mother,' said Rosalie icily. 'You make it sound as if I just go there each day to play about. There's a lot more to a servant employment agency than that, and I don't for one second think that Miss Edith and Miss Tabitha would want to employ her ... and even if they did she'd get even less than she did working in the pawn shop. And you know what Dasia's like – always expecting to be paid nearly as much as a man, even though she's still a chit of a girl with no proper experience.'

But luck was on Alice's side for the very next day Rosalie came back from work and announced that Tabitha and Edith, who ran the Servants Registry, were booked up for a trip across to the Isle of Man for two weeks with their lodger, Mr Bates, as his birthday surprise, and that Dasia could go and help, immediately.

'Just what you need,' said Hal when Dasia told him the news. For even he seemed to think she would be better off in a job of some sort – especially after seeing a man with some binoculars trained on her striped bathing costume one day.

Everyone was delighted – even Andrina, still toiling away in the pawn shop and dwelling rather morbidly on the fact that in a few months she would actually be a grandmother.

Suddenly the bell on the door of the pawn shop rattled and rang, and a very scruffy little urchin of about ten came furtively towards the counter.

Andrina stared at him suspiciously. People were up to all sorts of tricks ... like the old one of one person engaging you in conversation whilst another one cleared the decks of all your most treasured objects.

She waited a few seconds. 'Yes ...?'

The boy's pale face looked drawn and nervous. He had bare feet, torn trousers, and wore a filthy old jersey. He was clutching a small cardboard suitcase.

'Wanna buy a good case, missus? Only tuppence ...?' he looked at her pleadingly.

Andrina shook her head firmly. You had to be tough in this line of trade, no matter how heart-breaking the picture on the other side of the counter, or you'd sink out of sight yourself. Yet she just couldn't help staring at the case ... It was as if she knew it, as if she had always known it.

'Let's have a look, then. Where's it from?'

'Mi bruvver found it, missus, lyin' on a dump. Mi bruvver can read, see. It was 'im as told me to bring it 'ere. It's a very good case, Missus. Mi mam's sick and there's no food. Mi brother said fourpence, but ...'

She took the case and opened it. Inside was an envelope addressed to the shop. She peered inside and gently tugged at the folded letter. Yes, it was the self-same one, the one written by Adrien Shawfield to her father! In a corner of the case were some of Dasia's stockings, rolled up, some of the ones she'd given her ... A sudden cold shiver ran down her spine it was so uncanny.

'Here –' She rummaged in the big pocket of her canvas apron and drew out a sixpenny piece: 'Tell your brother – thank you very much for returning our lost property.' Then she said, 'Wait there and don't move an inch.'

The boy stood like a statue as she hurried to her bag, took out her lunch of meat sandwiches from it, and an apple – and gave them to him: 'Take these as well.'

When he'd vanished she looked again into the case and felt the stockings to see if they were damp from being left somewhere, and as she did so she felt a hardness inside them; something was wrapped there.

Her long fingers fished out the small leather drawstring bag, and as she looked inside she went quite faint ... What on earth were jewels like that doing in Dasia's small suitcase? Had they been specially placed there by a fence trading in hot goods? Perhaps it was left in a certain spot to pass on its rich, secret contents – and this ragged, half-starved child and his brother had unwittingly blown the plan.

Should she inform the police?

That night, when she got back to The Grove, she decided first to have a word about it with her lawyer fiancé, Sammy Tankerton, but just as she was getting ready after tea to go round to his house, she came face to face with Dasia in the hall.

Dasia stood stock still and gazed with disbelieving amazement at her suitcase: 'Where on earth did that come from? It was lost when the bailiffs broke in. I thought it had gone for ever!'

'It came into the shop today, brought by a young child. He wanted twopence for it.'

'Twopence! Is it empty?' Dasia held her breath ...

'Nearly. It had that letter in of Father's. I was going to give it him back, and ...' her rather plain face looked troubled, 'it had someone else's property in it – robbery stuff ... jewels: a very good diamond ring and a wonderful necklace. At first I was going to inform the police, then I thought I'd mention it to Sammy first. Although it's quite plain it isn't ours, I certainly don't want to be involved in a case of harbouring stolen goods.'

Dasia grabbed at the case and said urgently, with breathless relief, 'What a marvellous stroke of luck! It's not stolen, Andrina, it's *mine*! It's one of the Wrioth's family heirlooms, handed down since the year dot to every bride through marriage, and I thought I'd lost it. I didn't dare tell Hal!'

260

They both went upstairs to the dolls-house room in the attics and sat there on old chintz-covered chairs, and gazed at the contents of the leather drawstring bag.

'I just don't know what to say ...' murmured Andrina in awe. 'In some ways it's a wonderful honour, but in others it's a whole load of unwanted, unasked for responsibility. They're not the sort of things you're ever likely to wear with your present way of living, and where on earth can you keep them – except in a strong box at the bank? Would you like me to get Sammy to deal with it and go to the District Bank about it?'

Dasia nodded, picked up the small bag with the jewels in and handed them to her mother: 'You see to it Andrina, and ask Sammy to help. It'll be a real load off my mind. In the end they'll be as cumbersome as a load of pebbles off the beach, and just as useless if I have to keep worrying about them being mislaid. And especially as they have no sales value whatsoever as far as I'm concerned.'

Then she said tentatively, 'Are you going to give me grandfather's letter back, Andrina? I'm convinced they don't want anything to do with it themselves, but one day I'm determined to claim the inheritance for both our sakes.'

Tears came to Andrina's eyes as they both read the letter again. Then Andrina folded it up, put it back in its original envelope which protected it, and handed it to Dasia again: 'Don't for heaven's sake lose it!' Then she said, 'And while you're at it, you may as well have your birth certificate. It was never put with the family documents. I've always kept it myself.'

Andrina leaned over and kissed Dasia gently on the cheek: 'It's been a strange old world for you, hasn't it? But it could have been a whole lot worse, for both of us ... think of all the people in orphanages.'

They sat in silence for a few seconds until they finally went downstairs again.

Lady Wrioth was absolutely distraught when she casually came across the note, left by Hal after he'd taken the heirloom to give to Dasia.

She rarely opened the secret drawer in her jewel box, but one morning, as she thought tenderly and sadly about past days and prayed in her mind that Hal might soon meet a well-bred, aristocratic female, suitable for his bride, she pressed the groove where the curving rose leaf was, to look at the true Wrioth inheritance, held in safe keeping for a proper bride-to-be – and found nothing there!

She read Hal's scrawled words with horror. It was like a bad dream.

She went back to bed and told her personal maid, Miss Foster, to summon Lord Wrioth immediately.

'I shall be staying in my room for the rest of the day, Letty. Please let cook know. And I don't want to be troubled with any outside messages unless they are direct, family ones.'

'Very good, your ladyship,' said Miss Foster in her quiet, carefully modulated voice.

Thinny lay back against the pillows weakly, as her sharp brain sent her a thousand messages. She was in a dreadful dilemma. She knew she had to let Bazz know, but she didn't quite know how best to put it, for fear of bringing on one of his heart attacks. The worst thing, as far as she was concerned, would be for poor old Bazz to snuff it, so that she would become demoted to a mere dowager widow, mouldering away in a small apartment in the East Wing with this terrible little usurper becoming the mistress of Hyndemere.

'Yes? What is it? Miss Foster seemed to think you were feeling a bit off colour, Thinny. Don't keep me too long; I'm busy with some wrought-iron work, and young Dicky was just about to present me with a rather nice cup of coffee and a piece of chicken pie ...' Bazz frowned slightly, and gave her a curt appraising glance. Women were all right just so long as they didn't interrupt anything more important. 'Mmm, you do look a bit shattered, old thing. Any trouble with the staff?'

'I've just been thinking about Hal ...'

Bazz gulped with relief: 'Oh, is that all? I wouldn't worry too much. He'll survive. The Wrioths thrive on a spot of hardship – even though his true place is here, looking after this estate. He'll soon come to his cake and milk. It's just the old story of young uns sowing a few wild oats ...

'Once we've got that wretched girl sorted out over the baby, we can forget all of it, and she can trot off somewhere, find herself a nice young man, and settle down.'

'I've a terrible feeling it won't be quite as simple as that,' said Lady Wrioth with a grim face and tight lips. Then, throwing caution to the wind, she handed him Hal's letter.

'Married? How on earth can he be married? What absolute, confounded nonsense! Surely they haven't been doing a bit of blood-letting round a gypsy bonfire? The boy's a bloody lunatic!'

Then he cooled down and said, 'If it's true, it's going to be a bit difficult, especially if the baby turns out to be a boy, and he's absolutely convinced it's his. Yes, it's going to take a hell of a lot of thinking about is this ... and it's absolutely buggered mi wrought-iron work.'

Dasia was enjoying working with Rosalie at Sale in the Servant Registry, for the office was just a part of Miss Edith's and Miss Tabitha's comfortable home.

There were just Rosalie and herself, and a visiting

charlady, for the whole two weeks while Edith, Tabitha and Mr Bates were holidaying in the Isle of Man.

Some days she even managed to sunbathe in her striped bathing costume as she sat on a deck-chair in the old-world splendour of the rambling, mellow, walled back garden, where blush pink blossom covered every small gnarled twig of mossed apple trees, and old red brick paths were packed on each side with beds of lavender and cat-mint. On slack, uneventful days, Dasia had short periods of bliss as she looked up at the blue sky, and breathed in the heady scent of honeysuckle and sweetpeas.

Then, one day, when Rosalie had hurried off in her best floral georgette frock, ostensibly to go to the Maypole for some butter and chocolate biscuits, but really to visit Arthur Bolingshaw on Sale station where he'd been promoted to booking-office clerk, the front door bell began to ring.

Dasia, who'd been sitting in the garden, fortunately fully dressed in a neat, subdued blouse and skirt, with a navy blue silk bandeau round her red hair, and a large green tennis eye shade, went to open it, and was astounded to see Hal's mother!

It was obvious that Lady Wrioth hadn't even recognised her, as she asked to see Miss Edith or Miss Tabitha about some temporary help at Hyndemere Hall.

Dasia turned away quickly and led the way to the office with Lady Wrioth explaining in a loud authoritarian voice that she needed a good living-in under-gardener who was obedient, hard working, young and easily trained, intelligent, physically strong, polite, and of happy disposition and – most important of all – more interested in his job than financial reward, and able to take orders without arguing.

Dasia sat at the desk and looked at the list of people on their books requiring gardening work. The only person she could find was an elderly widow, who offered to water people's plants and take very small dogs for walks when people were on holiday.

'Excuse me ... but don't I know you from somewhere?' Lady Wrioth was staring straight at Dasia. 'You wouldn't by any chance be Miss Greenbow ... Miss Dasia Greenbow ...?'

Dasia felt herself trembling slightly with pervading nervousness: 'Yes ... I'm here to help my aunt Rosalie.'

'You don't happen to know where Hal's gone, do you? He seems to have left that little house ...'

'He's living with me, at our house,' said Dasia in a small voice. 'He's got a new job, now, a much better one ...' She began to cheer up. At least it was nice to be able to give some good news for a change.

'Living with you ...? What a naughty boy to be doing that when he knows quite well he can come home. Whatever must your parents think?'

'We shan't be there for long, Lady Wrioth. It's just until we find a small place of our own, in time for the baby being born.'

Thinny stiffened: 'Oh yes, Lord Wrioth and I wanted to have a word with you both about that. There's no need for either of you to be tied by it, you know. These things often happen even in the best of families, and I'm sure we can come to a satisfactory arrangement.

'You're both far too young to be anything more than friends – and of course we'll always contribute to a decent nursing home for you, and a small allowance for the child. There's no question of your being out of pocket.

'Time soon goes in this life, my dear, and soon, no doubt, you'll meet a nice young man of your very own.'

'Hal is my young man, Lady Wrioth. He's the first proper young man I've ever had.'

A smile of relief began to glow on Lady Wrioth's face;

at least her son hadn't landed himself with soiled goods for this unfortunate peccadillo. Loose women could send infections round like bush fires. 'How lovely for you to have him as your first young man,' purred Thinny.

Dasia suddenly took off her tennis eye shade and smiled with cool confidence at her: 'And, as *my husband*, Lady Wrioth; surely you know that? Surely Hal let you know that I am properly married to him and that this baby inside me is our legitimate child?'

Cynthia Wrioth's face flooded bright crimson then almost to a dull grey, half out of grief and half out of livid rage. Then swiftly turning away she hurried from the room, and found her own way out to her car – where Danny Elvers was patiently waiting.

When Rosalie got back from the Maypole grocery store with her butter and chocolate biscuits, her beautiful georgette dress was slightly crushed and her eyes were bright and shining: 'Have you had many enquiries while I was out? You look quite weary.'

Dasia told her about Lady Wrioth, while Rosalie listened to it all with eyes as round as gob-stoppers and her darkened eye-lashes, beneath her almost platinum blonde hair, as startled as Betty Boop's. 'The old bat ... She sounds as hard as iron. She'll never leave you alone from this second onward now she knows the full score. After all, you are now carrying the heir of Hyndemere, aren't you?'

And shrewd Rosalie was pretty well right ...

CHAPTER SIXTEEN

The Second Ceremony

August Bank Holiday was traditionally associated with the first day of August, and everyone looked forward to it, for holidays were few and far between. Many people took to trams, trains, buses, bicycles, and hiking boots to get away to the beauty spots of Derbyshire, Cheshire, Lancashire and Yorkshire in a brief, twenty-four-hour respite from general day-to-day toil.

Many a year, the weather would start off very hot and heavy with everyone hopeful for a nice sunny day. They had all dressed up in carefree finery, often paid for weeks in advance through a co-op savings ticket, with flowery cotton frocks, bright, shiny straw hats, and the men in light-coloured, baggy summer flannels. Families trailed round fair grounds, garden parties, agricultural shows, and village fêtes – often ending up at about seven in the evening in a mad rush through thunder and lightning, totally unprepared and dripping wet, in their deliberate gamble with the capricious heavens.

And so it happened that Dasia and Hal hurried from Wythenshawe Park, after a wet ending to the day, and called in at Sharston tea rooms for tea and buns.

They were in high spirits, with the golden tan of summer ripening their young faces, when Hal said out of the blue, 'I saw Mater and Pater quite by chance in Manchester last week, and they desperately want us to go and stay with them.

'I know it's hard to credit, Dasia, but they've completely changed their attitude. They both apologised profusely about the way they'd treated us both in the past, and asked for bygones to be bygones. I expect we could try it out some time: at least it would give your lot a rest from us.'

'But how on earth would you manage to travel all that way into Manchester for work every day, Hal?'

He hesitated: 'Father wants me to help him with the estate. It would be far more lucrative than being in Manchester, and it would help us to get money together more quickly for our own home. For, make no mistake, we shall lead our own lives. We won't just be going there to join the empire.'

For once, Dasia gave serious thought to the idea. Her ideas had changed a bit since the beginning of the year. She knew it was an extra strain for Alice and Horace having her and Hal around all the time, and that her grandfather liked to spread himself about the house when he was busy with his inventions. Also, as she expanded round her midriff, she knew that acquiring money to get themselves a proper little home of their own was getting more and more important.

But even so ... her memory wasn't quite as short as all that when she remembered the awful Christmas débâcle at Hyndemere, and how domineering and scheming his mother was. Oh yes, her own grandmother Alice was pretty tough, too, but at least Alice usually stepped in to help her in the end – whereas Cynthia Wrioth was only interested in protecting her one and only son.

'How about going for just one night, next weekend?' said Hal slowly. 'We could go on Saturday afternoon and return on Sunday – just so you can see for yourself how much they've changed their ways now they know we really are man and wife?'

Dasia nodded and tried to drown her misgivings. Quite often things didn't turn out as bad as you imagined, and nothing ever stayed the same in life. It would either be better or worse, and Hal was adamant that it would be truly better.

And so it was all arranged for the following weekend. They set off by rail, with Elvers to meet them in Chester; and Elvers even being promised to return them to The Grove on the Sunday.

Dasia began to feel like a new being. She marvelled at how well she had settled down this time, and the weather was gloriously well behaved. Later, on the Saturday, she and Hal sauntered through Lord Wrioth's wrought-iron trysting gates into the rose gardens, and took photographs of each other, sitting on an old stone seat, savouring the scented air hung heavy with the fragrance of creamy pink roses.

Thinny was on her best behaviour that weekend. She oozed quiet and tactful hospitality, and friendly kindness, and put them in the guests' suite which, she casually mentioned to Dasia, could make a most suitable flat for anyone. It was even large enough for a small family because of its several rooms, its bathroom en suite and its windows graciously placed to perceive the whole of the vast Hyndemere estate.

'It's such a healthy place, too ...' added Lady Wrioth, gazing at Dasia enthusiastically.

One thing about beautiful summer days is that it's always difficult at the time to imagine the horrors of winter; and so it was that Dasia forgot the feelings of isolation that she had felt there the previous Christmas.

For now, by the end of a short period of what appeared to be perfect and untrammelled freedom and luxury, alone with Hal, so happy at last in his childhood home and with the blessing of both his parents, Dasia began to waver towards Lord Wrioth's friendly plan for them both to go and live there for as long as they wished. Little did she realise that she was caught like an innocent darting fish in the inner pocket of their powerful net.

The news was met with caution when she returned home, but no one could really fault it. When all's said and done, she was merely getting what she so richly deserved – the trappings of a successful marriage 'catch', even though she had never seen it as such. And from her own point of view she had her own unborn child to think of and needed to give it the best possible start in life.

'And don't you be putting that pert little nose of yours in the air and forgetting us 'oo's brought you up,' warned Alice excitedly. 'And don't let Hal boss you about. Always remember you're on equal terms even though you're a bit younger. And remember that being a lady has nowt to do with whether you were born in gutter or great house. It's all a matter of your own conscience, to do what you think's best for you and that wee bairn that's growing inside you.' Then she said bluntly, 'And I 'ope to God they gives you some weekly wages of some sort for being 'is wife. For at least you 'ad your own scrap of independence when you was working at the pawn shop, and Marcia's and Baulden's. But now it'll be all different.

'Rich landowners like the Wrioths usually add to it all by pairing themselves off to others of the same ilk and make sure it's a woman of property or young heiress with plenty of potential ... someone with an inheritance.'

Dasia's face clouded over for a few seconds, then she

270

cheered up and said, 'Well, I've got an inheritance, grandmother.'

'You?' Alice scowled at her.

'The inheritance for me to claim – in that letter from my other grandfather, Adrien Shawfield, about my proper father Blennim dying and leaving me a small fortune in Canada of various items ...'

'Oh, that ...' sighed Alice with disinterest. 'The Shawfields always were a lot of muddle-headed romantics, and the best thing that happened to Andrina was not getting involved with them, or she'd now be dead herself from a broken heart. And you mind what you say, lady, about "proper fathers". Your proper father was the man who brought you up – and that was your grandfather Horace Greenbow, so don't you ever forget it. And as for that other saga, about claiming your rightful inheritance, we'll believe it when we see it ... whenever that is. Probably after the end of the world, if you ask me.'

August flew by, and Hal gave his notice in at J & N Philips and went to Hyndemere a week before Dasia to get the apartment ready for them both. Dasia helped spasmodically at The Servant Registry, went to see the doctor for check-ups and started knitting and planning the layette for the new arrival – even though to the casual observer she did not look pregnant but just seemed like an older woman with no waist and a calm unlined healthy face.

'Don't you fret, lass,' said Horace one day, 'by the time October comes you'll be looking like the back of a house and thinkin' you're in for twins. Your grandmother was allus like that. And by the time December's here again it'll've worked its way down and be sticking out like a camel's hump and you'll be glad to get shot of it.' Then he went to his oak bureau and, counting out

271

four five-pound notes from a tin box, handed them to Dasia and said, 'Keep that in reserve, lass, in case you ever need to escape from that dratted place ...'

At first, when Dasia bid all her family at The Grove a tear-stained goodbye, as if she was never going to see them again, and settled in at Hyndemere, everything went like clockwork. The staff were kind and friendly, and very excited by the thought of a new baby in the house. And they treated her with the utmost respect.

But one day in late September she got a sudden shock as Lady Wrioth asked to have a word with her in private.

'To be perfectly candid, dear, I've had this wonderful idea of you and Hal having a small and simple wedding ceremony here in the private chapel. I've been having a word with the Vicar and he's quite willing to perform the nuptials.

'I know you did say once as a bit of a joke that some people even in your own family didn't quite regard Gretna as the perfect sealing ceremony, and I thought that if you and Hal had a more spiritual rendering, here at Hyndemere, in preparation for the eventual christening of your child it would please everyone.' Thinny fixed her with a bright brittle smile. 'I haven't mentioned it to Hal yet, but I'm sure he'll agree.'

Dasia was completely taken aback. The wedding at Gretna Green now stood out in her memory as happy and romantic, and to start wanting to blot it out with a special Hyndemere rendering seemed to her to be insensitive and even sacrilegious, almost suggesting a sort of late shot-gun marriage to establish who owned the goods.

'To be perfectly frank, I don't think it's necessary. And it was my wedding, Thinny. Hal was the one who suggested it, and it worked out perfectly well.' She saw a streak of temper rise in Cynthia's eyes.

'Excuse me, Dasia, but I do think you can be rather

too arrogant for one so young. You must remember that life here isn't quite the same as life in places like Manchester and The Grove.'

'I'm quite aware of that. I'm not stupid!' Dasia's own temper began to smoulder, but she turned away so as not to show it and went to look for Hal who was in the estate office across the courtyard. Surely he wouldn't kow-tow to such a silly idea. Then, as she began to think about it further, it dawned on her that it could be even more awkward and embarrassing because of her own illegitimacy, and the fact that she had never seen her proper father. For although Hal knew she was the child of Andrina he had never questioned her on the subject, and she had never enlightened him on any other parts of her background.

But once Thinny began to get her claws into things it might be like stirring up a hornet's nest ...

Luckily there was no one else about in the office when she went to see Hal. He was sitting at a leather inlaid desk, in a light linen jacket and trousers looking perfectly at home and peaceful, his hair a mass of dark curls.

She knew he didn't really like her popping over to see him when he was working. The words he'd uttered only yesterday still hurt her heart: 'I'm doing a proper job now, Dasia. Just because we live on the premises doesn't make it any different, and having you popping in and out at odd times is a bit unsettling. I don't want to hurt your feelings but that's how it is. You'll have to make your own little life during my working hours. Mother will always help you, or give you advice. I know it must be hard for someone unused to our way of life ...'

She'd listened to him with mounting shock. Where was the Hal from their small home of Tipperary in Manchester? Was it true that only a few weeks of this other life could change him so much?

'It's not me who's changed, Dasia. It's our circumstances, our environment. When in Rome do as the Romans do – and all that. And the same applies to you.'

'You have changed – you have!' Tears had rushed down her cheeks, 'But *I* haven't changed.'

He suddenly began to chuckle like a father dealing with a small wayward child: 'Of course you have ... You're changing all the time or how else would our baby be managing to grow? Now go away there's a good girl and get on with a bit of knitting or something, and maybe this afternoon we'll go for a good walk round the woods. How will that suit?

'For God's sake stop looking so miserable, you make me feel quite guilty.' He put out his hand and stroked her glinting, auburn head of hair.

'Yes, what is it this time?' He looked up at her, and she knew it was only a joke, but it hurt her.

'It's your mother. She has this terrible idea of wanting us re-married in your private chapel ... it make me feel quite sick to think of it. It's almost like blotting out our own memories of our own true life.'

A faint frown came to his forehead, and he looked puzzled: 'Surely it isn't as awful and dramatic as all that? She means well. She's just concerned for us. She's making sure everything's done properly ... She's always like that.'

Dasia gazed at him in silence. What was happening? Was this the same man who'd pleaded with her to marry him and help him in his hour of need after the hospital fiasco, when she hadn't even wanted to get married for at least another ten years? Was this the person who had suggested going to Gretna Green and had forsworn his family and their ways for ever after the terrible way they had treated her?

'You're just like a chameleon, Hal. How can you

274

change so the moment you get here?'

'Look, Dasia, let's get this straight. I was offered a job by my father, and I took it. It's work I like and it's bringing us in a fortune compared to our life in Denmark Road. I accepted his offer for both our sakes, and to give our child a good start in life. I'm not the chameleon you think I am. It's just that I've come to terms with things. Everyone has to compromise some times, Dasia, and that includes both you and me ... *Got it*?'

She looked at him sullenly, and almost stamped away. Then as she crossed the courtyard again her own temper evaporated, and she saw Danny Elvers in white shirt-sleeves and a navy blue apron. He was bending down polishing one of the cars, and stood up and stretched both his arms in the air when he saw her and put his yellow duster on the bonnet. 'How's it going, Miss Greenbow?'

He knew as well as she did what the score was, and she often gave thanks for his calm, reassuring ways when she saw him going about his duties.

'When there's no one about, just call me Dasia and I'll call you Danny.'

'Right you are Miss Dasia.'

'How's Enid going on, Danny ...?'

He hesitated, powerless to escape her innocent un-calculated charm and wishing like some fool that he was fifteen years younger: 'Not too good at the moment, Dasia. She's been backwards and forwards to hospital for the past seven weeks and's due to go in shortly for what they call a rest and some new treatment.' He suddenly crumpled into complete sadness. 'But the family's a blessing, and the Wrioths are very under-standing.'

'They aren't in the least understanding with me! I feel like running away from Hyndemere every second. I

275

think Lady Wrioth is an absolute dragon – and wicked with it. There! I've said it! And you're the only one in the world who knows.'

'I understand you, Dasia. Yours is an entirely different situation from mine. But let's hope it all improves and ends up happier for both of us.'

Then he went back to polishing the car, and as she walked away from him she tried to be more reasonable, and see the other side of things. Maybe she was just being over-sensitive, because she was now the outsider. And after all, Hal had been a bit of an outsider in her family ...

But this ...? This was totally different.

Although Alice and Horace Greenbow never deigned to set foot in Hyndemere, Dasia was filled with joy the following Sunday to see Sammy Tankerton's Ford winding its way towards the house.

At first she could hardly believe it, for there had been no suggestion that they would call in the whole of these long weeks of September, yet now, as they drew near to the front entrance, she could see Andrina's new summer straw. It was a blue and cream weave with a huge curvy brim and a satin ribbon.

Dasia hurried to greet them in a fever of excitement almost like a captive seeing human kind again. But before she could even reach the front door, Partridge the butler was already there, and as she drew close to him he said, 'Were they expected, madam?'

She gave a gasp of scorn: 'They're always expected, Partridge. The lady's my mother. And the gentleman is her betrothed.' Then she added aggressively, 'And they can come here whenever they like just so long as I'm here.'

'Very good, madam,' said Partridge coolly, with a certain touch of ironic humour round the sides of his seemingly expressionless mouth, 'I will inform her ladyship to that account.'

'It was such a nice day, we thought we'd take the bull by the horns,' said Andrina as she and Sam got out of the car. 'What a magnificent place it is! We had no idea you were living in such a palace.'

'But it's so lonely, Drina ... And so cut off, and different ... And Hal's always so busy on the estate. His whole existence seems absorbed with it. They all lead their own individual lives, going round in their own small circles like little worlds within the universe of Hyndemere as if it's the hub of everything. I expect it'll be different when I've had the baby, because then I'll have my own little world too ...

'Anyway, come in – and I'll introduce you both to Lady Wrioth,' Dasia bit her lip, '... if she's available.'

Lady Wrioth was not available, and neither was Lord Wrioth. They were both out visiting some friends who'd bought some new horses and had racing stables, and Hal himself was about three miles away inspecting part of the river bank.

'On afternoons like this,' said Dasia, 'I usually have afternoon tea alone by the windows in the drawing room. So today it'll be an extra treat with you two here, and I'll be able to moan away to my heart's content. The trouble with a place like this is you can't really be yourself like you can at home ... but for Hal, it *is* home ...'

They all laughed, and soon Melanie, one of the maids, arrived with a full afternoon tea, with fresh salmon and cucumber sandwiches, small fingers of game pie, rich fruit cake, scones and quince jam, fresh fruit salad and cream, and a tray with a silver tea service.

And as they guzzled their way through it with rapturous delight, Dasia told them about Thinny and her awful plan for her and Hal to have another marriage ceremony in the private chapel, and how Hal seemed to be quite won over whenever his mother suggested anything.

'You see, he always takes her side and says both she and his father are doing it for our own good ... I just can't understand him.'

Sammy Tankerton bristled slightly. He was a man of few words, but very observant: 'You do have some personal rights, you know, Dasia. We know that a wife is, as yet, secondary to her husband, but I don't think you should be too much put-upon, or your whole life will be miserable. I know to my own cost that mothers can be very dominating, and so does Andrina. Let's hope that *your* generation won't be the same.'

Then Andrina said, 'So who's looking after your pregnancy then?'

'No one really – well, what I mean is that Thinny's own private Doctor, Dr Prancey, often calls round for a cup of tea and asks how I am. And sometimes he gets his private nurse to call in and take a urine sample, and check the baby's movements and take my temperature and blood pressure. But it's not the same as having my own doctor from childhood, like Dr Fothergill ...'

'That's just it then, Dasia. Why don't you tell Hal you want to stay with Dr Fothergill under the hospital's Penny-a-Week scheme? – seeing you've never actually said anything to Dr Fothergill about leaving him, ' said Sammy.

'Yes,' said Andrina eagerly, 'I could mention it to Dr Fothergill myself, and ask him to give me a list of your times for visiting him – then you could come and stay the night back at home sometimes, just for a change of scene.'

By the time they were ready to depart, Dasia was full of new cheerfulness and hope. What a wet blanket she must have seemed.

'Don't worry too much, dear,' whispered Andrina. 'Being a mother is a very tricky business, and it depends whose mother you are, but I'll try not to let you down.' Then she added in an even lower whisper, 'By the way – Sammy's mother is very ill indeed. She went into the Memorial Nursing Home yesterday with a sudden heart attack. She's said to be in her nineties though you'd never have guessed it, with all those outings into Manchester to meet her other old cronies, so she's had a real good innings. Sammy was her youngest ... He'll miss her terribly. I expect in some ways the old are ideal companions because you can rant away and they don't hear half you say, or even care, and so everyone is happy.'

The next day, when Dasia was mentioning to Hal and his mother about Andrina and Sammy coming out to see them for an afternoon run in the car, she said, 'Oh, and by the way, I've decided to keep to Dr Fothergill while I'm expecting the baby. He's always been our family doctor, just the same as you have your family doctor ...'

There was a sudden tense silence, then Lady Wrioth said in her most reasonable voice, 'But don't you think that's a little bit short-sighted, Dasia? After all, how would you get there for a start?'

Dasia's colour rose: 'I'd have to ask Elvers to take me and bring me back like he does for you when you go into Manchester, or Chester; or I could go on the train one day, and come back on the train to Chester the next day ... After all it wouldn't be happening every week, and it would probably make a bit of a change.'

'A change?' said Hal in amazement. 'We've only been here a few weeks and you're already talking about having a change. Anyone'd think you'd got St Vitus's Dance!'

'What a cruel thing to say!' gasped Dasia. 'Surely I can choose my own doctor!'

Thinny gave a deep, mock sigh: 'I'm afraid Hal's right, my dear. It's just not practicable. For a start, there's the wedding ceremony to be planned as soon as possible – hopefully next week on Wednesday afternoon, according to Reverend Bolt, the vicar. And when that's accomplished, it'll be a case of arranging where the baby is to be born, either at Dr Prancey's private maternity home, Babbitt House, or here at Hyndemere in the same room as Hal was born ...'

Nothing more was said, and then next day Thinny saw Dasia and said in honeyed tones, 'I've spoken to the vicar, dear, and it's quite all right for a week tomorrow afternoon in the private chapel. Hal is quite agreeable, and you can have Andrina or someone here if you want, as a witness. And if you want a specially nice frock for the occasion, even a real wedding dress, we can go to Chester and fix it up with no expense to you, dear. It will be my little treat. I've also ordered Mr Cringley from *Living Life* to come and take a photograph next to the altar.'

Dasia looked at her dejectedly and shrugged her shoulders: 'It's no good, Thinny ... all my family have to work during the week. They'd need far more notice of it all. And in any case they regard me as married already. They'd just regard it as a pure waste of precious time. It isn't as if Hal and I were some very old couple renewing our wedding vows or something because we'd forgotten ever having made any. And anyway, Andrina's fiancé, Sammy, has a very ill mother at present, and has more serious things to think about.'

Lady Wrioth went crimson, and it showed up quite frighteningly because usually she was very pale: 'This marriage ceremony is very serious, Dasia. Make no mistake. The Wrioths take their family commitments very seriously indeed, especially when there's a new generation to be born.'

Although no more was said, the effect of the coming ceremony was causing such deep pressure and stress for Dasia that she began to suffer griping pains after every meal, and to worry secretly whether she would even manage to carry the baby to full term. Yet strangely she kept it all bottled up inside her, and neither she nor Hal ever mentioned the second wedding, but rather tried to ignore it all and take it as lightly as possible, hoping by some miracle that it would never happen ...

But it did happen, on Wednesday afternoon, the fifth of October. The little private chapel was beautifully bedecked with flowers and autumn fruits as it was in the middle of Harvest Festival. Thankfully, because the chapel was so small, there was little room for many of the Hyndemere staff or others to be present.

Dasia was in a nervous and depressed state. She hadn't even sent Andrina definite word about it because she didn't want to burden anyone else with her own private worries and imaginings, and deep down she didn't want to let her grandmother down, because, according to Andrina, she was already over the moon at having a granddaughter married to a real lord's son. Alice would in some ways have been the very first to support Thinny in this second official splicing if it had been done in a less snobby way.

'Are you ready then, Dasia?' Hal came into the room all spruce and shining with a beautiful coppery-pink rose bud in his button hole, smiling like a school boy. It was obvious that to him it was just a general reaffirmation of their love and was rather like a jolly extra performance laid on to humour his parents.

His face changed and he stared at her: 'Surely you aren't going like that? You look ... well ... You look –'

'Yes ... How do I look?' Her heart began to beat nervously as she said with terrible tenseness in her voice,

'You know, Hal, in a *proper* marriage you shouldn't even be seeing me till I reach the altar.' She brushed her eyes hastily with a lace handkerchief.

He realised he had put his foot in it, and like a true gentleman farmer he made it worse: 'You look pretty enough, Dasia. Maybe it's just the shape of the frock ... all those frills and flounces. You look a bit like a nursery rhyme milk-maid – not that it's any detriment to you of course, and traditional milk-maids are known for their beauty.'

'A milk-maid? She went quite faint. She should *never* have let his mother choose it. Why was it she never seemed able to stand up for herself properly when Thinny was in on the scene? It had been outrageously expensive with rather too many pale blue ribbons slotted fussily through the broderie Anglaise. Yet at the time when the choice was made her humble pride had prevented her from asserting her own idea of suitability because of the price, which was far beyond an ordinary life style.

But if she'd had her mother-in-law's wealth she'd have chosen an entirely different version – beautifully plain and tailored in heavy silk satin. She wanted to look her best for both Hal's sake and that of her own family, and at first she'd even thought of wearing her old blue crepe-de-chine dress from the time she met Hal at Redman's – but to her unbelieving shock, it was too tight.

'You'll just have to blame your mother if you don't like me in it. It was her choice. I never ever wanted another wedding –' her voice cracked with misery.

He tried to comfort her, and put his arm around her: 'Come off it, Dasia,' he said gently, 'you know Mother told you you could have anything you wanted, and she'd pay. But if Mater chose this – then it must be all right. She knows more about these things than either of us.'

He gave her a long, loving kiss – but the damage was done.

Miserably, Dasia walked with him to the chapel in a state of depression and hysteria. Hysteria at the farce it all was, and depression because Hal looked so beautiful and had taken it all so naturally. Oh how she wished she could have done the same.

Just before they reached the carved doors she began to feel extremely ill, as she heard the organ playing 'Here Comes The Bride'.

'I can't go through with it, Hal. It's so pointless ...' Her voice was small and weak, and lost in the loud organ music. She leaned, trembling against his arm.

She knew nothing of the service or the remarks and looks of concern as she came in, but when the vicar said the words about having anything to say or forever holding your peace, she suddenly shouted, 'Yes, *I* have something to say ... I am already married to Hal, and I don't wish to take part in any of this charade.' And as she said the last word she fell to the floor in a dead swoon.

The first person she saw when she opened her eyes was Cynthia, with the vicar next to her, and Hal and his father standing worriedly in the background.

She herself was lying on the best tapestry *chaise-longue* in the small sunny music room, as words like, 'poor little soul', and, 'still an unworldly little schoolgirl', and, 'Not up to it ...' wafted through the air.

The following day, unable to bear any of it any more and on the pretext of doing some shopping in Chester for the baby, she took a lift in the car and, without a single thing except her handbag containing her five-pound notes from Horace Greenbow, and her precious letter about claiming her inheritance, her birth certificate, and her marriage lines, she set off to Manchester to find lodgings in secret.

'What on earth are *you* doing in here, Dasia?' gasped Rosalie, a few days later. Rosalie was in Bendal Hill's department store in Deansgate, having her hair roots kept up to their platinum blonde perfection with ammonia and peroxide in a white, frothing, stinking, bleach.

Rosalie liked places like Bendal Hill's. She regarded them as part of her spiritual home, whenever she got the chance. That was the problem with ordinary low paid men working in railways stations – how on earth could they keep women of expensive tastes in the manner to which they were accustomed?

'What are *you* doing here, you mean?' said Dasia leaning heavily on the shaft of her sweeping brush.

Her overall was far too tight over her swelling body, and she could hardly bend down some times to sweep all the different coloured locks of hair into the dust pan

As quickly as she could, and whisking the brush too and fro occasionally to show she was still hard at work, Dasia told Rosalie about the awful wedding ceremony, and how she'd run away only yesterday – in a mad panic in case she was trapped there for ever in Lady Wrioth's clutches.

'I've got these lodgings near Tipperary where we used to live – with a girl called Flo Monagan who found me this job. It's supposed to be temporary for someone who's in hospital, and it better had be or I'll collapse and roll about like a barrel trying to get at all the hair stuck under the chairs.'

They both began to giggle, and Dasia resumed her sweeping.

When Rosalie was ready to go she said, 'Do Mother and Father know?'

'No they don't. And don't you dare utter a word!

They'd only worry, and I feel as right as rain now I'm out of that terrible place.'

'What about poor Hal? He'll be worried out of his wits, surely?'

'I rang him up this morning and told him I wasn't going back. I told him it wasn't his fault, but I couldn't ever be happy at Hyndemere.'

Rosalie gave an inward gasp. She would have been happy with every second God sent her in a place like that – and she'd soon have got Lady Wrioth taped! 'Whatever did the poor boy say?'

'He just couldn't believe it. He said I *had* to go back and that I was his wife, and he loved me. And it was his baby as well as mine ...'

'So then what did you say?'

'I started to cry. I just couldn't help it. But I told him not to worry and that I'd keep in touch with him through his friend, Kenny Saville – the one whose Aunt Celia got us fixed up with our little house. He's still at the Infirmary and I'm sure that if I got in touch with him he'd stop Hal worrying too much until the baby's born. You see, what causes me most fear, Rosalie, is this dread of his mother trying to drag me back there again. If I can just manage to hang out until the baby's born, I feel sure things'll get better. It's due at the end of December.'

Rosalie looked worried: 'It's quite a while yet. There's the whole of November to survive. You've got two of the worst winter months ahead, full of terrible fogs, and streaming damp, and snow and rain – and even flu and other illness. I know I'm sounding gloomy, Dasia, but sometimes you strike me as totally impractical. You can't go through life just walking out of every problem.'

Dasia glared at her: 'You just don't know a thing, sweet Rose ... You've just no idea what I've suffered since I married Hal. You live a life of comfortable luxury compared to me ...'

Rosalie took a deep, smug, happy breath of relieved self-satisfaction, and thanked her lucky stars: 'I must honestly admit I don't envy you in some ways, Dasia.' There was a moment of silent gloom, then Rosalie brightened up again and said: 'Maybe Miss Edie and Miss Tabby would take you as their second lodger for a while seeing as how you helped out at the Servant Registry while they were in the Isle of Man. Then they could get on with their life's work of fussing over Mr Bates, and you could do the household chores.'

Dasia nodded eagerly. Anything – *anything* to get settled somewhere half decent until the baby was born ... Anything to escape the nightmare of Hyndemere.

She wrote down her present address at Flo Monagan's, and handed it to Rosalie.

CHAPTER SEVENTEEN

Grandson

Most of October was an Indian summer. The weather was warm and mellow with golden, sunny days and lots of wasps and flies about, so that every jug and jar was covered in net or muslin, weighted round the edges with rows of colourful beads, and in every kitchen and living room ugly-looking brown strips of sticky fly paper hung from ceilings.

At first when Dasia accepted Flo's kind offer of help she was amazed at her own good luck in being fixed up so quickly, and staggered by Flo's alacrity in finding her a regular job, even though the pay was abysmal.

The house Flo was in was a good size with cellars and attics, but was in poor condition and was rented from a landlord who never carried out any improvements of repairs. repairs.

'Tessy Watkins and I paid rent for it for three years,' said white-faced Flo, mournfully, 'but Tess 'as buggered off to get married to a feller oo's no better than a pimp. At least we never 'ad one of those devils in the background when we was working together.'

Dasia cursed herself for being so dim, for only after a few days of living at Flo's did it dawn on her what Flo did for a living. Flo never actually mentioned it in so many words, although her general conversation made it quite clear.

After a week or two with Flo, Dasia became very lonely. Rosalie had never been in touch about her going back to work in Sale and maybe lodge with Edith and Tabitha. And she herself had kept out of the way of The Grove, and the rest of the family, in case Hal should come looking for her.

But one thing she had done was to get in touch by phone with Kenny Saville and ask him to let Hal know she was perfectly safe and working in Manchester.

'Must say I'm frightfully sorry it hasn't worked out with the old coots at Hyndemere,' said Kenny over the phone, 'but I sympathise with you a bit. Quite a nice life and all that when you can come and go as you please, and do the old huntin', shootin' an' fishin once in a while. But a bit of city life's basically more in my line, Dace – even though I do go round this ghastly hospital quivering like a confounded jelly and expecting to be kicked out every second. I think I might try some mixture like medical orthopaedic, in the end – where I only have to deal with people with bad chests who are in plaster, and I just have to stare at their plaster casts and warn them about crumbs getting in, without actually having to do any wretched operations ...

'Anyway, Dace, old fruit, I'll remember what you've said, and I'll tell him to bury his nose in the old pheasants and horse manure till you tell him to do otherwise ...'

By the time November the fifth came, with its foggy black night and damp, biting coldness, Dasia was still living at Flo's. But on that night she suddenly had a visit from Andrina.

'Whatever's brought you here on this Saturday night of all nights, Drina?'

Andrina stared round Dasia's bedroom and said, 'It all looks very bare, and the place is terribly scruffy, Dasia. It looks most dubious ... almost the sort of property one associates with ladies of easy virtue. And those dusty old paper flowers on the window ledge are *dreadful.*' Then her face softened and she said, 'I've brought a bit of good news really, but first I want to ask you if you've been seeing Dr Fothergill regularly, although you do look amazingly well.'

'Pregnancy isn't an *illness*, Andrina.'

'I know it isn't, love, but a young girl on her own might not look after herself well enough, or even eat properly.'

'Well, I'm doing very well thank you ...' she hesitated; 'there is one thing ... I don't think I'm going to be able to work much longer at Bendal Hill's. A woman customer complained about me yesterday and said it was obvious that I was pregnant and that I shouldn't be there, even though I am only temporary.

'Naturally, I denied it ...'

'You *denied* it? Denied you were nearly eight months' pregnant! How on earth could you have had the cheek? It's plain for all the world to see.'

'It never is! One of the girls who works there in the ladies lavatories said she knew a girl who looked as big as me but it turned out she had something else wrong with her – so you never can tell.'

'Won't they let you sit down behind the counter some times?'

'Sit down behind the counter?' Dasia gaped at her. 'Didn't our Rosalie say what I did?'

Andrina shook her head nervously.

'I'm second sweeper-up in the hairdressing department.'

'How perfectly dreadful ... You poor little creature.' A tear came to Andrina's eye.

'It's no use looking like that, Drina. I quite like it, and it's certainly better than being stuck in prison at Hyndemere ... and the girls working there are good fun. We sometimes have some really good laughs about the customers.'

'How rude, and unkind. It all sounds really coarse. You were brought up to be better than that.'

Then, at last, Andrina got round to her bit of news; 'You possibly won't have heard that Sammy's mother passed away in hospital, and is now dead and buried.'

Dasia shook her head and felt sad; not for the plight of Sammy's mother but for the fact that she was so isolated from all the goings on in her own family circle.

'The result is that Sammy has been living in that huge house all alone, so I'm going to live there and be his –' Andrina gave a quick fluttery sniff, 'his housekeeper. But I shall still help Mother and Father out with the pawn shop. Then after a suitable time of mourning has elapsed Sammy and I hope to get married.'

Dasia flung her arms round her mother, delightedly. 'Congratulations. You couldn't be marrying a nicer man! I expect that's why his mother hung on to him, so long ...'

'And the other part of it, dear, is that Sammy and I would like you to come and live with us. There's loads and loads of room for you and a young baby, even if it bellows all day long, and we're both willing for you to have it born at The Cedars, so you'll be able to inform Dr Fothergill to that effect.' Then Andrina went rather sad, and said, 'There is only one complication; I think we'd better keep it a complete secret that you're living with us till the baby is actually born, even from Alice and Horace. I know it sounds almost impossible but they never go down The Grove past The Cedars, and with it being such a long avenue of a place, and with Sammy's home having that mews entrance at the side, and the neighbours all pretty well keeping themselves to themselves, we might manage to keep it really quiet for as long as possible. If we broke it officially to Mother and Father it would be a constant procession of visiting and publicity, and that is the very last thing we need – with Lady Wrioth waiting in the wings.'

Dasia was sad when Andrina finally had to leave. They both walked together down nearby Froddlesham Street, through the heavy pall of fiercely burning bonfires, with crowds of raggedly clothed young boys and the smoky, smut-ridden faces of others silhouetted against the burning, spitting wood. Every little street and byway tended its own huge mass of patiently collected rubbish which had been stored for weeks in backyards, and put together at the last minute so that no one should set fire to it before its time.

Andrina and Dasia were hypnotised by this annual ritual. Roman candles made fountains of glittering light in the dark air and rockets shot to the sky amongst the explosions from rip-raps and giant squibs, and Catherine wheels burnt themselves out on back doors, while everyone sucked treacle toffee and ate sticky ginger parkin.

Hal had met his friend Kenny Saville one day in Chester and decided, as Kenny had tactfully advised, to be patient and not do anything about trying to get in touch with Dasia until the baby was born.

'I know ... well I don't know *really*, old chap, but I suspect ... that it will all work out far better if you just let her be. She's promised to keep in touch with me, old sprout, so I can spread the gospel so to speak.

'Quite candidly, I think it was the country life getting her down and, looking at it from her point of view, who'd want to be preggars and sit knitting all day in a place like Hyndemere in the middle of winter? I mean, old boy, we must be honest and admit that most of us clear out to the South of France, or jolly old Italy – or at least Switzerland. Well, those of us not having to earn our bread and butter dragging out yards of intestines and then trying to get them back again in the right order.'

Hal managed to raise a glimmer of a smile but really he was dreadfully depressed and worried. His father had already had another minor heart attack which his mother placed fairly and squarely on poor Dasia's rather slim little shoulders for behaving so monstrously over the private wedding ceremony. There was no way Hal could think of chasing after Dasia this time, for by now he was thoroughly tied up in the affairs of the Hyndemere estate.

'I think you're right, Kenny. The baby's due at the end of December so at least all the usual Christmas fuss at Hyndemere'll help the time to pass quicker. Then, as you say, I can get something properly sorted out for the New Year. And at least I know that her own family will support her. My only hope is that Mother won't kick up too much of a din about it.'

'Well, as Robbie Burns said, old chum, The plans of mice and women goes aft awry, or some such rot. So let's hope it does in this case. Or was that what we were aiming for before we started on this bottle of Johnny Haigh?'

During December, when Dasia was finally settled in with Andrina and Sammy at The Cedars, it seemed inevitable that Alice and Horace would find out about it, but they were sworn to secrecy.

'It is absolutely essential for Dasia to have that baby in complete peace and quiet, Mother. Even Hal himself knows it. But if Lady Wrioth got a breath of where Dasia is, she'd be accusing us of kidnapping the child or something equally awful; and with poor Sammy being a lawyer it makes things even worse because he doesn't want to be involved in all our legal wrangles or his own practice will suffer, and that would be a tragedy.'

Alice grunted truculently: 'It's certainly a rum do ... Trust it to be that little madam that's causing it all. Why can't Dasia ever act normal, like other folk?

'All I 'ope is that the baby won't be as contrary as she is ... And God help the little devil if it's a boy.'

'A grand little lad, Dasia ... Seven pounds, six ounces and lungs like iron ... A good New Year present for tomorrow.'

It was Saturday, the thirty-first of December. It had been a quiet but pleasant Christmas, and the labour had taken about twenty-four hours from the start of the first griping pains which Dasia had put down to turkey rissoles.

Hal had sent her both a birthday card and a Christmas card with: 'To Dasia, my darling wife and sweetheart', written inside, but there were no messages, and both cards had been readdressed from Flo Monagan's.

Doctor Fothergill washed his hands in the bedroom wash basin, and beamed at Dasia over the top of his rimless glasses, while Mrs Brennan, the midwife on duty, wrapped up baby Alexander in his clean white cotton blanket and handed him, like a small firm parcel, to his mother: 'Lie him against you, dearie, it'll help your womb to contract.' Then she put a bit of extra coal on the fire in the bedroom fireplace and poked it to make it glow again, and put the big brass-edged fire guard round.

Dasia lay there gasping with happy relief that nine months of waiting and worrying were over at last, and that she'd be able to see her own feet properly.

All over once and for all – for she was never going to

suffer all that again. Then all the painful thoughts seemed to vanish like vapour as she gazed at this wonderful, wonderful miracle. This real live roaring baby with its tiny fingers and toes, and its huge bright eyes peering out at the new world.

He had damp black hair clinging to his small red skull and a strange dimple in his chin – just like her grandfather Greenbow. But apart from that, he didn't look like anyone but himself.

'And now the hard work *really* begins,' smiled Mrs Brennan when she visited Dasia a few days later and helped her to bath the baby, and replaced the pad of gauze over his stump of umbilical cord, so that it could dry off day by day, beneath the small flannel binder.

It was a time of acute happiness and searing anxiety as Dasia worried about every cry and whimper, and whether her new bundle of joy, baby Aleck, was overfed or underfed, whether her breasts were swollen from too much milk or not enough milk, and whether he was gaining weight or losing weight.

And where had those little red scratches come from on his face? And why had nurse put him in white lint boxing gloves?

And it was time for cards and presents for the new arrival: bibs, and teething rings, and hand-knitted matinee coats, and rompers, and fancy bonnets of silk with fluffy rabbits' wool round the brim.

But for Dasia the most touching present of all was a silver-plated spoon and pusher, with 'Good Luck for the future from Danny and Enid and family at Hyndemere'. The card was in Enid's own writing – even though she was seriously ill.

A son ...

A son and heir for Hyndemere ...

Hal felt a surge of heart-felt relief that the waiting

and isolation from Dasia were both safely over, and gave inward thanks to the Almighty as he trudged along frosty woodland paths holding the telegram which had just been delivered to him.

His own little son; a bundle of humanity weighing hardly more than a brace of pheasants, yet heir to all of this ...

Quickly he went inside and telephoned Kenny Saville: 'I must see the child, Kenny. It's ludicrous, now, not to know Dasia's proper address. And the agreement was only supposed to last until the child was born.'

'Congratulations, anyway, Daddy ...' crowed Kenny blithely at the other end. 'I quite envy you, old sausage. My own problem is, will I ever have the guts to grab a female by her thatch, and force her – kicking and screaming – into my own humble cave? Although I have spotted a rather comely and sympathetic widow aged forty with oodles of cash whose late husband was a coal merchant – but I'm dithering as usual ...

'Anyway, good luck old man. I'll get in touch with Dace – and find out if the stable's open to visitors.'

Hal replaced the receiver, his face wreathed in smiles for a few seconds before he thought about breaking the glad tidings to his mother and father. *That* was going to be the worst part, for goodness only knew what complications it would bring.

The first person he saw was his father, and he handed him the telegram. 'Your grandson, Father ...'

Bazz was tempering a bit of iron in his workshop next to his small furnace. A smile spread over his face: 'Boy, eh? Congratulations. Better let your mother know. She's doin' a bit of flower arrangin'. Better get her before she vanishes to see the horses.'

Lady Wrioth's face flooded with joy: A grandchild, at last ...

295

'And your own little son, Hal. Your own son and heir for Hyndemere. What a blessing. Thank goodness all this charade of keeping the child from us is over at last.

'We must have him christened here, and you must visit Dasia immediately and tell her so. She's had a nice long rest; we haven't troubled her, in fact we've been exceedingly patient with a young woman whom some might describe as over-excitable and grossly self-centred. Alas, only proper breeding can inculcate decent values . . .'

Hal sighed inwardly as he heard the bitter words. Nothing had changed as far as his mother was concerned.

'There's something else I wanted to mention, too, Mother. I expect you know Father's getting a new man for the estate, who trained as manager with Lord Bonsdale, plus two more extra staff. So it all ties in quite nicely really for me to relinquish the reins and go back to Dasia.'

Thinny's face went bright scarlet, and Hal was sad and embarrassed for, after all, she was his mother and had always worshipped him. It was just so terrible that she had this obsession about family dynasties.

'No – let me finish . . . *please*, Mother. It's obvious that Dasia will never settle down here, and I can't settle myself, without her by my side. So I just have to go back to her, at whatever cost. I just *have* to . . . for the sake of our son.'

'You stupid, stupid, boy,' moaned his mother softly with disciplined self-control. 'You just don't know what you're doing. She's ruining your whole life! Oh, if only you'd seen sense in the first place and married someone else more suitable, like Cordy Brighton, someone from your own circle – instead of a spoilt little ignoramus.'

With a huge shuddering sob, Lady Wrioth rushed from the room.

By February, Hal and Dasia and baby Aleck were living in apparent bliss, in a roomy flat in West Didsbury, as once more Kenny Saville's Aunt Celia came to their aid. She even arranged for the christening to take place at Didsbury Church, with Kenny as one of the God Parents. And although Hal's parents were invited neither of them arrived – due to a sudden attack of tonsillitis.

'Aunt Celia's a really good old egg,' beamed Kenny. 'There aren't many of 'em left. And what strikes me is, *she* never took the plunge either.'

For three whole years, Dasia and Hal lived in settled happiness in West Didsbury with their small son, and made lots of friends. Hal was lucky and had found a job in the laboratories of the British Cotton Industry's Research Association.

Dasia was no longer going out to work, but was fully occupied with baby Aleck and enjoyed her time spent at home in those formative years when he was developing so quickly from baby to infant. There was no real need to go out to any old job just for the sake of extra money to exist, which was a very fortunate situation to be in, compared to all those suffering from slump conditions who were grasping at anything which might help to save them from a starvation level of existence.

During this time Dasia was able to afford trips out to visit her own family and even to go with Hal to Hyndemere, for the past wounds had almost healed over now that life was on such a steady keel. Of course, both Bazz and Thinny adored their one and only grandchild, just as much as Horace and Alice did, for he was bonny, intelligent, bright and lively with dark curls and glowing brown eyes. By the age of three he was at his most endearing and his most exasperating. He explored everything in sight and drove the adults mad with his excess of liveliness and energy, and his never-ending whats, wheres, and whys.

Then one terrible day early in 1931, when Dasia was just twenty-one and Aleck was three, an accident happened ...

It was a lovely day in March, with purple and yellow crocuses growing above the winter grass, and the last of the snowdrops still under the hedges.

Alice Greenbow was taking her adored great-grandson for a short walk along The Grove. He was staying with her for the day while Dasia was in Manchester getting some new curtain material in Crighton's at All Saints, where Arnold Kimberley, Louise's ever faithful boyfriend, still worked.

'We'll just walk along The Grove as far as Gran and Gramp Tankerton's garden,' said Alice (for Andrina and Sammy Tankerton were now married). 'Then we can feed the donkey over their back fence with a few carrots.'

Aleck loved feeding the donkey. He also loved the old cedar tree, with its firm spreading branches which came right down to the ground, and were like ladders. He ran to the tree and scrambled triumphantly amongst the heavy, bare rungs. He was far ahead of Alice and as nimble as a small elf.

But this time he overstepped himself as he climbed too high and toppled to the ground.

At first, even though he howled and screamed enough to wake the whole neighbourhood, Alice thought it was just a bit of bruising. But soon it turned out to be more serious, and she had to get him back home and phone for Dr Fothergill. By this time it seemed that he might have broken his arm.

'It could be a green-stick fracture,' said Dr Fothergill.

'It can often happen with young bones. Sometimes the bone bends and breaks slightly – like a young green twig. I'm afraid there'll need to be a hospital check-up. I'll take him in my car to the Memorial Hospital.'

Alice was all of a weak flutter. She tried to get in touch with Louise at Baulden's where she was now a chief buyer, but had no luck. Then finally she rang through to Crighton's on the off chance that Dasia was actually in the shop ... And she was!

'Do come at once, Dasia. Dr Fothergill's taking us both to the Memorial. Yes, Aleck's calmed down a bit now, but hurry. And you'd better tell Hal.'

The panic in Alice's voice made Dasia so nervous that she hurried back straight away – her mind full of all the worst things that might have happened to her little son, and quite unaware that no great harm had been done – nothing that a light splint and crepe bandage wouldn't cure. Whereas she herself, when stepping off the tram near The Grove, tripped and fell like a stone, right into the path of a drayman's heavy cart full of timber, and was rushed unconscious to Wishington Hospital with multiple injuries.

Everyone was in a complete state of shock, disbelief, and disarray, as Hal went immediately to Wishington and was informed that she was too ill to receive any other visitor than himself – her next of kin.

That evening, the Greenbow women and Hal discussed what to do, while poor Horace, who was devastated, hid himself away in another part of the house.

'Aleck had better stay here with Mother,' said Louise to Rosalie. 'Andrina obviously can't manage him, with Sammy being away in London and her working at the shop.' She looked at Hal: 'And you've got your work to attend to, Hal, as well as having to get time off to visit poor Dasia. Maybe you could stay here with us, in The Grove for a while with Aleck, then at least he'll be with his father, and it will be happier for him.'

Hal nodded bleakly: 'I'll have to let them know at home, too . . .' He looked as white as a ghost.

The sense of shock was much the same at Hyndemere, as Lady Wrioth broke the news to Bazz: 'So poor old Hal is staying with Aleck at the Greenbows' at present – and all his spare time'll be taken up with hospital visits. She's terribly, terribly ill.

'I've just been on to them at the hospital, myself. I explained who we were and said that we were extremely concerned and would like to speak to Dr Mortingworth the chief medical officer, but he was out at a meeting. However, Sister Kemp did say in complete confidence that the outlook for Dasia is very grim indeed.'

Lord Wrioth stared at his wife in silence, then Thinny said, 'I wonder if we should offer to look after the child?'

Bazz shook his head: 'I'd let things run their course, Thinny. We've had enough trouble in the past . . . Let Hal manage this lot. He's older now – and it is his child, and Dasia's . . .'

'I know dear, but –'

'But, but, but!' said Bazz angrily. And he left the room.

Three weeks went by – and still Dasia was in a state of semi-coma. She had sunk to almost a skeleton, and her red-gold hair now framed a pale, lifeless face with half-closed eyes. Day after day, week after week, she lay there, her bony frame being given constant nursing care to guard it against bed-sores. Nurses patiently fed her, using a small white pot feeder with a spout on it to suck through with her dry, scaly lips. Sometimes she would take small spoonfuls of easy-to-digest slops.

Then, as if this wasn't enough to cope with, Hal was

promoted to a completely different job within the Cotton Industry's Research Association, and was asked to go to India for three months.

He was in an agony of indecision. How could he possibly go with Dasia lying there so ill? Yet how could he turn down the chance of a lifetime? As he saw it, it would bring long-term prospects of security and hope for him as a married man and bread-winner, and guarantee him and Dasia complete independence from Hyndemere and its clutches. He decided to see the specialists who were watching over Dasia's condition, and to ask their advice about the general prognosis.

The verdict was depressing and inconclusive. 'She could be in this state for as long as a year, old chap, or by a miracle she could suddenly start to improve. It's all in the lap of the Gods. There's nothing to do except wait and hope ...

'But quite naturally it's up to you to decide what you might do ... a very tricky situation indeed. Yet life has to go on, even for the sake of those lying in semi-comas. A man's work is of prime importance. You can't be chained to the bedside for ever. This is in *complete* confidence, of course, old chap ...'

When he got back to The Grove, Hal spent hours and hours, driving himself almost to madness, wondering what was best – and his pillow was wet with tears of worry for Dasia. But he knew only too well that if an offer of promotion was turned down it was usually regarded as a direct snub, and the same chance never came round again.

'You must do what you think's fit, Hal,' said Alice Greenbow. 'Poor Horace and me has faced a lifetime of family problems.

'I'm an old woman now, and I've got mi work cut out keeping an eye on the pawn shop, looking after Horace, and visiting poor, darlin' Dasia. That's just about all I can possibly manage.' Then she softened a bit and said, 'But don't worry, son. You've got to go to India and that's a fact. We'll keep an eye on Dasia and let you know any news. And your mother can look after Aleck, for a bit – then all us grannies will 'ave done our proper stint.'

There was no one there to see Hal sail to India from Southampton, except his father.

'It'll do you good,' said Bazz. 'Just what a youngster of your age needs. And don't worry about the boy. He'll be in good hands.'

For the first time in her life, Lady Wrioth had actually called round at the Greenbows, to collect Aleck to take him back to Hyndemere, and she was quite amazed to find that they lived in such a salubrious area. She was the sort of woman who made her own private assumptions right from the start and was so wrapped up in her own important and ordained life that she never really bothered about anyone else's. They were not her clan and that was all there was to it. Yet now, as soon as she and Alice came face to face they recognised a streak of like meets like . . .

They were both, in their own ways, schemers; women who had their own private incomes to back up some form of independence and decision making. And, even though Alice Greenbow's income was minute compared with Cynthia Wrioth's, they had a bond of experience more in common with each other than with young Dasia.

Thinny and Alice sat there supping tea and eating chocolate marshmallows. The frills and furbishes of class convention were swept away, for they were both beyond the competitive strife of grabbing a man or acquiring property.

'The point is, Cynthia, I can't possibly manage to look after Aleck now that Hal's in India. And our Andrina is far too involved in business to give him the background he needs at present. It would be different if he was of school age ...'

'Now don't worry for one single second, Alice. You couldn't be doing a more sensible thing than to send him to us. Hyndemere is in his blood, and already he adores horses. I think you'll find that every one of us will be a lot happier when he's settled in his spiritual home.'

Then she said very seriously, looking at Alice from her pale oval face and dark eyes, 'I think we should come to a financial agreement, too, Alice. A special one – just between the two of us.' She lifted an envelope from her beautiful lizard-skin handbag and took out a hand-written form with a place for signatures on it: 'We're both women of the world ... It's a sort of unofficial "adopting" really – but it'll give us all a proper sense of security. Now, how would it be if I arranged to pay you a quarterly allowance?'

'Me, Cynthia – whatever for? It's us should be paying you summat, for going to all this trouble.'

'No, Alice,' insisted Thinny, smiling brightly, 'You must take the quarterly allowance towards helping out with Dasia. You might well need extra funds if she ever recovers a bit and needs nursing care at home.'

'Oh, I don't think we're at that stage yet ... and anyway, Hal'll be home in three months.'

'All the same, Alice, I do think I might be right. Life plays some very strange tricks on us all. How would it be if I paid you a quarterly allowance of two hundred pounds?'

'– But it's a fortune, Cynthia! Most folks 'ud be able to exist for over a year on –'

Cynthia waved her hand dismissively: 'Nonsense, we musn't always drag up the lowest common denominator,

303

and you can always stop receiving it if you choose to ...
Why not try it anyway? After all, Alice, you as a business
woman know you can always put it in the bank to gain
interest, and not even have to bother with it if you so wish.
It would then always be at hand if you ever felt your
conscience required you to return it all.

'And ...' Thinny made a rather wry, coy expression,
'We are pretty solvent at Hyndemere whatever the rest
of country estates are like; so I'll let you have the first
two hundred pounds next week.'

Alice was secretly horrified. She wasn't a woman to
be bought, and it all seemed strangely back to front. She
knew it was foolish to look a gift horse in the mouth, and
she even agreed with much of what Thinny had just
said. All the same ...

She sat very still and stuck her chin out as she stared
silently at Cynthia. Then automatically she folded her
sturdy arms across her chest and smiled slightly: 'No
thank you, love. It's not my style.'

'No thank you?' Thinny looked completely puzzled.
She'd always imagined she could buy anyone off in the
final show-down.

'You didn't *really* think that a woman like me would
swallow all that stuff from a woman like you ...? I
wasn't born yesterday any more than you were. To put
it bluntly, Cynthia, I don't need the likes of you to feed
me with scraps of bread and butter ...'

'But of course not! I quite realise that. I was just
trying to do what was best for everybody –'

'Because that's what you're used to doing, isn't it?'
said Alice getting a bit rattled; 'doing your bloody best
for everybody – whether *they* think it's the best or
not ...'

'That's settled, then,' said Thinny as the two of them
stood up and stiffly shook hands.' I take it you enjoy
making the worst of a bad job – when there's no need to.'

'If that's how it looks to you, *yes*,' said Alice. 'Anyway it's been nice talking to you Cynthia, and getting the whole bloody thing sorted out. All the best to 'is Lordship.'

When Lady Wrioth and little Aleck had gone, Alice wept a few tears at the temporary loss of her great-grandson – even though it appeared to be for the best. But she decided not to mention the money rumpus to Andrina, or anyone else. For in some ways it was Andrina with whom Lady Wrioth should have dealt. Yet somehow Andrina was avoided or ignored – probably because Alice never regarded Andrina as the mother of Dasia in the true, conventional family sense. All those years of secrecy made it too late, in Alice's ledger-book of life, for her to be properly counted.

And so, as Dasia languished in hospital, little did she know how quickly her own little world, so hard won, was being dismantled.

CHAPTER EIGHTEEN

The Accident

The day Dasia opened her eyes properly to encounter the real world once more came as quite a shock to everyone.

She was suddenly aware of sunshine from one of the windows in the hospital side ward where she'd lain for all the past weeks in a semi-conscious state. She didn't know where she was, but her thoughts immediately went to pale yellow primroses surrounded by their stout green crumply leaves, and to the wonderful golden cowslips that might soon be out on the grassy banks of West Didsbury.

She put out her hand in a slightly puzzled way, to feel if there was anyone in the bed with her, and knew at once that it was not her bed at home. As she lay there she began to perceive that the smells weren't the same either. It almost smelt like the public lavatories after they'd been doused with Jeyes Fluid ... and there was even a whiff of carbolic soap in the air. And there were strange clanging sounds which, unknown to her at the time, were the noises of hospital porters pushing heavy trucks and trolleys about on the echoing stone corridors.

She tried to turn her head but her neck seemed weak, and she just lay there helplessly staring at the greyish white ceiling. It was, somehow, reminiscent of washing day ceilings at The Grove in their outside wash-house. For there was also a touch of Dolly Blue whiteness about it all.

She lifted her hand slowly and looked at her thin fingers. Her wedding ring was so loose that someone had put a ring of sticking plaster just below it to stop it from slipping off. She brushed her hand against her hair. It was there all right but it felt strangely tousled and matted, as if it hadn't had a proper brushing in years; and it felt shorter – almost as if it had been chopped off at the ends with a bread-knife. Then, as she gingerly placed her hand towards the back of her head, she found that her hair was pressed as close as the texture of a felt hat on the starched pillow.

'Good gracious, Mrs Wrioth ... Are you awake?' It was a brisk, breezy, kind-hearted voice, full of undisguised amazement.

Dasia closed her eyes and fell into a deep, natural sleep.

When Andrina got back from the pawn shop on the day Lady Wrioth had taken Aleck back to Hyndemere, she was in a state of great excitement. She'd just received news that Dasia had regained consciousness!

She hurried round immediately, with Sammy, to give Alice all the details: 'She just woke naturally as if she'd been sleeping very heavily and wanted to know where she was ...' sobbed Andrina thankfully, as she clasped her hands together and thanked God for their good fortune.

Then a bit later, when they'd all calmed down, she said, 'It means that Aleck'll be able to go to the hospital to see his mother at least – even if it's only to wave at her through one of the windows.'

Alice nodded with relief.

'How long was he supposed to be staying over with the Wrioths, then?' said Louise, 'because he won't need to now that Dasia's taken a turn for the better. He'll be far better back here so they can see each other more often. It will help her to recover, and show her how important it is to get better.'

'Their place is with us now, Mother,' said Andrina firmly. 'I feel it's my job to look after them both, and so does Sammy.'

Rosalie and Louise nodded in agreement.

Then Alice said bitterly: 'Well, you'd better talk to her bloody ladyship then, because my days of bargaining with Cynthia Wrioth are over after today's palaver. As you rightly say, Drina, he is your grandson. It's really between you and 'er.'

So eventually it was decided to write to Hyndemere telling them that the situation had now altered and that it would be possible to take Aleck back to be nearer to his mother and maternal grandmother.

With cold reluctance and a curt but polite note to say they were both delighted that Dasia was recovering, Bazz and Thinny accepted Sammy's and Andrina's plan to call and collect Aleck again that weekend.

'I expect the poor child will just grow into a football in the end,' said Thinny to Bazz, 'kicked about from pillar to post when all the time he could be here in his true environment.'

This idea was reinforced, when Andrina and Sammy arrived – and Andrina in the course of the conversation enthusiastically revealed her own plans for looking after her grandson. 'He'll be in good hands. I shall take him with me each day to the pawn shop. It'll all work out very well, really ... We have this neighbour there called Tilly Mattison who sells savoury pies and she'll be a boon. Her fourteen-year-old daughter who's just left school would look after him sometimes and give me a hand. It's all going to work out beautifully.'

Thinny and Bazz sat there and listened impassively, their faces expressionless. But when Andrina and Sammy and Aleck had gone, Cynthia was overcome with fury and grief.

'The *ignorance* of them. They'll totally ruin that poor child's life. My poor, poor son – having his one and only offspring brought up in those conditions ...'

The tirade went on for a good quarter of an hour until Bazz disappeared to his workshop to think about a complicated wrought-iron pergola.

In those days the huge red brick Wishington Hospital, where Dasia was now gradually recovering, was still part of a past but slowly vanishing Victorian era.

Dasia was now able to walk about and was in a main female ward with many other women, who occupied the tubular-framed, metal beds. Each had her own wooden, well-built, but often ant-infested, locker.

Wishington stood near to the cemetery and still had, within its own out-dated territory, the old workhouse, where people had been deposited from years back and which was still open, as a last resort for paupers. It was a well-ordered place from the outside with flower beds and cleanly swept paths. White-haired old men and bowed women sometimes sat outside in carpet chairs in blue workhouse pinafores or aprons, and they made up the work force for keeping the place in order.

The laundry, with its huge chimney, and all its machinery, provided a constant stream of clean, bleached, starched and ironed bedding, as well as thousands of freshly laundered night gowns and light flannel dressing gowns for males and females.

The sewing rooms, where all the nurses' uniforms and cloaks were fitted, were staffed by female machinists who turned out made-to-measure uniform dresses of good quality, hard-wearing material in different colours according to staff status. Starched caps in cotton muslin and white starched aprons in tough cotton completed the nurses' uniforms, with scarlet cloaks in thick pile wool for out of doors.

But there were some less pleasant features: the underworld of ants and cockroaches (which they sometimes called steam flies) and the darting wriggling insects known as silver fish.

The first news Dasia had to assimilate, when she'd recovered sufficiently to realise how long she'd been ill and what a miracle it was she'd survived, was to read all Hal's letters and to see the photographs and postcards he'd sent from India.

Her bodily injuries were now almost healed and she was walking about the wooden floors of the ward quite comfortably, and carrying out small tasks, like fetching drinks of water to help others who were in a weaker state.

And all the time, on her own locker top, she kept the smiling portrait of her infant son, Aleck.

Oh how she wished she could see him more often. For only once had she glimpsed him through the hospital windows, for children were not allowed in the hospital wards and visiting periods were as rigid as in any prison.

'As soon as you're out of this place,' said Andrina one day, 'you'll be with him for good. He's living with us at the moment and he's as happy as a lark.'

Dasia felt a terrible stab of sadness. All she wanted, now that she was recovering, was to see the back of this place before Aleck forgot her entirely. But she put a brave face on it.

Then one day when she was reading a letter which had arrived from Hal in India she could hardly believe what was written:

'... And so my darling, I think it will be for the best. Aleck will be getting the best kind of upbringing he could possibly need at Hyndemere and there will be no financial worries for any of your family.

... We shall both be able to rest in peace – knowing that his every need will be met and his education seen to. I notice that Mother said in her last letter she has already engaged a tutor for him until he goes to prep school ... What a blessing she has been ...'

Dasia brushed her thin hand across her forehead, as small beads of feverish perspiration began to surface. What on earth was he going on about?

The letter had been written some weeks ago, just after Dasia had shown her first signs of recovery, for mail from abroad often took months to arrive by sea.

That evening when Andrina arrived to see her she was completely up in arms. 'Why didn't anyone *tell* me? Surely I should have been the first to know?'

'There isn't anything to tell, dear. You must remember that you were seriously ill and we were all trying to do what we thought was best for Aleck – with you being here and Hal abroad. So we took it in turns with Hyndemere for him to stay. It seemed only reasonable. But since you've recovered, all that's changed and he's with me and Sammy all the time. So for goodness sake stop sending yourself mad with worry. Honestly, Dasia, you have just no idea how ill you really were. Often we didn't think you would last out another night.

'But it'll all be better now. They say you can come out in about two weeks.' Andrina suddenly fished in her handbag and produced a photograph from her leather

311

wallet: 'See, here he is, taken in the garden. I've just had them developed at Boots.'

He was standing there, his round chubby face wreathed in smiles as he held hands with Andrina and Sammy beside a small, ornamental, stone birdbath.

Dasia broke down and started to sob: 'When I get out he won't know me . . .'

Andrina began to look distressed herself, as she tried to comfort her heart-broken daughter: 'Stop torturing yourself. You ought to be glad he's been in such good hands, and happy that he's a sturdy healthy boy and that you are nearly better yourself. If you hadn't been so ill I'd say you were thoroughly spoilt compared to some . . .' Andrina pointed to the other picture on Dasia's locker: 'And that's a much better one of him, next to your bed. Cheer up, beloved. All three of you will be back together again soon.'

'Elvers is taking me into Manchester today, Bazz,' said Cynthia Wrioth. 'There are one or two small things I want to do.'

She was feeling extremely restless, and brooding over Aleck not visiting them so frequently. And the picture of him standing by the birdbath with Andrina and Sammy had quite set her teeth on edge. It wasn't a patch on the beautiful one Danny Elvers had taken of her and Bazz standing on either side of him in the rose gardens, next to one of the trysting gates.

'I thought I'd just go and visit my little grandson and see if he's at that pawn shop before I go on to Marshall and Snelgroves,' she said.

Elvers nodded respectfully but his heart was heavy with the agony of Enid being even worse in health, and the five children all still young. For now, in 1931, Maria the youngest was six, Robin was nine, George was eleven, Beth was twelve and Amy was thirteen.

He wondered for a few seconds how Dasia was going on. But thought it wise not to broach the subject as he knew the whole path was full of thorns. He and Enid had sent her some flowers when she was in hospital but from all accounts she was unconscious – though he'd heard that now she was recovering.

Well, at least there was still some good news left in the world.

Danny Elvers was ordered to park the new green limousine in Aglioni Street behind an ancient red brick laundry with loads of steam coming from it.

'Yes, I'll be quite safe, Elvers. But come to the shop if I'm not back in thirty minutes.'

When she arrived at the pawn shop, there was only a boy there, with his leg in irons, who told her that Mrs Tankerton had gone on an errand to town, and that young Aleck had gone to the local 'rec': 'It's over the main road near the catholic church. Eva's took 'im.'

'Oh yes ...?' She fixed him with cold brown eyes. 'And who exactly is Eva?'

'Ma Tilly Mattison's daughter.' His eyes lit up at the thought. If only he was there too, at the rec with fourteen-year-old Eva. She was a real card ...

'They won't be long, either, because she's going to call back 'ome and bring us some pies in.' He licked his lips slightly.

What a drab insalubrious area it was with all the poky little street houses each with a chimney almost as big as the house and smoke pouring out of every one, even in the midst of summer. She took out a delicate lace-edged Swiss handkerchief and blew her nose. It left a sooty mark.

Fancy having to see her one and only grandson spending his time in an atmosphere like this.

With determined haste she hurried to the rec, her

313

whole being repulsed by the awful surroundings, until she saw the green grass of the small park and rough football ground with tennis and bowls beyond.

And there, in the far corner, near the municipal bowling green there was a small wooden see-saw and some swings.

Thinny's heart melted slightly. It was quite nice really ... But as she drew nearer her heart turned to steel; for there, playing alone on the see-saw, while his temporary nurse-maid Eva and her pal Violet flirted and ogled at a group of boys, was Aleck.

And just as she drew near he tried to stand up on the sloping plank, gave an unholy yell and fell off.

'Bloody 'ell!' shouted Eva – 'Andrina'll kill me.'

The whole group of them stared in consternation, as they saw blood streaming from one of his knees (for it was rumoured he was the grandson of a lord) and Charlie Frimley produced a grey-coloured hanky with a butterscotch still stuck in the corner to tie round his leg.

But in a flash Cynthia was at his side: 'My poor, poor chicken. Come to grandma ...'

At first they all watched in silence, glad of an adult to take over, but when she began to drag him away the mood changed.

'Ay – what d'yer think yer doin', you bloody old cow. Leave 'im alone ...' But even then they didn't actually stir themselves too much except to yell at her, and then hold a post-mortem on what had happened.

''Oo the 'ell does she think she is?'

'I'll swear she 'ad a diamond ring on.'

'Did you see the way she grabbed 'im?'

By this time Eva decided to try running after Thinny and Aleck, but it was difficult because she was wearing a tight pair of Tilly Mattison's high-heeled shoes and no way was she going to run barefoot. So she and Violet hobbled and scuttled as quickly as they could, just

314

managing to keep Aleck within sight; while all the boys drifted away and began to talk about football.

'Where are we going, grandma?' said Aleck.

'Home to Hyndemere, dear. But first we're going to find grandpa's new green car and the First Aid Box, and Elvers will put some iodine on your knee and a bandage.'

'No! I don't want iodine. It stings.' Then he said, 'Did you say it was a *green* car?'

'Yes, dear, a beautiful, shiny green car and you're going to drive all the way back to Hyndemere in it with me and Elvers.' She smiled at him and squeezed his hand.

'Is Nanan Tankerton coming, too?'

'Not this time, dear. Maybe some other time.'

'What about Mama?'

'What about her, sweetheart?'

'Will Mama be coming?'

'Not just now. Don't be a Silly-Billikins – you know she's still in hospital, so how can she? But when she's better she'll certainly be able to come and see you.'

'What about Daddy?'

'Daddy's still in India, chick – but he'll soon be back.'

'Will he be back tomorrow?'

'Not *quite* tomorrow but very, very soon.'

Elvers was sitting in the driving seat, waiting ...

'I went to the shop, madam, and Mrs Tankerton said you weren't there – so I thought I'd better come back here for a while in case we crossed paths.' He smiled but deep down he was very puzzled by the sight of Aleck because Andrina had said the child was out at the local park with the young girl from the pie shop.

'He just needs something putting on his knee from the First Aid Box, Elvers, and then we'll get straight back to Hyndemere.'

315

Danny sat Aleck in the back of the car and attended to his knee, but all the time he was trying to think what he should do for the best. For this was surely a case of kidnap.

When he'd finally got some gauze tied round the grazes, and they were ready to go, he told Aleck to stay where he was, and said to Cynthia, 'Excuse me, m'Lady, but could I have a word with you outside the car?'

'Indeed you can't. We're going back right now, and no nonsense. Whatever you have to say doesn't need me to have to get out of the car again.'

'I think it does, Madam.' His voice was cool and firm, as he stood there on the worn stone pavement, with people going past giving them quick, inquisitive stares.

'Get in *immediately*, Elvers and take us *home*,' hissed Lady Wrioth.

But he stood his ground: 'There's something urgent I must discuss with you before we set off, m'Ladyship.'

Reluctantly, Thinny got out of the car again, and stood with him on pavement. 'Well . . .?'

'We can't just *take* the child . . .'

' *We*? What on earth do you mean – "we", Elvers? I'm ordering you to take us back home this minute, and you can decide for yourself whether it is better to do as I say, or be sacked on the spot and find your own way back home by train, not forgetting finding somewhere else to live.'

Never in his whole life including his days in the Great War, out there in the trenches where death was cheap, had he felt like murdering anyone as much as he did now. He looked into the calm, confident, self-righteous face and had to contain himself from knocking her to the ground: 'As you wish, your ladyship.'

Slowly, the car moved away from its drab surroundings with majestic grandeur, and was soon speeding along the open roads away from the city centre.

316

But back at the pawn shop, and at Ma Mattison's pie shop, it was pandemonium.

'I'm not sure what she looked like,' wept Eva to Andrina, with Violet by her side. 'It was all so quick. She seemed like a nice old lady – same as you. Then she just walked off with him when he started to yell from falling off the see-saw. We did follow 'em didn't we Violet? But then I got this blister on mi heel and 'ad to stop.'

Violet stood there, white-faced, and nodded.

It was a great day when Dasia was finally discharged from hospital, unaware that Aleck had been taken back to Hyndemere. There was quite a celebration at Andrina and Sammy's for it had been decided that she should stay with them at The Cedars until Hal finally returned from India – which everyone now reckoned would be in late July.

Alice had even gone to the trouble of making a beautiful fruit cherry cake covered in marzipan and layered with almond paste – like the celebration simnel cakes, eaten at Easter or Mothering Sunday. And she'd written 'Welcome Home' on it, in white icing.

But the happy day had a great gap . . .

It was Aleck.

'They promised to bring him over,' said Andrina shamefacedly, 'but apparently they already had this other important engagement, so they're up in Scotland visiting Hal's great aunt Katherine.' Everyone seemed really nervous at having to break the news, especially after Alice had been so confident that she'd seen Cynthia off with a flea in her ear – on that day when she'd tried to buy Aleck for ever.

'Anyway, not to worry . . . you'll be seeing him very soon, dear. I expect he'll have grown quite a lot, too.'

For the next ten days Dasia did nothing but mope about, mourning the fact that even now she hadn't seen

Aleck, although she'd spoken to him on the phone.

'Hello Aleck, my precious, this is mummy,' she had said, 'I've been in hospital, but I'm home again now. I'm coming to see you on Sunday, with Nanan and Grampi Tankerton.'

There was total silence, then a small thin voice said, 'Oh.'

'I'm bringing you a lovely cuddly lamb I made for you when I was in hospital.' Dasia's eyes filled with joy.

'Oh ...' Then he said, 'I've got a *real* pet lamb ...' Then he perked up even more and said in a very authoritative, perfectly enunciated voice, 'You'd better ask Lord Wrioth first.'

Dasia replaced the receiver, with a leaden heart.

A *real* lamb ... How on earth could an ordinary town-bred mother compete with Hyndemere on that? She felt as if her heart would break, for she knew that children of that age absorbed their surroundings like blotting paper. Yet she had never imagined her own beloved firstborn son sounding like some complete little stranger.

Ruefully she thought of the time she'd spent in hospital sewing away with determination and hope, to make him the small token of her motherly affection, only to have it dashed on the phone by those three condemning superior words ... 'a real one'.

As the time for her to visit him arrived she felt an overwhelming sadness and became quite obsessed. Would he even recognise her again? Supposing he never even spoke? And what if he actually loved his Wrioth grandparents better than herself and Hal?

The trip to Hyndemere the following Sunday was not a particularly happy one. It was only after a quarrel between the Wrioths and Dasia, Andrina and Sammy, that it was eventually agreed that Aleck could go home with them.

'All that can be said,' sighed Cynthia, 'is that he is

318

actually going home to his proper mother at last and isn't going to be anywhere near that dreadful pawn shop again, being looked after by a child skivvy.'

'How dare you say that! How DARE you!' screeched Andrina. 'The sooner the poor little devil's away from this awful prison the better. He had far more freedom when he was with me and Sammy.'

'Freedom isn't what they need at his age,' said Thinny scornfully. 'They need security; to be seen but not heard too often. And a good grounding in Latin and Greek, outdoor activities and the basic civilities of a cultured society.'

As usual, the two men kept silent. Lord Wrioth because he knew Hal would soon be home again and he had forgotten what little pests three year olds could be, who lost all his perfectly kept workshop tools round the rose gardens, and yelled in the night with nightmares, crying for their mothers. Yes – he was quite glad to see Dasia after all and give her back her son for a while.

In the end Aleck had said a rather tearful goodbye to Bazz and Thinny, who said he would soon be back with them again. On the way back to Manchester Andrina tried to comfort him, telling how much everyone was looking forward to seeing him again, and how daddy would soon be back and then the three of them would be in their own home once more ... But he remained pale and quiet and said nothing.

The following day, when she was alone in Andrina's house, Dasia was surprised to receive a letter from Hal posted well over a month ago in Delhi. She sat down on the flowered chintz sofa for a few minutes to read the letter. To her horror it was all about Aleck, and about the time she was ill, and it revealed all the things she hadn't known but which she now realised her own family had chosen to keep quiet about:

My Darling Wife,

How my heart has yearned to be home, and close to you and Aleck all these past long weeks, for there is something urgent I have to say to you about an arrangement I made at the time you were hovering between life and death.

You may not be aware of it, my dearest heart, but I gave permission for your Grandmother, Alice Greenbow, and my mother, Cynthia, to arrange an adoption for our son Aleck, so that he would be able to be totally brought up at Hyndemere.

At the time I did it with great pain, but considered it to be for the best, as there is some hint that I am needed to take on a permanent post over here.

All I can hope, my loved one, is that you will forgive me and try to see what sort of a predicament I was in while you were so ill. But now you are on the road to recovery, and when I come back home on leave I'm hoping you will be fit enough to come to India with me, knowing that Aleck will be looked after well – all his young days in the house he will eventually inherit.

Do not grieve too much, my darling, and have faith.

Love to our little one,

Your ever loving husband,

Hal.

The first thing Dasia did when she'd finished reading the letter was to go and walk round the garden. She was almost in a daze. It was too much for her brain to take.

She went and stood by the beautiful rectangular garden pond with its white and yellow water-lilies as she watched huge golden carp swimming idly in the dark, cooling gloom. Andrina and Sammy had designed and made the pool themselves . . .

They had designed this, thought Dasia, while down in

320

another part of The Grove her own grandmother Alice Greenbow was wilfully designing Dasia's own life.

She stumbled back inside with tearful eyes and poured herself a glass of lemon and barley water. She sipped it slowly.

It was three o'clock. There was just time to go round and see Alice before Louise and Rosalie, and Andrina and Sammy got back from business. For she knew that Alice rarely visited the pawn shop in the afternoons.

As she walked along The Grove in the hot, dusty sunshine, she went over the letter again in her mind.

Alice and Cynthia had actually started it off then? – by making a secret pact ... How awful! Fancy her own grandmother stooping to such terrible deceit.

And even Hal, her own husband, had agreed to the adoption – with not a single person saying a word about it to her.

But there again, perhaps Andrina and Sammy and the others didn't even know.

But the Wrioths themselves knew all right ... No wonder they were so cool and distant, and domineering when Dasia and Andrina and Sammy had brought Aleck back here.

By the time she reached the Greenbows' back door she was seething with rage as she thumped her way into the kitchen.

The room was as quiet, cool, empty and sun-dappled as in a fairy-tale. The grandfather clock was ticking loudly and peacefully: Tick ... Tock. Tick ... Tock, in the corner – like an eternal blessing. Everything was neat and tidy, and a small glass vase of snap-dragons was on top of the corner cupboard. But there wasn't a soul about – not even the cat or the dog.

She went upstairs to her old bedroom and found it absolutely cluttered up with wire, metal piping, and welding equipment. Piles and piles of battered old books lay on the floor. Even her wardrobe had vanished. The only thing that remained unaltered was the large brown stain from the leaking ceiling.

She stared at it all knowing it was the final end of girlhood, and the severing of family ties linked with The Grove.

'Is someone up there?' It was Horace's voice. He'd just come in from the garden with some lettuce for tea.

''Oo is it? Get thissel down 'ere, 'oo ever y'are, an' let's 'ave a look at thee.'

'It's only me, Grandad, it's Dasia. I came to see Grandmother.'

'She's int' gardin. What's the idea of suddenly comin' 'ere at this time?'

'Nothing, really. Just thought I'd take a walk. In the garden, you said?'

'Aye, she's pickin' some strawberries.'

Dasia faced him at the bottom of the stairs: 'I've really come to see what's been going on over Aleck while I was ill ... I had a letter from Hal today, and he says Aleck's been adopted by the Wrioths. I just can't believe it ...'

Dasia sat down on the stairs and began to weep.

'There, there ... Dinna fret thi'self – lass.' Horace patted her shoulder, and sighed.

'Sometimes these older women overstep the mark. They allus claim to mean well at the time, but often it turns out to be a bloody pain in the backside. But from all accounts there wasn't much 'arm done. Alice be'aved very well when the thin one wanted to buy we out. She refused point blank and almost told 'er to bugger off. It was all a damp squib, lass. All over and done with long afore you got out of 'ospital.

'Anyway, Dasia, allus remember that where Alice Greenbow is concerned I 'ave no power whatsoever – an' if you want 'er, she's with the strawberries.'

Suddenly Dasia hugged him. She knew it was true. One thing was certain, she could never blame him for any of it.

She walked down to the strawberry beds, which were covered in bits of white curtain netting, and saw Alice there on a rubber kneeling mat, with a big pale green fruit bowl by her side on the ground.

'What brought you along?' said Alice sharply.

'This letter from Hal.' Dasia shoved the letter in Alice's face, aggressively. 'This letter – telling me how you and Thinny Wrioth worked out a plan behind my back – giving *them* the power to take *my* child away from me!'

Alice looked at her askance: 'It wasn't a bit like that, love. You don't know the half of it . . .'

'No, I certainly don't know the half of it, do I? I – the child's mother wasn't told any of it!'

Her grandmother got up slowly then stood squarely and angrily on her two stout, flat feet, facing her granddaughter. 'You listen to *me*, madam. It 'appened because we was driven mad with what was best to do.' Her grey eyes suddenly took on a pleading look: 'We could've 'ad a large amount of money by now being paid into a fund for you alone, Dasia, in case you needed it. But never fret – you haven't got a bloody penny there, lass, because I refused!

'I'm not back to buying and selling children yet, lass – even if I does run a bloody pawn shop!'

There was a moment's hesitancy, and somehow Dasia sensed Alice's isolation as she stood there next to her half-picked strawberries.

Suddenly she moved up close, flung both her arms round her neck and smothered her with kisses.

'The only thing you can do at the moment,' suggested Sammy, 'is to try and keep calm and think about getting a job, to keep your mind occupied. Otherwise you could end up getting more and more depressed and worried, and be forever brooding about something. Particularly over this problem of whether you'll be going back to India with Hal, when he gets back – and leaving Aleck here with us.'

Dasia agreed. For, apart from those sound reasons, there was the one of finance. She needed an occupation which paid some sort of regular wage to help her save up – to give her a bit of independence. Money she could really call her own, even though she was well off compared to most women with Hal now earning a good salary that kept her secure and all the bills paid.

Deep inside her was the feeling that never would she want to go to India and leave Aleck again after all this past trouble, so finding a job and some sort of personal income was doubly important.

As soon as the *Manchester Evening News* arrived through the letter box, she began to look in the vacancies column for an advertisement which was there at least twice a week: 'Brilldecker Private Nursing Home, Seven Hedges Road, Hale, Cheshire; Qualified nurses and nursing care attendants required for both day and night shifts. Only genuine carers need apply. Applications in writing to The Matron, Miss Agnes Buttlehampton, Brilldecker Nursing Home.'

The advertisement was almost an institution, and she remembered Rosalie telling her that they were very fussy and loads of people tried to get jobs there, but never succeeded.

So Dasia decided to try her luck.

CHAPTER NINETEEN

The Inheritance

Late in June, when Dasia was watching the post ever hopefully to see if anything would arrive about the job in the nursing home, she was surprised to receive an entirely different communication which had been re-directed to her.

It was from the solicitors looking after the affairs of her true father Blennim Shawfield, and was about the items of sentimental value she was supposed to go and collect in Canada with all expenses paid, and with no time limit set as to when she should go.

She started to read it carefully, with excitement and anticipation. For as the years flew by, the strange instructions remained like a kernel of hope for the future, and the rare chance to visit a faraway place that she hadn't a hope of getting to otherwise, now that all her domestic problems entangled her.

But after only a brief glance at the letter, she knew that everything had changed. For these instructions were from a firm of well-known Manchester solicitors called Ailmar, Trantham and Hazlehurst, with words to the effect that her grandfather, Adrien Shawfield, who was still alive and living in Monte Carlo, had himself arranged for the items due to her to be forwarded to Manchester. This was to save her the 'bother and inconvenience' of having to trail across half the world, especially as he had received a short note from Horace to say that Dasia was very ill in hospital after being knocked down and severely injured by a dray cart.

'What right had he to meddle?' said Dasia petulantly to Andrina as they both read the letter again later that day.

'Think yourself lucky you were ever remembered in the first place,' said Andrina ruefully. 'Because I wasn't! Me, your true mother, wasn't even offered a single rose petal.' Then she cooled down because the letter from Ailmar, Trantham and Hazlehurst also mentioned that Adrien Shawfield had plans to come back to Manchester and visit his old birthplace in Salford, and visit all the haunts that he and Horace knew when they were young – and all his other friends and relations, before he had to meet his maker. He also planned to call and see his great grandson, and his only granddaughter, Dasia – sadly assuming that by now she would be more of an invalid than he was.

'We'll wait until it all happens,' said Andrina with a touch of irony; 'seeing the last lot faded out, this could well do the same. Life is full of lost causes, so cast it completely from your mind, Dasia, and stop hankering for what might never be.'

It was just two days later that Dasia got the news she was genuinely waiting for: the offer of a day job as a nursing attendant at Brilldecker Nursing home.

She began work there in July, thinking it would be fairly light work.

'This is a very select place, dear,' said the elderly Miss Buttlehampton in kindly tones. She was not in uniform but wore a florid silk dress with a coffee-coloured, V-shaped modesty vest in heavy lace which covered the cleavage area between her well-developed breasts, and which, far from being a disguise, pin-pointed the area with alarming boldness.

'You will find, Mrs Wrioth, that your duties are light and pleasant, and mostly concerned with setting the meal trays for our patients; doing a small amount of mending and darning in the afternoons, and generally being a pleasant and kind person for them to talk to.'

Dasia was quite impressed with the place for it stood in lovely grounds with aged spreading beech trees and green velvety lawns and white wooden summer houses. Inside the house itself there was a wonderful dining room with a grand piano in it and marvellous rosewood dining furniture.

The whole place was owned by the Buttlehampton family who had their own luxurious self-contained quarters, in stark contrast to the rooms upstairs which had been made into nothing but cubicles by dividing the former spacious bedrooms into extra small pockets of valuable income.

Many of their residents were extremely rich and very old.

The Buttlehamptons were beguilingly pleasant, but they always locked all the food cupboards in case hungry nurses broke into them, and one girl was severely reprimanded when she was seen to have an extra slice of turkey on her plate at Christmas.

Often, when the nursing staff sat in their own 'nurses room' with its sturdy kitchen table, made in the year dot, and covered in a brown chenille cloth, they would talk about why they happened to be working there at all. Their reasons varied, for they ranged from female helps as young as fifteen, to elderly widows, or maiden ladies in their sixties. Some were the only family bread-winner and some had handicapped children or relatives who needed their financial support.

They would have brief cups of tea as they met each other coming and going off duty, or changing into uniform; and some would flop into the battered old armchairs amongst piles of unread, ancient *Nursing Mirrors*, to read newspapers, or do a few minutes' knitting, or crochet, or write a letter to someone, often in pencil – or half smoke a cigarette, then stub it out and save it for later.

At first Dasia viewed it all through rose-coloured spectacles, for the pay she received was threepence an hour more than any job as a nursing attendant in a proper hospital. But it soon dawned on her that she was already carrying out proper nursing duties such as helping to give enemas, taking temperatures, giving out medicine, and dressing wounds. She was also expected to lay out dead patients and do all the domestic chores associated with looking after sick people – and gallop up and down the winding back staircase like a beast of burden, umpteen times a day.

As far as Dasia was concerned it was her way to a struggling sort of independence, but, like all the rest of them, she found it a hard, narrow path.

She was just about settled in to it when Hal arrived home on leave from his three months' stint in India. He had taken an earlier ship than expected and his father was the only one there at the quayside to greet him – for he wanted to cause as little fuss as possible after hearing of all the traumas caused by Dasia's illness.

Their reunion at Andrina's was strangely quiet. It was a day when Dasia had been helping to lay out an elderly patient at Brilldecker, and she was feeling very tired and depressed. Aleck hadn't made the day any better either, by breaking Sammy's greenhouse window with a heavy toy aeroplane which wasn't even supposed to fly.

Dasia fell into Hal's arms, as if there was no tomorrow. No words could describe the feeling of thankfulness, in that first embrace. Oh the joy of feeling warmth against warmth as their bodies pressed silently against each other and Dasia lost herself against the familiar shape of him; all the months of longing and hoping melting into this moment of true rapture. She stretched her hand across his face, suddenly aware that he'd changed slightly, for his hair had receded from his temples, like the tide going out, and his skin was taut and slightly yellow from a bout of malaria.

And as for herself, she knew only too well how thin and spiky she'd grown, with her golden red hair so boyishly short as she stood there in a plain dark green dress – smiling at him.

'One of the main things to get fixed,' said Hal next morning at breakfast time when Andrina had taken Aleck with her to the pawn shop and Sammy had gone off to work, 'is our flat ...

'It's been unoccupied so long.' He suddenly took her in his arms and kissed her gently: 'We'll just have to let it from now on – and use it when we're *both* home on leave.'

Later, on her way to work, as she sat in the third class railway compartment with men smoking their pipes, and young college ladies with flat leather music cases, and gazed idly up at the thick mesh luggage racks and the oblong framed water colour prints of other parts of Great Britain, she thought back – not to Hal's passionate love making, nor her first relief at being able to fall once again into his welcoming arms, but to the moment this morning at breakfast when he'd talked about renting the flat – 'when we're *both* home on leave ...'

Was it just a mistake, or did he mean it?

329

She was pleased when he called to collect her that evening at six o'clock from the nursing home – his face wreathed in smiles because his car was working. Then with sudden swiftness he turned to Mrs Lester, one of the nursing sisters, who was just passing them in the hall and said, with casual inbred authority: 'Where can I get hold of Miss Buttlehampton? I just want to have a word with her. Tell her it's Henry Wrioth.'

Sister Lester hesitated, and her long neck stiffened in its rigid starched white collar. 'I'm not sure whether ...'

But Hal didn't seem to have heard her: 'The name's Henry Wrioth. I don't mind waiting for a minute or two.'

'... I'll just check ...' She hurried away towards the Buttlehamptons' private apartment.

Dasia almost curled up with shame. What an indignity, to have this happen. Her face was now scarlet as she stood there like some small child with its father – waiting to see the headmaster.

'What on earth are you *doing*, Hal?' she whispered. 'You're making me really embarrassed. I feel a complete ninny!'

He turned to her with a solemn face – then deliberately winked. But she was not amused. The wink irritated her even more as she sank deeper into humiliation.

'Ah, Mr Wrioth, what can I do for you ...?'

To Dasia's amazement, Agnes Buttlehampton was flowing towards them like a ship dressed overall. She strode across the thick Turkish carpet waving a plump, expressive hand which grasped Hal's. 'Sister said you wished to see me.'

It was just as if Dasia didn't exist. She went and sat on an old carved oak chair behind a plaster column, just within earshot – and heard Hal swiftly outlining the fact that he was home on brief leave from India, and that his wife would no longer be able to continue her duties.

'Er ... From when? Mr Wrioth?'

'From now – actually, Miss Buttlehampton.'

'From *now*, Mr Wrioth?'

'From this minute, Miss Buttlehampton.'

Agnes Buttlehampton peered round uneasily as she suddenly realised that the main subject of their conversation was about somewhere. 'I must say, your wife never mentioned anything like this happening. And we're *desperately* short of staff at present. Ladies of her calibre are few and far between.'

'I'm sure they will be.' He nodded his head with a quick grunt of sympathy: 'Well, I won't take any more of your valuable time, and you know her address – with regard to the salary owing. Thank you very much, Matron. I know that my wife has enjoyed every moment of her time with you.' This time he grasped *her* hand.

Dasia sat there in dumb misery as they drove back to Andrina's. The first proper job which she had actually managed to get for herself, on her own initiative – squashed like some small, soft greenfly with the flick of a finger. Her one small sign of independence blotted out in that one terrible wink, as if he was virtually doing her a favour, and without any warning or discussion. A shuddering, sighing sob rose within her.

She caught a sideways impression of Hal's face as he drove along. It was smooth and untroubled.

'Well, that's that, then,' he said cheerfully. 'I must get to Hyndemere tomorrow, to see Mother – and all of them. We'll go together; you, me, and Aleck.

'Father was saying how they miss seeing so much of their grandson. Absence makes the heart grow fonder, and all that.

'But never fear, they're quite prepared to take him on again while we're away. Continuity in his life is essential. He'll be able to have a private tutor until he's seven, then he'll be sent to Ten Keys Prep school in Cheshire ...' His eyes caught a glimpse of her alarm: 'Surely you know it's for the best, Dasia?'

'No ...' She shook her head vehemently. 'No, I *don't* know! But what I do know is – I want to stay right here, close by. And I've also got my own job, now –' She suddenly shut up like a trap. Her job was gone ...

Hal's face whitened slightly. He slowed the car down, and stopped.

'I know you don't like what I did at that place, but I had to. It was them or me. It's ludicrous for a man to have to compete for his wife's attention against a nursing home!

'Thank goodness I never did finish my medical training, when I see what goes on ... And it isn't as if you even need the job!

'And as for Aleck, once he's at boarding school he'll be of an age to fend for himself. It'll be the making of him.

'Then – when we're back on leave – he can be with us, and live at home in West Didsbury at weekends. Everything'll work like clockwork.' His face shone with boyish enthusiasm and hope as he turned and hugged her.

Dasia tried to stifle her anxiety. 'I can't bear to think of going out to India, Hal. My heart is here on this island. You just said he needs continuity – and that's just what he's got at the moment. But now it's all going to change again. I just won't be able to stand it.'

'But you're my *wife*, Dasia. Remember?' He looked at her ruefully.

He started up the car again, and they drove back to The Cedars in complete silence.

★

The next day, Hal was up bright and early, but to his amazement, Dasia was still lying there with her eyes closed. She wasn't asleep, but all the anger of yesterday's episode lay inside her like an unexploded grenade ...

'Come on, Dasia, what about our breakfast? Aleck's already twittering about his clean starched shirt. He says there are some creases ironed into the sleeves. He's a really fussy little blighter – takes after his grandfather Wrioth.

'Dasia?' his tone sharpened and grew more bombastic. 'Don't say you're going to lie there all day, woman. It's nearly twenty to eight. If you'd had to go out to that wretched job you'd have had to be out by now –'

Suddenly Dasia sat up, wide awake. 'I know that, Hal,' she said in a hard toneless voice. 'But I was deliberately prevented from ever going there again wasn't I? I was carried off like some naughty infant who'd escaped from home – not like an adult being rightfully employed. Not in the least like a mature, responsible human being ...' she hesitated then said sarcastically, 'like – *you*, for instance.

'I shall remember that moment, when you dragged me from my work at the nursing home till the day I die. The pure indignity of it – as if I was just your bundle of personal property; like some slave who couldn't even speak for herself. It was appalling ...' She lay back in the bed and closed her eyes.

But Hal's own eyes flashed with anger: 'Less of the histrionics if you don't mind, Dasia. You'll never convince me you actually liked working in that hole when you could be back here with me and Aleck where your proper life is.'

Dasia sprang out of bed, her cheeks burning with fury: 'That's not quite the point is it? It's up to *me* to decide. Just as I've had to decide all the time you've been away.'

'All right then. Point taken ...' he said through gritted teeth. 'Now get up, there's a good girl, and sort things out for Aleck, and get our breakfasts. We want to get an early start. Mother likes everything arranged to the dot.'

Dasia pretended not to hear. Instead she went to a small bookcase of Andrina's in the bedroom and took out a sixpenny paperback book. 'You can see yourselves out,' she said, 'I'm going to have a special day of rest and please myself for once – to make up for yesterday. I shall probably read novelettes, like women are supposed to do, and eat chocolates. Then, when I'm fed up with that in a couple of hours, I might even look round for another job. One thing's certain, though, I'm not coming with you to Hyndemere.'

She felt a sudden overwhelming sense of relief that she had at least asserted herself.

The effect was catastrophic. Hal looked ready to strangle her, but didn't because Aleck was calling him. He thumped out of the room like a small child himself, muttering and sighing and growling evilly to himself about her stupidity: 'We should never have married. I knew it wouldn't work the moment I asked you. You're just a self-centred melodramatic little madam!'

And as he left the room and thudded down the stairs Dasia yelled for all the world to hear: 'And you, Hal Wrioth, are a cowardly jumped-up snob – tied to his mother's apron strings and hardly able to lace up his own shoes. If I hadn't married you when you *implored* me to, you'd have wilted away to *nothing*!

'But you won't catch me wilting away – in spite of dragging me from that job. Never, never, NEVER!'

An hour and a half later, Hal and Aleck set off for Hyndemere alone, planning to spend a full week there, while Dasia moped about at Andrina's in a fever of uncertainty.

'Why didn't you go with them?' said Andrina. 'Oh but of course, you won't be able to get the time off, will you? Anyway I must dash.' Then Andrina hurried away to the pawn shop.

In desperation and longing for someone to talk to, Dasia decided to take a chance and call on Dolly – even though she knew she wasn't always welcome there, in spite of Dolly saying she was.

But when she got to Derbyshire Lane, she forgot all her own troubles, as she walked straight into a complete fiasco. Dolly was standing talking to Marcia at the gate, and a workman was removing a large piece of drainpipe and some guttering from Dolly's small patch of garden outside her front window. Everyone looked unusually solemn, and Marcia had three huge scratches on her face.

'Isn't that your Dasia? I think she's coming here,' said Marcia to Dolly. 'My ... she isn't half turning into a skinny-ribs.'

'I couldn't care a tinker's cuss what she's turning into,' mumbled Dolly mournfully. 'All I want is my Mr Corcoran back here under this roof, like he's been for the past nine years.

'An' *I'd* get some of that Dr Fox's pink ointment on them murderous-looking gashes, Marcia, before they turn septic from that new maid's fingernails. She must be the worst one you ever took on in the whole of your born days.'

'That's not her fingernails, Dolly. It was your marvellous Mr Corcoran pushing me into next door's wire netting while he escaped with her.'

'I can hardly believe it, even ten hours later, Marcia. *My* Mr Corcoran ...' Dolly's top lip trembled. 'He just doesn't know what he's let himself in for. She's a regular little praying mantis where innocent men's concerned. And what eyes, Marcia, as big as Lilian Gish's when she's just escaped the rail track, and enough butter melting in her little rose-bud gob to spew out all down that satin dress. All I hope is that Mr Corcoran realises that he'll be nailing his own coffin, when they get to that caravan at Rhyl ... and she leads him off the straight and narrow. Honestly Marcia, I feel too weak and ill to even lift a finger – even though I am expecting that new lodger any minute. I feel as if I shall have an instant collapse.'

'Well, just think of *me*, Dolly, with no staff except the charwoman and that new Mrs Lucas who borrowed Mr Frandle's hanky to wipe jam off two of the clean plates ... and wouldn't help me out unless she was allowed to keep her moulting Persian cat in the bedroom ... for believe me, Dolly, I'd even be driven to taking your Dasia back at this moment.'

'Wouldn't we all, Marcia? Wouldn't we all ...?'

Their voices faded away and they stood there looking quite dreamy as Dasia came close.

'Now, Dasia, love. And what can we do for you, on this bright sunny day?'

She hesitated. She hadn't bargained on Marcia being there. But Marcia just narrowed her green eyes into catlike slits and gave her a warm purring smile: 'Long time no see, lovey. I was just saying to your aunt that the standards of domestic help are falling rapidly. Even since your day.'

'Yes,' said Dolly, 'we were just this minute thinking about you and wondering how you were going on. Is Hal back yet?'

Dasia nodded: 'He's just taken Aleck to Hyndemere for a week.' Then she added quietly, 'He was in a bit of a huff.'

'That'll be nice then ... You'll be glad to see the back of him. I sometimes wish someone'd take my gentlemen away for a week.'

'Except for – you – know – who ...' said Marcia staring extra hard at the length of drainpipe lying in the front garden.

Dolly pretended not to hear and looked hard at Dasia as Dasia expounded on the heated climate between herself and Hal.

'Maybe it was a bit much for you, dear, him coming back then him immediately swanning off there for a whole week – leaving you on your own. You did quite right to come here to get it off your chest.'

'I'm not really on my own. Andrina and Sammy are always there when they get back from business. But I dare say I'll miss Aleck – especially with my no longer working ...'

'No longer working, dear? Why ever not?' murmured Marcia. 'Not by any chance another little ...?'

'No, nothing like that. It's just that Hal wants me to go back to India with him – and for us to leave Aleck behind with Lord and Lady Wrioth while we're away.' Dasia dabbed hastily at the corners of her eyes.

'Why on earth don't you take him with you?' said Dolly.

'Good Gracious, Aunty. Not that! It just wouldn't be suitable for any of us. I couldn't bear it. I'm his *mother* ... I want us both to stay in our own surroundings.'

'How do you know you wouldn't be able to bear it, if you haven't even been, love?' said Marcia. 'It's a *very* luxurious life out there.'

Dasia stared at her coldly: 'Even Hal admits it's a bit dicey. There are all sorts of risks with a young child.'

'So you mean to say you'll stay back here with your one and only offspring parked at his place, with no job of your own – and with him waltzing off to India again?' said Dolly bluntly. 'If you ask me, that's just *asking* for trouble.' She and Marcia exchanged shrewd, knowing looks ... 'You want your head seeing to, lass.'

337

'So what is it then?' said Dolly later that afternoon as they sat alone in the front room in the leather, metal-studded arm chairs – with the brass ash trays draped in their ribbons of weighted suede over the arms.

In seconds, all Dasia's fears and sadness came tumbling out as she told Dolly all her troubles. Finally she said, 'It's Hal ... Wanting me to go to *India* ...'

'Only you can decide all that, dear ... Look, Dasia, that child is yours and Hal's – not his parents'. It was quite different when you were ill, but now it's all changed. You'll just have to stand up to them all, dear, or they'll swamp you out. But only you can find the best way to do it. Whatever happens you must keep him with you and Hal. Or with you, his mother – when Hal's away.'

The conversation ended abruptly as Dolly heard voices talking outside. She stood in the middle of the room and peered: 'That must be Harold Solway, my new lodger, arriving. He only looks the age of your Tommy, though he's got a bit more weight on 'im, and a bit more 'andsome in the manly sense. Not that I'm decrying your Tommy, Dasia, but he always seems to remain a bit of a school boy ... Whereas this one ...' Aunt Dolly's eyes glowed. Mr Corcoran was fast fading from her mind for ever.

'You spent the week at *Dolly's*? Acting as her unpaid skivvy?'

Hal glowered at her in ill-concealed anger: 'Why do that?'

'I was lonely.'

'Lonely ...? When you know full well you could have come with us to Hyndemere. But instead, after me going to the trouble of getting you freed from that job, you chose to be thoroughly awkward and let your husband and child go on their own. Honestly, Dasia, I just do not understand you.'

He turned to Aleck and said lightly, 'What on earth should we do with her, Aleck?'

Aleck smiled up at his father, silently.

'Did you enjoy it at Gran and Grandpop's?' Dasia pulled him to her for a big hug and a kiss but he tried to wriggle free.

Then he said, 'Yes, and there's another pony there, specially for me. And I'm calling him Snowball. Grandpa let me have a ride on him and Elvers is going to feed him all the days I'm not there.' Then he went to Dasia and dragged at her hand and said, 'Why can't we be in our proper home, then I could keep Snowball there.'

'Hyndemere is your sort of "proper" home,' said Hal gently.

A fearful, simmering rage welled up in Dasia: 'No dear,' she said just as gently, 'Daddy doesn't *quite* mean that. Hyndemere is Gran and Granpop's house, and *your* proper home is our flat at Toppyford Mansions in West Didsbury – where we're going on Monday, for the rest of Daddy's leave.

'There won't be room for Snowball, but you'll have lots of fun when you see him again, just as you'll have lots of fun when you come back here to see Nanan and Nunky Tankerton, and Great Mama and Pa Greenbow.'

Hal's eyes and Aleck's fixed her in a startled gaze, then Hal said, 'It's the first time I've been told my own plans in advance – before I've even decided them. Actually I had no intention of opening up the flat.'

'Well we *are*, Hal ...' There was an uneasy note of hysteria in the pitch of her voice. 'I am staying there with Aleck in our rightful home, until you return on your next leave in three months' time.'

And so, on the following Monday, he opened up the flat and gave her the keys.

'Are you sure you'll be all right on your own?'

'I shan't be on my own shall I? I'll have Aleck. And they are service flats with a beautiful garden. It isn't as if we're living in a broken-down old tenement.'

Her heart was leaping with tearful joy as she explored the place, and noted all the things that needed improving upon since they last lived there, before her accident. It all seemed so much brighter and lighter than she'd remembered. And so convenient with it being on the ground floor. She gave thanks to God in Heaven that she'd lived to get back to it, and that all three of them were here, for the time being, together.

It was a time for true conciliation, and so it proved to be, for in spite of having to iron out day-to-day differences the rest of the leave went well. Dasia even enjoyed a brief weekend visit to Hyndemere, hearing, with sadness, that Danny's wife Enid was still in very poor health.

Danny put on a cheerful face and won Aleck's heart with Snowball the pony. 'Pr'aps one fine day I'll bring Snowball to see you at Toppyford Mansions,' he joked. 'I'll bring a tent and camp along the way – and he can crop your grass in the garden before he goes back again.'

Aleck's eyes shone with delight, for there was no doubt in his mind that it would happen, and for a fleeting second, as Dasia herself caught Danny's eye, she got caught up in the fantasy of it.

A few days after the tearful farewells of Hal's return to India for a further three months, Dasia received another letter from Ailmar, Trantham and Hazlehurst – the Manchester lawyers dealing with her father's will.

It informed her that in a month's time her grandfather, Adrien Shawfield, was coming over from France with his housekeeper, to stay at the Midland Hotel for a few days in order to meet everyone. An initial meeting about the will had been arranged, to take place at The Grove with the solicitor present, to hand Dasia her long-awaited bequest.

'. . . But in no way, madam, can it be deemed to be of a very substantive nature . . .'

'Which implies,' said Andrina when she saw the letter, 'that they think it's almost a waste of time your claiming it at all. But it's not up to them to put that in a letter. Sammy was most annoyed when he saw it.'

Nevertheless, Dasia could hardly wait as she counted the days to her grandfather's arrival.

It was the gathering of a lifetime at the Greenbows' in that golden October. The roomy houses of The Grove were deep in the vivid shades of fallen autumn leaves, of nut brown, orange, yellow and vivid scarlet. And the shadows of slim lime trees fell across white pebble-dash, and mellowed bricks and slate-blue roofs.

Horace, now seventy-eight, and Adrien, aged eighty-nine and in his wheelchair, met and embraced each other like long-lost brothers, while Alice stood alone with tear-filled eyes and Andrina turned her face deep against Sammy's ever-steady shoulder.

And as they sat there in the sun-drenched quiet of the drawing-room, with its ancient French windows, and Rosalie brought them refreshments, the full details were revealed to Dasia about the bequest from the dead father she'd never seen – Blennim Shawfield.

'This is a photograph taken of him, when he was about your age,' said Adrien, handing it across in a strong, sun-burned hand, with just the slightest tremor. 'You are very much alike . . .

'Years ago, when my dear wife, your grandmother, died, I went out to Canada and America for some time while your father was there and worked as a jeweller. But it's hard, meticulous, tiring work, especially if you work with gem stones and jewellery design. It's a great strain on your eyes, working in glaring artificial light all the time and using magnifying glasses. So when poor Blennim died, I dug up my roots again and went to the South of France, and I've never regretted it – except for wonderful moments such as this. And now I'm due to go back down memory lane with old Horace.' He smiled at Dasia and shook his head slightly in wonderment. He was a handsome man with a beaky nose, very deep-set eyes and, even now, a fine head of silvery hair.

Then he and Horace got together again to look at snapshots and press cuttings. They talked about the Manchester and Salford of yester-year in the days of Queen Victoria, often going back to times when Horace was only eight and Adrien was eighteen, when the Shawfields and the Greenbows lived close to each other near Greengate, Salford.

Adrien's father was a bookkeeper, and Horace's a cloth merchant, and Adrien had once nearly married Mollie, one of Horace's older sisters, but sadly she had died in her late teens.

'It seems like only yesterday when you dragged me safely from a watery grave at Ardwick pond, all covered in weed and slime, when some of us little uns were over there fishing for jacksharps ...' said Horace dreamily. 'The dangerous things we got up to was nobody's business. I often wonder we're still alive to tell the tale.'

'I can even remember back to seeing watchmen in heavy cloaks and carrying swords and great knives along with their night lamps as they went round the city,' said Adrien, 'and even your Horace'll remember the police in those tall top hats, surely? And the old Dog and Duck in Charter Street, Manchester, with its coloured lamp and known to be a den of thieves ...'

342

Then Mr Trantham interrupted the flow of reminiscences, turned to Dasia and said, 'The final part of your father's will is concerned with the small cottage left to you here, in Flixton, Lancashire.' He then proceeded to read the details.

Here . . .? They could hardly believe it.

'I just can't understand why my father wanted me to go all the way to Canada to claim my bequest when all the time the main part of it is here,' said Dasia excitedly.

'Don't get too carried away,' admonished Andrina, 'we've yet to see it . . .'

'I think the reason he wanted you to go to Canada,' said her grandfather Shawfield, 'was to give you some inkling of the main part of his life and what it had been like. But there you are . . . things never turn out quite the way people imagine and, who knows, but you might go there at some other time in your life after this.' Then he smiled and said, 'Well, at least I'm grateful it's worked out this way – or I'd never have got back here to see you all.'

Then they all began to talk about the background of Dasia's new acquisition – the deeds to this small cottage, close to St Michael's church and the Greyhound pub in Flixton, where the Jubilee Tree was, and where Blennim claimed, much to Andrina's embarrassment, Dasia Greenbow had been conceived.

'Never in a month of Sundays did I have any idea that he'd secretly bought that cottage,' gasped Andrina. 'It had belonged to his friend, Brian O'Hara, but he left just after Blennim went to Canada and there was a tenant in it. So I never knew what happened to Brian . . . And now it seems Blennim bought the place with some money his mother left him. Right now it's empty and going to rack and ruin – according to the solicitor.'

That next afternoon, Dasia, Andrina and Sammy went to see the cottage. They offered to take Adrien and his housekeeper with them, but Dasia's grandfather refused apologetically, saying it would be too much of a strain and that they would be packing to get back to France the day after.

They wound their way through Urmston along Flixton Road and past the Bird in Hand pub, then past Squire Wright's with its huge weeping copper beech tree and all its chaffinches and thrushes and blackbirds dotted about in peaceful tameness. As they crossed over the railway bridge at Flixton station and into Flixton village, a great sense of peace enveloped Dasia. What a wonderful bequest – a place of one's own!

But when they saw it, in its patch of overgrown weeds and nettles and coarse field grass: a small, isolated little farm labourer's peeling, whitewashed cottage of the one-up-one-down variety, with no indoor lavatory and small cracked window panes covered in spiders webs, Andrina said, 'Surely this wasn't the place you were conceived! It was never like this in my day ... And it looks so *small* ...'

Sammy glanced fleetingly at Dasia's slightly crest-fallen face. 'It's got quite a lot of potential you know. Its saving grace is that it's got that half-acre of land with it and you'd be able to modernise it and even build an extension.'

Dasia nodded meekly. It was all a lot to take in in one go, a place of her own; especially as she had no income of her own to do repairs or alterations.

'We'll see you right, won't we, Sammy?' said Andrina smiling, as they went to collect Aleck from the Green-bows and took him and Dasia back to West Didsbury.

'One of these days it'll all come right, dear ... Just you wait and see.'

CHAPTER TWENTY

The Cottage

The following month, no sooner was Dasia settled down into a patch of contented, untrammelled life at West Didsbury, with Aleck happy at his kindergarten, and loving letters from Hal in India, than Horace Greenbow died suddenly and peacefully of an acute heart attack, in his bed without any warning illness.

To say that the whole family was devastated was an understatement – for he was a linchpin in everyone's day-to-day existence as he ploughed away with all his ideas and inventions, and discussed the future of mankind with his old pals and cronies, as they played chess and smoked their pipes, and sat on park benches.

There was an immediate panic as to what was going to happen next, as Alice swore she could never live in the big house in The Grove, without him.

Horace was not a religious man in the formal sense and always asked that one of his pals, Charlie Spinnet, should conduct a non-religious sort of memoriam when he died, and said that he would like to be cremated: 'Tha can do what tha likes wi mi after that, but never let mi ashes float anywhere near Dawson's 'ouse – what turned down my ideas for electric lawn-mowers . . .'

It was a freezing foggy day in November when the service took place and the small chapel was packed out with friends and relations, many of them old men in mufflers and overcoats and complete strangers to the rest of the Greenbow family.

'He always had an assortment of mates – that's for sure,' wept Alice, after they'd been treated to a reading from the *Ragged Trousered Philanthropist*, the poem 'To a Skylark' by Shelley and a vigorous rendering of 'The Red Flag' followed by a gramophone recording of 'Nymphs and Shepherds' sung by 250 Manchester schoolchildren recorded in 1929.

Notice of his death was put in the *Manchester Evening News* and the *Manchester Guardian*, and the Wrioths sent a huge wreath of deep red roses – even though it was requested that there should be no flowers, but money instead to the Society For Inventions (rudely called the sieve heads by many).

'You've got to hand it to him for being a bit of a character,' said Dolly to Marcia as she joined the throng heading for the Co-op assembly rooms for a ham and tongue funeral get-together.

They were both dressed from top to toe in black; Marcia wore black silk stockings with decorated 'clocks' ornamenting their sides and high-heeled ankle strap shoes with very pointed toes and a hat which was a mass of black polka dot veiling and black feathers so that she resembled a rather thin black crane. Dolly looked like a small round black liquorice allsort in her thick black 'funeral' coat with its bit of mock astrakan on the collar, and wearing her round black pill-box hat covered in black beading.

'Harold Solway was quite taken with me in this getup,' Dolly whispered to Marcia as they helped themselves to mustard. 'He's the best lodger I've ever had ... Always so caring and attentive. It's as if we were both born into the world at the same time. We're exactly on the same wave length . . .'

'Except that you must have been waiting about forty years in the midwife's little brown bag,' murmured Marcia, maliciously.

That evening, when Dasia returned from the funeral, there was a letter waiting for her with the Hyndemere crest on it, and her heart sank. This was hardly the time to be hearing from them. But to her surprise it was a note of sympathy from Cynthia saying how sad they both were to hear of Horace's death and that she wanted to apologise for having sent the wreath of red roses, when no flowers had been requested. There had been a strange muddle, for the roses were for Enid Elvers's funeral – as she'd died in hospital at almost the same time as Horace.

She ended the note with the hope that Dasia would soon be bringing Aleck to stay with them again.

Enid Elvers . . .

Even though Dasia knew she'd been ailing for years the news of her death was still a terrible shock. She thought of Danny's motherless family, for his eldest girl was only thirteen.

Next day, she made arrangements to send flowers from herself and Hal, along with a card of sympathy to the Elvers family. But oh – how little it really expressed the depth of her feelings.

Then she went round to see how Alice was getting on. No one was at work that day. Rosalie and Louise were both at home to console their mother and there was so much to do, settling up Horace's belongings and estate, and an insurance fund he belonged to.

'Your grandfather left summat for you,' sighed Alice when she saw Dasia. She went away and came back almost immediately with a large, much bashed-about ancient wooden tool box, and a letter.

★

347

Dear Dasia,

My one and only, precious grandchild – the enclosed bit of metal and wire, and other attachments is for you.

It is an electric motor. A versatile invention specially designed by me for fixing to small bits of kitchen equipment.

Maybe it could be incorporated into a potato peeling machine – or summat like that.

Never say that man hasn't tried to help woman. Take no notice of Alice.

Good luck in life, dear.

Always yours,

Even in heaven,

Your loving Grandfather, Horace Greenbow.

Dasia gazed through tear-blurred eyes at the mechanism. If only – oh, if only he had still been here with that triumphant twinkle in his eye, and that enthusiastic timeless optimism.

The gadget meant nothing to her at the moment, but in the back of her mind she was already determined to see if something could be made of it.

The following May, when the weather was dry and sunny and beams of golden colour shone on the sylvan glades of spring, and the evenings were light and long, Danny Elvers brought the piebald pony and a small, immaculate gypsy caravan to Toppyford Mansions in West Didsbury. Lord Wrioth had insisted that, after all, something more than a tent was required and had come across this relic of the past in one of his own fields, under a huge oak tree down by a brook. He had arranged for it to be cleaned and painted and the wooden-spoked, metal-bound wheels to be repaired and made roadworthy.

Everyone was delighted and the staff at Hyndemere turned out to wave Danny and his young daughter, Maria, off on their adventure, while Bazz took a photograph of it all. The rest of Danny's family were being cared for whilst he was absent by the new young assistant housekeeper Shirley Badell, who was in her mid-twenties.

Aleck and Dasia were completely dumbstruck when they saw the caravan actually arriving at the flats and being parked in the vast grassy garden. And when Danny and young Maria came inside to get some water for Snowball, Aleck could hardly believe it and stood there with wide and wondrous eyes, watching his pony drink.

Dasia looked back on the whole episode as one of the happiest in her life. It was so wonderful to have Danny actually staying there the night. So secure, so carefree and restful – not to be on her own. Late into that first evening they talked of their own personal joys and sorrows with a freedom neither of them had ever known before.

'There's no doubt about it,' said Danny sadly, 'that the ideal life is one with a man and wife sharing the joys together ... and we are both missing that just now.' Before he went to bed, he hesitated slightly, almost as if he was going to speak – then went on his way.

But just before he left to take the two children back to Hyndemere he stood close to her and said, 'Thank you. It's been terrific, and the children have had a great time.'

She laughed, and spontaneously put her hand on his arm. 'It was your idea in the first place, remember? You said it to Aleck once, and you kept your promise.'

At first he turned away from her, then swiftly he turned, and taking her in his arms he swept her against him in a gentle kiss. Before she could stop herself, she was kissing him back with equal fervour before drawing back in embarrassment.

A sense of shame and treachery flooded her heart as she hurried out to the caravan ahead of him, waving to the children and telling Aleck that Mummy would be calling at Hyndemere for him in a few days and to be a good boy. Then she gave both children a kiss and told them to give her love to Grandpops and Grandmama.

She turned past Danny again, but she did not dare to look at him but merely wished him a safe journey, then she hurried back into the flat and sat alone in the kitchen in a sudden well of desolation.

What a fool she'd made of herself. How could she possibly bear to meet him again when she went to collect Aleck – and what an unfaithful thing for a married woman to do. Whatever had induced her?

She looked up at the sash window and saw the sun streaming in and the leaves waving on the trees, and sighed. Then she sat down and wrote a letter to Hal in India and tried to forget it, telling him only that Aleck had just departed for a few days to Hyndemere.

Dasia had hardly time to arrange with Andrina about going to bring Aleck back from Hyndemere when her worst fears were realised. Although she'd spent a day or two wondering how she would have the courage to meet Danny face to face again, and how she could have succumbed to that moment of love for a man so much older than herself, she now discovered that she would not be going over to Hyndemere after all.

For there, on the table in front of her, was a letter from Hal to her, and when she read it she could hardly believe what it said.

'... I've been having second thoughts about his education ... so I've planned with Mother and Father to have him entered for a place at Klintersdene in Scotland which is a highly progressive, well thought of, modern

350

boarding school which specialises in outdoor pursuits such as sailing and equestrian sports – as well as the academic side. They take children from kindergarten right through to university entrance.

'... I hope he will be admitted this coming Autumn term and meanwhile Mother is arranging for him to go with her to Aunt McAnzie's at Inverdrendy Castle ... and stay for a while ... only a few miles from the school ... meet some of his relations ... aware of more of the world than ... Manchester ... or even Hynde-mere ...'

It sent Dasia quite weak at the knees.

Not another bout with them! She couldn't stand it ... Was this battle going to be waged over her one and only child for the rest of their lives?

But there was worse to come, because next day a letter came from Thinny herself, telling Dasia not to bother collecting Aleck again just yet, as he was all set to travel up to Scotland with her – to her sister's for a few weeks, close to where Hal wanted him to be properly schooled. Even Lord Wrioth wouldn't be at Hyndemere, as he was off to India to pay Hal a visit.

Dasia didn't know what to do. She felt completely shattered, her whole world suddenly snatched away again without so much as a by-your-leave, as if she was nothing but the nanny who was of no account. Had she *no* rights to her own child? Would he actually have gone already?

She wiped her tear-stained face and decided to ring up and find out.

It was a fresh voice at the other end; 'Hyndemere ... Miss Badell the assistant housekeeper speaking. Can I help you?'

'It's Dasia Wrioth. Is it possible to speak to Lady Wrioth please – or my son?'

The voice softened to tactful sympathy: 'I'm sorry,

madam, they caught a train for Scotland early this morning.'

'Is Lord Wrioth there, then?'

'I'm afraid he's away too, madam. He'll be away in India until he returns with his son on his son's next leave.'

'Is Mr Elvers there ...?'

There was a cautious hesitancy: 'I'll just go and see, Madam ...'

A few minutes later Danny was on the phone, saying what a shock it had all been – even to him.

'Whatever shall I *do*, Danny?'

'I just don't know ...' he sounded really upset, then he said, 'Look, I've got to come to Manchester tomorrow on a personal matter for Lord Wrioth. I'll call in on you tomorrow afternoon.'

Next day, Dasia couldn't settle to anything as she waited for Danny Elvers. All she could think about was the way Aleck had been taken from her once again, to be used for some family destiny. She paced nervously round the flat gazing out of the windows in lonely isolation.

Then, at last, she heard a vehicle turning into the drive, and saw the green saloon car pulling up outside.

It was the first time she had ever seen Danny in a car without his uniform. He was wearing a light tweed jacket, flannel trousers and an open neck cricket shirt.

'I came straight here, in case you wanted to come with me into town. It might do you good – and take your mind off things a bit.'

She nodded and went to change into a floral summer frock and a small velvet jacket. But when they'd set off towards Manchester, and she was sitting beside him, her brain kept turning towards Hal ...

How could he, her husband, have arranged to have Aleck removed from her loving, motherly care without even any discussion – and so obliquely?

It was like a dagger in her heart, and for an instant it was as if all her love for him was dead.

When Danny had posted off the parcel of special silk underwear and a good quality mosquito net to Lord Wrioth, he said quietly, 'Is there anywhere in particular you'd like to go? ... Anywhere special that would make you a bit happier?'

She hesitated, then said shyly, 'There is one place. It's a little cottage my father left me in his will. It's in Flixton village about ten miles away, and quite easy to find. Pr'aps we could have a sort of picnic there.

'Andrina and me and Sammy are doing it up – by degrees. It's ever so tiny; just about the size of one of the Hyndemere stables but at least it's my very own.

'I think I was actually conceived there!' She went slightly pink.

He smiled at her consolingly: 'Of course we'll go. Good idea. We'll stop at Yates Wine Lodge and get a bottle of sparkling Bavaria, and I know a place where they'll pack us some fresh salmon patties and some fruit.' He looked almost like a schoolboy as the worry lines cleared from his face.

There'd certainly been improvements since the first time Dasia saw Bequest Cottage. The grass was now neatly cropped and the small pink Dorothy Perkins rambler roses were flowering profusely round the newly whitewashed walls. The broken window panes had all been replaced and many bits of pointing and grouting done. Inside was a very pretty pastel-coloured carpet square from the spare bedroom at Sammy's, two chintz-covered armchairs from a second-hand furniture auction, and a little wooden table, three chairs and a stool from the pawn shop. Upstairs in the bedroom was a brass bedstead, and a feather mattress from a cousin of Alice's who'd changed over to a modern sprung mattress. Meanwhile, Aunt Dolly had donated all the curtains from a batch given to her for a jumble sale in aid of the Salvation Army.

There were six wine glasses in the cupboard, put there by Sammy who was extremely civilised and couldn't bear to drink wine, or even ale, out of chipped cups or bent tin mugs. And there was a blue and white check table-cloth.

Dasia put the cloth on the table, but that was as far as she got – for, almost as if they had read each other's thoughts, they were as one in each other's tender arms, as she submitted to his passionate embrace.

Oh what a relief it was to throw off the chains of convention, as Danny led her gently up the stairs.

She followed him without a single qualm; she had thrown caution completely to the winds, as they lay locked in each other's arms on the dipping feather mattress, in their inevitable passionate embrace.

Hours later they drove back to Toppyford Mansions in quiet, comfortable, thoughtful silence. Dasia had not felt so calm and fulfilled, since the time Aleck was born.

But as they bid their final farewells and Danny was back in the car to set off to Chester, he said, 'It was a moment of madness, Dasia. How can you ever forgive me?'

'Forgive you? Whatever do you mean? It was a moment of pure love ... Oh Danny – how can you say such a thing?'

'I'm far too old ... I should never – it was violation. I was looking for comfort ... with Enid going and –'

'Sh ...' She placed a finger gently on his lips. 'It just had to be. How could it have been otherwise? We both needed each other. We both gave and we both received. Don't forsake me, Danny. Don't let it spoil our friend-

354

ship. Please come and see me again while they're all away ...' He nodded and waved ...

But he never came again, even though he wrote once or twice to tell her how Aleck was getting on in Scotland, and when they'd be due back. ·

A few weeks later, Andrina, who also had a key to Bequest cottage, said, 'I never knew you'd been there recently, Dasia? I drove there with Sammy last Sunday to take a small six-piece tea service, and I met Minny Taylor from Trellis Yard. She was walking along the field footpath, and said she saw the bottom curtains drawn, and a big green car there ...

'The only person with one of those is the Wrioths ...'

She looked hard at her daughter: 'I wondered for a moment if Hal had suddenly come back from India unannounced. It's very upsetting for you to have him forever going backwards and forwards to another country. He almost leads a double life in some ways, and it's a very unsettling situation for any faithful wife.

'Yet on second thoughts there would hardly have been time for him to be back again now – unless it was by aeroplane!' Andrina stared down at the ground – waiting ...

Dasia felt herself going scarlet: 'You know full well it wasn't Hal. It happened to be Danny Elvers. He came to Manchester on an errand and asked me, out of politeness, if I'd like to go anywhere special, and I said – there ...

'We had a glass of wine. . . . A sort of picnic ...'

'Picnic?' said Andrina sharply. 'Picnic – inside, with closed curtains?'

'Why shouldn't we have closed the curtains?' said Dasia defensively? 'I closed them for that very purpose – because of nosy people like Minny Taylor.

'Just imagine me and Danny sitting there having a

355

simple glass of wine, and seeing her great moon-like mug peering through the window.'

Andrina said no more. But they both knew the truth.

'I'm a bit worried about Dasia,' said Andrina to Sammy one evening when they'd taken her back to Toppyford Mansions. 'Poor dear. She doesn't half suffer with that absent husband of hers. But at least Aleck is back with her for good, now – after that disastrous trip to Scotland with Lady Wrioth.'

Sammy nodded tactfully.

A few weeks later, both Hal and Lord Wrioth were on their way home. Bazz had been taken ill with a mild stroke and Hal was taking some extra unpaid leave, accompanied by one of the secretaries out there called Lucille Quigley who lived in Bowdon.

But just at the time when the excitement of Hal's arrival in Manchester again should have been uppermost in her mind, Dasia was confronted by more troubled thoughts. Her monthly period had entirely disappeared . . .

CHAPTER TWENTY-ONE

Daniella

People say that when you are pregnant you take on a serene and beautiful look ... or at least, many men say it. But Dasia didn't feel in the least serene or beautiful as she stared at herself in the mirror with a woebegone face full of inner fear.

Now, at the beginning, her weight was eight and three-quarter stone – much the same as it had always been over the past year. Yet she knew her face had almost lost its rounded, youthful bloom and was less fleshy. And her clear grey eyes seemed larger and ever-changing as they caught up the blues and greens of light and shade.

Her red-gold hair was longer, less tidy and efficient-looking, still glinting as it curled its way across her head, as she sat there waiting for this first meeting with Hal.

She was thankful that Aleck had settled happily once more in his kindergarten close by, and she had assured him a hundred times that he would never be taken away again to go to boarding school. 'And if you're lucky and work hard, you might even win a scholarship to Manchester Grammar School.'

★

Dasia was astounded when Hal arrived home to find
that he was not on his own.

'This is Lucille Quigley,' he said, 'I think you've
heard me mention her. She came back with me to help
with Father.'

Lucille stepped forward with a brisk, self-assured
smile as she and Dasia shook hands.

She was a matronly thirty-five or thirty-six, dressed in
dark grey with a necklace of pearls and an aura of
polished sophistication. A person adept, it seemed, at
making herself indispensable as she explained in cut-
glass tones that when she was on leave she lived with her
widowed brother, but hadn't gone back to Bowdon yet,
as she'd been helping Hal at Hyndemere.

'We thought it was best, didn't we, Hal?' She looked
at Dasia with limpid eyes: 'We women always get let in
for it don't we?' She turned back to Hal, smiling
radiantly: 'I think Hal knows how I feel, don't you, Hal?
We have a sort of natural interaction . . .'

So that was what she called it! Dasia's temper began
to simmer. All her hopes for a warm, intimate, family
home-coming to allay her own hidden fears and anxieties
had been well and truly scuppered.

'I expect I was cut out to be a nurse, really – rather
than a highly graded civil servant,' she joked. And she
passed rather swankily close to Hal, swaying her plump
hips.

But who was she to talk – with her own dreadful
skeleton rearing itself from the dark confines of its
cupboard? She wondered whether she could, after all, be
making a mountain out of a molehill, imagining she was
pregnant when all the time it was caused by something
else – like filling her bladder with too much lemonade
and gobbling down too much tinned salmon and bread
and butter, and chocolate truffles.

And was that morning sickness merely due to a sudden early morning longing for a fried breakfast? And was the absence of her monthly curse due to a lack of exercise?

When Hal finally arrived home again after taking Lucille back to Bowdon, Dasia said, 'Why on earth did you bring her here? How terribly thoughtless ...'

She saw his temper begin to rise, and how tired he looked. But she felt tired too.

'Don't be silly, Dasia. She was just being socially polite when she said she'd like to meet you – so I thought it was better to get it over and done with in one fell swoop, rather than elaborate invitations later.'

'The direct opposite of polite, if you ask me, Hal. Wasn't she even sensitive enough to know that it was Aleck's and my first meeting with you in weeks and weeks?

'Why did she need to pry? To put it plainly she's just a downright nosy parker with the skin of a rhinoceros.'

There was a deathly silence, as all sorts of thoughts passed guiltily through Dasia's mind: back to the first time Hal had gone to India, and how glad she'd been that he'd found a decent job at last. And how happy they were, living in this flat with baby Aleck before her accident.

She remembered, sadly now, how she'd refused point blank to go with him to India because she loved England and her own family in The Grove so much. She felt herself almost crumpling inside as she remembered how she had betrayed him with Danny ... and was haunted, even this moment, with the fact that she could be pregnant.

That night in bed they welcomed each other for different reasons: Hal because he was home at last with his wife and son in his own domain, and Dasia because all she wanted was to escape what might be some awful future fate – and live for one brief night in Hal's caring arms as they made passionate love.

But the next day was different, as Aleck regaled Daddy with tales of the awful place Grandmama had taken him: 'It was Jack and The Beanstalk's Castle, Daddy – where the horrible giant lived, and Alistair shot me with his bow and arrow and I had to have seven stitches in my bottom. I'm never, *never* going there again!

'And Mummy says when I'm big I can go to Manchester Grammar school ...'

Dasia smiled at him with almost a warning look: 'Why don't you go next door, that's a good boy, and show little Ruth your new Indian soldier doll?'

Then, when he'd scampered away clutching his new gift in its flimsy grey cardboard box, surrounded with its clouds of thin white tissue paper, she said to Hal, 'It was terrible of you never to have even told me properly what you and Hyndemere were planning for *him*, my only son.

A guilty flush rose in Hal's forehead: 'Nonsense, Dasia. It's only natural for any family to want the best.'

She sighed wearily, 'Well at least it's all settled now – once and for all. Thanks to young Alistair.

'Your mother will never get Aleck up there again. I'll see to that – even if I have to follow them. But no, there won't be a next time!'

He turned away in exasperated anger. Then after he had eaten a leisurely breakfast and spread his toast very thickly with Frank Coopers Oxford marmalade, and read *The Times* from cover to cover, he said coolly, 'I promised to call round and visit Lucy today.'

'Lucy?'

'Yes ... You *know*! Surely you haven't forgotten Lucille so soon? She's known as Lucy to all her intimates. I said I'd pop over this afternoon and meet her brother, Ronald, who's an expert on Early

360

Mediaeval History.

'I'd have asked you to come too, but there'll be Aleck to see to, won't there? And I don't think either of them are particularly child orientated.' He smiled at her with traces of his past student devilry.

'What time will you be back, then?'

'Can't say for sure. It all depends on her diary, and what she's planned.'

From that moment on, Hal's leave turned out to be a disaster for Dasia. He spent his whole time running round in circles after Lucille, even to the length of attending some of her brother's lectures at the university, and being hypnotised into buying an obscure book on the history of Danegeld, going back to Aethelred the Second, which he never even opened. Finally, on the night before he was going back to India, there was a terrific row to end all rows – played out with calm coldness.

'It was hardly worth your being here at all, seeing you were with her and her brother all the time. Aleck still doesn't know he's got a real father ...'

Hal's eyes darkened with anger: 'Don't fret. This'll probably be my last visit. You never wanted me to go abroad in the first place and it's caused nothing but trouble all round. But you're quite willing to take the pickings aren't you?

'Quite willing to live here in this flat; quite willing to try and stunt your son's education, out of your own selfishness; quite willing to make him into a little namby-pamby mother's boy ... not allowed to move out of a circle of ten miles' radius.

'You're so – so *ignorant*, Dasia. So provincial ...'

'What wicked, WICKED things to say after the way I've slogged and slaved in the past. And it was you who wanted to marry me, remember – on your bended knees.

361

I *never* wanted to get married early. I always wanted to see a bit of life first . . .'

'Don't make me laugh. Only those who've been to a place like India know what life is . . .'

'It's you that doesn't know what life is, Hal. I certainly don't need to go to India to find out.'

Then she drew herself up and said, 'So go there! Go back for good. I don't care if you never come here again!'

The words were empty threats full of bravado, but the reply was even worse – and she'd asked for it:

'I probably shall, Dasia, and maybe you'll think differently when your wifely allowance stops.

'I might even live with Lucy, too, if it comes to that. Worse fates have been known in life and at least she has an open mind.'

'– And knows all about India . . .' said Dasia drily.

'To be perfectly honest,' he said in stern, dignified tones, 'she's fallen in love with me – and I feel honoured. Which is more than you ever seem to have done over the years.'

'What a terrible lie . . .' Her face went white. Then she said, 'We can all have people who love us. I have someone who loves me . . .'

He stopped in his tracks. 'Loves *you*? How on earth do you reckon that?' A slight touch of amusement lingered at the sides of his mouth. He knew her too well, knew she was incapable of . . .

She nodded silently with tear-filled eyes for she was aware that no one seemed to love her, not even Danny who now retained a very formal relationship and always mentioned Shirley Badell, the new housekeeper – almost as a warning. He'd done that again when she spoke to him recently on the phone on the pretext of getting through to Lady Wrioth, to enquire about Bazz.

'I have a man who would do anything for me.

Someone who worships the ground I walk on.'

'Come off it, Dasia. That's a bit thick . . .' Her protestations seemed to soothe him; his anger left him and for some reason he saw the funny side. 'We're both being utter idiots . . .'

But they knew it wasn't true. And she knew it even more than he did.

The baby was premature. It was born in February 1933.

The first to know about her pregnancy was Aunt Dolly, just before Christmas, when Dasia was still facing alone the guilty secret of the new child in her womb.

Dolly had sent her a lovely birthday card and a small locket for her twenty-third birthday.

'I just had to come and thank you, Dolly, and hear all the news . . .' she said, trying to be extra joyous and bouncy.

But gradually, her own bit of news had to come out . . .

'Another little stranger. Well I never . . .' said Dolly getting her wits together to winkle out all the details. 'Who'd have thought it. Was it a shock, dear, with Hal being away such a lot . . .?

'Mind you, I sensed something the moment I saw you at the door. "I think she's expecting a baby girl," I said to myself. "Her face has a very calm look . . ."

'I shall have to get the gold ring out and swing it over your belly before you go – just to make sure.

'Anyway, let's have a nice cup of tea while it's quiet, and I'll show you some snaps of me and Mr Solway at Belle Vue Race track and the beautiful coney fur muff he's bought me . . . He's a real gem, that man . . .'

'Have you ever seen anything of Mr Corcoran, since –?'

'Not a sausage, Dasia, and it's good enough for me. What slyness . . . Though Marcia did once reckon she caught sight of him in the Tower Ballroom at Blackpool, steering a woman twice his size round the floor, who dragged him about as if he was her pet poodle. So it's good riddance, *I* say.'

She looked Dasia up and down. 'Nobody but me could possibly know you're expecting, love. You've actually gone a bit thinner – over all. Haven't you even let on to Andrina?'

Then she said, 'You'll have to put Hal some french letters in his Christmas stocking. Though I do know that lots of men say wearing rubbers is like washing your hands with gloves on. But it's not them as has to face the consequences is it?' She gave Dasia an exceedingly penetrating look and made her feel so uncomfortable that she bent down to adjust her shoe and wondered if Dolly had guessed the truth.

'So when did you say it was due, dear? Some time in March?

'Well at least it's a good time to be confined – when all the snow and ice is about. Will you have the midwife? Or will it be hospital?'

Dasia sighed: 'I'm hoping it'll be the midwife. I expect to have to break the news soon because Aleck will need looking after.'

'It will have been from the time when Hal was home earlier in the year won't it?'

Dasia nodded and Aunt Dolly poured her a second cup of tea and offered her a chocolate marshmallow.

'And haven't you even let Hal know either? What do you think he'll say?'

'I expect he'll be quite pleased, really. At least a new baby'll mean less spoiling for Aleck. He's beginning to get a bit too much like an only child.

'But at least Hyndemere haven't tried to interfere in our lives lately. And Aleck's got lots of his own friends at home and at school now – so when he goes on visits there he never really wants to stay for ever like he once did, even though he misses Snowball the pony a bit.' Then Dasia coloured up slightly and said briskly, in case she actually blushed, 'But Danny Elvers sends him little notes about it from time to time.' And to her embarrassment she felt her whole face flaming up the moment she mentioned Danny's name.

'Oh yes, that's right,' said Dolly pretending not to notice, 'he's their chauffeur isn't he? The one whose wife died and left him with all those children.'

Dasia nodded and stood up, then said she must just dash to the WC before she set off again.

'If you wait another few minutes, love, Harold will be back and he'll drive you home. There isn't a thing he wouldn't do for me. But of course, by the same token, there's quite a lot I do for him.'

Then she came up to Dasia and put her hand gently against her cheek and said, 'Try not to worry too much, lovey. I know it's easier said than done. But I'm always here if you want help, and I shan't say anything about it to your Tommy, or even to Alice. I'll let it all come from your end.'

When Dasia came back from the WC, Dolly made her lie down on the sofa while she swung the gold ring on its fine cotton thread over her bulging stomach and proclaimed that it would definitely be a girl, then the new gentleman of Dolly's life, Harold Solway, drove Dasia home.

'Dasia, I think I may be coming back for good. It all depends on this new managerial post they're making in the export department in Manchester, starting next September. Lucy thinks I should apply for it, then she could be back here as my secretary and able to look after her brother.

'It could be a very good move especially with them

365

getting a bit long in the tooth at Hyndemere, and Father being a bit peaky.'

Hal appeared to have cut Dasia out of his plans completely; even though they were always civilised and friendly, never once did he mention the coming child – except to tell her to keep her pecker up.

'Mummy? Why is Daddy always rushing off to Aunty Lucy's and never has time to play with me?'

'Because he's very busy, dear, and his leave's much shorter this time. But we're busy too, because we've got our new baby coming.'

'And, we've got our potato peeler,' said Aleck solemnly.

'Yes, we certainly have ... We've always got Spud the potato peeler to think about.'

This invariably did the trick where Aleck was concerned, because he knew all about the plans his great grandfather Greenbow had left for Mummy, and how they were going to turn it into the greatest potato peeler in the world with the help of Uncle Tommy and an engineer at Metro-Vicks called Mr Delders who Uncle Tommy once brought round for tea and who could do card tricks.

The blueprints for the amazing potato peeler fascinated him, and often he would go to the cupboard where they were rolled up and spread out the finely textured glazed cotton with the plans on, and stare at them. Then he would roll them up again and put them carefully back like the map to some hidden treasure.

Life was more secure for him these days for, although they had visited Hyndemere with Andrina and Sammy, there was never any suggestion now that he should stay for any length of time – or any heavy hints about his future education. Although he missed Snowball, Danny always saw to it that he had a ride, and kept him informed with small notes on Snowball's progress: 'Dear

Aleck, just a jolly postcard to say that Snowball galloped all the way down Silcock's Lane today when he shouldn't have done, and splashed six sheets on the line. Love Danny.'

The baby was born at home, even though it was a bit premature, and Dasia sent Aleck off to stay with Alice and Rosalie and Louise.

'How you managed to get yourself stuck with another one, when Hal's away all the time, beats me,' said Alice bluntly. ''You'da thought he'd've been more thoughtful and gentlemanly and used summat, seeing as 'ow much work you 'as to do for yourself these days.' She shuffled into the kitchen to make a steamed jam roly-poly, and never said another word.

If it hadn't been for the midwife, the birth of Daniella Alicia Dasia Wrioth would have been a heart-breaking affair for Dasia, for she suddenly felt so isolated and alone as the painful contractions took over.

Deep down, she was wondering what the baby would be like because it wasn't Hal's, even though all babies could be as different as chalk and cheese no matter who their parents were.

'She's the image of you when you were a baby,' said Andrina when she saw the tiny little red, five-and-a-half-pounds scrap of humanity with its black silky thatch of hair.

When Lord and Lady Lord Wrioth saw a christening photograph – whilst they were in Juan Les Pins – they looked at it very carefully through their new glasses and argued as to whether it had any of the Wrioth character-istics.

'It reminds me terribly of someone we know – but I can't quite tell who ...'

'Those skinny little monkeys in Zanzibar,' joked Bazz. Then he said, 'They're all much the same at that age – you can't tell anything till they begin to put on a bit of flesh.'

'And at least Hal had a boy first, dear ...' said Thinny with meaning.

St Patrick's Day in Manchester was always a great day for the Irish as everyone took to the wearing of the green, and shamrock was everywhere.

It was barely a month since Daniella was born, but Dasia felt that she would go mad if she didn't have some sort of a change. She seemed to spend all her time feeding the baby and her breasts were so laden and oozing with milk that the flat smelt like a sour milk dairy and she felt like some heavily weighed-down cow. Surrounded by a small byre festooned with rails and clothes racks of nappies and baby nighties, she miserably ruminated on her condition.

'The baby's an absolute little cherub, Dasia,' said Sheena, a friend of Dasia's who had always remained beautiful, and childless – with a sylph-like figure. 'I really envy you some times.'

Then she said, 'Why don't you come out with me and my young man to Chorlton Palais – just for a bit of fun? The bright lights and music u'd do you good. I'll get my sister Ada to sit in for you for a couple of hours, so just do as I say for once. Go and revel in a good hot bath, put on your best bib and tucker, and I'll set your hair up in a new style with some creamy roses and shamrock in it. You'll look a peach.'

Once she was persuaded, Dasia took on a new lease of life, and in due course, with both her offspring bedded down, and Ada there to watch over them, she set off with Sheena in her boyfriend's shiny grey saloon car. Soon she was sitting at a small table for four in Chorlton Palais, as Irish reels filled the air and the company was alive with jokes, songs and laughter.

Then a voice suddenly said quietly, 'Fancy seeing you here, Dasia!'

She looked up, startled: 'Danny! And fancy seeing you here.'

'Do you want to dance?'

'No – no thanks. It's not long since I've had the new baby and quite truthfully I feel a bit weak. This is my first real time out, and I shouldn't really be here at all – but my friends said it would take me out of myself a bit.'

She looked into his face as if she was reading a map, and their eyes met. 'How's life with you, and the family?'

He hesitated. 'Not too bad. I mustn't grumble. The children are very sensible, and Shirley has been an absolute tower of strength. We're supposed to be getting married in December ... Lady Wrioth has taken it upon herself to arrange it all.'

The silence said more than words. Then Dasia said, 'Supposed to be?'

He looked away ... 'I shouldn't have said that. She's a wonderful young woman to be taking on six of us to look after. But she keeps telling me she's young and strong – and she's talked me into it. All children need a mother ...'

Then he looked at her and said, 'What's your latest one like then?'

Dasia smiled, and was suddenly glad she was wearing the roses and shamrock: 'Sheena – who's out there dancing – says she's an absolute little cherub, so I suppose she must be ...'

They both laughed.

'What have you called her?'

a sort of fear '... Daniella ...'

Why oh why had she called her that? Why hadn't

369

she chosen something less obvious like Miranda or Mary?

'Daniella?' Then almost without thinking he said, 'After me ... and our time at Bequest cottage?' He stopped suddenly and stared at her in horrified shame. 'What am I saying! Forgive me. I must have gone completely mad. Whatever will you think ...?' Then he muttered quickly, 'And even if anything *had* happened you would not have told me ... Oh, Dasia, how I rue that day. I betrayed you like some creature of no feeling.'

She looked at him calmly as the music blared all round them and Sheena waved to say they were staying on the dance floor for the next round.

She felt very calm. It was as if she were floating on a cloud (although later she put it down to not having had enough to eat and worrying about Daniella's next feed). 'Don't torment yourself, Danny, it was a perfect day, and I'll always remember it.'

Neither of them mentioned the name again, but one day six months later, just before Hal had finally decided to come home for good, she saw the likeness in the precise downward tilt of the small firm nose, and took her baby from the pram and hugged her gently, for she was a true love child.

It was very hot weather when Hal finally came back for good.

Everything had worked out well for him. He had been given the new managerial post and Lucille had been found a post as his personal secretary.

He looked handsome, and well. And so did Dasia who was now firmly established in her own way of life with the two children.

And the first thing Aleck greeted his father with – was The Potato Peeler.

'Why on earth does he keep mentioning that thing?'

said Hal irritably. 'He seems to have a complete fixation. It isn't normal for a small boy of his age.'

'It isn't a fixation,' said Dasia defensively. 'It's a real proposition. And our Tommy and Cyril Delders are doing wonders with it and soon hope to get it patented.'

'And where's the money coming from then? The allowance that I've been giving you?'

'Certainly not. The expenses will be shared between all the Greenbows and Cyril Delders. And if you want to invest in it, now's your chance.'

'You must be crackers, Dasia! Why on earth would I want to be mixed up in some footling thing like that?'

'From acorns, do large oak trees grow … You once told me that, yourself.' She thought sadly how much he'd changed – or perhaps it was that she'd never really known him properly.

Then he said, 'By the way, if I marry Lucy there'll be the question of you leaving this flat, and returning the Wrioth family heirloom.'

She was absolutely astounded: 'Marrying her? Surely you don't mean it? You've never said that before!'

'Well, I'm saying it now – aren't I?'

'Does she know? Has she agreed to it?'

'She doesn't know officially – but I know she'll agree to it.'

'What about her brother in Bowdon, that she drools over?'

'He's going to Milan University for two years, and he's letting their home to a religious organisation for a holiday exchange residence. That's why we'll need this place …'

She felt quite sick. He had clearly gone out of his mind. He seemed to have no idea now that they were still a married couple, and that this was their permanent home.

Then he added more fuel to the fire: 'I don't suppose

Father will last much longer, and when the worst happens it will be my duty to return to Hyndemere and take over. And we all know how set against all that you are. But with Lucy it'll be different . . .'

'Never, never will I agree to a divorce,' sobbed Dasia. 'Why should I have to suffer all that just when the children are happy and settled? And as for your wretched heirloom I got rid of that ages ago!'

'Got rid of it?' His face went ashen.

'I put it —' She was going to blurt out that it was in a special bank deposit box for Aleck, so that he could have it when he was twenty-one, for the jewels had never brought her any luck whatsoever and were a complete liability. Maybe her own son's future wife would fare better with them. But quickly she checked herself from telling Hal all this.

'I — well I didn't quite get rid of them, and they're safe. You gave them to me your wife as part of the Wrioth tradition, and that's how it's staying.

'What were you hoping for? . . . To pass them on to her, your great big purring puss on the rich downs of Bowdon?

'Oh — no, not yet, my darling. I don't give in that easily.' Dasia's eyes flashed with sudden fire and her face shone with searing anger.

That evening Hal departed to his lady love's at Bowdon. And that night Dasia lay in bed thinking about it all . . . but this time she didn't cry herself to sleep. This time a steely hardness to match Hal's own was growing inside her . . .

CHAPTER TWENTY-TWO

Hal

As soon as Hal arrived at Lucille's he was consumed with remorse.

It was dusk and tall silk-fringed standard lamps gave a welcoming, golden glow through the drawing-room windows.

Hal hesitated for a moment. He could see the grand piano with the silver rose bowl on it, and heard music from His Master's Voice as Lucy's brother stood there, beating time gently with one hand and smoking his pipe with the other.

Hal put out a tentative finger to press the bell, almost wanting to turn and run – run back to his beloved and maddening Dasia. But the thought vanished immediately as Lucille opened the door and welcomed him in, taking care to kiss him in a manner that suggested a lasting and intimate association. 'My goodness, Hal, I quite thought you'd got lost. I'll get you a drink. What's it to be? Gin and It?'

'No thanks ... really. We used to drink far too much in India.' It suddenly occurred to him that his drinking had been the main trouble at Dasia's ... back at his home – he must remember that: it was still *his home.*

He now saw that it was a back-log of steady, topped-up drinking that had made him say the things he did when he was there with her. And the very thought of her face, so passionate and fiery, brought an ache to his loins.

'I've had to move our bedrooms round a bit, because of the decorators, dearest. You're on the landing right next to me from now on, as quite honestly Ronald likes to have the third floor all to himself as a self-contained flat, and he's got a lot of sorting out to do when the awful moment of his going to Milan happens – and leaves me like a little orphan ...'

Hal's spirits were dropping as quickly as a thermometer in a freezing blizzard.

The whole ambience of life was so different now they were back permanently. When they'd been abroad there were always others there in close perceptive contact, to heighten the drama of living and charge it with a thread of excitement, so that if one was bored – God forbid – one had hundreds of ways of curing it.

But here, in Bowdon ... with her all the time. And at work ... Well ...

'I think I'll turn in early, Lucy, if you don't mind. It's been a tiring day and it didn't go too well with Dasia. We never seem to hit it off at all these days.'

'I don't wonder, darling. You see, you got yourself embroiled with her a bit too early and hastily, didn't you? Before you'd fully matured.

'It's a jolly good job you met me, Hal ... I've saved you just in time, *and* managed to get you fixed up in your brand-new export job, with my cousin Hiram being on the Board of Directors and him realising what a good family background you have ...'

He yawned wearily and wondered how the baby was going on. It was a handsome child and a bit like Dasia, but with no red hair. He thought of Aleck and how pleased the child was to see his Daddy; a real little Wrioth if ever there was one. Then he looked at Lucy sitting there smiling at him with her smooth chubby unlined face and her beautifully tailored sea-green dress. A credit to any man in the world.

Yet she too hadn't always had it so good. She made no secret of the fact that she had a son in his teens at Winchester and was finding it very expensive to keep him there, in spite of all the money left by her father, Ambrose Grange, a corn merchant.

She never mentioned the boy's father, and Hal never asked her about him.

Later, as he lay in bed thinking, it became more and more obvious that he was getting himself tangled up in a very tricky situation which certainly Bazz and Thinny wouldn't approve of.

Just as he was wearily closing his eyes, a familiar apparition in a long white satin nightgown and lace robe came tiptoeing into his room and kissed him on the cheek.

'Do you want to come back to my room, my angel, or shall I stay here?'

He lifted up the covers to let her in beside him, and felt her fulsome body press towards him. He gave a heavy sigh: 'Yes ... it's been a very long day. Bring on tomorrow and let's both get a good night's sleep.'

When Andrina and Sammy heard about Hal's threats to evict Dasia from the flat they were flabbergasted.

'Whatever possessed him?' said Andrina. 'What wanton cruelty to even suggest it, and to his wife of all people; a wife with two small children. I would never have dreamed he was that sort of man. Perhaps it was the heat of India. They do say that if you stay there long enough it sends you mad.'

'*She's* at the bottom of it all,' said Dasia as she

gathered the last of the plums from the fruit trees in the garden at The Cedars. 'But I think he's getting a bit fed up. He sent Aleck a beautiful train set the other day, with "Give my love to Mummy", on it.

'But the damage is done, Drina. The fact that he's even thought of getting us out of the flat has really taken the wind from my sails, even though it was probably empty threats. All I want to do now is to take Aleck and Daniella and leave there, for good and all – and let him do what the hell he likes with the whole bloody shoot, and I hope he rots in Hades ...'

Andrina looked at her in horror: 'You mustn't take on like that, Dasia. It isn't the least ladylike. After all, he is still your lawful wedded husband, and you said yourself you wanted it to stay that way.'

Dasia lapsed into silence as they took the deep red Victoria plums inside to the kitchen and spread them on some white cloths to check on their condition.

Then, just as they'd finished their work, Andrina said, 'If you feel so unsettled there, why don't you go back to Mother's for a while till it's all sorted out? She's so lonely in that big house now Horace has gone, and the children would keep her livened up.

'I suspect that both Rosalie and Louise will soon be slinging their hooks and getting married, and when that happens all sorts of other plans about the house will have to be made ... but meanwhile ... Anyway it was just a thought ...'

Dasia brightened: 'Unless I went to live in my own little place ... In Bequest cottage.'

Andrina gave an exasperated sigh: 'It's far too small for anyone with two children.'

'People live in far worse places in Manchester ...'

'But not usually from choice, Dasia.'

The whole subject was then left in abeyance until one Sunday when Dasia went with Louise to Southern

Cemetery to put some flowers on the family grave in front of the flat, ancient gravestone where Horace Greenbow's ashes had been scattered.

They both wept slightly and as they turned to leave Louise said, 'I was just about to get married to Arnold when Father died and it had to be put off for a while, but we never told anyone. Mother seems quite desolate at times, always trying to rake up memories from the past which are too far gone. It's just a question of Rosalie and me holding the fort, at present.

'I think it might be better if you did come home for a bit like Andrina said – that is, if you really are set on leaving the flat.'

Then she cheered up and said, 'And did you know our Tommy's just been snared into getting married to Maureen Sanderson next year, and's going to Samuel's to buy her an engagement ring?'

During early November, Dasia finally decided to take the plunge and go and live back in The Grove.

The amount of furniture in the flat was absorbed quite comfortably into the Greenbow household, and what didn't fit was packed into outhouses and attics in place of much of the stuff Horace had once stored there.

The only person who really grumbled about any of the turmoil was Aleck who was losing his friends.

'He'll soon make some more at his new school,' said Alice with newly found cheerfulness. 'That new urban primary is the very first decent council school they've ever had round here, so you'll not have to cough up for private ones.'

She had greeted them quietly when they first arrived. She'd aged a great deal; her stomach had spread out as if she were pregnant, and her shoulders were bowed forward beneath a much thinner face so that she looked the old lady she was. But a bit of the old spark was there as she said, 'Well there's one thing, love, folks'll not be licking round *me* for a fortune when I go. My friends'll be real friends judging by how much Horace *didn't* leave us all.'

'Except for Mummy's potato peeler,' blurted out the voice of a small boy listening, unobserved in a corner of the kitchen.

'Moved? Where've you moved? When was it? And what in heaven's name for?' Hal sounded completely pole-axed.

Dasia had made the phone call to his private office at work, and as soon as she got through she had recognised Lucille's dulcet voice of saccharine sweetness.

'Mr Wrioth is out of the office at present, who is it speaking please?'

Dasia hesitated, wondering whether to make up some false name; then in cool, challenging tones she said, 'His wife, Mrs Wrioth. When will he be back?'

'Just one moment, Mrs Wrioth,' said Lucille as if she'd never heard or seen or spoken to Dasia in the whole of her life. 'He's just come back to the office. I'll see if he's available.'

'What on earth made you do it? You must have been mad ...'

'Just like you were when you told me to —'

'Look, Dasia, this is neither the time nor the place. I'll call round to The Grove tonight. All right?'

He rang off abruptly, and it struck her that it was the fastest reaction she had ever had from him in the whole of her life.

'Hal's coming round tonight,' she said to the others when they were all in at tea-time.

'Oh goodeeee,' whooped Aleck. 'He's been away ages, Mummy. Is he going to live with us here?'

Everyone pretended to be stone deaf as they kept

asking each other to pass the bread and butter and did anyone want any more corned beef hash? And watch that Daniella didn't tip her jelly over old Periwinkle.

They were all very tactful when he arrived; Rosalie whipped Aleck away to play Snakes and Ladders and Louise began to get Daniella ready for bed.

Dasia took him upstairs to where she had made herself a comfortable bed-sitter from the very room with the leaking roof and the po full of rain drops which had been her bedroom all those years ago.

As soon as Hal was in the room with Dasia in one of his own armchairs, hand-me-downs from Hyndemere and relics of his own childhood, he relaxed into a semblance of his old normality.

'I know I've been an absolute bloody fool, Dasia. I've just got myself into this terrible tangle with Lucy. She's making a meal of it and saying that when her brother gets out of their place she'll be a complete orphan Annie – and she's clinging to me like a limpet. I was going to come home and try and make it up – but I felt so guilty about what I'd said when I was half stewed, that I simply hadn't the courage.'

He looked at her with the same appealing eyes.

'Well, you've still got the flat, haven't you Hal? It's yours and it's completely empty now – to do exactly what you want.'

'Don't be like that, Dasia ...'

'How else should I be?'

'Isn't there anything left between us?'

'Why should there be? You made it plain enough I wasn't wanted any more the moment she came home from India with you that very first time.'

His temper began to rise: 'Come off it – the whole of our married life you've been a little tyrant about coming with me to Hyndemere and letting Aleck stay there. You're just an inverted snob.'

'It's your mother who's the tyrant, and a *proper* snob! I never knew what a proper snob was till I met her.'

He went very quiet and formal: 'You realise of course that as soon as you rang today I finished it entirely with Lucy. I haven't actually told her yet, but I'll go over there this evening and then come back here to you and the children. And over the next few weeks we'll get something sorted out and start afresh. It can be a true beginning again, with us both being together in the proper sense and my being back in Manchester for good.'

Dasia felt herself weakening. Another true beginning was all she really wanted, and a good life for the children.

'I expect it all depends if we can really forgive each other,' she said slowly.

'I can forgive you everything and anything,' he said cheerfully as he saw her beginning to waver. 'I expect I just have to admit that men are the weaker sex when it comes to straying from the straight and narrow, but it has to be admitted that they're often in very vulnerable positions – especially if they have to go abroad. I don't want to rub it in, but I pleaded with you to come with me to India in the first place.'

She nodded. Then she said, 'You've never been to see the cottage my father left me in Flixton have you? It's very small but Andrina and Sammy and I have been doing it up, and quite frankly I've been thinking of going to live there with the children. It's a pleasant little place, and if I could get some sort of a job there ...'

He looked at her askance: 'Jobs, jobs, jobs. Why must you always bring those in? If I was a woman I should be jolly thankful to be in the position of not needing one.'

'But I do need one – because you said you wanted to divorce me and marry Lucy and you wanted us out of that flat.'

'Not *again*, Dasia. I told you ... I was drunk ... It was all the aftermath of adapting to England again. And you know full well that if the worst had happened, which it couldn't possibly have done, I'd always have provided you with an adequate allowance for yourself and the children.'

That night, Hal left The Grove to go back to Lucy and break the news that he was going to West Didsbury to live in the flat on his own. Lucy seemed thoroughly delighted. She didn't seem to cotton on at all to the fact that he wanted to finish their 'after hours' relationship and go back to being a proper family man.

'How wonderful that Dasia got out so quickly and left the place completely clear to furnish it our way, Hal. There's loads of stuff we can use from this end. It's a godsend in a way because it means that all my most precious treasures will be kept safe for the next two years while this house is let out.'

Then, furnishing him with a camp-bed and bed clothes plus a flask and some food, she sent him back to West Didsbury and said she'd see him at work the following morning.

That night, as Hal shuffled and shivered, and turned about in his cramped camp-bed, in his cold, bleak, empty flat with a gathering fog thickening the night skies, he felt as if he was in a complete no-man's-land, and wondered what on earth to do.

CHAPTER TWENTY-THREE

Lucille

During the following week at the end of November, Hal's life was a positive misery. He saw Lucille's smooth, carefully made-up face looming up at him reproachfully every single second, as she carried out her secretarial duties like a paragon of virtue.

She had speedily and skilfully moved into the West Didsbury flat within twenty-four hours, with the help of a huge pantechnicon, and now had it furnished to perfection as if it had been hers for a century. Hal himself, in desperation, retired to a seedy, private hotel in Rusholme, little knowing that there was even worse to come.

For Lucille Quigley was already pregnant.

A private specialist had assured her she was in fine fettle but, recognising her predicament, mentioned fleetingly that if complications cropped up in the early months, sometimes ... on very, *very* rare occasions ... there *might* be a case for early termination.

The very next day, at work in Hal's private office, she pleaded with him to come and see her at West Didsbury.

He refused point blank. He'd had enough of women,

and was planning to go to Hyndemere for the weekend.

'It's something serious, Hal.'

'Can't you tell me here?' His voice was icy cold. 'I'm travelling back to Hyndemere tonight for the weekend. It's not much cop living in a down-at-heel commercial travellers' shack.'

'... You aren't *forced* to live there. You know jolly well you could be living with me at West Didsbury in our own place. Shall I come with you to Hyndemere, then? At least I won't be kicking up a fuss about the place – like Dasia did ...'

It was the last thing he wanted now, as with ill-concealed annoyance he cancelled his plans for Hyndemere and went back with her to his own flat with a sinking heart, to find out what all the secret fuss was about.

'Where's he gone?' said Thinny to Bazz. 'He was supposed to be popping over for the weekend ... Don't say he's having problems with Dasia, again ...'

They were quite unaware of the rapid change in his life, and Lady Wrioth's mind was deep into other things at present – like getting the housekeeper, young Shirley Badell, married as soon as possible to Danny Elvers so that there would be a proper family with a mother and a father in his home once again.

They were to be married in the private chapel at the beginning of December before the Christmas house party began.

'Any woman willing to take on five motherless children needs the Victoria Cross,' said Bazz.

Lucille Quigley drew the yale key out of her snakeskin handbag to let Hal and herself into the flat.

He looked round the place.

No sign of child life now ... No dirty nappies left there by Dasia to soak in a bucket.

He sat down dispiritedly on a pink and grey plush sofa.

Roses again, in that same silver bowl from Bowdon on a glass and stainless steel occasional table, in part of the corners of the room now pervaded by Art Nouveau.

She reached for the decanter, but he shook his head.

'I advise you to have a drink, Hal, because you might need one when you've heard the news.'

He frowned and was slightly puzzled. The fact that she was 'advising' him, grated on him.

'... a father? I'm already a father ...'

Then it all began to dawn, and he went slightly pale and decided to have a large whisky and soda.

'Yes. I saw Mr Bolsover the specialist two weeks ago. I wondered what to do. I never expected to have another child so many years after Eustace.'

'Are you actually *sure*? We've always taken precautions ...' His mind began to flood with all the jokes about one in every packet having a deliberate hole in it.

He left her a couple of hours later to go back to Rusholme, but they were still in a complete deadlock because he refused to return to the flat – even though he assured her that if what he called 'the worst' came to pass he would give her an allowance towards the child.

... or even pay the fees, if anything else transpired.

He left her in a flood of tears, protesting at the way she was being treated, stranded here in the flat without either him or her own brother who was already packed and ready to go to Milan.

But she knew she was talking to a brick wall.

When Dasia heard about the wedding of Danny and Shirley she was both pleased and sad.

Danny had sent her a short note that it was about to

happen, and she'd gone into Lewises in Manchester to find them a present.

She wondered if Hal knew about it?

There'd been silence ever since the day he went back from The Grove to the empty flat at West Didsbury. Yet she'd still wanted desperately to know what was happening to him, even more so because of Aleck who kept asking where Daddy was.

But pride refused to let her give in and find out.

Oh, how her views had changed since she moved from their flat ... Oh, how she chided herself and wished she hadn't moved out in the first place – and that they could all be together again as a family.

She stood in Lewis's and looked at some small silver trays and some gilt-edged mirrors. Surely the present should be coming from both Hal and herself?

She bought the silver tray, but it was so expensive she felt he should have subscribed to it – seeing that Danny and Shirley were part of his Hyndemere life.

Then on a sudden impulse, she decided to catch the bus to West Didsbury to find out for herself what was happening.

It was dark when she got there, and she was startled when Lucille opened the door.

'I was wondering if Hal was back from business yet,' she said abruptly. 'It was just to ask him if he knew Danny was getting married at Hyndemere.' Already she was feeling a complete fool.

Lucille's face set into a placid gaze of superiority: 'What a strange time to call, Dasia. I'm sure he will know ...

'Would you like to come in? He isn't actually here at the moment.'

Dasia couldn't resist the invitation as she drank in the luxurious transformation of her own recent living quarters. 'When will he back back? I expect I could wait ...'

'It's no good waiting, dear. You see, he doesn't actually live here any more. He's at The Abbot's Elbow in Rusholme.'

Dasia was astounded: 'Whatever's he gone there for? It's a terrible dump.'

'Don't ask me, dear. The world would be a different place if we knew the reasoning of men.'

But Dasia reckoned she did know. It was clear that even though he'd burnt his boats in the first place like she had – he had changed his mind.

'I won't stop then. I'll try and root him out at his hotel.'

'There is one thing before you go,' said Lucille coolly. 'I happen to be pregnant.'

'Oh . . .?' Dasia froze.

'Yes – I've seen the specialist.'

'Oh . . .'

'It's absolutely Hal's of course. There's never been anyone else.'

'Oh . . .'

'He says he'll support me whatever happens.'

'Oh . . .'

'Mind you, we'll just have to see what happens.'

'Yes – of course.'

Dasia's mind was in a complete whirl as she caught the bus home. Somehow she'd never ever in her life expected it. Maybe she'd just been too much wrapped up in her own guilty predicament about Daniella.

She hurried back to The Grove planning to go tomorrow to see him, then began to waver.

So she wrote to him instead:

Dear Hal,

Just a line to say did you know Danny is getting married to Shirley?

I bought them a wedding present from both of us

386

yesterday and took it round to our flat but found you
no longer live there.

Lucy also said she was pregnant.

Your ever loving wife,

Dasia.

Hal picked up the letter and re-read it. He didn't know
what to make of it. Yes, he did know Danny was getting
married, because Mother had invited him and Dasia to
go to the wedding. As Shirley was a person without any
strong family links it left the field clear for Thinny's own
plans. All the same, he decided he'd better call in at The
Grove that night, just to put Dasia straight about Lucy –
seeing the cat was out of the bag.

It was an evening when only Dasia, Alice and the
children were at home, as the rest were at the pictures,
and he was greeted as if nothing much had happened.
'Come on in, stranger, and have a bit of supper with us,'
said Alice helping Dasia to dish out some vegetable soup
and dumplings.

Afterwards, he and Dasia went into the drawing room
and sat in silence for a few seconds as Dasia moved the
glowing red coals about in the fire with long steel fire
tongs then poked it until more and more flames shot up
the sooty chimney.

'I'm glad you got the letter anyway,' she said finally.
'I was wondering whether it would ever reach you.'

He half smiled: 'So what's all this in the letter, about
your going round to our flat?'

'Do you mean to say Lucille hasn't said anything?'

'She mentioned you'd called, but nothing much
else. She didn't say she'd told you about ...' His face
flushed, 'The fact is, Dasia, I've completely finished
with her, and this baby is as much a shock to me as
anyone ...

'I just don't know what to do. She's in there now for

good or bad – for the next two years – unless some knight in shining armour comes and carries her away. I've been such an idiotic fool.'

'Haven't we all ...?' said Dasia sadly. 'I should never have taken off from the flat like I did. It was from sheer temper and a feeling of desperate hurt over what you'd said ...'

He hesitated: 'Couldn't we get together again?'

'You mean – you'd come and live here with me?'

'Yes if needs be. After all, you are the innocent one, and you've had a raw deal from it all.'

Dasia looked hard at him: 'The two children are the innocent ones. They're getting the worst deal. The *three* children, soon, counting hers ...'

'Of course they are. And from now on we must be fair to them.' He nodded vigorously.

'All the children,' said Dasia.

'But of course. It goes without saying. No need to keep stressing it, Dasia.'

'It doesn't go without saying, Hal ... I can't keep it back from you any longer ...

He frowned slightly: 'Can't keep what back? There's no need to talk in riddles.' Then he went paler as he felt a tenseness and desperate seriousness in her voice, and saw her eyes almost pleading at him. And a quiver of fear shot through him.

'Daniella isn't your child, Hal.'

He stared right through her as if he'd seen a ghost then his chin sank towards his chest and he put his hands over his face. 'Jesus Christ ...' he muttered. 'What's happening?

'How much more is there to take? I just can't believe it ...'

'You might as well have it straight. Daniella is Danny's child, and it wasn't his fault – it was mine. She's a true love-child, Hal.'

388

There was a long, bleak, terrible silence.

'Does he know?'

'I've never actually told him, or anyone ... not in so many words. You are the only person I've admitted it to.'

Then she said, 'Does that make it all different? Will you still want to come back to me and the children?'

For some time he sat there restlessly opening and closing his hands and sighing and blinking tears from his eyes – then he said, 'You're all I've really got, Dasia. All I've ever really wanted. And I thought it was the same with you.'

'So it was until *she* came on the scene. Maybe it was my own fault for letting you go off to India on your own. But the damage is done, now – and there's no turning back. It's all in the past.'

He began to pace round the room in an agony of shock. 'What shall I do? How could you have been so damned disloyal – you, my true wife? The only woman I've ever honestly loved? Oh – Dasia ...' His voice broke down to almost a whisper.

'We've just got to try and start afresh, Hal. For the sake of all the children.'

He stared at her with temper suddenly rearing in his eyes: 'Got to start again ... just like that? Got to start again with an offspring of Danny Elvers fastened on to us? You must be mad!' Then he said with cold scorn, 'He'll have to be told. It's only fair to both him, and to the child. He might want to bring it up.'

Dasia tried to keep silent, but not for long: 'She's mine, Hal. All mine. Just supposing you had chosen not to come back to us. Supposing you'd stayed over there with Lucille – or even some other woman ... I would still have been here looking after my children.'

Then they said no more. The shock of all these revelations had been too much. But in the end Hal agreed to come back to The Grove and be with her.

And the Abbot's Elbow, the seedy hotel in Rusholme, never saw him again.

Just after Christmas, Lucille Quigley was lying in a cubicle in the Private Patients wing of the Infirmary.

It had been a terrible time for her, a time of pain and despair. For not only had the baby miscarried, but she also knew that she had lost Hal for ever.

For all her faults, Lucille accepted the inevitable with sadness and stoic calm. Perhaps it was, after all, the best outcome.

CHAPTER TWENTY-FOUR

Wedding Feasts

1934 came in like a lamb. Hal was now home for good, and still living at Alice's with Dasia and the children, but, as March arrived, the year was more like a lion, for there'd just been an urgent message from his parents.

'I want you both to come over with the children and help us out for at least a week,' demanded Thinny in dramatic tones. 'Something dreadful and entirely unexpected has happened.'

'What now ...?' groaned Dasia suspiciously as Hal hurriedly secured an unpaid week's leave of absence from work.

Lord and Lady Wrioth were on the terrace at Hyndemere, with the spaniels, talking about their problem: it was Danny Elvers.

'How *could* he have done it, after all these years?' said Thinny gloomily as they waited for Hal, Dasia and the children. 'What on earth was he thinking of to drag a beautiful young wife like Shirley Badell away to the back of beyond to live under such terrible conditions?

'Our best and most faithful chauffeur ever, and our

391

best housekeeper in twenty years . . .

'Why can't people *know* when they're really well off? What could have been more comfortable for them than staying here with us . . .?'

Bazz sighed. He knew men sometimes came to an age when they looked back on their lives and began to take stock, often desiring some sort of change or second chance before it was too late.

Perhaps Danny was like that. Perhaps the man needed to start afresh, now that Enid had gone.

For Danny and his new wife and family had suddenly departed with the speed of common city 'flitters' to the outskirts of Southport, to join Danny's cousin Michael in a car repair shop and garage – where they'd be living in very cramped conditions in rooms at the back of the premises.

'Don't worry too much, Father. It'll turn out all right, now we're here to help,' said Hal reassuringly, in a confidential talk in the library, 'Dasia and I will always hold the fort.

'We've come to a complete understanding on the matter, and if anything ever happened to you – God forbid – we'd come here, straight away, and I'd take on my proper family responsibilities of managing the house and estate.

'Meanwhile we'll do our best to help you out over this week until you get your staff problems sorted out.

'I'll do some driving for you, and Dasia can help with the house-keeping whilst you and Mother do one of your usual batches of interviewing.'

As luck would have it, a man and his wife in their early thirties called Hatty and Bradwell Mallow from Runcorn – who'd worked for the Baldermain Estate until it was recently sold off to World Aviation as a private conference centre – fitted the bill.

They were childless, business-like, and knowledge-able.

Bradwell had a thorough grasp of all vehicles from humble Rudge motor bikes and Swallow Side-Cars to Rolls-Royces, and Hatty knew every piece of domestic silver from the mustard spoon to the punch bowl as well as every item of the bed chamber from the feather bolster to the brass-panned bed warmers.

They were even obliging enough to come in for a few days while Hal and Dasia were there, to get to know the ropes.

For the first time in her life, Dasia realised with some amazement that she was regarded by all and sundry as a lady of the house in terms of general authority.

Suddenly all the terrible past of the place and her youthful fears about Lord and Lady Wrioth, and her heartache about Aleck being taken from her melted away. It was as if she had grown strong enough to cope with it, and never needed to worry again.

And that night, in the gold-fringed, four poster bed – in a room which hadn't changed its furnishings one iota over the years – she and Hal made love with a passion even stronger than their first flush of youth.

But when they got home again at the end of the week, and she remarked how strange it seemed for Danny and his family to have upped and left so suddenly, Hal was very quiet.

Then, at last he said, 'I never told you this, Dasia, because I didn't want to upset either of us, but I met Danny one day in Manchester near St Peter's Square, and we went for a bite to eat.

'He was very straight with me. He mentioned Daniella, and we both got down to the truth, then and there.' He hesitated as if what he was going to say next was a terrible effort: 'I told him how you felt about the baby being your love child . . .'

393

Tears came to Dasia's eyes and she looked down hastily and tried to blink them away. 'It was only that one solitary day, Hal ...'

'Anyway, he said he was willing to contribute to her upkeep, but I turned it down. All the same, he plans to put money aside for when she comes of age.

'I think that's why he decided to move out so suddenly. It would have been very difficult for us all to have kept meeting with a secret like that always in the background.'

They both stayed silent as Dasia thought of her own background, and the shock it had been when she'd discovered that Alice and Horace weren't her true parents. Yet now it was happening again to her own baby daughter, and she had no solution. All she could do was hope that time would become the great healer, for at least Danny already had a family of his own, and Daniella had brought nothing but love, joy, and liveliness for herself and Hal and young Aleck in their own small family.

In May, Dasia's thoughts turned again to her potato peeler and she called round at Aunt Dolly's with Aleck and Daniella to have a talk, and ask Dolly if she'd tried out the prototype yet. It had been resting in Tommy's room at her lodgings, surrounded by paper and cardboard and pieces of dark red, cloth-covered, electric wire flex – along with an assortment of brown Bakelite electric plugs and sockets, and an itinerary of future selling plans, carefully supervised by forty-five-year-old Cyril Tobias Delders, the engineer from Metro-Vicks.

And now it was just waiting there to take Dolly's cooking scene by storm in a trial run.

But when Dasia arrived, all hell was being let loose. There was a terrific row going on between Marcia and Dolly, as Marcia burst out of Dolly's front door with a squawk as loud as a peacock.

'Let the children go and play on the grass at the back, Dasia, love,' said Dolly as she hastily found a battered old play-pen, once used for three rabbits Mr Corcoran had brought her years ago as pets – but which had been quickly bought by Marcia and turned into rabbit pies. 'We'll sit in the back kitchen where we can keep an eye on them.

'... Eeh, Dasia – I feel quite weak after all that lot. It isn't often Marcia gets her full dander up ... But she's very jealous of me at the moment ... *Very* jealous.

'The wonderful truth is, love, Harold Solway has proposed to me and we're getting married at the church – near the war memorial.

'Marcia has been extremely nasty about it all. She reckons he'll do the dirty on me and disappear – just like Corky did. But I don't believe it for one second. He says I have eyes like bluebells, and skin like ripe peaches, and he'd like to take me on a tandem bicycle to the edge of the world. Talk about romantic – when he feels like it.' Then she added, 'Which reminds me I must get a new set of false teeth that don't rattle, and a really good, new pair of pink corsets with strong bones and good back lacing.

'Harold says there's nothing a real man likes more than unlacing a pair of really good strong corsets and the more knots the better.

'Not that it's ever happened yet, of course,' she said hastily. 'It was something he saw written by a married man in a book translated from French when he was in the Great War called Male Confessions, with some other rather disgusting things in it ...' Then she stared at Dasia and said, 'But that sort of thing is more for older people, love. You've not got enough there to even lace up. You need to have plenty of spare tyres and things like me. And even Harold bulges all round his braces ...'

Slowly and tactfully Dasia brought her back to the

potato peeler: 'Has it *ever* been fully tested out yet, Aunty?'

Dolly looked vague, then began to get a bit irritable. 'Look, love, I'm sure I don't know what goes on in those scientific places. All I'm interested in is looking after my own gentlemen properly.'

'When will you be trying it out in your kitchen then? Because when we know it'll work properly in an ordinary kitchen –'

'Excuse me, Dasia, my kitchen is not "*ordinary*". I'll have you know that Harold has just done it all out with pale green Eau de Nil distemper with a very expensive embossed paper frieze of pears and pineapples in purple, and –'

'Aunty – I didn't mean it like *that*.'

'What *did* you mean then? Just you watch your step, young woman.'

Then she cooled down and said, 'To be quite candid, dear, I think it'll be a total flop. For a start you have to have a special power plug, to plug it all into for the electricity, and my kitchen is all gas, and the fire range, except for the electric lights.

'I couldn't possibly afford to have all the walls ripped to pieces, and all those special bits of wire running everywhere. And where would I be if rats and mice gnawed through them? And the whole place all set on fire, just for the sake of Horace's one little electric potato peeler invention and me able to peel the damned things myself as quick as lightning if the daily help isn't here?

'No, Dasia, pet, I think your grandfather had a heart of gold and good intentions when he left you the plans, lovey, but like everything else he did it was always a bit too early for the market place.'

Dasia's heart sank: 'But Aunty,' she pleaded, 'surely we must always look on the bright side when it comes to new inventions? More and more people are beginning to use electric gadgets. Think of all the vacuum cleaners.'

'A Eubank carpet sweeper is still good enough for me, love, and cold tea spread on carpets then brushed off with a stiff brush. Plenty of elbow grease never killed anyone. Though I must say I do like cars ...'

'And Cyril Delders has been marvellous, aunty. He's ever so clever and he's done all the work getting it made up into something like a working model. It would be dreadful to let it all fade away. He says that once you've tested it out in your kitchen he'll be able to see if there are any practical flaws and make it even better. Then I'll be able to go round all the big shops like Lewises, getting orders for it.

'And I'm sure we could all subscribe to getting you fixed up with a proper power plug.'

Dolly hesitated, then smiled slightly: 'Well, dear, the only person I know with electric plugs is Marcia – and just look what a state *she's* in at the moment.'

But by the end of the afternoon, and lots of tea and biscuits, and a bandage on Aleck's knee because he'd fallen down from a tree, it was arranged that Dolly would try and get Marcia in a good mood by getting Tommy to slip round one evening with Cyril Delders – who was a bachelor.

'He needs a good woman like Marcia,' said Dolly generously. 'It would stop her being jealous of me and Harold – and then, who knows, love, maybe we could have a twin wedding?'

'But I thought she was married?'

'Not so as you'd notice,' said Dolly drily. 'Her private life would fill a book, and marriage has never really come into it.'

And a few weeks later the Greenbow Electric Potato Peeler was tested out at Marcia's, and acclaimed with such enthusiasm by both Marcia and Cyril that Cyril deserted his lodger status at his cousin Desmond's house in Edge Lane and came to stay with Marcia instead – and proposed marriage the moment he got there.

The year Dasia and Hal moved to Timperley, to a fresh house and a completely fresh start, was the year Alice died.

Sadly, Alice never saw any of her daughters, or her son, married, but passed away quietly one day when sat in her rocking chair – from what the doctor described as a rare form of anaemia, which he said she'd had for years.

There was then the problem of what to do about the house, as the will said it was to be shared by Andrina, Louise, Rosalie and Tommy. Dasia was to have a choice of furniture and was left Alice's one and only bit of real wealth: two beautiful Chinese Ming vases once deposited at the pawn shop thirty years ago and never claimed.

Inevitably some family squabbling arose. The general consensus was for the house to be sold and the money from it divided out, but Rosalie wanted it converted into flats for family use, for when she was married to Arthur Bowlingshaw; and Louise half agreed for when she was married to Arnold Kimberley. But Andrina's Sammy most certainly did not agree and said it had to be sold and shared out as stipulated in the will, and Tommy and Maureen, his wife, agreed with him.

The day the house was sold at public auction, Dasia wept buckets. For although she was the one to leave it first – when she'd run away that day to Aunty Dolly's – she was the one who longed for it to be kept.

Their own house in Timperley was bought through a building society mortgage, and was along Park Road, well past Timperley railway station not far from a lovely old farm where they could collect their own fresh milk.

It was a large bungalow-type dwelling with a

verandah and five bedrooms. It was painted white with black wooden beams and stood in its own grounds set back slightly from the road and surrounded by mature trees.

Timperley at that time was one of the places where the corn fields were just being taken over for new houses, and all the farms and small moated manor houses, like the one along Heyes Lane where they sometimes went for walks, were vanishing.

But the canal was still there alongside the railway line, with its colourful painted barges and butty boats being towed slowly along by huge cart horses on the tow paths. You could walk to Broadheath along the canal bank, while in the other direction from Timperley station you could walk along to Brooklands and Sale.

1936 was the year when King George V died, and men wore black ties and women sewed small black cloth diamonds on the arms of their coats and costumes as a mark of respect.

And in 1937 a memorable wedding occurred ...

It was the double one for Dolly and Marcia, with Dolly all out to become Mrs Harold Solway, and Marcia with talons well embedded into Cyril Delders.

The small church in Stretford was packed out for the great occasion in June, and small box-like Austins and Jowetts and Fords parked all along the narrow road at the side, beneath the sycamore trees.

It was dazzlingly hot and sunny outside and the wooden pews in the cool, stone-floored church were packed with whispering, shuffling, excited people all turning their heads about.

All the Greenbows were there as well as Dolly's ramification of family tribes, plus Marcia's relatives: the Prendergasts, Mullanders, and O'Dwyers, mingling with a few of the more stalwart gentleman lodgers past and present.

Harold Solway's brother was his best man, and four of his heavy-looking sisters were there with their gigantic husbands and children with legs like tree trunks. Whilst Cyril Delders's rather skinnier lot – all from Stretford and numbering at least twenty – were a load of bright-eyed scallywags with numerous children clutching flat wooden spoons and kitchen mugs of Porelli's ice cream which they'd secretly brought with them. The ice cream cart had just been and they lived only a few yards from the church.

Cyril Delders and Harold Solway were immaculate in dark grey suits with cross-over waistcoats and spats over their shoes as they stood trembling in front of the altar in front of the Reverend Paxley in his white surplice.

Dolly made a real meal of it. She was in a dazzling white crinoline decorated with artificial pearls almost the size of bull's eyes, and she was wearing ankle-length pantalets.

Dasia was her matron of honour and wore dark blue taffeta, and Daniella and Aleck were squashed into the same outfits they'd worn for Louise's wedding with a few hem lines lengthened, and some darts let out.

And all the time, as Dasia walked slowly down the aisle, she was hoping that none would notice that she was pregnant again ...

In 1938 Dasia and Hal were living happily in Timperley – gradually doing up their home and looking forward to a new baby. In spite of dire newspaper reports on the world political situation in Europe and articles about Adolf Hitler, the leafier suburbs of Manchester and Cheshire remained calm. But thousands of people were extremely fearful, especially those who'd fought in the last war, and people who had come to Manchester as refugees, or immigrants from Europe.

Aleck had delighted everyone, including himself, by winning a scholarship to Manchester Grammar School which was a huge place with well over a thousand boys. But Dasia viewed it with a contrary suspicion as she had become drawn to the idea of a freer type of education with boys and girls being taught together in co-educational schools. She realised this was not the time to make such views known and she must be truly thankful for his getting to such a good school.

It was like a new era with all the Greenbows married and the family house in The Grove gone. Even Andrina and Sammy at The Cedars had suddenly sold up and moved out to Plumley near Knutsford to a smaller, more modern detached house, with an acre of land and greenhouses suitable for a small market garden business, as a side line.

And as for Hyndemere, it had mellowed in its old age and was managing very well with its new chauffeur and housekeeper. And from all accounts Danny Elvers and family were still thriving in the used car and repair trade near Southport.

It was also the year when Dasia took courage in both hands and, although pregnant, went round all the big stores demonstrating and advertising the Greenbow Electric Potato Peeler and giving out leaflets about it.

Then, one day in April, she visited Baulden's where, for a fee, she was allowed to stand in a special display area in a corner of the Hardware department explaining to all who would listen the virtues of this unique machine and how it could revolutionise and cut the time spent in potato drudgery for the average housewife.

She was amazed at how much Baulden's had all changed in the past ten years. Some people looked so much older she hardly recognised them, and it suddenly came home to her that if they appeared to have changed so much, she herself must have changed too.

About fifteen minutes after she had got her stall set with the gleaming new potato peeler in its enamel-coated basin, and a fan of leaflets and booklets on display – she noticed someone hovering at the back of the crowd, staring hard at her. She felt her cheeks getting flushed as the stares persisted . . .

It was Mr Fanshaw in a pair of brown overalls, and he hardly looked a scrap different except that his fringe of hair was very white and he looked a bit thinner. Then he disappeared.

As the crowd dispersed and Dasia was writing down some orders for the potato peelers in her order book, she was amazed to see him coming back again. He was carrying a cup of tea and a biscuit.

'I've brought you this, Miss Dasia,' he said. 'My . . . how you've changed. I hardly recognised that little innocent girl I helped out all those years ago. You're looking quite buxom round your middle . . .'

His sharp, beady eyes stared at her non-existent waist. 'There's never been anyone quite as nice as you to sit and eat mi sandwiches with, lass. I expect you know that Miss Davina is now dead and gone? But all my family are doing well – thank the Lord – except that mi wife can't work any more due to a rupture.

'I must say I admire them as gets off their backsides and works like I see you're doing, and if I can ever 'elp you again I'll be glad to do so.'

She was quite touched. After all, the cup of tea and the biscuit were just what she needed as she was getting quite hoarse. And honestly, just what would she have done all those years back if he hadn't stepped forward to help her out?

'Thank you very much, Mr Fanshaw. You look just the same.'

Then a bit of the devil got into her and she said

solemnly, 'Can I sell you a potato peeler? They truly are a marvellous invention. It would be a boon for both you and your wife.'

He looked quite startled: 'Not a boon for *me*, Miss Dasia. The others is the ones who does all that sort of thing, and it's too dear for an ordinary working man like me to buy when all the others can peel 'em.'

'You could have it at cost price, on instalments?' she said with a grin.

He shook his head and smiled slightly. 'It's ever so kind of you, but I'm only a poor humble man with hardly a penny in the world, but as I say, to know that your own father invented it has quite made my day, and I 'ope you gets lots and lots of orders.' Then he swiftly disappeared.

When Dasia got back home, she felt completely worn out. She lay on the bed and thought about the new baby lying in her womb, and looked at her order book. There were hardly any empty pages and orders had come in from all the richest places in the area like Hale and Bowdon and Higher Broughton and Victoria Park.

Then she opened her large leather handbag and took out a small framed snapshot.

It was a picture of her grandfather, Horace Greenbow; one that Alice had always kept – from when he was a man of about forty. He was clean-shaven and smiling. A man in his prime.

She looked at it fondly for a few seconds then kissed it gently and put it back in her bag, reflecting that he was not just an idle dreamer, but a man with ideals and ideas.

A man of foresight ... and practicality ...

She felt an overwhelming sense of pride. Pride that she herself was persevering to get the peeler established in the face of past family disbelief and scorn; carrying on something good and worthwhile to a new generation.

Some time later, when Dasia and young Aleck were walking in the bluebell woods, he said, 'So will you really be going to places like America and Australia to sell your potato peeler, Mum?'

She burst out laughing and hugged him as best she could for she was nearly nine months' pregnant with baby Mirabelle.

Her red-gold hair sparkled in sudden sun through tree branches: 'You bet your life, son,' she said with gusto, 'and not just me ... but all of us.'

EVE'S APPLES

Lena Kennedy

Twelve-year-old Daisy Smith steals a carrot for Jackie
Murphy, an Irish barrow-boy, and so begins a love affair
which will last for both their lives. Even when Jackie's
family leave for Australia, Daisy cannot forget her
childhood sweetheart – and she determines to follow her
beloved to the ends of the earth, if need be!

In Australia they both make their fortunes – Jackie in the
opal mines and Daisy through the outback bar she runs
with her husband. On his death she returns to England to
be with Petal, the illegitimate daughter born out of her
love for Jackie. But restless Petal is determined to forsake
her East End life for a modelling career in New York.

Though Daisy and Jackie are destined never to marry,
their various children, like Eve's apples, will spread out
across the world to create new lives thousands of miles
away from their East End roots.

Also by Lena Kennedy:

MAGGIE

NELLY KELLY

AUTUMN ALLEY

LADY PENELOPE

LIZZIE

SUSAN

LILY, MY LOVELY

DOWN OUR STREET

THE DANDELION SEED

THE INN ON THE MARSH

FICTION

THE HARSH NOONTIDE

Sara Fraser

In 1848 – the most ruinous year of the potato famine –
Grainne Shonley and her husband, Con, leave their
native Ireland for the promise of the New World.
Arriving in Liverpool, gateway to America, they
encounter the squalor of Paradise Alley, the most
treacherous part of the docklands. In this corrupt world
no one can be trusted – especially their sinister landlord
Tom Tracey and his henchmen. But their passage
overseas is soon confirmed and the Shonleys leave with
relief.

As *The Florida* sets sail Grainne feels sure that their luck
has changed. But she hasn't bargained for the vile
conditions below deck, the tyrannical Captain Lockyer, or
for the fearful night when disaster strikes the ship . . .

TIME TO LOVE

Beryl Kingston

From the dark alleys of Whitechapel to the genteel luxury of Finsbury Square, from the hop fields of Kent to the bloody fields of Ypres, Beryl Kingston's compulsive novel captures the atmosphere and the spirit of a forgotten age . . .

Ellen Murphy was born to a world of rotting slums and starving children. Determined to escape from poverty and from fear of her drunken Irish father, she takes a job as shopgirl on Shoreditch High Street. And then she meets David Cheifitz.

The only son of devout Jewish parents, David has grown up with his future mapped out: an honest trade marriage to a nice girl, and a handful of grandchildren for his mother to enjoy. But David is an artist and a rebel. When he falls in love with Ellen Murphy, he turns his back on the old ways.

Confident in the dizzy happiness of first love, they marry. But as time passes, religious differences, rejection by David's parents and domestic strife throw up barriers between them that their devotion to the children of their love cannot overcome. Only when David is drawn into the Great War do they realise how precious their marriage is . . . and by then it may be too late to find . . .
A TIME TO LOVE

Also by Beryl Kingston:

HEARTS AND FARTHINGS
KISSES AND HA'PENNIES
TUPPENNY TIMES
FOURPENNY FLYER
SIXPENNY STALLS
LONDON PRIDE

FICTION

Warner now offers an exciting range of quality titles by both established and new authors. All of the books in this series are available from:
Little, Brown and Company (UK) Limited,
Cash Sales Department,
P.O. Box 11,
Falmouth,
Cornwall TR10 9EN.

Alternatively you may fax your order to the above address. Fax No. 0326 376423.

Payments can be made as follows: Cheque, postal order (payable to Little, Brown and Company) or by credit cards, Visa/Access. Do not send cash or currency. UK customers: and B.F.P.O.: please send a cheque or postal order (no currency) and allow £1.00 for postage and packing for the first book, plus 50p for the second book, plus 30p for each additional book up to a maximum charge of £3.00 (7 books plus).

Overseas customers including Ireland, please allow £2.00 for postage and packing for the first book, plus £1.00 for the second book, plus 50p for each additional book.

NAME (Block Letters) ....

ADDRESS..

....

☐ I enclose my remittance for _____

☐ I wish to pay by Access/Visa Card

Number ⬚⬚⬚⬚⬚⬚⬚⬚⬚⬚⬚⬚⬚⬚⬚⬚

Card Expiry Date ⬚⬚⬚⬚